GUILTY PLEASURES

G·K Hall &Co.

This Large Print Book carries the
Seal of Approval of N.A.V.H.

GUILTY PLEASURES

Stella Cameron

G.K. Hall & Co.
Thorndike, Maine

Published in 1998 by arrangement with Zebra Books,
an imprint of Kensington Publishing Corporation.

G.K. Hall Large Print Core Series.

The text of this Large Print edition is unabridged.
Other aspects of the book may vary from the original edition.

Set in 16 pt. Plantin by Juanita Macdonald.

Printed in the United States on permanent paper.

Library of Congress Cataloging in Publication Data

Cameron, Stella.
    Guilty pleasures / Stella Cameron.
        p.   cm.
    ISBN 0-7838-0114-9 (lg. print : hc : alk. paper)
    1. Large type books.   I. Title.
[PS3553.A4345G85   1998]
813′.54—dc21

#38354325

98-5509

For a fabulous team: Kensington.

One

The boy who scribbled, *"Least Likely to Succeed,"* beneath Polly Crow's high-school-yearbook photo had proudly signed his brilliant comment. He'd also laughed in her face when he handed back the book. Why not? After all, he had nothing to fear from a girl who came from nothing and was going nowhere.

Polly folded her white cashmere cardigan tightly about her and breathed deeply of the stiff late-summer breeze off Lake Washington. Back then she'd begun to believe Brad — she couldn't recall the other name — and his friends were probably right. And if there'd been a least-likely-to-succeed award, she'd have won with no contest. She hadn't been eligible to win any other prizes.

But they were wrong. They were all wrong, including Polly, because she had amounted to something. And because she'd made good, someone was trying to frighten her to death.

As she liked to do at the end of each day's filming, she walked along floating docks at the southern end of the town of Kirkland's waterfront. Leggy impatiens, luminous pink, orange, purple, and white, slumped in wooden planters. Ivy geraniums faded by weeks in the sun trailed

7

from baskets suspended on poles. Before long it would be time for chrysanthemums and winter pansies.

The smell was coming-of-evening rich, sleepy-silk-sway-of-water mysterious.

Polly's long cotton skirt whipped about her legs. Too bad she couldn't ignore the other, the menace she'd lived with for days.

Just some obsessive creep getting a cheap thrill from threatening a TV personality. It happened all the time.

And sometimes these freaks acted on their obsessions.

She wouldn't change her lifestyle, wouldn't start locking herself inside the condo, wouldn't tell anyone who didn't already know what was happening.

If she said aloud: "Someone leaves messages on my answering machine. No, I don't know who — he whispers. He says I only made one mistake in my life, but he's forgiven that, that I used to be really good and I need him to make me good again," it would all become too real. Polly didn't want it to be real. She didn't want to voice, "I want you with me, or I want you dead." If she did, she'd have to admit she wasn't imagining the calls, imagining the worst threat of all: "I know you'll do what I want, what we both want, and get rid of anyone who stands in our way. Otherwise, I'll have to make sure you do."

Good?

Only one mistake?

She was twenty-seven years old. An ex-addict. Never married. The single mother of a seven-year-old son. Daughter of a single mother.

Sam Dodge, the handsome rebel who'd wanted her because she made him look good, had taken her so low she should have been dead by now. But she hadn't died. Polly smiled at the wind, smiled at the watery sting in her eyes, smiled at the jumble of bittersweet memories.

Having Bobby had saved her. Of all things, rather than adding another stone to the weight dragging her down, getting pregnant at nineteen had stopped the fall.

"I ain't gettin' slowed down by no brat. If you wanna keep on being my woman, get rid of it," Sam had demanded when she'd told him about the pregnancy. And when she'd refused he'd said, *"No account piece of trash. You'll never amount to anything without me."*

Even as she shuddered, Polly smiled. Sam had given her a choice between drink, drugs, abusive sex — and Bobby, dear, serious Bobby. No choice. Thank God what was left of herself had made the decision so easy.

The whisperer called Bobby a mistake. That had to be what he meant, and he threatened to get rid of him.

Bobby hadn't questioned being sent to stay with Venus Crow, Polly's mother, who lived in nearby Bellevue. He'd accepted the story that the show was going into a production crunch and this was a great time for him to run free at the artists' colony that had once been his home. Venus ran Hole Point, and Bobby loved the place.

Venus hadn't questioned Bobby's visit either.

Some members of the cast of *Polly's Place* had been with her when she got the first message. She'd laughed it off and never mentioned the continuing calls.

The uncomfortable thud of her heart made Polly open her mouth to swallow. She ought to ask for help. The police wouldn't do anything unless something happened. Her heart leapt again. Unless she was hurt in some way — or someone she loved was hurt — they'd say there was nothing to be done.

She continued walking. Rafted boats jostled at moorages. Gusts of laughter and raised voices erupted from cabins and deckhousing. The wind was enough to send most of the messers-about-in-boats below for their happy hour.

These people weren't what drew Polly this way so often.

The real reason was something else she ought to pack away in her heap of shouldn't, and never-will-be's.

But a woman could look at a man, couldn't she? Especially when that's all she would ever do — look?

She strolled to the very end of the farthest dock from shore and searched about. No sign of the big, black rubber dinghy. No sign of the man in his wet suit doing whatever he did at the end of his day. Maybe he wouldn't come so regularly as fall and winter approached.

Polly rolled her eyes at the disappointment she felt; disappointment because she might not get more chances to take furtive glances at a man she didn't know.

He'd never looked her way — not deliberately. He didn't know her, and she didn't know him. She'd never even heard him speak.

Polly stopped and narrowed her eyes to focus on the distant, snow-dusted Olympic Mountains. She'd never heard the big man with his sun-bleached hair and curiously light brown eyes say a word, even to the black cat who rode with him in his dinghy filled with diving equipment.

She knew his eyes were brown, and that they were remote — cold even. She knew because he had met her gaze occasionally. Each time their glances had crossed for no more than a few seconds. Polly always looked away first.

Her walks weren't at exactly the same time each day.

Usually the dinghy appeared. It just appeared, floated into sight from shadows around the dock. No engine noise. The engine didn't burst to life until she'd retraced her steps to the park that edged the waterfront.

As if he waited for her to come, watched while he pretended not to watch, then left once she was gone.

Rubber fenders squeaked between the rafted boats.

Mooring lines creaked.

The man had strong teeth. She'd seen them between his parted lips as he pulled a mask from his lean face. And he chewed gum. Polly had always disliked watching someone chew gum. Not this time.

Gavin Tucker, an artist who appeared on the show with Polly, said the man ran a dive shop. Gavin had also questioned the diver's reason for hanging around this section of the waterfront when his shop was a mile away. Anyway, Gavin had pointed out, the scuba lessons advertised by Room Below — the dive shop — were held in Puget Sound, not here in Lake Washington.

Ferrito. She knew his name was Ferrito, that he chewed gum and liked cats. And he limped. Funny how you noticed some things. Even moving around in his boat, his limp was evident.

Kirkland wasn't a big town, and the show pulled in people from the community. Polly and the rest of the cast were friendly and open. Finding out about any of them wouldn't be so hard — including their phone number.

Once more Polly searched about.

Finding out a person's habits wasn't so hard, either. But Ferrito wasn't here today.

He liked cats. He wouldn't make threatening phone calls. She didn't know what he would do; they'd never even exchanged a smile. Exasperated by the power of a stranger to frighten her, by her own weakness, by the ridiculous leap in logic she was making, Polly turned back.

She'd never heard him speak . . . or whisper.

Startled, Polly couldn't move.

She hadn't heard the approach of his bare feet on the wooden planking of the dock.

"Hi," Nasty Ferrito said. "Nice evening."

Her blue eyes stretched wide open. Very blue eyes, but he already knew that from watching her TV show.

Apart from dropping her hands to her sides she didn't move. Polly Crow, bubbly singing star of *Polly's Place*, the most popular children's show to hit the box in a decade, stared at him with her mouth open. If he didn't know how ridiculous it would be, he'd say she was afraid of him.

"Getting colder." Talking about the weather. He'd finally decided to quit stalling and force a meeting with the woman, and he was talking about the weather.

She nodded, almost imperceptibly. On television her straight, thick hair appeared lighter. In person it was a dark honey blond. This evening she wore it pulled back into a band at her nape. Her skin was pale. He'd found out from watching her on the docks that she was thinner than she appeared on the screen. Average height, but small.

He preferred more substantial women — stronger women.

Or he had.

Hell, he felt shaky.

This wasn't close enough. Nothing would be close enough. He wanted to touch her.

"Are you cold?" he asked. Sounded too personal.

Polly Crow shook her head. Her neck was slender, the bones at its base delicate. He'd read about seeing people's pulses beat. This was the first time he'd ever noticed.

She bowed her head and looked up at him from beneath dark lashes tipped with gold.

And Nasty's heart stopped beating. He hadn't imagined the effect she had on him — no, he hadn't imagined that. A man shouldn't be able to feel protective and predatory at the same time. So? he was breaking new ground. He'd like to cover her up and protect her from the world — and be inside her while he did it.

Good thing he'd spent almost as much of his adult life wearing a wet suit as he had anything else. Wet suits were great. Short of armor, they were the best way he knew of masking an erection. The hard-on inside his suit felt as if it had the power to punch holes in concrete. He dropped to sit on his heels and stroke Seven, who had, as usual, followed him up the steps from the side of the dock where he'd tied up the dinghy.

This wasn't the way he'd rehearsed this meeting, but then, he was no expert at approaching women he thought he could fall in love with. In fact, he'd never done this before.

He'd never fallen in love. "Fall's coming." *Hell.*

"Yes," she said. Her voice wasn't breathy on television.

"Beautiful time of year."

"Yes."

Oh, great. "Am I bothering you?"

Her shoulders rose. She gripped one of the standards that supported a hanging basket.

Nasty picked up Seven and bounced to his feet. "I wouldn't want to intrude." Yeah, he would. "Excuse me if —"

"No." She shook her head emphatically. "No. You excuse me, please. You took me by surprise, that's all. It's pretty quiet out here."

A nice voice. More than nice. Sometimes he closed his eyes to listen to her on TV. Laughter hung out somewhere in there. And she could sing. All those kids songs he listened to. He smothered a grin. Nasty Ferrito, ex-Navy SEAL, tough veteran of more life-on-the-line covert operations than he could remember, made a point of tuning in *Polly's Place* and listening as if he was into Down and Out the Main Monsters, and watching Gavin the Paint Man. Ferrito's crusty partner, Dusty Miller, had plenty to say about that. Ferrito passed it off as practice for when Junior, an old friend's little girl, came to visit. Dusty wasn't fooled.

"Nice black cat."

Her spontaneous comment surprised him. He stroked Seven's sinuous body and long tail. "Unlucky for some," he said. "We get along."

"That's thirteen."

Ferrito squinted at her. "Seven."

"Thirteen — unlucky for some. Not black cats

are unlucky for some — or seven."

Definitely not the way he'd rehearsed this encounter. "Communication gap," he said. Each time he looked into her face, that look lasted a little longer. He risked stepping closer and turning until the cat faced Polly Crow. "Her name's Seven."

"Ah, I see." Polly laughed. Her fingernails were short and devoid of polish. She smoothed Seven's head. "Why Seven?"

"Always liked the number, and I found her — scratch that — she found me on a Sunday. Seventh day of the week. What are you afraid of?" He'd have to put that off-the-wall question down to rusty social skills.

"I'm not afraid of anything. What makes you think I am?"

He slung Seven into her favorite position, draped over his shoulder. "Hell, I don't know. Just a feeling." Another sense you developed when you lived largely on your instincts for a long time.

Her eyes became unblinking. She nailed him with that stare. "Why do you come by here each evening?"

"Do I come by each evening?"

"Yes, you know you do."

"Maybe I live on one of these boats."

"Do you?"

Triumph shouldn't be what he felt, but he did. She'd noticed him — noticed what time he came, and how often. "I live on a boat. But it's in front of my partner's house." He hooked a thumb over his shoulder. "Farther up the shore. I come in the evening because I like it here."

"Why?"

"I just told you why."

She crossed her arms. "No you didn't. The whole waterfront is lovely. But you always come right here." She pointed downward and crossed her arms again.

Not a big woman in any respect, but nice, very nice. Keeping his eyes above her breasts wasn't easy. "Why do you come here every evening?" he asked.

"Because . . ." Pink swept along her cheekbones, and the soft skin of her neck. "It's calm. Quiet. I like that."

"Calm and quiet on this dock rather than, say, that one?" He pointed south, then north. "Or that one?"

"I like this one."

"Know what I think?" Dusty always came out with the truth, swore he could live with letting the chips fall where they might. "I think you come here because I do. I think you come out here each evening hoping to see me."

Her lips formed a silent, Oh!

Smugness didn't suit a man. Nasty felt smug anyway. "You walked out here tonight expecting to see me. You were looking for me when I came up behind you."

She planted her feet in her flat brown sandals and her face worked through one expression after another. "Crumb! Well, I've never met a man with so much — *ego*. I certainly don't come out here to look for you. We just happen to come at the same time, that's all. It doesn't mean a thing. Not to me."

He wouldn't remark on *crumb* as an expletive — yet. "How old are you?"

"Twenty-seven." Another silent, Oh! "Crumb! I can't believe it. You sashay up here, accuse me of taking walks because I want to see you, then ask me how old I am."

Nasty shifted Seven to his other shoulder and unzipped his wetsuit to the waist. Despite the wind, he was feeling increasingly hot.

Polly Crow looked at his chest.

"Sashay, huh? No one ever accused me of sashaying before. Sounds cute."

"There's nothing cute about you," she told him, glancing away, then back at his chest. "Nothing."

He'd swear she was responding to him. "Good. Cute wouldn't suit me." Maybe his thoughts were wishful, but he doubted it. "You're cute."

"You're pushy. How old are you?"

"Fair enough. Thirty-six. Is that too old?"

"Too old for what?"

"For you."

Polly Crow made a lot of silent Oh's!

"You watch me, Polly Crow. You come out here and watch me in the dinghy almost every night."

"Crumb!" Again expressions washed over her

features. "You know my name."

"Don't you think everyone in Kirkland knows your name?"

"No."

He spread the fingers of his right hand on his chest, inside the wet suit. "You're on TV every afternoon. Sing the song for me."

An amazed frown was all he got.

"Come on. *Everybody needs somebody. Everybody is somebody. Somebody needs everybody.* Sing it for me."

"No." She took a step backward. Her fascination with his chest was undeniable. "Are you telling me you watch *Polly's Place?* In the afternoon? A children's program?"

"Yep, yep, and yep. Quite often."

"Then you come over here to watch me in person."

"I come over here."

"Grown men don't make a habit of watching children's programs in the afternoon — probably almost never."

"Lots of grown men would if they knew they'd see you." He'd said it. No taking back the words. "You do hope to see me when you come here, don't you?"

Another pink rush rose up her neck. She spun away and gave a startled yelp as a scatter of seagulls came in for a landing.

"Don't you?" Nasty persisted. "I come to see you, and you come to see me."

Their heads jerking, the gulls strutted across

19

the decking. Seven spared them a glare but knew better than to take chase. "Hey," Ferrito said softly. "I have scared you. Damn, I'm sorry. I didn't mean to do that. Would you like to see my boat?"

Polly turned to face him again. "You've got to be kidding. Would I like to see your boat? I guess it's more original than etchings."

He doubted she'd laugh if he told her he had some etchings on the boat. "Let me take you out in the dinghy, then. Peaceful out there."

"You think I'm going to get into a little rubber boat with a man I don't know?"

Smiling didn't come easily, never had, but he managed. "You might. Never any harm in asking."

"No, thank you."

"I'm good with boats. Safe. I'll take care of you."

Where there'd been a blush, pallor seeped in. "I don't need taking care of — by anyone."

This was not going well.

She said, "I can keep myself safe." But she didn't try to leave. "What do you think of answering machines?"

A flurry of activity passed between the gulls, and they took off, crying and swooping, their wings battering the air.

"Did you ask me what I think of answering machines?"

"Simple enough question."

"Okay. I think answering machines are great."

"Because you can leave messages you'd be afraid to give in person?"

He couldn't begin to guess where this was going. "Because they make it possible to make sure you don't miss a call. And you don't have to be tethered to the damn phone all the time."

"I've got to get back."

"No you don't. You're through for the day."

Her hand went to her throat. "You don't know that?"

"Sure I do. When you leave here you'll go to your condo. Alone. Your boy's not with you at the moment."

A sharp breath made a scraping sound in her throat. "Good night."

Automatically, Nasty stepped aside. "Yeah, sure."

When she drew level, she paused, and whispered, "Leave me alone, please. I haven't done anything to you."

By the time he rallied she was several yards away. He caught up easily. "Polly? Look, if I upset you, I'm sorry. Of course you haven't done anything to me. I thought it was time we talked. Nothing more complicated than that."

She stopped and stared toward the sky. "Time we talked? Now why on earth would it be time we talked?"

"I put that badly. I guess I haven't had a whole lot of practice at this" — he spread his arms — "and before you ask me what 'this' is, I mean coming on to women without at least asking them

21

to dance or buying them a drink first."

"Charming," she said through her teeth. There was fire in those blue eyes now. "If some woman is stupid enough to dance with you, or let you buy her a drink, you think you can *come on* to her."

"Geez, not exactly. I mean, not —"

"She's supposed to understand you expect sex? Men like you are a menace."

"I do not —"

"Well, you and I haven't danced, and you haven't bought me a drink."

"Would you like a drink?" He groaned aloud.

Polly wrinkled her nose. "That's disgusting."

"You looked at my chest."

She covered her mouth.

He should have stayed in the dinghy. "I mean, I think you find me attractive, too. I think I turn you . . ." *Great going, Ferrito.* "We may have a mutual appeal."

"You are absolutely unbelievable. And if you're doing what I think you're doing to me, stop it. I don't have any proof yet, but I'll get it."

He gaped at her.

"Oh, I know about scrambling numbers for anonymity, but sooner or later you'll make a mistake and get caught."

"Er, sure. Anything you say." Most people might be wholly confused by what she said. Nasty also knew about scrambling numbers — and a great many other covert procedures. "Polly, we've gotten off to a bad start."

Her laugh cut him. "We haven't started, period!" With that, she set off at a brisk pace.

Nasty followed. "I guess I've said everything wrong. Will you give me another chance? Can I see you again?"

"Not if I see you first."

He strode along beside her. "That's a cliché."

"You ought to know. It's about the only one I haven't heard you use." She glanced at his face, then down. Most people glanced down when they met him. They couldn't help reacting to his limp.

"If you knew me, you'd like me."

"I'd hate you. I already do."

The venom in her tone stopped him, but only for an instant. He fell into step as she turned to walk along another of the bobbing docks. "All I can say is sorry, again. I'll go away now."

"Good."

"You're very beautiful, you know."

When she looked sideways at him he could swear there were tears in her eyes. She said, "You just told me you were going away."

"I am. I wanted to tell you how beautiful you are, though."

"Thanks. I'll tell my husband you said so."

"You don't have a husband."

"Who are you?" Her voice rose. "Who *are* you?"

"Ferrito," he said quietly. "Nasty Ferrito. Nasty to my friends."

This time her voice was faint. "Nasty?"

"You can call me Nasty."

"Nasty?"

"Sure. And don't ask me why that's my name because I don't discuss it." He didn't even think about it. "Dusty Miller and I run Room Below. It's a dive shop. We're trustworthy people. I'm trustworthy."

A woman in red climbed from a motor cruiser and set off toward land. The flash of relief on Polly's face was impossible to miss. "You really are afraid of me, aren't you?" he asked.

"Good night, *Nasty*."

"Aren't you? Doesn't matter. I'll find out why."

"You'll leave me alone." Trotting now, Polly followed the woman.

"If you're scared, it isn't because of me. Let me help you."

"No!" She started to run.

"Lock your doors, Polly." Jesus Christ, she was terrified. Something had crawled inside her skull and ripped up her nerves. He'd just happened along when she was ready to break. "Do you hear me? Lock yourself in."

Her strides lengthened, but he kept the same distance between them with no effort.

As she reached the grass verge at the shore end of the docks, Polly paused and looked back at him. Her eyes were dry but wild.

"It's okay," he told her. "Talk to me. Let me help you. Tell me what you need, and I'll make sure you get it."

She didn't answer, but sped away once more.

Nasty threw up his hands and said, "Okay, you win. For now. But remember to lock those doors.

24

A lovely woman alone is always vulnerable."

He let her leave him behind.

So he wasn't smooth. Maybe he'd handled things badly even. But not badly enough to warrant her behavior. She was scared shitless about something, and he wasn't through asking what it was. Next time he'd just have to be more forceful.

Yeah, next time he wouldn't take no for an answer.

When she ran, her long, white skirts flipped up around her knees. Even at a distance he noted how pretty her legs were. She had narrow feet. Nasty Ferrito was a foot man on occasion. Like now. He'd like to kiss Polly Crow's feet. He'd start with the toes, spend a lot of time on her instep, go slow, very slow — work his way up.

Bless the wet suit.

"Hello, Pretty Polly Put the Kettle On."

The light on the answering machine still flashed, but a click came, then a buzz.

Polly felt so sick she had to sit down. That was it, the whole message. She pushed strands of hair from her forehead and felt moisture. She was sweating, but she'd been sweating since she left the hard-muscled, cold-eyed diver behind on the waterfront. ". . . remember to lock those doors. A lovely woman alone is always vulnerable."

Another click.

"Polly, where are you? It's your favorite super-model sister. I'm so sick of being an *object*, my love. All these pushy people *pawing* me. Can we

25

meet? Puhleeze? Call me."

Fabiola. Polly smiled with relief at the sound of her twin's blessedly familiar voice and reached for the phone.

Click, buzz, click.

She peered at the counter on the answering machine. Six calls and she'd only heard two.

"Oh, Pretty Polly, you haven't been listening to me. I'm going to have to get very angry with you if you don't stop disobeying me."

Click.

She let her hand fall back into her lap. He as much hissed as whispered. Who was he? The clock on the equipment no longer functioned. Why hadn't she fixed it or bought a new one?

Buzz. Click.

"Heavenly child, I feel you are in need of me. Come to Festus and to me. You are always so calm at Another Reality. I'll make you some of my latest tea. Soar to Serenity. It's a Belinda special, darling child."

Belinda and Festus of Another Reality, a crystals, incense, taro, tea, and Wiccan-wannabe shop, had become good friends to Polly and Bobby.

Click.

"You should be there by now, Polly. You've had time to leave the studio and get home. Ah, but I mustn't be too harsh with you. Perhaps that dreadful producer has kept you late. He is much too involved. Producing. Writing. Directing. *Controlling.* Be very careful of him, Pet, he wants you,

26

you know. He wants your body, not your mind. I want your mind . . . and your body. Bye."

The scream Polly heard was her own. Shaking desperately, she stared at the readout that should have given her the caller's identification. Blocked. Every time it was blocked.

Who could she ask for help? Venus was out of the question. Fabiola would panic, too. Belinda and Festus already knew and had suggested incense and a goddess to do something or other.

Once more the buzz on the line was followed by a click, and the whisperer said, "You have tried my patience, Pretty Polly. Why can't you understand that I, and only I, am to see the woman you really are. That thin, white skirt" — he gave a grating moan — "with the light shining through. And the wind blowing. You know what that does. You do these things deliberately. Light and wind. Showing your legs. Oh, yes, your legs . . ."

The connection broke before the final message began. First there was only panting, then he said, "I've given you chances. I told you there is a connection between us. But you have denied me again. Others saw you on the dock, flaunting yourself. Disgusting. But don't worry, little Polly, I'm going to save you from yourself."

Two

"Starstruck fool," Dusty Miller muttered. "God-damn idiot groupie. Man of your age ought to know better. If Roman was here, he'd have your ass for —"

"My love life — or lack of it — is my business," Nasty pointed out.

"It's your business till you let it mess you up, then it's mine, too, partner." Dusty's brush of short, white hair and his jutting brows empha-sized leathery skin burned to a permanent ma-hogany color by years in the sun. An ex-Navy SEAL himself, he'd been Nasty's instructor when he'd first gone into training for an Underwater Demolitions Team. Roman Wilde, Nasty's clos-est friend, had also been a new recruit. Currently Roman was Dusty's absent show-and-tell in the paragon-for-a-man's-life department.

Nasty was edgy enough without Dusty's nee-dling. "Let's get down to business."

"You need a clear head for business. Right now your brains are in your pants. That's not the kind of clear head I want from you. Roman would say —"

"Roman would point out that you don't have the best track record with women." The instant the words left Nasty's mouth he regretted them,

28

but there was no going back — ever. "Don't interfere, Dusty, okay?"

Dusty shuffled through dive cruise brochures on the shop counter. Opening time was ten, still an hour away. "My record with women is just fine, bucko. If some sonovabitch hadn't thrown a grenade into that schoolhouse, Sammy'd be here with me today." Sammy had been Vietnamese and the love of Dusty's life.

"Hey," Nasty said. "Pax, huh? I shouldn't have made that dig. You didn't have any control over what happened to Sammy."

"Drop it," Dusty said shortly. "That was then. This is now. I gotta stop what I see happenin' here."

"Nothing's happening," Nasty pointed out. He ripped open a box of valves and started stacking them. "Maybe that's the problem."

Flexing his arthritic fingers, Dusty came from behind the counter. "What does that mean?"

Situated in a recessed area of shops fronting Marina Park at the north end of the Kirkland waterfront, Room Below was an airy space. Yellow, Dusty's hallmark color, dominated the decor. The shelves were painted yellow, the counters were yellow, yellow plastic chairs were provided for customers to sit in and try on wet suit boots, or fins — or to shoot the breeze with Dusty. Yellow slatted blinds hung at the windows, and yellow tiles covered the floor.

"Yellow," Nasty muttered. "Hate yellow."

"I asked what you meant," Dusty said, advancing. Despite his wiry, white regulation cut, no one would look into his laser blue eyes and take him for a man in his mid-sixties. "Nuthin's happenin' and maybe that's the problem? What the fuck does that mean?"

"I thought you were trying to give up swearing because of Junior." Junior was Roman's little girl and Dusty's favorite human being.

A smile instantly drove ripples of lines into Dusty's thin face. "She ain't here, more's the pity. I don't see her often enough. Answer the question."

"Forget it. I don't know what I meant." He meant he wasn't cut out to be a shopkeeper — even if the wares were related to his occupation of choice.

"You miss bein' in the service."

Nasty flopped into one of the too-bright chairs and shoved his long legs out in front of him. He unwrapped a stick of gum. "We both miss the Navy."

"That ankle givin' you problems?"

Nasty looked dispassionately at the knotted scars webbing his left ankle. "It never gave me enough problems to warrant them trying to stuff me behind a desk."

Dusty grunted. "You gotta adjust."

"I have adjusted. How're the sign-ups for the next classes?"

"Full. The regular series and the fast track. We got three for the rescue course, too." He flipped through a ledger. "You still got two weeks off.

But then it's back out there with the newbies."

"Dandy."

"Shit!" Dusty pulled a chair to face Nasty's and sat down. "Okay, we're goin' to do this now. No punches, bucko. Damn, but you've got cold eyes."

Nasty laughed. "Where the hell did that come from?"

"It came from in here." The older man thumped his chest. "I'm used to you. I forget what an icy bastard you are. Nuthin' shows on that face of yours."

"Useful in my line of business. You're sneaking cigarettes again."

"It *used* to be useful in the line of business you *used* to be in," Dusty reminded him. He ignored the reference to cigarettes. "For the business we're in right now it might be nice if you could crack a grin now and then."

"I'm not a stand-up comedian. Trust is what I need to inspire, and I do that."

"Yeah, yeah." Inside his khaki bush shirt, Dusty's chest expanded. "You're bored. That's what you're tellin' me. I twisted your arm to come in here with me because I was lookin' for a way to get your mind off bein' mad at the Navy — and the rest of the world. I should've let you be mad and get it over with. You got plenty of money. You don't need this place. Never spent a dime on anything as far as I can remember — except for that damnfool boat you hole up on. Nuthin' but a damnfool, ornery cat for company."

31

Nasty stacked his hands behind his neck and stared at the ceiling. He shifted his gum to a cheek, and said, "I like my boat. And my cat." But they weren't enough.

"I might have to cut down on the classes I offer and get someone to stick around the shop, but I could manage some of the classes on my own."

"Meaning?" Nasty asked, snapping his attention to Dusty's frowning face.

"Meaning if you want out, you got it. I ain't going to try to tie you down if you need to move on."

The sun was up. Pale and lacking warmth, but up. A winking path of silver speckled across the lake. "I don't want to move on," Nasty said honestly. "It isn't that. Something's changing for me. There's more than what I've got — what I've always had. Just myself. And you, of course. But I want more. You know what I mean?"

Dusty's sigh gusted before he coughed. He'd tried for years to quit smoking, but habits of forty some years died hard. "I know what you mean. You're picky, but your cock's sending you signals."

Nasty shook his head and jerked forward to bury his face in his hands. "You don't get it at all." Not entirely true. "Well, I guess I mean, that could be a small part of it."

"You said it, not me."

"What does that mean?" Nasty looked at Dusty, then laughed. "Oh, yeah. Very funny. I think I could find some witnesses to tell you there's nothing small about me. Geez, could we get some other color in here? Like black, maybe?"

"No. Don't change the subject."

"This place is so damn happy, happy. It makes me want to puke."

"Yellow's Junior's favorite color."

"Junior isn't a partner in this business. She comes once a year. And yellow is *your* favorite color."

"Yeah, that's right. Yellow is my favorite color. It was Sammy's, too. We always said we'd have a house full of kids, and a lot of yellow."

Nasty decided to leave that alone. "We're doing well here, Dust. It's a success."

"Uh-huh."

"I'm glad. For both of us. You ought to have Rose down for a visit. Take her out. We'll hire some help like you said for when we're both away from the shop."

From the town of Past Peak in the nearby foothills of the Cascade Mountains, eccentric, reclusive Rose Smothers was a friend of several years. There's been a time when Nasty had acted as her sole watchdog. Now Dusty shared the job.

"Getting Rose out takes dynamite," Dusty said. "You know that. And you're changing the subject again."

"Coffee?" Nasty levered himself to his feet and went to the coffeepot that was always hot. "Geez, I need a jump start this morning."

"I'm coffeed out." Dusty's gnarled fingers drummed on a bony knee. "What happened last night? You said you talked to the girl."

"Polly Crow's a woman, not a girl. Women don't like being called girls these days. You've got to catch up with the times, buddy."

"Shit. Woman, then."

"Rose can be persuaded out of that house of hers. She's got a soft spot for you. And she has good ideas about things like making a place look good. Like this shop."

"Nah," Dusty said, but he avoided Nasty's gaze. "Rose is one of the best. She knows I'll never let her down if she needs me. I can't . . . well, y'know, expect her to come running because I ask her to."

"If you say so," Nasty said. "But think about it. One of these days you should give her a call and lay a guilt trip on her. Tell her you're hurt because she hasn't come down to see our shop."

Dusty wrinkled his nose and furrowed his brow. "Nah." This time he didn't sound so certain. "You saw that *woman* last night? That Polly Crow?"

"I told you I did."

"And?"

"Did that shipment of decompression tables come in?"

"Yes, *dammit.* What happened with the woman?"

"Nothing happened," Nasty said, and wished his gut didn't take a nosedive every time he thought about Polly.

Dusty extended a hand. "Gimme some of that coffee, too."

"Sure." Nasty poured a second mug. "It's like mud."

"Tastes good to me," Dusty said, taking a deep swallow and closing his eyes. "You messed up, didn't you? Probably asked for her autograph and couldn't think of more'n two words to say."

"Gimme a break, Dust!" Despite himself, Nasty laughed. "What do you take me for?"

"You didn't ask for her autograph? And you had a nice, long chat, then?"

"We talked."

"She as pretty up close as she is on the television?"

"Prettier."

"Hah!" Coffee spattered as Dusty gestured triumphantly. "Gotcha. You're smitten. Stars in your eyes. What time is that fool show on? I gotta get a better look."

"Mind your own business. She doesn't like me, anyway."

Armed with paper towel, Dusty wiped up the spilled coffee. "They sleep around, y'know."

The logic took a second to follow. "You mean you think Polly sleeps around? Watch what you say, Dust."

"Or what? I'm worried about you is all. These movie types sleep around, I tell ya. She'll screw you and move on to the next candidate. I know all about it."

The seething, jumpy agitation beneath his skin made no sense. Nasty took a calming breath. "Do you? How?"

"I read all that stuff. Married to one poor schmuck. Screwing whoever they're screwing in the movie. Marry the guy they're screwin' in the movie, then screw the guy in the next movie." Dusty considered his analysis before saying, "You're a good-looking guy. What they call a real stud."

Nasty looked at the clock. "It's almost time to open."

"Yeah." Clearly enamored with his revelation, Dusty put himself in front of Nasty and did a thorough head-to-toe. "Yeah. A stud. Good-lookin' if a woman likes tall, blond, muscle-bound men with cold eyes."

"I'm not muscle—"

"Roman always said you could have any woman you wanted."

"To hell with Roman."

Dusty smirked. "Losing your temper. Now I know I'm gettin' to you. You gonna see this Polly tonight?"

"Not if she has her way."

Dusty's impressive white brows rose. "Didn't take the bait right off, huh. Smart girl."

"Woman."

"Smart woman. Geez. The smart ones never want to look too easy. You oughta know that. They tease a little. Play it like they aren't interested. She wants you."

This was a conversation Nasty would rather not have, not while he was still raw from being so close to her, from wanting her — and from seeing that he'd accomplished nothing other than making her frightened.

"She was there, wasn't she?"

"Yes." He couldn't get her fear out of his mind. It had filled her eyes, tightened her face, driven every word she'd spoken, every move she'd made.

"And you said she always goes there the same time you do."

"I always go there the same time she does."

"Okay." A march to the door and back didn't soften Dusty's irritated expression. "You both go there at the same time. Yesterday you said you thought you were both doing it deliberately. You changed your mind?"

Nasty thought about it. "I'm not sure."

"Well I am. Take it from me, I know about these things. I've watched people all my life. The pair of you want inside each other's pants and you're doin' the courtin' boogie to get there. Time to —"

"Don't say that about Polly."

"Oh, excuse me." With exaggerated steps, Dusty backed away. He picked up a feather duster and flipped along the tops of air tanks. "My mistake. I mustn't talk about the princess as if she was an ordinary female."

"She isn't. She's something else."

"Is that so? What's different? Ain't she got tits and —"

"That's it!" Nasty put down his mug and scrubbed at his face. "Okay, okay. I've got a case on Polly. And I'm touchy about it. Dust,

37

she's . . . she's different. I don't know how else to put it. She's different, and I want her."

Dusty screwed up his eyes but didn't reply.

"You know you said she was scrawny?"

Still Dusty didn't respond.

"Well, you did. She's even smaller than she looks on TV."

"Really scrawny, huh?"

Nasty gritted his teeth and said, "Really *slim.*"

"You don't like small women."

Sometimes winning was out. Nasty exhaled. "I know I've always said I like women . . . Well, I may have said —"

"You've always said you liked plenty of woman to hold on to."

"Thank you, Dusty." This wasn't going to be simple so he might as well wade on through. "I do, on some levels, like more — *substantial* women. But Polly's . . . She's . . ."

"Different," Dusty finished for him with a flip of the feathers over the cash register.

"Exactly. Her hair's not as blond as I thought. More a kind of gold color, I guess. But all that's not important. Nice figure. Her eyes are that kind of blue that's kind of dazzling. But, well —"

"But all that's not important?" Dusty suggested.

"Exactly. What's important is that I can feel who she is inside."

"Sure you can. She's a stranger you've been watching on TV and sneaking around in the dinghy to stare at."

38

Patience was a learned quality, and Nasty had learned it from necessity. There had been too many occasions when impatience could have cost his life. *Patience.* "Polly Crow's strong inside, but she's also under pressure."

"So now you're a goddamn mind reader."

"Do you want to go on with this conversation? Or shall we check the deliveries?"

"What makes you think she's under pressure?"

A beige Mercedes convertible, its top down, pulled into a slot in the parking lot out front, and a man got out. Nasty watched him without interest. "I felt it. She's frightened."

Dusty nodded. They both knew better than to really question the potential power of intuition.

"I think someone's bothering her. She made some off-the-wall comment about scrambling numbers."

"Yeah?" Interest sparked in Dusty's intense eyes. "Like what numbers?"

"Telephone, I think. She talked about knowing how you can scramble numbers to keep anonymity. I can't think of anything she'd mean but one of those scramblers people use to block telephone ID."

"Why would she say that to you?"

He wished he hadn't spent a good part of the night thinking that one over. "She must have decided I've been calling her up, I suppose. Using the answering machine from what she said. Maybe she's getting crank calls."

Dusty regarded him for a long time. "Maybe

you were right. Things didn't go so well between the two of you. Maybe this is one of those times when you walk away before anything gets started."

"Nothing has got started."

"Yeah. Just as well if she's a kook."

"She's not a kook, Dust. She's scared."

Dusty tossed the feather duster behind the counter. "Paranoid, more likely. Look, if you've got an itch, scratch it. That's what I always say. Find yourself a nice woman and take her to bed. You'll forget your little songbird."

The man from the Mercedes had strolled to the shop and was studying ads posted in the window. "I'm not going to forget her. But you can. This is my business. I'll deal with it."

"Everybody needs somebody. Everybody is somebody. Somebody needs everybody." Dusty sang the theme from *Polly's Place*. His singing voice wasn't great, but he could carry a tune. "You could just tell her you're taking notice of her theme song, and you've decided she's the somebody you need."

"Thanks, Dust. If I can't think of a better line, I'll use that."

The guy outside looked fortyish. Stocky. Strong, with the kind of moves that said he knew his strength, that he was sure of himself.

"Maybe we should open up," Dusty suggested.

A shaved head, eyes so dark brown they were almost black. A flash of gold when he parted his lips from square teeth with a wide space upper

40

front and center. "Thinks he owns the world," Nasty commented. "Must have cost him a fortune to look that casual."

"City type," Dusty said. "In shape but lives soft."

Automatically, Nasty studied the man's hands. "Yeah. Why would a guy shave his head?"

" 'Cause he's tryin' to pretend he doesn't care if he's losing his goldilocks."

Nasty hid a smile. "Maybe we don't like him, huh?"

"Maybe." Dusty laughed from his belly. "Just sizing up the unidentified male. Old habits die hard."

"Let him in."

Taking plenty of time, Dusty worked the bolts loose from the top and bottom of the doors and flipped open the lock.

The man sauntered in immediately and stood in the middle of the shop. A whiff of spicy cologne contaminated the rush of cool, clean morning air through the doors.

"Mornin'," Dusty said.

"Good day."

Affected bastard. Nasty ground the gum between his back teeth and said, "Need some help?"

"I might." The man's dark eyes took in Dusty and moved instantly to Nasty, who got the long, slow, insolent treatment. "The diver, huh?"

The diver. "I dive. You?"

"Name's Spinnel. Jack Spinnel."

Spoken as if Nasty — and everyone else in the

world — ought to be impressed. "Nice to meet you, Jack." Any man could be allowed an occasional lie.

Jack Spinnel ambled along the mask display, idly picking up first one, then another. "How's business?"

"Great," Dusty said, and dislike glinted in his eyes. He raised his brows at Nasty. "Looking for anything in particular?"

"How long have you been around here?"

Nasty's trouble antennae rose. "This is our second year."

"Winters must be slow."

"People dive in the winter."

"Yeah?" Spinnel dropped a mask back — into a tray of snorkels. "I'd have thought it was too cold."

"We're talking scuba. Wet suits. We do avoid taking people through ice." Not a ghost of a smile touched Dust's lips. "Person could get hurt — or lost — diving through ice."

Spinnel looked toward the lake. "Hell, I didn't think it ever got that cold here."

Nasty moved the gum from one side of his mouth to the other and said nothing.

"You been here in winter?" Dusty asked.

"Last winter." Spinnel sounded vague. "Most of it, anyway."

"That a fact?" Very deliberately, Dusty retrieved the misplaced mask and put it back where it belonged. "And you're planning on taking up diving this winter?"

"No. I'm a producer."

The coffee Nasty swallowed was cold. He didn't ask what Spinnel produced. Neither did Dusty.

"And a director, and writer," the other man continued. "I'm from Los Angeles."

"Figures," Dusty said.

Jack Spinnel frowned. He used a well-manicured forefinger to stir around in a box of rubber washers. "We might be able to use this place. It'd be good for your business."

Too little sleep and too much tension had shortened Nasty's temper. "Maybe you'd like to explain who you are and what you want," he said. "I've got a feeling you think we know. We don't, Mr. Spinnel."

"Jack, please." His smile endowed them with a flash of gold. "I produce, write, and direct *Polly's Place*. Sorry. I should have mentioned that up front."

"Yeah." Dusty glowered as washers spilled into lengths of hose. "Might have been a good idea. My granddaughter watches the show when she comes." His unwavering stare warned Nasty to keep his mouth shut. Since Junior didn't have a grandfather, Dusty had appointed himself surrogate.

"I've got a cowriter for some segments. Mary Reese. You've probably seen her name. But it's my show. My idea."

Nasty lowered himself back into a chair and tented his fingers. In time this guy would get to the point.

43

"I asked about you around town," Spinnel said, addressing Nasty. "Everyone's seen you. No one knows you."

Slowly, Nasty met Spinnel's eyes. "I guess I'm not gregarious."

"You're silent, that's what they say about you. Not easy to talk to."

Nasty took in a long breath through his nose. "Sorry to hear I'm not a likable guy."

"Expensive sailboat, I'm told. And you live aboard."

"Am I supposed to be impressed because you ask questions and get answers."

"I always get the answers I want," Spinnel told him. "People in this town like me. They like the show. They're glad we chose this location. It brings a lot of money into Kirkland."

"Bully for you," Nasty said. "Your point?"

"I may not be the only one who wonders about you."

"Give me names."

Spinnel turned the corners of his mouth down and shrugged. "It's not important. I can make my point without naming names. But if you make enemies in a small community, it could get hard for you to do business here."

"That's a threat," Dusty said explosively. "Where do you think you get off coming in here and threatening us. Fuck off, asshole."

"Charming," Spinnel said, without bothering to look at Dusty. "My point is that you'd better work at staying in line and getting along with people."

"Or you won't spotlight us on your show?" Nasty said, amazed at the man's balls.

"Most businesses in this town would do anything to be featured on *Polly's Place*. The print shop says their business has quadrupled since they were on. And ask those crazies who run the voodoo dolls and tell-your-fortune joint. Belinda and Festus. We had to do that one carefully — stick to the homemade soaps, and candles. Feel-good herbal tea. That kind of thing. But they've never had it so good."

"I'm happy for them. Is this the way you approach all your prospective features?"

"You aren't a prospective feature — yet. I just want you to think about making sure you don't offend anyone. Especially me. I can be a bad enemy. I could also be really easy to get along with."

"Maybe I don't care about getting along with you." Nasty didn't want to play this game anymore. "Maybe I'm just not a very friendly guy."

"But you like good-looking women."

The pieces of this puzzle dropped abruptly into place. "What man doesn't?"

Spinnel's laugh wasn't pleasant. "That's not the point. The point is what you do about it. I've seen you before. And so have some members of the cast and crew. Nice Zodiac."

Subtle as a tank in a churchyard. "I've got a Zodiac. I use it — a lot. But I don't have the only Zodiac in Kirkland."

"You've got the only Zodiac that hangs around

the docks in front of the condos where Polly lives." Spinnel's humid brown eyes turned hard. "She takes walks on those docks in the evening. And you hang around there every night at about the same time, *Ferrito.*"

"Hey —"

"Don't worry, Dusty," Nasty said rapidly. "This is between Jack, here, and me. I'll handle it."

"She's high-strung," Spinnel said.

Nasty tapped his fingertips together and squinted through them. "Is that a fact?"

"I know her very well."

How well? Nasty didn't say anything.

"What troubles her, troubles me. Do you understand what I'm telling you?"

"Sure. You're concerned about the welfare of your star. No Polly, no show. In other words, you hope I don't plan to knock her off the dock one night and drown her."

From the corner of his eye, Nasty saw Dusty close his eyes.

Spinnel squared his shoulders. "Is that supposed to be funny?"

"Yeah. But I never was much good at cracking jokes."

"Polly's more than a TV personality to me," Jackie-boy said. "Much more. Am I getting through to you now?"

Nasty regarded the man. He subjected him to the kind of careful scrutiny he'd received himself, and said, "I'm trying to be real open. I'm trying to see what you're telling me, or what I think you're trying to tell me." And he couldn't picture Polly Crow with this joker. If he could, he wouldn't like it.

"Don't tax yourself. It'll come to you." The heavy gold ring on the small finger of Jack's left hand needed careful adjustment. Then he looked sharply at Nasty. "I make it part of my job to be sure nothing upsets Polly. She's temperamental — most actresses are. And she means a great deal to me. If I thought someone was interfering with her peace of mind, I'd have to step in and sort that out."

The man might be strong. He was not, and never could be, any match for Nasty Ferrito. Very slowly, Nasty gathered his feet under him and rose. "What made you decide to come here this morning?" he asked softly. He had a head and shoulders on Spinnel.

"I'm the one asking questions."

"You *were* the one asking questions," Nasty corrected him. "Now I'm asking. There's no law against taking a Zodiac along the waterfront."

"There's a law against stalking women."

Nasty stepped close enough to make the other man have to raise his chin. "Do you want to rethink what you just suggested?"

"You don't frighten me." The sound of Spinnel swallowing made a liar of him.

Nasty smiled. "Of course I don't. Brave dude like you wouldn't be scared of anything. Too important, right? Too used to getting your way.

47

Too used to pushing people around and having them be grateful for the honor."

"I didn't come here for a fight."

Dusty snickered.

"Just as well," Nasty remarked. "You'd go away disappointed. You will anyway, but only because I make it a rule not to hit weaker opponents. Get out. Don't come back."

"Look here —"

"Out," Nasty said, turning away and opening a door.

Spinnel's attempt at nonchalance failed. His hands shook as he pushed them into his pockets. "I'll go. Because I want to. I've got a show to direct. I've said what I came to say. I'm heading you off at the pass. Just remember that."

"I can't seem to make out a word you say."

"Stay away from that dock, or I'll have to warn Polly not to walk out there."

"Did Polly ask you to come here?"

"Just stay away."

"In other words, she didn't. You'd lie and say she did anyway, but you're afraid I'd find out you were lying. What are you afraid of?"

"I'm not the one who needs to be afraid." The sun shone on Spinnel's impressive dome. He walked out, but jammed a foot in the door when Nasty would have shut it behind him. "You're being watched. Remember that. Every move you make, I'll know about it. Don't go near Polly again."

Either Polly had mentioned Nasty's approach

last night, or her boss made it his business to watch every move his star made — and every move made in her direction.

"I'll have my assistant call you about a segment. Do we have an agreement?" Tension tightened the skin around Spinnel's eyes. He really didn't want anyone going near Polly.

Nasty had never walked away from a challenge. "We'd love to talk to your assistant," he said. "We'll look forward to it." And he intended to find out if Polly enjoyed having Jack Spinnel as a personal keeper.

He heard Jack let out a breath as if he'd just won the battle. "Great. Just great. I knew you'd see this my way."

"Oh, I see everything real clearly now, Jack."

Jack giggled. "Yeah, well, we'll be talking. I've got a lot of clout around here, Ferrito, a lot of clout."

"I'll just bet you do."

"People do what I tell them to do." Spreading his arms, he backed away. "They know better than to mess with me." He bumped into the wing of the Mercedes, and sent a lopsided grin in Nasty's direction before vaulting into the driver's seat.

Nasty let the door swing shut and turned his back as the powerful engine burst to life.

"Better not mess with Jack," Dusty said sweetly. "He might hurt you."

Three

Gavin Tucker paced back and forth on the set, stopping from time to time to glare in the direction of each door into the soundstage. He tossed aside one of the big brushes he used to paint scenes live on camera.

"Can't you calm him down?" Mary Reese asked Polly. "I don't know what's got into him. He's always so laid-back. Gavin! Cool it, will you?"

"Piss off, Mary, darling," was Gavin's response. He didn't as much as check his stride.

"And the same to you, *darling*," Mary said. "Why don't you whitewash the john while you're at it. If that won't tax your talent too far."

Gavin rolled his brown eyes and extended a hand pleadingly toward Polly. "Shut her up, pet. My nerves are stretched to the max this morning. I didn't sleep a *wink* last night."

The camera crew lounged around their equipment, and makeup hovered near Polly. "Where's Jack, anyway," she asked Mary. "He's never late."

"He is today," Mary said through her teeth. "He knows we've got a tight schedule."

Polly stopped herself from asking Mary what was holding her lover up. She assumed everyone knew Mary and Jack lived together, but the fact was never mentioned.

Mary looked at her watch. "This is costing money." She snapped her fingers. "Places, people. Let's at least be ready to go. We'll take a walk-through."

Grateful to stop watching Gavin pound to and fro, Polly assumed her spot beside a park bench and ducked her head while a hairdresser draped hair behind one ear.

Makeup brushed blush over her cheekbones, powdered her nose, and went to repeat the process with Gavin.

"This is about fall," Mary called. "About getting ready to go back to school. Saying good-bye to kids who visited their divorced parents for the summer. Children coming back after visiting a parent. Acceptance. Caring. Learning to appreciate the positives. Supporting the underdog. Being open to change. Love and friendship."

"Sickening," Gavin murmured. "Sugar drips around here."

"You were saying?" Mary shouted from out front.

"Sweet," Gavin said loudly. "I was saying this is going to be a really sweet segment. Give me a big kiss, Polly, pet. In the spirit of love and friendship."

Polly had fallen into Gavin's love and friendship traps before. Just thinking about his tongue in her throat made her feel ill.

"Come on, pet," he wheedled, approaching

51

with outstretched arms. "Just to pass the time. I'm sooo bored."

"Cut it out," she told him tersely.

He came close and hitched his slim rump on the back of the bench. Tall, whip-thin, and deceptively languid, sharp intellect and a devilish grin saved Gavin's long face from being unremarkable.

"Polly, you are driving me nuts," he told her. "Let's go to bed."

She didn't bother to answer.

"You know you want me," he said softly. "Why keep holding out?"

Polly laughed. "Save the jokes for the camera."

"Did I say something funny?"

"I'm sure you meant it to be funny."

He touched the side of her face, and his lips tightened when she flinched. "You're the only thing that makes this job bearable."

"Thank you." Her skin crawled. When he wasn't making a pass, Gavin could be a nice guy, likable. "You're fabulously gifted. I like working with you." That was true.

His features softened. "Ditto, pet. Oh, ditto, ditto. Wouldn't you like to try your wings outside this little burb?"

"No," she told him honestly. "The show's national. I don't have to go anywhere. I like this little burb. I like the show — and what it stands for."

"Family values? Honor and truth?"

She wished she could put more distance between them without drawing the attention of the crew. "I think those are great values to present to children. It'll all start with them."

"What'll start with them? Slow death by sugar-coating?"

"If you hate it so much, why do you stay?"

He smoothed the backs of his fingers along her jaw. "I've already told you. I'd like to paint you, pet. Preferably nude."

"Stop it," she whispered. "You're a very talented man. You're the most talented person on the show. They need you, and I hope you stay. But I don't want this from you."

"This?" He raised one sandy brow. "What can you mean? A little harmless, friendly patter? Surely you don't begrudge a man some entertainment."

Polly made a great deal of ensuring her striped shirt was tucked into her jeans.

"Come to LA with me, pretty Polly."

She froze. Her scalp prickled.

"Hey, hey," Gavin said, looking closely into her face. "You okay? You look ill. Or are you overwhelmed with excitement because I've just suggested what you've always wanted to do?"

". . . pretty Polly." As she looked at Gavin, his eyes seemed to expand.

He took her by the shoulders. "Polly? What is it?"

She shook her head. "Nothing. Nothing at all." Pretty Polly was something she'd been teased with all her life. She was starting to see bogeymen everywhere she looked, and it had to stop.

"Calling Polly!" A crew member approached with a cordless phone in hand.

Polly smiled at him and took the set. "Polly Crow here."

She heard a sound as if the caller clicked his tongue. There was a short laugh, then a dial tone. Polly waited a moment, then looked at the earpiece. "Are you sure someone asked for me?" The unpleasant flip in her stomach was too familiar.

The man frowned. "Sure I'm sure."

Polly shrugged. "They hung up." She handed back the phone, hoping she looked more unconcerned than she felt. "Thanks."

Encased in red-and-yellow-striped spandex, Art Loder wandered onto the set, with his sister Jennifer trailing behind. Carrying their shaggy red costume heads, they were dressed as Down and Out, the much-beloved Main Monsters of *Polly's Place* fame.

"Oh, goody," Gavin murmured. "Here come the cutesy Aussie twins. It's shew time, folks."

"Put a sock in it," Polly told him. Who was tormenting her? Why didn't he stop?

Gavin kissed her cheek, and let his mouth linger near her ear. "I bet you didn't say that to the dive boy, my pet."

She jumped away from him.

"Hey, mates," Art said before Polly had a chance to ask Gavin what he meant. "What's the bother, then? It's bloody hot hanging around like this. Where's Jackie?"

54

"How should we bloody know where your old mate is?" Gavin asked, aping Art's accent.

Brother and sister were close to the same height, close to six feet, and very athletic. Among their credits were stints as circus performers in their native Australia and around the world. The show provided a perfect forum for spectacular acrobatic and dancing skills.

Jennifer grinned at Polly. The other woman had a wry sense of humor and had become a good friend. Jennifer had been with Polly the first time she heard the man on the answering machine. Jennifer had agreed that the less said about it, the better.

As she'd done so often, Polly considered who might be making the calls. Yet again, she came up empty of ideas — except for the ridiculous notion about the diver.

An outer door opened and thundered shut again. Frowning ominously, Jack strode through the jumble of wardrobe, props, equipment, and crew and fell into his chair. He ignored everyone and picked up the day's script.

All eyes turned to Mary.

Mary advanced on Jack. She tossed back her curly auburn hair and swung her hips with each exaggeratedly deliberate step.

"Uh-oh," Art said very quietly. "Might be time for us chickens to go on a walkabout."

"And miss the show?" Jennifer said. "Never. She's going to chew the bastard up and swallow him. Rather her than me, mates."

Colorful language — and fantastic physical power and grace — added up to the Loders' considerable, but only outstanding features. Hazel-eyed and brown-haired, with pleasant but ordinary faces, once out of the red-and-yellow costumes they'd never be noticed in a crowd.

Polly shrugged away from Gavin and sat on the bench. Thank God this wasn't a day when they were doing a live shoot — and that they already had several shows in the can.

"I had business to attend to," Jack shouted suddenly. "Am I supposed to ask your permission before I make a move?"

"Keep your voice down." Mary didn't. Fury emanated from her short, voluptuous body. "It could have waited — if it was something you had to do at all."

"I had to do it. Let's get on with this."

Art and Jennifer put on their heads and broke into a series of tumbling falls.

"Cut!" Mary swung toward the set. "Take the day off."

"Places," Jack shouted. "Now!"

"Clear the goddamn set," Mary said. "Go on. Clear out."

Jack shot to his feet. "We don't have time to take a day off. And you don't give the orders around here."

"If you don't want . . ." Mary's remarkable turquoise eyes glittered. "Don't turn this into a bigger mistake than it already is, Jack."

He threw the script on the seat of his chair and stalked to brace his weight against a wall. "I hate jealous bitches," he ground out. "This is my show. Get it? Mine. You don't like it — I find another writer."

"Like hell." Brilliant color suffused Mary's pale, freckled skin. "You're full of it, Jack. You may be the producer and director. I'm the story chief. And I'm your skin, Jack. Without me, you bleed."

Jennifer and Art dropped to sit on the floor. The camera crews drifted toward the back of the soundstage.

"Children," Gavin called sweetly. "Why don't we all play together nicely. We're going to teach the little darlings about love and acceptance. Isn't that right, Mary, dear?"

Polly held her breath. She wanted out of here, and she wanted to stop looking for crazies around every corner.

Jack and Mary ignored Gavin's interruption.

"Don't stir it up," Polly told him, letting breath out again. "Maybe we should just melt out of here."

Mary stood very close to Jack, and said, "Where were you? Who were you with?"

"None of your . . ." Jack tilted his chin up. "Give it up, Mary."

"Why are you doing this?" Mary asked. "It was something to do with her, wasn't it? You ignored what I told you and went to talk to him about —"

"Shut up," Jack told her, his teeth bared. "I

don't need your permission to do what the hell I like."

"Don't you?" Mary closed in on him. "Are you sure you don't want to revise that? You do if you want things to keep running smoothly around here."

"Ugly beast, is jealousy," Gavin commented. "Makes the shrew forget to be careful what she says."

"What is she jealous of?"

Gavin sat down on the bench and put an arm around Polly's shoulders. "You really don't know, do you? Amazing. That's what I like best about you. You're so naive."

"I don't have a clue what you're suggesting," Polly said, edging away.

He gripped her shoulder. "Let's just say it could be a great idea if you and I showed Mary she's got nothing to be jealous about."

Polly stared at him. Then she stared at Jack and Mary.

"Yeah," Gavin said. "That's what I mean. That's what she thinks."

"But I'm here. I've been here. How can she think he's been with me?"

"She doesn't. Not this morning, anyway. But I think I know what she does think. Let's change her mind."

"There's nothing to change her mind about."

"She thinks there is," Gavin said. "She thinks Jack's in love with you. Lust with you. We can make her feel a whole lot better by showing her we're the swirl flavor of the month."

Polly turned her face up to his — and gasped as his mouth closed over hers.

Daylight felt so much safer. Daylight and lots of people around. Polly crossed to Lakeview Drive and strolled along the shop fronts. Cars jammed the narrow street. The day was warmer than any during the previous week. Bare tanned arms and legs were in evidence again. Young laughter rippled among sidewalk throngs. Kirkland's quaintly trendy atmosphere drew gaggles of well-heeled people from the surrounding areas.

Relaxing took deliberate effort. She let her shoulders drop and concentrated on breathing from her stomach. The morning's shoot had been an almost complete disaster. Gavin's segment had gone well enough. He'd painted a backdrop of trees, their leaves turning gold, while Down and Out pretended misery at being shunned. Then war broke out again between Mary and Jack.

Polly had excused herself and left.

She couldn't put the latest telephone contact out of her mind.

The smell of fresh-baked bread drifted from a patisserie to mingle with the aroma of good coffee. Normal pleasures on a normal day. She had to stop letting that creep get to her. That's what he wanted — to make her miserable.

Polly stopped to look at paintings in a gallery window. Seascapes were big here. And wolves.

She stared at a pack of wolves among bare sapling trunks, in the snow. The desolation, and beauty of the scene tightened her throat.

Another browser stopped beside her, and she felt a harmony in their joint silence.

Above the group wolf painting, hung another of a single animal peering from the shelter of a rock. Polly looked from the animal's light, piercing eyes, to the eyes of the person beside her.

He looked back at her.

"Crumb," she said very faintly, scarcely able to breathe. "You just . . . appear." She glanced down, half-expecting him to be barefoot. He wore tennis shoes.

"I followed you here," he said with no sign of remorse on his coldly handsome face. "You were preoccupied. That's why you didn't hear me."

"Did you leave messages on my answering machine?" she asked, blurting out the question before she could consider the wisdom of caution. "Did you call me this morning and hang up?"

He shook his head. "No."

"As if you'd admit it." Gathering what poise she could muster, Polly walked on.

Mr. Nasty Ferrito, with his definite but oddly appealing limp, walked right beside her, his hands crammed into the pockets of his tight, many-times-washed jeans. "I owe you an apology, Polly," he said.

"You owe me privacy."

"Everyone has a right to privacy. I don't want to make a nuisance of myself."

She could feel him. Darn it, she could feel him in places she shouldn't even be aware of on a bright, sunny day, on a very public sidewalk — with a total stranger.

What a stranger.

What a man.

"You're a nuisance, Mr. Ferrito. Thanks for the apology. I accept it. Good-bye."

"I've never done this before."

She stopped.

So did Nasty Ferrito.

"You're bothering me," she told him. "You may be a perfectly nice person, but you frighten me." No, no! Why did her mouth keep saying things she'd had no intention of saying? "I mean —"

"Oh, Polly." Distress actually softened his cool, brown eyes. He slipped a big, warm hand beneath her arm. "I'm sorry. You're going to let me buy you some coffee."

"I don't drink coffee." He made her tingle, actually tingle. This was nuts.

He smiled. No man should look that appealing just because he smiled. "Beer?" he suggested. "A martini? A fuzzy navel? Sangria? A missionary's downfall? A tropical itch?"

She wrinkled her nose in distaste.

"Lemonade."

"No, thank you."

"I'm a pussy cat. Honest. Ask anyone. Ask my partner, Dusty."

A pussy cat? A six-foot-something, blond,

brown-eyed, tanned, all-muscle pussy cat? "I don't think so."

"What do you drink?"

"Tea," she said without thinking — again.

"Tea it'll be," he told her, smiling — again.

The result was the same as before, her mouth opened but she couldn't think of a thing to say. He couldn't be the one making the calls. Distracted, she let him steer her along the sidewalk.

"I guess the place on the corner serves tea?"

"I'm going to Another Reality," Polly told him, gathering some of her composure, but still not enough to be as discreet as she ought to be.

"Voodoo dolls and fortune-telling," he commented. "I know the place."

"Belinda and Festus don't sell voodoo dolls," she told him, feeling defensive on her friends' behalf.

He held her arm a little tighter. "I'm sure they don't. I was just repeating something an idiot told me."

His remark mollified her slightly. If he was dangerous, threatening-type dangerous, she'd feel it. All she felt was . . . She felt hot.

"They go in for tea there, don't they? Didn't I hear that?"

"Yes," she told him. "But you won't like it."

"How do you know?"

Without missing a beat, they both turned down Kirkland Avenue toward an area of shops fronting the water.

"I like tea," Nasty persisted. He pointed along

the first of three sides of store windows. "Our shop's over there. You'll like my partner Dusty. Once you get used to editing his language."

"He doesn't speak English?"

"He speaks English. Colorful English, if you know what I mean."

What would Nasty Ferrito, who thought he had to warn her about "colorful" English, think if he knew what she'd once been? Polly hummed softly. No one must know about that, not here. Parents wouldn't want their children to watch a show hosted by a woman who'd once been considered an undesirable. And the man on the answering machine? What would he do if he found out? Leave her alone at last — or decide she was even more of a challenge, even more a creature to be saved?

"Penny for 'em, Polly."

She stopped walking. "I didn't say I wanted to go anywhere with you. So, if you'll excuse me?"

"Do you find me really objectionable."

"No."

"Ugly?"

He wasn't going to give up. "No." She shouldn't be glad, but she was.

"Is there a boyfriend somewhere?" His gaze became too intent.

"No," Polly said, and crossed her arms.

"Would it be terrible to sit in a nice, safe shop and drink tea with me?"

She thought about it. "I guess not."

Nasty's smile did its magic act again. "Terrific.

After you." He reached around her to open a door.

She hadn't noticed they were already outside the dream-catchers-, crystals-, and dusty books-filled windows of Another Reality.

Nothing terrible could happen to her in Belinda and Festus's shop.

Sounds of thunder rolled from speakers high on the walls of the crowded shop. Lightning crackled. Coyotes howled. Burning incense raised a pungent, vaguely blue haze overall.

"Hokey," Nasty remarked without inflection. "Maybe they do carry voodoo dolls."

"Polly!" Belinda, joint owner of the shop with Festus, flew toward her — a remarkable feat for a woman as stately as Belinda. "You came just in time. Another minute and I intended to send Festus to find you. Where is our darling Bobby? He isn't back in school yet, is he?"

"Not quite." Polly raised her voice over a fresh rumble of thunder. "He's with my mother at Hole Point."

"Ah, dear Venus. How are the belly-dancing courses doing?"

"Very well," Polly said, avoiding looking at Nasty. "She told me to remember her to you."

"Festus is upstairs. I'll call him down in a moment. He's like a child with his new dome. The silly man stays up almost all night watching his beloved stars."

Polly didn't know Belinda or Festus's last names, and she wasn't sure of their relationship to each other. They did share the living quarters above Another Reality, and, in an enclosed loft space, Festus pursued his passion for astronomy.

Belinda fluffed out the yards of tiny purple-and-orange pleats in her floor-length gauze skirts. She made an odd face at Polly, then hitched at the voluminous, hooded tunic she wore over the skirt.

Leaning toward her friend, Polly raised her brows in question.

"I expect you'd *both* like tea?" Belinda asked. Her fulsome voice vibrated with emphasis.

"Oh." Flustered at her own omission, Polly grasped Nasty's very substantial upper arm and said, "This is Nasty Ferrito."

"I know," Belinda said. "The shop with all those things for under the water."

"Dive shop," Nasty said, pleasantly enough. "Interesting place you've got here."

"We like it," Belinda said regally. Her narrow, green eyes made sure she'd never forget an inch of Nasty's person. An audible sigh issued from her full lips before she picked up a small hemp bag tied with green twine and pressed it into Polly's free hand. "Carry this with you at all times."

Polly knew better than to ask what it was.

"Sexual stamina," Belinda announced as she turned away. "I swear by it. And you're obviously going to need it."

The flaming heat in her face mortified Polly, but not as much as the fact that she dropped the bag.

65

Nasty picked it up and gave it to her again. He didn't say a word, and he didn't grin. Polly liked him for that.

"Sit down, sit down," Belinda instructed, waving them toward three rickety card tables arranged around a potbellied stove in the center of the shop. "I'm going to have to rethink Serenity."

Nasty pulled out a metal chair for Polly and took one for himself. "Serenity? Is that code for something?"

"It's tea," Polly told him. "Soar to Serenity tea."

"Let's get off to a better start." He sounded so earnest. "Last night was a disaster."

"We didn't get off to a start at all."

"But we'd like to, wouldn't we?"

Would she? Yes. Yes, darn it all, she would. Polly couldn't hold his gaze. She looked at his mouth. The bottom lip was much fuller than the top, the outline very distinct. The corners turned up a little. Ironic in a man who rationed his smiles. When he did smile, dimples in his lean cheeks were an irresistible surprise.

"Wouldn't we, Polly?"

He wore a soft denim shirt very well. With a physique like his, he'd wear anything well . . . or nothing.

She hummed and hefted the little hemp bag in her palm.

"You hum a lot," he said.

"Do I?"

"Yeah. You do it on the show when you're

demonstrating something, too. And you would like to start something with me."

"You have incredible nerve."

"Only when I need incredible nerve." He hooked his arms over the back of his chair. "And only when it's worth what it costs me to do what doesn't come naturally."

A man's chest wasn't supposed to be so fascinating to a woman. In fact, men always said women weren't turned on by men's bodies.

Polly sniffed, and murmured, "Shows what they know."

Nasty looked around. "Who?"

"No one," she said, amused at her own behavior. Whatever sex appeal was, this man had enough for an army of men. His legs pressed against the jeans, made hard ridges where very developed muscles flexed. The fabric was bleached in places — places more prominent than other places.

Another rush of heat to her face embarrassed Polly. "What doesn't come to you naturally?" she asked, covering her own awkwardness.

"Making the moves." Not a shadow of humor touched his features now. "Saying the right things, in the right tone of voice. Flattering a woman. Doing the things a woman needs and wants from a man — if he wants to mean something to her. That kind of thing."

Polly had often been pegged as a chatterer. No smart words came to mind right now, but she couldn't help liking his direct approach.

"I was out of line last night," he said.

A stick of incense smoldered in a holder at the middle of the table. Polly picked it up and sniffed, then coughed.

"It wasn't because I meant to be out of line. Like I've said, I haven't had much experience saying the right things to a woman."

"I believe you."

"Ouch. I deserved that, I guess."

Incense nauseated her. She put the holder on the next table.

"It never mattered before."

Polly studied him.

He tipped his chair onto its back legs and jiggled. "It matters now, and I don't care if I make a fool of myself telling you."

"You don't know me."

The sight of the tip of his tongue, curling over his top teeth, made Polly swallow hard. He said, "One day I'll explain why I do know you. Not all the details, of course, but a good deal. Everyone has special skills. Judging people is one of mine. I'm good at it."

"You're humble, too."

"I'm honest. You're a very special woman. All the more reason why I shouldn't have pushed you the way I did."

"Why did you?"

"I wasn't getting through to you. And I didn't want you to go. I didn't handle the situation well. I'm going to do better from here on."

From here on. He didn't know anything about

her, but he spoke as if they had a future. "You've picked me. That's what you're telling me. You've picked me and, as far as you're concerned, that means I'll automatically pick you. Interesting theory."

Nasty leaned across the table so suddenly she jumped. He pulled her hands out of her lap and held them beneath his on top of the table. "Desperate theory," he said. His voice was deep. "I've never thought I could fall in love before."

The rush Polly felt was as if ice had passed across her skin. Goose bumps shot over her arms and legs. Deep inside she trembled. "You can't say something like that," she whispered. "You can't."

"I just did."

"But you shouldn't."

"I did."

"You don't think you could love me. Crumb! That sounds mad."

"There's nothing mad about me."

"There has to be. I'm a stranger."

"I've watched you for weeks."

"But you don't *know* me."

"I'm going to."

This was the stuff of movies, not Polly Crow's life. He sounded — obsessed? *Oh.* "I've got to go."

"I've scared you. Again."

"Please let me leave."

"If I do, I'll have blown it. You'll never let me talk to you like this again."

69

How right he was. "No." How much she wanted him to be wrong. How much she wanted . . . what did she want? They were strangers. He was a fantastically beautiful stranger, but facts were facts. He behaved as if he was obsessed with her — like the whisperer on the answering machine.

"Polly, forget I just made an ass of myself by saying something you can't be expected to take seriously. Just tell me you'll see me again. And again. And again."

"I'm a —"

"Please?"

"I've got a son."

"I know. I've seen you with him. He looks like a nice kid."

"The best. He didn't have an easy time of it when he was little. Now he's my life, and I intend to make sure he knows it. No one's ever going to be more important to me than Bobby."

"Little boys grow up into men. Then their mommies had better have someone else to love."

"I'm used to being alone."

With his forefingers, he followed the tendons down her wrists and over the tops of her hands. "I'm used to being alone, too. I do it real well. No challenge anymore. I shouldn't have assumed you didn't have a husband just because I haven't seen him."

Her hands trembled. "I don't have a husband."

"Somehow I didn't think you did. What did you mean about numbers? And scrambling numbers? You're talking about someone making crank calls, aren't you? A man?"

He was steadily lulling her into careless trust. "It doesn't matter what I meant. Some things go with the territory. They aren't nice, but they don't worry me." The occasional fib could be excused.

"You could have fooled me. You were as jumpy as a cat. Come to that, you still are."

"I'm never jumpy. You catch me off guard is all. One minute you're nowhere, then you're right in front of me — or behind me."

"Sorry. In future I'll whistle or something."

"Don't!"

"You don't like whistling?"

"It's creepy."

"Yeah?" He seemed fascinated by any revelation about her, no matter how insignificant. "Do you like to swim?"

"Sure." Polly couldn't swim, but it embarrassed her to admit as much.

"Ever done any diving?"

"No."

"Would you like to learn?"

"I don't know." Even if his eyes were cold — or remote, maybe — he looked at her as if she was important. "Here comes Belinda."

"If some crank's making calls, I want to know about it, Polly."

Now he sounded possessive as well as obsessive. "There's nothing you need to know." He'd actually told her — a woman he was speaking to for only the second time — that he thought he could *love* her. "Belinda! You didn't have to bring food, too."

"Of course I did, child." If Belinda was a day over forty-five Polly would be amazed, but she often treated Polly as if she were her granddaughter. "Taste this." She set down a tray, placed cups in front of Polly and Nasty, and poured pink tea from a black pot scattered with silver stars and moons.

Polly drank some of the sweet, fruity-tasting brew and watched Nasty over the rim of her cup. At times like this it might be nice to have his gift for expressionless stares.

"What do you think?" Belinda asked. She tossed her long, dark, single braid behind her back. "Be honest with me. I've been working on this a long time."

"Interesting," Nasty commented.

Polly pursed her lips to contain a giggle.

"You're the first to try it."

"We're honored," Nasty said, still deadpan.

Belinda set a plate of small, dark red cookies on the table. "These are made of the same ingredients. Baking intensifies the color."

There was nothing for it but to try Belinda's offerings. The taste was similar to the tea, but stronger.

"Good," Polly said. Not great, but not bad. Sometimes kindness became more important than comfort anyway. "What are they?"

She held her breath and felt Nasty do the same.

"Cherry," Belinda said. "I dried them myself.

And honey, lots of honey."

Polly stifled a giggle of relief.

"And ginseng, and powdered deer antler," Belinda continued. "The libido is bound to find a new wellspring of vitality. You will let me know if I've got the proportions right?"

"Will do," Nasty said promptly. "Won't we, Polly?"

Belinda raised her chin regally. "I'm going to call the tea, Ever Ready."

Polly's laughter joined Nasty's. She popped a whole cookie into her mouth.

Umbrage expanded Belinda's considerable bosom. "Why that should amuse you, I can't imagine. No matter. I have a little gift for you, Nasty. What a very odd name that is."

"It suits him," Polly said, smiling into her tea and feeling increasingly bold. She'd try to forget his ridiculous declaration. "He likes to do and say awful things to get people's attention. Very nasty."

"Really? How unusual."

Nasty waited until Polly looked at him. "If that's what you want to believe?" He gestured submission. "How about one of those diving lessons? We'd start in a nice, warm pool."

"I'll think about it."

Belinda dug into a concealed pocket and produced another small hemp bag. This she dropped, very deliberately, into Nasty's lap.

He looked at it.

So did Belinda.

So did Polly.

"A gift," Belinda said. "It could not have been for anyone but you."

"How kind," Nasty said.

"Because you belong to Polly."

"Belinda!" Polly choked and coughed.

"Thanks," Nasty said, all serious gratitude. The bag still rested on his fly. "My very own supply of sexual stamina."

"Oh, no," Belinda said. "You don't need any more of that. Your talisman is quite different. It's called, Inspiration. Men can be such unimaginative lovers — not that I suppose you are. But tuck that little bag under your pillow and remember the magic word."

Nasty and Polly waited.

"Foreplay," Belinda caroled.

In the thick silence that followed, Polly picked up a second cookie and took a bite. She dared another peek at the bag on Nasty's lap and choked — again. The bag jerked and slid sideways.

Nasty grabbed it and scooted his chair under the table. And then he drank his tea as if he loved it and held out his cup for more.

Something caught Polly's attention. A curving iron staircase led from a back corner of the store to the second floor. The movement she'd seen was willowy, gray-haired Festus getting to his feet and climbing down. She hadn't even noticed him sitting up there on the steps.

Fortunately, today Festus wasn't robed as the warlock he fancied himself to be. A gray silk shirt and soft, gray corduroy slacks fell in folds around his tall, thin body. He advanced on the group by the stove and said, "Glad to see you, Polly," but didn't look glad at all.

"Hi, Festus," Polly said, disturbed by the concern in his blue eyes. "Belinda says you're having fun with the new dome."

"Fun?" His narrow nostrils flared. "Fun is for dabblers. My study of the stars is of an entirely different nature."

"Yes," Polly said. "Well, Festus, this is Nasty Ferrito."

Festus took a pair of horn-rimmed glasses from his shirt pocket, perched them on the end of his very long nose, and peered at Nasty. "Athletic-looking specimen," he remarked. "One of those, are you? Ballplayer, or whatever?"

"Festus," Belinda hissed. "He's from the shop that sells the water things. Room Below, it's called."

"Whatever." Festus turned all of his considerable intensity on Polly. "If I'd known you were going to be here I could have said so."

"Who wanted to know?" she asked.

"He didn't catch up with you then?"

Belinda shifted irritably. "For goodness sake, Festus, you might as well get on with it. I'm sorry, Polly. I should have mentioned it as soon as you came, but I do so like the look of your new beau — and I don't see why *convention* should stop a woman from enjoying herself."

"He said he's had trouble getting you at the condo. He tried to reach you at Hole Point. No luck. The studio told him to try Another Reality."

Polly felt light-headed. She also felt Nasty watching her.

"Sounded nice enough. Obviously can't wait to get his hands on you again."

Belinda's furious, *"Festus,"* drowned out Polly's nervous gasp.

"Any hope of you getting to the point?" Nasty asked Festus. "You may be having *fun* with this. Polly isn't — and I'm not amused, either."

"Neither am I," Belinda said.

"Such a fuss," Festus muttered. "Fuss about everything. Who else would be coming back to look for you? Desperate to put things right again. Hardly able to wait to see Bobby. Sam, of course. Your husband."

Polly closed her eyes.

"He said you made a mistake, but everyone gets to make one mistake. He just wants to help you put it behind you."

Four

Cell phones were a blessing and a curse.

Nasty stretched out on the V-berth in his forty-five-foot ketch, and resigned himself to an interrogation, Roman Wilde style. Roman didn't pull punches.

"So tell me all about it," Roman said.

Dusty had talked. Damn Dusty, anyway. "You called me," Nasty said. "You've gotta be the one with something to tell."

"Don't play dumb with me," Roman growled. "Dusty called."

"You amaze me. He did? Why would he call you? Aw, shucks, I expect he wanted to ask about Junior. Ain't that cute?" Wait till he got his hands on the old troublemaker.

"Sure he wanted to ask about Junior. He calls every week and checks on her. And on Marta. He's an equal-opportunity grandpa."

Roman and his wife, Phoenix, had two little girls now, the youngest about eighteen months old, but Dusty had spent a lot of time with Junior and almost none with Marta. Sometimes he tried to hide his partiality, but not often.

"How's Montana?" Nasty asked scrambling for safe ground. "Funny, I still can't peg you as a fledgling rancher."

"I can't peg you as running a dive shop, but you do. Tell me about this —"

"How's that foolish woman who married you?"

A sigh gusted into Nasty's ear. "Phoenix is wonderful. Phoenix is always wonderful. She loves bringing the kids up here. I don't deserve her."

"You're right there, old buddy. Never could figure out what she sees in you."

"Neither can I," Roman said, too affably. "You aren't pulling it off."

Still wet from the shower, and buck naked, Nasty scooted down the bunk, propped his crossed feet on the bulkhead, and locked his knees. He deliberately looked away from his left ankle. "You do know this is expensive, don't you?"

"Huh?"

"Long-distance."

"I called you, friend."

"On *my* cell phone. My bill, in case you've forgotten."

"You don't give a . . . Darn, you've got a way of making me digress. You don't care how much this call is costing you. What does matter for some reason is getting out of telling me about this woman you've fallen for. Dusty says you're pining away because of something you won't tell him."

"Dusty talks too much."

"Dusty says he's worried about you. You've been avoiding him for three days."

Nasty yanked a pillow beneath his head. "This isn't simple, Roman. Give me a chance to think."

Three days since he'd left Polly with her friends at Another Reality. Three days when he'd tried to figure out why she'd told him she wasn't married if she was.

The only reason for her to say she wasn't married would be because she was interested in him and thought he'd be put off by discovering she had a husband. When he'd forced the first meeting she'd mentioned telling her husband. He'd said she didn't have one because he couldn't find any record to suggest otherwise. Another point that irked him. He didn't make careless intelligence mistakes like that. He'd have been dead a long time ago if he had.

Water still glistened in the hairs on his legs. That water was cooling, and it didn't feel great on a not-very-warm morning. "I need to get dressed," he told Roman. "We'll have this conversation later. Dusty's worrying about nothing. So are you."

"Are you telling me there isn't a woman? You haven't turned into a groupie over the star of *Polly's Place*?"

Nasty tended to forget the show was nationally syndicated. He'd rather forget permanently. He didn't like thinking about so many people watching Polly.

"You're not very talkative," Roman said.

A possessive woman wouldn't make the cut with him, Nasty thought. He couldn't expect

79

Polly to feel less protective of her independence.

"Hey, Nasty?"

"Yeah. I'm here. So far I haven't clawed my way up any fences to get at her, screaming and crying all the way," he said. "And I haven't sent her my underwear."

That announcement shut Roman up — momentarily.

"What are you talking about?" he asked at last. "Who said anything about sending underwear?"

"Isn't that what groupies do?"

Roman cleared his throat. "I've never been a groupie."

"Neither have I. Give my love to Phoenix and the girls."

"Not so fast," Roman said. "What about this woman?"

"You never did know when to leave things alone." Nasty made a fist over his eyes.

"Nasty?"

"Yeah. I'm here."

"The woman?"

He ran his fingers through his short, thick hair. "It's none of your goddamn — crumb!" Polly didn't like bad language.

"Huh? What did you just say?"

Nasty stared up at the deckhead. "I'm losing it — starting to sound like her." Geez. "No, no, forget I said that. I'm in perfect control."

A clattering sound came from up top.

"Buddy?" Roman said. "I don't think we should put this discussion off."

More clattering. Nasty covered the mouthpiece and shouted, "Who's there?"

Seven launched herself through the cabin door and landed on Nasty's belly. He winced as twenty pointy little claws dug into his skin.

"Nasty?"

"Yeah, yeah," Nasty said into the phone. "I'm here. Cat's in one of her mad moods. My belly's never going to be the same."

Seven walked delicately up to settle on his chest. He heard a female voice call, "Hello?" probably from the steps down to the saloon. He lay absolutely still.

"Nasty?" Roman said again.

Nasty whispered, "Shut up."

"Hello?" the very familiar female voice said once more, much softer, and even more unsure than the first time. "Are you here?"

He'd tossed his clothes in the hamper. His wet towel was in front of the open door to his cabin. "Shit," he said, with feeling.

"Something's going on there."

He lifted the phone and glared at it.

"Um, Nasty?" she whispered this time, a hoarse, nervous whisper that reached him clearly in the quiet interior of the ketch. The only other sound was of water gently lapping at the hull.

"Answer me," came from the phone, agitated. "Are you in trouble? I'll call Dusty."

"No," Nasty whispered into the phone urgently. "Hold on. Just shut up a minute."

He heard Polly say, "I knew I shouldn't have

81

come," then the sound of her feet on the carpeted deck in the saloon.

She was leaving.

"Polly! Hey, Polly, don't go."

"Polly, huh," Roman said with too much amusement in his voice. "What's she like in the flesh?"

"Later," Nasty told him, "and don't call me. I'll get back to you later."

"Why —"

"Later," Nasty said. "Do this for me, friend. Don't call back, okay?"

"Okay."

Nasty hung up. "Polly! I'm in here. Polly, don't leave, please."

"I'm not. I thought you weren't" — she stared at him, openmouthed, from the doorway — "I thought you weren't here," she finished faintly.

"Ah, excuse me. I just got out of the shower."

"Uh-huh." She held his gaze as if looking into his eyes would make them both believe he wasn't naked.

"I got a phone call."

She nodded, kept on nodding.

He smiled at her and rolled his hips, very slightly, away. "Roman Wilde. He's a very old friend. We were in the service together."

Great, now all she'd have to do was glance, and she'd get a perfect moon view.

"The service?" Her voice cracked. She looked toward the skylight. "You were in the service?"

"Navy."

"Um, I'm sorry, I must be embarrassing you. I thought you called me in. I'll go."

He laughed and winced at the hollow sound of it. "Embarrassed? Me? No way."

"Of course not. But I'll just . . . I'll come back another time."

Seven chose that moment to stroll down and settle in his lap. Nasty closed his eyes.

"Yes, well, good-bye then," Polly murmured.

"Please don't leave. I want to talk to you. Maybe you could find some place to sit down out there and wait?"

"It's not a good time."

Nasty pushed up onto his elbows. When he put a hand on Seven, those claws went to work again. He sucked in a sharp breath.

"What's the matter?" Polly took a step toward him. "You're hurt!"

"No, I'm not. I'm fine."

Her gaze shifted, as he'd known it would, to the cat. Seven peeked back at her over his hip. "Nice cat," she said, swallowing loudly enough to sound like a trigger snick.

Nasty fell back. He fell back, draped a forearm over his eyes, and laughed. Seven's weight departed abruptly. Nasty kept on laughing. He fought for breath and wiped tears from his eyes.

Polly's rapt attention was on his face again. She pointed over her shoulder. "I'll . . . I'll wait in there, if you're sure that's okay."

He found enough air to say, "Yes. Yes, please."

She spun away, the wrong way, and bumped

into the bulkhead. Her faint, "Oh," was all Nasty heard before she rushed from the cabin.

Swinging his feet to the floor, he listened closely, afraid he'd hear her leaving the boat. If she did, he'd run after her — with or without clothes.

He didn't hear a sound.

She'd come looking for him. She'd found out which boat was his and where it was moored and actually come.

The nearest locker yielded a pair of wrinkled jeans shorts. He tore them out, stuffed his feet through the legs, and hauled them up — and gritted his teeth when he closed the zipper too carelessly.

He ducked his head and stepped through the doorway. Polly stood in the middle of the saloon with Seven brushing around her ankles.

"Hi." She gave him a wiggle-fingered little wave. "Your partner told me where I might find you. I should have called, but I didn't think there were phones on boats."

"Cell phone," he said. "Radio works, too. And you can hook up phone lines when you're at moorage."

"I see." She saw him, from head to toe, and parts in between, and then she blushed. "I don't know much about boats."

"What do you think of this one?"

"It's very nice. I didn't know you could have wood-burning stoves, and" — she indicated the teak and brass and leather, and Oriental carpets

— "and all this. Like a comfortable house. You've got great taste."

"Thanks."

Yellow butterflies were scattered across the high-waisted white dress she wore. When she shrugged her shoulders, the waist became a sweet halter for her pretty breasts. He'd like to see her breasts, to hold them, to do what it would take to make them respond to him.

"Look, I really apologize," he told her in a rush. "When you live alone you get careless about things like clothes."

"Oh, you don't have to apologize."

"Yes, I do. I'm sure I shocked you."

"Not at all," she told him. "No, I wasn't shocked."

He wrinkled his brow. "You weren't? I thought you might not be too thrilled to be confronted with —"

"No, really! Honestly, you looked very nice."

They stared at each other. Nasty couldn't keep the question out of his eyes. He saw the confusion in hers.

"Perhaps you want to say you didn't really mean that?" he suggested.

"No" — her tilted smile was wry — "no, I don't. I shouldn't have said it, but it's true. Doesn't that make me a forward woman?"

"It makes you exactly what I felt you were. You're a woman who tries to say it like it is."

"You can say that after the other day?"

Nasty checked the old ship's clock on the bulkhead above shelves of books. "It's noon. We could . . . No, you don't drink anything but tea, do you? I'll make tea if you'll drink it."

"I like white wine."

"I've got white wine."

"I guess it must be fate then, again?" She slid into the dark green leather banquette that curled around three sides of a teak table. "This is so lovely. Have you lived here long?"

"No." The wine was cold — thank god. "Since last year."

"Longer than I've been in Kirkland."

"You've been here almost a year."

Her chin came up. "You've done some homework on me."

"I've tried. Believe it or not, I'm a cautious man. About some things."

"What things?" she asked, as the cork popped from a bottle of chardonnay. He was no connoisseur of wines, but Dusty was, and he never gave up trying to educate Nasty.

"Let's just say I don't take chances with the really important stuff — like getting involved with a woman." He poured two glasses of wine and gave her one.

"Why is the boat called *April?*"

"For a friend of a friend. She was very brave. She died. I never knew her, but I wanted to do this for the people who did."

Polly looked thoughtful but didn't comment further. She drank some wine. "I tried to persuade myself I shouldn't come looking for you."

"I'm glad that didn't work out." She wasn't oblivious to him. Not oblivious at all. "If you hadn't come to me, I don't know how much longer I'd have held out."

"In spite of Festus's announcement the other day? You didn't stick around afterward."

The wine didn't do much for him. He leaned against one end of the banquette and swung the glass by its rim. Words needed to be carefully chosen. "You didn't want me to stick around, Polly."

She considered that.

"You told me you had business to attend to."

"Until Festus dropped his little bomb, nothing would have made you go away. That's how it seemed." Her color heightened. "Then all I had to say was that I ought to go home, and you couldn't get away fast enough."

True. He'd needed to think things through. "You didn't ask me to stay."

"How could I? I hardly knew you — hardly know you." Her voice faded away.

"But it does feel as if you know me, doesn't it?" he said gently. "I feel as if I've known you a long, long time. Polly, your business is your business. You don't have to explain yourself to me."

"Don't I? Is that your way of saying you want to start something with me, and you don't care whether or not I'm free?"

Was that what he'd meant? "No. It's my way of saying that I want to start something with you if you want to. And I don't think you're the kind of woman who'd do that if she . . . Hell, I don't know what I mean."

"I'm not married."

He exhaled through pursed lips.

"Do you believe me?"

Nasty gazed at her intensely blue eyes. "Yes, I do. But what was all that about? The call. Your friend Festus sounded as if he believed the guy. The *nice* guy."

Her regard wavered. "I don't know. Freaky things happen in this business. People get fixations on you. It's one of the trade-offs."

"I don't like it."

"I don't like it either. But I do like this job. Apart from Bobby, it's the best thing that ever happened to me. It's changed our lives. Before we were . . ." She averted her face. "None of that matters. Forget it."

"Is this the guy who made the other calls? The ones to your answering machine, or whatever?"

Polly scooted around and got to her feet. She toured the saloon, smoothing wood paneling, studying the black-and-white etchings he'd collected over the years. And while she stepped from one to the other, she hummed something complicated, classical, maybe. "Places you've been?" she asked, tapping a picture frame.

He'd let her avoid giving answers for a while. "Yes."

"Paris. Sydney." She pointed to the next picture and raised a brow in question.

"Amsterdam," he told her. "Then Hong Kong,

Wellington, Bogotá, Madrid. London, of course."

"You've traveled a lot."

"It used to go with the job."

"When you were in the Navy."

"Yeah." The less said about that the better.

Her gaze dropped to his left ankle. She didn't comment on the scars, hadn't mentioned his limp.

"Ugly, huh?" he suggested.

"No. But it must have been painful when it happened."

"It's over now." And he was lucky to be both alive and relatively unscathed. "You are getting threatening calls, aren't you?"

She laughed.

He wasn't convinced. "Aren't you?"

"No, not really. It's just silliness." She returned to pick up her wineglass and stood near Nasty. "The guy who said he was my husband. Sam Dodge. He's Bobby's father." The announcement was defiantly delivered.

"But you're not married anymore?"

The shutter came down. Her eyelids lowered, hiding her expression — except for the fixing of her mouth in a tight line.

"You could have told me the truth before."

"I didn't owe you the truth. I don't owe you anything."

"True." But she was here, and she'd already let him know she'd come to set the record straight — and that she was less than indifferent to him.

She rested an elbow on one crossed arm and touched the glass to her lips.

He felt her, felt her body heat, the tension in her muscles, her rigid stance. And he felt her awareness of him.

Nasty set down his own glass. He shrugged away from the banquette and stood over her, very close.

Polly's fingers tightened around the glass. Her lashes flickered, and a nerve near her left eye.

Half-expecting her to run, he touched the tips of his fingers to that fascinating pulse at the base of her throat.

She held absolutely still.

"I'm not the enemy," he told her.

The breath she took was deep.

He took the glass away and put it down beside his own. "You don't believe me." Was that what he was seeing — feeling? "That first night on the docks . . . You decided I was making these calls, didn't you?"

She looked at him then, and he absorbed the shifting emotions he saw, the wavering between suspicion and wanting to trust.

"I've never called you on the phone. When I do, you'll know it's me."

Her pulse beat hard. The skin he touched was soft and warm. She had come to him. "You are frightened by these calls, aren't you? They aren't just something that goes with the territory? These are different?"

Still she hovered on the edge of believing her instincts.

"You came to me alone. You'd be no match for me if I was the kind of man to take advantage, but you came here. Are you willfully stupid, or are you trying to persuade yourself I'm a good guy?"

The look she aimed at him held everything she felt, doubt, anger, confusion, fear, the need to trust. She needed to trust him. He took her hand in his and she didn't resist. Polly Crow needed a friend. Whatever roles the people in her life filled, they didn't fill the one that had brought her to him this morning.

Nasty sat on the end of the banquette seat. He tugged gently on Polly's hand until she let him bring her to stand between his knees.

Today she wore her hair loose. Straight and silky, it swung forward over her shoulders. Dark lashes contrasted with the honey color of her hair and her light skin. The hand he held trembled, and she tightened her fingers around his.

"You and I are on the same side, Polly."

She raised her eyes to his. Such searingly blue eyes, so vivid he almost had to look away.

"Friendship would be a good place for us to start." Whatever it took, he was going to break through her defenses. She wanted him to, or she wouldn't be here. "Do you need a friend, Polly."

At last she broke her silence. "I've got friends?"

"A different kind of friend."

Her throat moved. "I stopped thinking about it a long time ago. I thought I had, anyway."

"Would you like to make that clearer for me?"

She raised her free hand as if to push back her hair, but made a fist and settled it on his bare shoulder instead.

She didn't look away from his face.

Neither did Nasty look away from hers. "What did you stop thinking about a long time ago?"

"I don't know how to say it."

"You're not frightened of me, are you?" He'd frightened a lot of people in his time, but only people he'd wanted and needed to frighten — Polly wasn't one of them.

"I'm frightened of me. Of what I'm feeling. I haven't let myself . . . I haven't let myself think about — about me, I guess. It's been easier that way."

"Polly —"

"I'm not sorry for myself." The defiance was there again. "It's just the way it is — the way it's had to be. I had to make my way. For Bobby and for me. I've had a lot of luck, too. Some really good people have come my way."

One by one, he loosened her fingers. Her hands were long-fingered but narrow — the nails short. Graceful but capable hands. He turned her palm upward, stroked it with his thumb.

"Should I be scared to be here with you?"

"I think you know you shouldn't." The feelings were new to him, feelings he'd never expected to have, never even considered having. "No more scared than I am with you."

The fist on his shoulder unfurled, and she spanned the muscle there, rubbed tentatively to the base of his neck and back.

His erection was instant. So was the desire to pull her into his arms. Sexual urge and tenderness. These weren't the reactions he'd practiced dealing with. Survival required different skills. But this was another kind of survival, wasn't it?

If she knew the power of his response to her she'd run. "This Sam Dodge. Your son's father" — he didn't want to call the man her ex-husband — "does he keep in pretty close touch?"

"No. I haven't seen him for several years."

"I'm glad." Pretending indifference wasn't in the cards anymore. He'd already declared himself.

"It's fine with me. Bobby still thinks about him, though. I know he does. Children need to feel wanted — by both of their parents."

"Sometimes one is as good as it gets," he said. A reflex. He didn't want the topic to get personal. "Did Sam reach you on the phone?"

She hesitated before saying, "Yes. We talked."

Cautiously, trying not to think about Sam Dodge, or the fact that just the sound of the man's name made him jealous, Nasty bowed over Polly's palm. He pressed his lips there and closed his eyes. If she bolted, he'd just have to start all over again.

Polly didn't bolt.

He felt her hold her breath.

She smelled of roses, the wild kind that grew in hedges in old gardens — in the sun.

When he kissed the base of her thumb it jerked.

At the touch of his lips on the inside of her wrist, she drew in a sharp breath.

And he drew in just as sharp a breath when she stroked his hair so very lightly. She stroked his hair all the way to his nape, and her fingertips stayed there.

He tensed all the way to his gut. Concentration got tougher. "Did you get together with Sam?" He had no right to push her for the personal stuff.

"Not yet."

Yet. "He'd be a fool not to want to get back with you."

"Sam and I never worked. We never could. He's in Florida, and I haven't invited him to come back here."

A man couldn't be blamed for feeling satisfied when he got the answer he wanted. "I'm glad you decided to come to me."

"Are you?" she said. "We don't know much about each other. I don't know anything about you."

"You know some," he told her, raising his head. He glanced at the rise of her breasts above the low neckline of her dress, at her throat — and into her face. "I told you I'm thirty-six. Ex-Navy. Co-owner of Room Below — and this boat. A car. Not much else. I never was interested in things."

"What did you do in the Navy?"

He'd never be able to tell her, not really tell her. "I was a SEAL."

94

She frowned, then her expression cleared. "Oh, sure. Diving, right?"

Among other things. "Yes, diving."

"I used to be a cook."

It was his turn to frown, before he laughed. "A cook? You?"

"A very good cook," she told him. "For an artists' colony in Bellevue, the one my mother manages now. A friend of mine, Bliss Winters — she's Bliss Plato now — she owns it. She was very good to me when nobody would take a chance."

"I can't imagine anyone saying no to you."

Pleasure tinged her smile. "I can be flattered, you know."

"Most of us can. What did Sam want?"

Her smile faded instantly. "According to him, just to talk. For old times' sake." She made a disbelieving sound. "As if I'd want to remember any times with him."

"Weren't there any worth remembering?"

The question earned him a direct stare. "No. Not one of them. I was never married to him."

So his intelligence hadn't been faulty. He probably shouldn't feel glad, but he did, mostly because the man, Sam Dodge, had never had any legal claim to her.

"Does that shock you?" It was a challenge.

"Does it shock me that you had sex with someone you weren't married to? That's the question, isn't it? The answer's no. I never was into double standards. I've never been married. I'm not a virgin, either."

She smiled. "Why doesn't that surprise me?"

"Because you only had to look at me to know I was that kind of a guy?"

Polly smiled again. "I'm not sure what kind of guy you are — but I can't seem to stop wanting to find out."

Reading too much into what she said would be easy. "Then we're even." Overreacting could be disastrous.

He pushed back her hair and framed her face lightly. For a long time they just looked at each other.

"What kind of a name is Nasty?"

"A nasty name," he said, flippant before he could regroup. "A name I picked up as a kid, when I probably deserved it. It stuck."

When he didn't elaborate he saw her decide not to press him.

He looked at her mouth. Soft, pouty — a sensual mouth whether she liked it or not.

Polly folded her hands over his forearms. She had to know he wanted to kiss her. Was she signaling him to stop? He shifted forward on the seat a fraction.

Abruptly, her eyes closed. She slid her arms around his neck and buried her face there.

For a moment he hesitated, then he held her, eased her close and held her, smoothed her back through thin cotton, crossed his arms around her and hugged as tightly as he dared.

The sensation of her fingers in his hair, on his neck, slipping down his spine and back across his shoulders made him shiver. He was glad he hadn't put on a shirt. He'd like to pick her up and carry her into his cabin, undress her, stretch her on top of him. She would be all softness to his tough angles.

He'd be happy with that. Hell, he'd be goddamn delirious with that.

It'd be enough for now.

Her smooth fingertips began their trip all over again.

Nasty shivered again.

Getting naked and lying together would be great. It wouldn't be enough, ever.

With a sigh, she pushed back far enough to see his face again.

He inclined his head to study her. "I want to have a relationship with you, Polly."

"I know."

"What do you want?"

"I'm not sure."

Not exactly the response he'd hoped for. "How can I make you sure?"

The circles she made in the hair on his chest drove him wild inside. He pressed his lips together and willed himself to be patient.

Slowly the circles widened. Then they narrowed. All the time she watched, until she used only her thumbs to trace around his nipples.

Surely she knew what she was doing to him. How could she not know? The rapt concentration on her face made him unsure. Almost as if she was somewhere else, watching herself touch him, and gauging his reaction to those touches.

Nasty made fists on his thighs. No longer completely calling his own shots, he leaned toward her and pressed a kiss into the soft flesh above the neckline of her dress. He felt her shiver this time.

This wasn't a one-sided attraction. "We could start really slow," he said, pressing his mouth to the hollow beneath her collarbone, to the pulsing beat above it, to spot, after spot, on the side of her neck and across her jaw to her earlobe.

Gentleness fled. She drove her fingers into his shoulders and clutched.

A whisper was all that separated his lips from hers. He whispered, "I'm going to kiss you," and sealed the promise.

The first joining was a series of glancing brushes. He opened her mouth. Quickly, repeatedly, he slipped the tip of his tongue just inside to moist skin.

Polly kissed him back. For every move he made, she had one of her own.

She wanted him, too.

If he hoped to take this where he wanted it to go, he must help her to have no regrets. *Take it slow.* Shoot, this was what he got for spending most of his adult life alone. A bunch of raw edges and not a lot of finesse.

His breath came in pants.

So did Polly's.

"We're . . . Every word that comes into my head sounds like a line from an old movie."

Her eyes were closed. He kissed the lids. Keeping his hands off the rest of her should earn him an award.

"Maybe they just sound like old lines, period?" she suggested.

"Maybe. But I mean this. We don't have to take things fast. I'm a patient man." He was becoming a routine liar with her.

Warm. Her breasts were warm against his chest. Her hips fitted snugly between his thighs. If she didn't feel what she was doing to him, she wasn't feeling anything.

She felt what she was doing.

Nasty watched Polly glance downward and let out a shaky breath. "I didn't think too much before I came. I wasn't sure why, except I knew I wanted to see you. And I wanted you to know I hadn't lied."

"Thank you," he said. "I haven't thought of anything but seeing you for weeks."

"I'm not oblivious to what this is doing. It's hard on you."

He grinned. "Nice girls try not to notice things like that. They certainly don't mention them."

"I didn't mean —" Outrage blossomed and died before she dealt him a playful poke.

"Can we see if it would work with us?" he asked, seeing an advantage and deciding to push it. "I mean, will you let me? . . . Could we spend time together?"

"My life isn't simple. I come with baggage."

"I don't care what you come with, as long as

you come — to me," he finished weakly.

She ran her nails delicately along his thighs.

Every move she made imprinted itself on his brain. He wanted a chance to have all the moves again, and then he wanted to return the favor. "We'd start *really* slow, Polly. We wouldn't jump right into bed." *Hell.*

Her crossed arms and hunched shoulders confronted him. He'd either angered or shocked her. Probably some of both.

"Seriously, I'm not the kind of guy to rush a woman."

"You're not?" She took a backward step. "Are you joking?"

Women. How could any man know how they'd react to an honest attempt at tact? At least, he'd thought he was being tactful. He leaned toward her. "Maybe I'm misreading the signals here. Have I offended you? Do you want to go to bed? . . . Do you? We can, of course." Boy, could they.

Polly spun around. Her laughter first puzzled, then mortified him. Frustration hovered a hair away.

A thud sounded from the deck, followed by rapid footsteps.

"No one ever bothers me here," Nasty grumbled.

Polly's laughter subsided to a chuckle. "Until today."

Sharp rapping on the hatch set his teeth on edge.

"Mr. Ferrito?" A rich female voice bellowed down the stairs. "This nice Mr. Miller told me to come here."

"Venus?" Polly said, her eyes screwed up.

Nasty walked past her. "What did you say?"

"Venus. My mother. It sounds like her."

The hatch doors swung open and sunlight flowed in. Feet clad in bead-studded gold sandals appeared, then ankles in leopard-patterned tights and draped about with many pointed lengths of floating, black-and-gold skirts. The rest of the woman came rapidly into sight.

She clinked.

Coins and bells strung around her waist and hips, more coins at the neck of her cropped, gold silk top — they all rustled and rang and clinked. Crowned with a curly chignon of red curls, the woman's florid face was handsome.

"Venus," Polly said again, sounding resigned.

The woman approached gracefully, her ample hips swaying. "There you are," she said to Polly. "That lovely man said he thought you might be here. And he insisted on bringing me all the way here himself."

So, Dusty was "lovely" to opulent ladies dressed for a little belly dancing. Nasty noted that Dusty had opted to remain on deck — not a good sign.

"Why are you here, Mother?"

Nasty wasn't disappointed to note that Polly didn't sound happy at the intrusion.

"I've done my best," Polly's parent said. "I

wasn't always perfect, but I learned. I worked hard."

"Mother, what —"

"And I've been a good grandmother."

"You're a wonderful grandmother," Polly said.

"You can't imagine how I felt when I got back. There I was with a bag of junk food and two videos, just like I'd promised."

"What *is* it, Mother?"

"It's taken me two hours to catch up with you, my girl."

Nasty braced his feet apart and crossed his arms. The newcomer tilted her head to examine him very thoroughly. "I suppose this was why you did it, Polly. I'm not saying I can't see the attraction, but really, you might have some consideration."

"Make sense!" Polly said so sharply her mother flinched.

Just as quickly, the woman produced a daunting scowl. "There are many boats. There is only one Venus Crow. Just because you met one of these" — she swept a hand in Nasty's direction — "these *film* stars of yours with fancy boats, you forget to respect your own mother."

Nasty sympathized with Polly's obvious confusion.

"Well," Venus said, sighing gustily, "I suppose I shouldn't expect any better. Children never do appreciate their parents."

Polly scrubbed at her face. "Please, Mother, what have I done to upset you like this?"

"Oh, don't give it another thought. I shall get over it. But you might ask yourself if it's kind — or if it shows simple gratitude, and courtesy — to use me, but to keep the most intimately important things in your life secret from me."

"Where's Bobby?" Polly asked, her voice strained. "You got junk food and videos for you and Bobby?"

"Whom else should I get them for?"

Polly took a step toward the stairs. "This is something to do with Bobby. Something's happened to him."

"Nothing's happened to him." Venus Crow's tone was tart, but her gray eyes shone — anxiously, Nasty decided. "He's up there with that nice Mr. Miller. Bobby's never been on a big boat before. Listen to him up there."

Footfalls overhead wiped away some of Polly's apprehension.

Venus's eyes continued to gleam. Skin puckered between her thin, red brows. "I had a phone call," she said. "Such strangeness in the world. To one such as I, these bizarre people are a mystery."

Polly said nothing. What Nasty might have said about people like Venus wouldn't help.

"The police . . . Hah, the police. We know how little you can expect from them at such times. They told me they can't help. *Yet.* Not unless someone's actually been killed."

Polly's face turned chalk white and she said, "Mother!" with her blue eyes wide open.

"It's something to do with all this," Venus Crow said, indicating the boat, and Nasty again.

He said, "Mrs. Crow," gently, and touched her arm. "Something's upset you."

She sniffed and drew herself up. "I should say it has. The police said a single threat doesn't mean a thing. Not without a body."

Polly's fear was palpable. Nasty caught her eye and winked. She didn't wink back.

"This is number one, and the fun will soon be done!" Venus's breathing grew short. She wound and unwound her hands. "On the phone. That was it. I answered the phone, and that's what I heard. Then they said, tell Polly her new friends are bad for her health. They'll make her sick if she doesn't get rid of them."

Polly touched her lips. "Who said this to you?"

"I don't know," Venus told her breathlessly. "But you know what a memory I've got. I remember every word. She said if you weren't careful, your new friends would kill you. Then she hung up."

Five

Reality had a way of smacking the unwary. So much for a brief fling, a careless brush with Passion. While she'd indulged desire, the rest of her life had flirted with disaster.

"Hurry up, Polly." With Dusty's help, Venus had already clambered from the boat to the dock.

Nasty followed and offered Polly his hand. She shook her head and put Bobby ashore before hopping from the gunwale herself.

"You doing okay?" she asked Bobby.

"Okay." He sucked in a cheek. "That's his boat?" He hung back and jerked his head toward the *April.*

"You know it belongs to Mr. Ferrito," Polly said. "When he brought you here, Mr. Miller told you it was Nasty's boat."

Bobby's tow hair stood on end. The worry in his brown eyes twisted Polly's stomach.

"What's up?" she said. "Can you tell your old mom?"

He pushed his thin hands into the pockets of his jeans and avoided Polly's eyes. "Nothing's up." He peered at Nasty, who stared ahead, expressionless, as if he couldn't hear every word. Bobby said, "Who's he, anyway? Nasty? That's weird, Mom."

"And that's rude," she told him.

Shifting the gum he was rarely without, Nasty looked unsmilingly at the boy. "Nickname," he said. "I got it when I was a bit older than you. When I grew up I went into the Navy. I was in one of those special forces. We all had nicknames then, too, so I'm really stuck with mine."

Bobby frowned. "If you didn't like it, you could make people call you something else."

"Geez, outta the mouths," Dusty Miller said with his barking laugh. "You got it, Bobby. Nasty here's a pretty scary dude. You'd have to be crazy to mess with him. Know what I think?" — he didn't wait for a response — "I think Nasty likes his name because he's really a softy, but he doesn't want anyone to know."

Bobby sucked in the other cheek and thought about that.

"Right," Nasty said, very softly, gifting his wiry, white-haired buddy with a mildly amused look. "Soft. That's me."

Holding the arm Dusty Miller had gallantly offered, Venus hurried along at his side. A fit woman, she puffed nevertheless, a sign that she was deeply agitated. "I want you to call the police yourself, Polly," she said. "Put your foot down. Insist they do something at once."

Another second and her mother would be spilling the exact details of the nuisance phone calls. "We'll go back to my place," she said, planning rapidly. "Don't worry. These things happen."

"Not to me!" Venus checked her stride. "Not to Venus Crow or her daughters. Not before you insisted on this — this flim-flam existence of yours, my girl."

"Of course not." Anything to keep Venus from revealing everything. "I'm sure Mr. Miller needs to get back to his shop. And Nasty must have things to do." She couldn't look at him.

"Dusty," Dusty Miller said. "Call me Dusty." He had to be younger than the white hair suggested. He exuded energy. "I gotta get back, but we're gonna go to my place first and make sure you ladies are taken care of."

Nasty coughed. Polly expected to see him grin at his partner's old-world chivalry. He didn't.

"Put it down to training," Dusty continued, settling a bony, deeply tanned hand on top of Venus's on his arm. "Nasty and me have spent a lot of years taking charge in this sort of situation. Must have been fate sent you our way."

"Fate," Nasty murmured, his cool brown eyes making fleeting contact with Polly's. "D'you think that's what it was?"

Rather than answer, she made a great deal of locating her keys.

"I called Fabiola," Venus said. To Dusty and Nasty she remarked, "My other daughter. Polly's twin. She's a model. She's as worried as I am. She said she'll meet you this evening, as planned, Polly. I told her I didn't think you should go anywhere while there's a maniac after you, but she —"

"Please, Mom," Polly said, too aware of Bobby's tension. "Later, okay?"

Undeterred, Venus continued. "Fabiola insisted she'd meet you as planned. Seven at Park Place. TGIFriday's. Something about public places being safest. I'm sure I don't know that I agree with her. But who cares what I think? I'm just a mother who worries about her children."

"And a very good mother, too," Dusty said, patting her hand. "I'm sure your girls think the world of you."

They hurried from the dock, where Nasty's was the only boat moored, to the lakefront gardens behind Dusty's home on Lake Drive.

"Can I come back to the condo now, Mom?" Bobby asked. "I want to come back."

She settled a hand on the nape of his neck. "We'll talk about it."

"I can't think of a *worse* time for him to be here," Venus said, puffing even louder. "Dangerous. I won't sleep a wink if he's in this place. You ought to walk away from it all, Polly. Come back to Hole Point. Bliss and Sebastian would be tickled to know you were helping me."

"Stop it, Mother, please. If I walk away, this isn't going to stop, don't you understand that?" The rush of blood to her head ebbed. "I'm sorry. We shouldn't be boring other people with our problems." And Bobby shouldn't be loaded up with reasons to worry. He worried too easily, and too much inside himself.

"Why isn't Bobby with you anyway?" Nasty asked. He didn't have to hurry to keep up.

Polly saw Bobby's face pinch.

"Not because I'm a bad mother," she snapped. "Bobby likes it at the Point."

"We're getting overwrought," Nasty said, so reasonably she felt furious. "You and your mother have had an unpleasant experience. As you once told me — some of this goes with the world you live in. We'll work it through."

His take-charge, take-over attitude silenced Polly. Almost anything she said would sound defensive.

Venus clung to Dusty as if they were old friends. "I always told you it was a mistake to be so much in the public eye, Polly. But did you listen to me? No, of course not. I'm only your mother. Why would you listen to your mother? She doesn't know anything. She hasn't lived in this world long enough to know even a smidge more than you do."

Venus had suffered a shock, Polly told herself. Now wasn't the time to tell her mother to put a sock in it. And Venus had never been good at worrying about more than her own flamboyant existence.

Polly stood still. She kept a firm grip on Bobby's neck while she told Nasty, "Thank you. Don't worry. We'll take it from here."

"What exactly will you take from here?" His eyes were as remote as they were cool now. Gone was the heat she knew could flare. "You need help. I can give you some. Dusty can give you some. Take it."

Venus labored up crazy-paved steps between terraces in the gardens. She said, "We'll just have to think this through. Surely you've got some idea who this woman is. Maybe she's a friend of the man who's been —"

"Don't make guesses," Polly said, trying, and failing to catch Venus's eye.

Windows in Dusty Miller's canary yellow, two-story house glittered in the sunlight. Geraniums and blue lobelia still bloomed in boxes lining a big patio.

"Home, sweet home," Dusty said cheerfully. "Come on in. We'll find a soda for Bobby, and whatever you ladies would like." He produced keys and unlocked a side door.

With a sense of doom, Polly scrambled for an out and failed to find one. Venus followed Dusty through the door, and Nasty stood back to usher Bobby and Polly before him.

Inside, a combination mud and laundry room opened into a big, overwhelmingly yellow kitchen.

Venus clapped, her countenance one of ecstasy. "Dusty, this is beautiful. Such an expression of inner self. You are a sunshine man in a sunshine home. Truly, truly beautiful."

Dusty's smile was pure satisfaction.

Nasty passed his partner, and said, "Excuse me, sunshine," on his way to the refrigerator. "Come and get what you want, Bobby."

"I don't want anything." Bobby stood just inside the kitchen. "When can we get Spike and go home, Mom?"

"You don't want anything, *thank you*," Polly said, on automatic pilot. To the room in general, she commented, "Spike's our dog. I told you we'll talk about all that later, Bobby. We ought to get going, Mom. We've taken enough of Dusty and Nasty's time."

"Crap," Dusty said, with feeling. "I mean, garbage. Lovely ladies like you could never take enough of our time, could they, Nasty?"

"Oh, no, never." The kettle clattered on the stove, and Nasty set out cups. "Where's the tea?"

"Tea?" Dusty's nose, with its crooked bridge, folded into ridges. "Who the hell drinks that swill? Nah. I'm gonna celebrate."

"Celebrate what?"

The older man glared at his friend. "You don't have any" — he waved his hands — "You just don't have it, buddy. No *savoir faire*," he finished, looking satisfied.

"That's me," Nasty said, popping the top of a Coke can. "*Savoir faireless*. Must have gone to all the wrong finishing schools."

"I'm gonna break out the Wild Turkey," Dusty said, his frown ominous. "You'll join me, won't you, ladies?"

Venus fluttered her fingers. "I suppose I could have just a teensy bit — for my nerves."

"Not for me, thank you," Polly said, her mind in turmoil. If she brought Bobby back to Kirkland, she'd have to watch him every minute. A *woman?* A woman calling Venus to make death threats? Someone who made references to "new friends." Did she mean Nasty? Was this person jealous of Polly and Nasty being together?

The answer was almost definitely, yes. And surely it all meant that Nasty couldn't have anything to do with the calls.

Venus accepted a hefty glass of bourbon, and said, "Oh, this has been a terrible day. I don't even remember driving here. I'm so frightened."

"There's nothing to be frightened about," Polly said, ever conscious of Bobby. "Cranks are everywhere."

"No, they aren't. Even the police said I should call at once if you were attacked."

"For cryin' out loud," Dusty muttered.

Polly went to Bobby and put an arm over his shoulders. She was grateful when, instead of shrugging away, he slipped a hand around her waist. "It's okay, Bob," she told him. "You and me, together, just like it's always been. We'll be fine."

"So I can come back?"

She'd fallen into that one. "We're going to work it out. I want you with me just as much as you want to be with me."

"He can't be on his own," Venus said, smacking her lips. "Not for a moment."

Nasty had become a still, silent presence. He sat on a high stool, one heel hooked over a rung, the opposite leg — the one with the terribly scarred ankle — stretched out. She shouldn't find it so impossible not to stare at him.

It was impossible not to stare at him.

They'd known each other, been speaking to each other for only a few days.

And they'd kissed — and so much more than kissed. She was right to regret that. She'd been wrong to give in to lust. What did she know about him? Virtually nothing.

But, how they'd kissed . . .

And he'd told her he could love her. The flush she felt was inside, a building pressure in places made for sensations that were so good, and so dangerous.

Venus talked. So did Dusty. Polly heard their voices, but not the words. Bobby seemed contented to stand beside her.

If Nasty Ferrito was a foe, what a foe he was. Formidable in every way. The more terrifying because he'd touched her as she hadn't been touched, perhaps ever.

He watched her. She felt him watch her.

Yellow tile countertops, yellow appliances, yellow chintz curtains at the windows, and yellow chintz cushions on chairs. Even the floor tile was yellow. In an attempt not to meet Nasty's eyes, Polly studied every inch of the overpoweringly cheerful kitchen.

Then she met his eyes anyway.

Cool. So cool. So distant. He snapped his gum between his strong teeth. Not a blink. Arms crossed over that very nice chest with which she had far too intimate an acquaintance. The hair on his chest had different textures depending on where . . .

She couldn't look away. He drew her, pulled her inside himself where the still, cold center waited. The coldest things burned.

He'd been hard. She'd felt him hard, and heavy, and ready against her pelvis. Polly couldn't stop herself from glancing downward again.

She swallowed, and heard her throat contract.

His erection pressed against the soft jean fabric of his shorts.

When she slowly, unwillingly, raised her eyes to his face again, he stared back without expression. As if he didn't care that she knew he wanted . . . Polly swallowed again. He looked at her, and wanted her — wanted to be inside her.

"Dusty's right, Polly," Venus said loudly. "We're going to have to take precautions."

Her attention was dragged back to his straining penis. "Yes. Yes, we'll have to take precautions."

"You got a job, Bobby?" Dusty asked.

"No."

Why didn't everyone feel the energy arcing through the room? Polly tingled. Her breasts tingled, and the dark places deep inside, and the moist folds between her legs. A blush flamed on her cheeks.

"How long before you go back to school?"

"A couple of weeks," Bobby said.

Dusty poured more bourbon for Venus. "How

about coming to work for me? If your mom and grandma will let you?"

Bobby didn't answer.

"I've been looking for a strong kid to help out. We've got a dive shop. D'you swim?"

"Yeah. I love —"

"He swims," Polly said quickly, her eyes locked with Nasty's again. "But he's not ready for diving yet."

"He will be," Dusty said. "How about it, Bobby? Help me stock the shelves, pack orders? Pay'll be good, and there's lots of neat stuff in the shop."

"He isn't old enough," Polly said faintly.

Dusty slapped his thigh. "Crap. Right, Bobby? This'd be an apprenticeship." When Polly finally managed to look at the other man, he winked. "Great place to be while your mom's at work. Till you go back to school. And if we make good partners, you can come after school once you do go back."

"Well" — Bobby removed his hand from her waist and raised his face to hers — "Could I, Mom?"

What did they really know about these men? "We'll see."

"Aw, *Mom*."

"May I use your bathroom?" Polly said. She had to get away from Nasty. She had to squash the ridiculous notion that he could make love to her from across a room.

"Sure," Nasty said. "Through there. Turn

115

right. There's a study. First door on the right. Bathroom off that."

"Just a minute," Venus said. The liquor had relaxed her shoulders and her tongue. "That woman said your new friends were dangerous. What new friends?"

She had to go to the bathroom. "Later, Mom, okay?"

"Not okay. How long have you known" — she raised her glass to Nasty — "how long?"

"Mom, please —"

"How *long?*"

"Hold on, Venus," Dusty said, all smiling good humor still. "Polly and I met for the first time when she came across to the shop this morning. Belinda and Festus sent her. You know Belinda and Festus at the voodoo shop?"

"New Age," Venus said severely. "Festus would never allow anything to do with voodoo inside his doors. Neither would Belinda."

"Just the odd bag of Inspiration," Nasty said in an innocent tone that didn't match his still watchfulness.

Fortunately Venus was too preoccupied to hear him. "Good friends, they are."

"Like I said," Dusty persisted. "You know them. And they sent Polly to me."

Venus gave up trying not to return Dusty's smile. "But you aren't anything to do with the movies."

Polly groaned. "I don't work in the movies, Mom."

"You're not a movie star," Venus said to Nasty. "I thought you were."

"Thanks." He'd make a great straight man. "Not guilty, though."

"You and Dusty own a dive shop." She made the statement in a less than enthusiastic tone.

"You'd rather I sold bags of . . . incense?"

Venus wasn't to be diverted. "It wouldn't be natural if I wasn't worried."

"Well, I haven't known Polly long," Nasty said helpfully. "In some ways. In other ways I feel as if I've known her a very long time."

"Can I work for Dusty, Mom?" Bobby said, clearly too enamored of the idea to think of anything else. "He's a friend of Uncle Festus and Auntie Belinda."

"We'll see," Polly told him, hanging to thin threads of resolve.

"What exactly do you mean by that?" Venus asked Nasty, raising her chin as if it would make her taller. "Either you've known her a long time, or you haven't."

"You can trust Nasty," Polly heard herself say, and knew how desperately she wanted to trust him. "I do." Her heart told her she was being honest, her head warned her to slow down.

He parted his teeth, and she saw his jaw lock. She couldn't have drawn her attention away if she'd wanted to. Polly didn't want to.

Nasty Ferrito could make love to her from across a room.

When someone wrote of a ghostly smile, this

elusive smile of his must be what they meant. It shook her and she wished she could stay shaken, just this way, forever.

"No one has a name like Nasty," Venus said, sounding as if hyperventilation was imminent. "Silliness. What is your name, young man?"

Polly sighed.

The corners of Nasty's mouth tilted up a little more. "Ferrito. Xavier Ferrito, ma'am."

Polly blinked. *"Xavier?"*

She'd said she trusted him. Now was the time to pocket those few wonderful words and push until she gave in and let him into her life.

Nasty allowed Polly a couple of minutes before leaving Dusty to charm Venus and Bobby. He went to the study that was his favorite room in Dusty's home and closed the door behind him. He had keys to the house, and Dusty's permission to call this quiet room his own. Outside a bay window, red maples screened off everything but a glimpse of distant mountaintops.

Xavier Ferrito.

What a name to stick a little kid with.

He prowled to a wall of books that belonged almost entirely to him, and pulled out first one, then another volume. Books had been his refuge, still were. Throughout years when he'd acquired none of the baggage other men collected, he'd always balked at the idea of getting rid of a book or two.

The toilet flushed in the small bathroom.

Water ran, and the sound of Polly humming made him smile. No ordinary, predictable woman, this blue-eyed dynamo. Endless surprises. Never a reaction he could totally expect. Bach, Beethoven, something from a show? — he wasn't an expert on music, but he could become addicted to the sound of Polly's voice.

The bathroom door opened. She jumped at the sight of him and didn't mask her anxiety quickly enough.

"Sorry," he told her. "Didn't mean to scare you."

Her nervous little smile angered him, angered him at whoever had singled her out for the wrong kind of attention.

"I'd better collect my family and go home," she said, glancing at the closed door to the hallway. "We've really messed up your day."

"You've *made* my day." Any move toward her might be a mistake. He stood his ground, but didn't like it. "Any day with you in it would be a better day."

Polly expelled a huge sigh and let her eyelids drift shut. "You can't go around saying things like that."

"I just did. And I intend to make a habit of it."

"Don't . . . Just don't get hung up on me, Nasty. I'm not a good bet. I never was."

He hadn't expected her to throw herself at him. Neither had he expected the answer he had got. "Another only semihealed spirit. Who'd a' thunk it? Polly of *Polly's Place,* national success, every mom and dad's dream helper. And she's got an ego about an inch high — on a good day."

Her frown darkened her eyes. "I didn't ask for psychoanalysis."

"Didn't give psychoanalysis. I just said it like it is. I may not be really quick, but I'm not stupid, not if you wave flags with messages on them in front of my eyes."

Polly's eyes were suddenly too bright. She went to the window and faced the branches of trembling red leaves outside. "Xavier's a great name. Distinguished."

"Thanks." The less said about that, the better. "Nasty suits me."

"I'd say you're wrong, but in a funny way I suppose it does." Her backward peek at him came as close to being coquettish as any move he'd seen her make. "It's cute. And before you try to tell me how cute you aren't, I think you are. Tough, but cute — and too sexy for my good."

He wasn't considered garrulous, but he could usually hold his own verbally. Not at this moment.

"It's definitely time to say good-bye, Nasty."

He found his voice. "No way."

"Yes." With a flurry, she spun from the window and made for the door.

Nasty cut her off. "You've got to be kidding. I went out on a limb the other day. I said something most people would think was suicidal."

"Wasn't it?"

"I meant it. I still do. More so. And evidently

you don't find me grotesque."

The tilt of her head, the way her lashes shaded her eyes, brought on some of that sexiness she'd talked about.

"Unless you can think of a way to convince me I shouldn't, I'm going to stick to you like glue," he said. "I'm taking care of you."

Her lips came together in a straight line. "Thanks for the white-knight sentiments, but I've been taking care of myself for a long time. I wouldn't want to start letting the side down now."

He reached for her. "You're important to me, Polly. Some fool's decided to make you a victim. He — or she — hasn't reckoned with me." The announcement that he was a pro in the covert attack area would probably freak her. "I'm a strong man. There are some who might say that when God made me He forgot the blood and nerves — and maybe the heart, too."

"They're wrong. About the heart."

Nasty grinned. "I guess I asked for that. You need to be careful, okay? Careful, but not frightened. As long as you do what I tell you to do, nothing's going to go wrong." He'd made it through situations where no one should have lived, situations that pitted him against the kind of professional killers who had mistakenly expected to bury him and grow old; he could handle any amateur terrorists.

"It could be nothing at all, couldn't it?" The quizzical widening of her eyes warned him she needed encouragement as much as honesty.

"It could be," he agreed. "The important thing is to think of ourselves as Boy Scouts. We've got to be prepared — just in case we've got a real live nut on our hands."

"I don't know how to react with you. You frighten me. Then you make me . . . You make me feel things I shouldn't feel. Not when we've known each other such a short time."

Exultation was a great sensation. "Point one: You're not alone. I frighten me, too, sometimes."

That, at least, earned him a weak laugh.

"Two. Who the hell decides what people should or shouldn't feel? The feelings police? Polly" — he caught one of her hands and pulled her toward him — "what I feel for you scares *me*."

"That's what I mean. This isn't rational — not to me, anyway."

His tug brought her closer. "And you think it feels rational to me? Just in case you think I go around making declarations to women, forget it. I thought I'd sewed myself in real tight for life. I never expected to . . . I never expected this. I'm a loner, Polly. Dusty and Roman are as close to family as I've gotten — and that includes during my childhood."

"It's too much." Her eyes closed again. "Too much all at once."

"Go with it. You don't get to tell me I can't watch over you until this other thing fades away. I'm going to anyway."

"You can't just —"

"You can't stop me." He inclined his head, searching for the right words, strong enough words. "There's no law against a man *being*. I'm just going to be. You won't even see me. But I'll be somewhere around you."

She pulled her hand away and wrapped her arms around her middle.

Nasty looked at her middle. A lovely middle. Even though he hadn't seen it without clothes, he knew how lovely it would be.

"I'll be looking for you all the time," she said.

Reluctantly he ended his contemplation of Polly Crow's waist. "Good. I may even let you see me sometimes, just to make sure you don't forget I'm around."

She wrinkled her brow. "Isn't that some sort of harassment?" Despite her best effort at seriousness, the quirky grin crept in. "I'm becoming an expert on harassment, you know?"

"I'm becoming an expert on you. I hope."

They paused together in that time and space, a space where even the air ceased to move.

With his two index fingertips, Nasty explored Polly's face, her jaw, from the point of her chin to the dips beneath her ears. The sides of her neck were smooth and soft. Her delicate collarbones felt as if he could break them between finger and thumb. She shivered, a steady, all-encompassing shudder.

"How did you get here?" he asked her. "To the *April?*"

"I walked. I like walking."

"You won't be walking back."

Her eyes opened, but almost sleepily. "My mother will drop me off."

"I'll take you. Why don't you keep Bobby here? He'll be safe, Polly. Probably much safer than with your mother. He won't be the first child Dusty's protected. He's good at it."

Something close to terror darted into her eyes. "Bobby shouldn't need protection."

"And maybe he doesn't. But be grateful it's here just in case."

"What time is it?"

"I don't want to stop looking at you to find out."

She breathed deeply, expanding her breasts.

A man was only a man. He studied her breasts.

"Don't look at me like that."

"I've got to. I'm always going to have to look at you."

"Fab will be expecting me at TGIFriday's."

Her mouth was a magnet. "You'll be introducing me as a date."

"She . . . Nasty, Fab and I share everything. I haven't said anything to her about a man in my life."

Gripping her shoulders, he slowly lowered his lips to hers, and said, "You're going to say something about me tonight," before he sucked her top lip, very gently, between his teeth.

He felt her coming apart in his hands. She filled her fingers with his cotton shirt and clutched him closer. Her moan filled his brain. They kissed ferociously, driven by the power of fear — her fear, and his desire — for her.

She tore her mouth away and rested her brow on his chest. "We've got to stop this. We've got to stay away from each other."

"Why? Because we both want the same thing."

"No —"

"Yes! I've been hard for days."

"Please."

"Anytime," he told her, deliberately twisting her meaning. "I can lock the door. We'll have each other here. Now. But it'll only be a start. You're a drug to me. I can't get enough of you, and I'm never going to get enough of you."

"This never happened to me." With her palms flat on his chest, she raised her face. "I'm not like this. I know I got pregnant when —"

"You don't have to talk about that."

"Yes, I do. If you think you want me so badly, you need to know who I am. Who I was. I was a wild kid. I thought I had something to prove. Getting pregnant was the best gift I could have had. I was on my way to the end of my world until Bobby. But I wasn't promiscuous. Sam was the man who got me when I didn't have anyone else. He made me feel important. I'd never felt important before. But then I grew up. There isn't a man who doesn't think I'm cold, Nasty. I don't lust after . . . Sex." Her lips remained parted.

"But," he said softly, "you lust after sex with me, don't you?"

Her hands became fists.

125

He said, "That sounds so calculating — so self-indulgent. I lust after you. All I have to do is think of you, and I spring to attention, love. When I look at you, I'm in pain. When I touch you" — he framed her face — "torture of the best kind is what you do to me. I want to take your clothes off."

She cried out, then covered her mouth.

"Don't worry. They're too busy making their own plans to miss us."

She shook her head.

"Love, love," he murmured, and cupped her bottom. He was a great deal taller than Polly. He had to all but lift her off her feet to bring their pelvises together. "You're going to keep on seeing me, Polly. And every time you do you'll know I'm thinking about this. I'll be thinking about putting my hands between your legs and opening you up. And I'll be thinking about slipping inside you."

"Stop it."

"D'you want me to?"

She held her tongue between her teeth.

"Do you want me to stop?" he repeated.

Polly unbuttoned his shirt. "We've got to go back to the kitchen." She pulled the shirt open and kissed his chest. She kissed with her mouth open and used her tongue and teeth, and she forced her hands between them to seek out the part of him that throbbed and strained.

"Kiss me," he ordered, gathering her hair in one hand at her nape to pull her head back. He didn't wait for her to comply, but took what he wanted.

She jerked her face away. "This is mad." Her hands shifted around his body. "Mad."

"Yeah. Completely mad." Deliberately, with the kind of willpower no man should be expected to have, he pried her hands loose and settled them on top of his shoulders instead. "And you're right. We'd better cool it."

Instantly, her eyes filled with tears.

"Hey! Hey, what is it, love? Hey —"

"Nothing," she said, sniffing. Tears overflowed. "I don't understand any of this. Someone's threatening to kill me. I'm scared about that. But all I can really think about is . . ."

He held his breath.

"All I can think about is making love with you."

"Yes!" He let it all out. "Oh, yes. Me, too. In every possible way."

"Nasty —"

The kiss he allowed himself, one kiss, left them both gasping for air. "Now," he said when he raised his head again. "First we get your mother safely on her way home. Then we have Dusty take Bobby over to show him around the shop. Then I take you to TGIFriday's to meet your sister. I'm looking forward to meeting her."

"Just a minute. Please. You're going much too fast."

"It couldn't be fast enough. After we've met with your sister, I'm going to take you home."

"You can't plan my life like that."

"Watch me."

"Bobby —"

"I haven't forgotten Bobby. I'm a responsible guy. Even when I'm having difficulty thinking of more than one thing, I'm still responsible." When in doubt, attack.

Her hands slipped from his shoulders to his chest once more. "I love touching you," she said, talking as if to herself. "I love the feel of you."

Some things had to be taken care of or a man might die of needing them. "I'm going to take you home from the restaurant, Polly."

"Mmm."

"You've seen where I live. It's only fair for you to show me your place."

"Okay, I guess."

"Okay, I know. And after we get there I'm going to take my time loving the feel of you. We're going to take our time. We're going to make love."

Six

The older model black Porsche didn't give Nasty enough room. His bent knees amused Polly.

So far he'd done exactly as promised. Venus had returned to Bellevue and Hole Point — happily accepting Dusty's offer to "take the boy and go meet some old friends." Bobby remained with Dusty to learn about the shop.

And Polly sat beside Nasty while he drove through a pretty evening into the crammed lot at Park Place, the bustling shopping center and movie complex on Central Way.

"Next comes Fabiola," Nasty said as if he could crawl inside her mind.

Polly smoothed her thin cotton dress over her bare legs.

He looked sideways at her. In this light his eyes turned oddly amber. "Is she like you to look at?"

"Taller. Prettier."

"Not possible."

She smirked. "Of course she can be taller."

"Smartie."

"I love this area. It feels sort of San Francisco to me."

He regarded riotous blooms cascading from planters, brightly filled windows in an eclectic array of shops, little tables arranged around a fountain and crowded with coffee-drinkers, and he made an assenting noise. "Coffee aficionados and microbrew junkies all. Readers and talkers — walkers and bikers — and boaters. Civilized renegades. Or maybe domesticated mavericks. People here remind me of settlers with a lot of respect for having found nirvana. I love this place, too."

"Are you from here?" She'd been waiting for an opening to see if he'd be protective of his background.

"Nope."

One more "nope" and she'd know how protective he was. "So you've only lived in the area since you came to Kirkland?"

He swung the car into a slot not far from a line of waiting moviegoers. "Nope."

Okay. "I was born in Marysville — that's a little town —"

"North of here on I405 — just the other side of Everett. Pretty place. Rural, really."

"So you know Washington well."

"Well enough." He pulled on the emergency brake. "I spent some time in Issaquah when Dusty used to live there. That was while my friend, Roman, had business connections at a . . . a sort of health club in the mountains. Foothills of the Cascades. In a place called Past Peak. Have you been there?"

"Of course." She turned sideways in her seat to look at him. "I like to ski. In the winter Bobby and I go up to Snoqualmie. It's not far from Past Peak. Do you ski?"

He stared straight ahead. "I used to."

His ankle. "I'm sorry. I didn't think."

"I'll ski again. I'm already a hundred percent better than I was after it happened."

"That's great." Relief at his optimism eased her breathing. "How long ago was the accident?"

"Twenty months. Not that I'm counting." He faced her. So enigmatic. So compelling. The final rays of a setting sun turned him gold.

"Did you do it skiing?"

His lips flattened. "No, Polly, I didn't do it skiing. Are we ready for beer and noise?"

She'd hit yet another of his nerves, this one very raw. "We've got a few minutes." She should know when to quit. She did, but wanted to know more. "You sound as if you've been to TGIF before."

"Yeah." He ducked his head to see up to the second-story balcony, and the red-and-white striped canvas awnings over the windows of the restaurant. "Cheerful."

"Good American food. I have simple tastes."

"So do I. In food. Not in women."

He had the power to stop the blood in her veins. "What does that mean?"

"It means I don't have a simple taste in women. Not if the woman's going to be important to me. I've had a lot of difficulty making any choices at all. But now I have, and she isn't simple. I choose you, Polly."

Nasty did everything he did so well. He

speared her easily in place with a clear, unwavering gaze.

"Do you have folks?" she asked.

"Everyone has folks."

"You know what I mean."

"Yeah. You mean you're curious about me. I take that as a compliment."

Polly rubbed her cotton skirts again. "And you also take it that I'm nosey. Isn't that what you're suggesting?"

"I want to know about you, Polly. That doesn't make me nosy, it makes me interested. I want you to be interested in me, too — it means you care. I was born in Montana. On a ranch."

She wrinkled her nose. "You're kidding."

"Why would I be? Don't I look like a guy who'd be at home in the saddle?"

Polly considered. "I think you're a guy who'd be a heartbreaker in the saddle. With one of those hats tipped over your eyes, and worn jeans. Scuffed boots. An oilskin duster that looks like someone had a war in it. Yes, I —"

"You've got quite an imagination." He stroked the bridge of her nose. "I left Montana a long time ago. I was seventeen. I've never been back."

"Why?"

"You and Seven should be great pals."

"What does that mean?"

"You both want to know everything about everything. I haven't had a reason to go back. I may now that my friend Roman and his wife live there. Wanna come?"

Polly blinked, and shook her head. "You just keep dropping things on me. Get serious."

"I've never been more serious in my life than I am right now, with you."

He wasn't giving her a chance to weigh what had happened between them.

"Cool it," he told her, and spread his big, right hand on her thigh. "I'm not going to try to drag you off to Montana tonight, or anywhere else, except to bed."

"Nasty!" Her heart smote her ribs. "You know you don't mean that."

"Okay. I don't mean it." That warm, hard hand rubbed her leg to the knee and back to the groin. And that's where it stayed. He didn't even let his small finger quiver, but it rested where it shouldn't rest — and they both knew it. His grip tightened. "I do mean it."

"Fab's zany," Polly said, making a grab for safe ground. "She says the first thing that comes into her head."

"I've got a one-track mind."

Polly eyed him quizzically.

"I can only think about you, right now. For the rest — I'll just be going through the motions."

She'd missed safe ground. Every second took her farther down the slippery slide toward crawling into his arms and taking whatever they could have together, and to hell with the rest.

"What's that look about?"

She started. "We should go into the restaurant."

133

"Did the guy who left the pep talks on your answering machine make any comments about you having dangerous new friends?"

She shrugged and prepared to brush the questions off again. Instead, she averted her head and frowned unseeingly at the windows of nearby Park Place Book Company.

"That's a yes," Nasty remarked conversationally. "Isn't that interesting? New friends. Who do you think these people are talking about?"

In some cases she had no idea. But when the man had berated her for the thin cotton skirt, he'd been talking about her walking on the dock and meeting Nasty. He'd been jealous of Nasty seeing her, that much had become very clear to Polly. And she no longer believed this man could be a threat, not the kind of threat she'd originally feared.

"You aren't afraid of me anymore, are you?"

"Not the way . . . No."

His short laugh held no mirth. "You're afraid of me, but differently from the way you used to be afraid of me. Great. How about explaining that to me?"

"I've got to meet my sister."

When she reached for the handle, he shot out a hand, palm up, inviting her to hold it.

Hesitantly, Polly rested a hand on his.

"You don't have to say anything," he told her. "I think I understand. You're afraid being around me is bad for your health. That it's making someone jealous."

"Something like that." *Why continue to avoid the truth?*

"What do you think happens next? In this setup?"

"I don't know."

"I do. If I'm out of the picture, your champion watches for any other man who looks in your direction, and threatens you until you get rid of him, too. And so it will go. Until or unless this creep gets the balls to approach you himself."

"Don't!"

"There's no point in pretending. That won't make it go away. The time to make a stand is now — with me to help you. But you've got to stop walking around smelling of fear."

"If I keep to myself, he might be satisfied."

"You're not listening. It's not *me*, Polly. It's anyone you might get close to. You do see that?"

"I guess so. But I feel helpless. You can't fight an enemy you don't know."

He took her hand to his lips and kissed it. He closed his eyes and kissed each finger, each bone in the back of her hand, her wrist.

Polly stroked his hair, she couldn't help herself. He raised his face and settled the side of his head against the rest. "I can see the enemy. Not his face. I don't have to. But I can see him — or feel him's a better explanation. That's what I'm trained to do. To get you, he'll have to come through me. The guy's a coward, a sneaky coward. He won't risk coming face-to-face with me. And wherever you are, I'm never going to be far away."

"You've got work to do."

"I run the diving classes, and we're between sessions. Dusty doesn't like my shopkeeper efforts."

"So you can squeeze in saving Polly before the next set of diving lessons." She sounded disgustingly petulant.

Nasty put her hand back in her lap. "However long it takes to get my hands on this clown, that's how long I'm going to take. I'm going to flush him out and bury him."

Alarm unwound in Polly. "Violence never solves anything."

"Wrong." The cynical downward turn of his mouth shook her. "Violence often solves a lot of things. Unfortunate, but true. But don't worry, I'm not planning to kill this jerk, just maim him for life."

"Nasty —"

"I've got to live up to my reputation. Keep in practice, too. Nail-pulling is an art. I'd better get my pinking shears sharpened, too."

Polly felt her eyes widen. "Pinking shears?"

"Most effective tool for an attractive circumcision."

She screamed. She couldn't help it.

"As I said," he told her when she'd covered her mouth. "You don't have a thing to fear, Nasty's here. So's Dusty. God help this dickless little bastard. Whoops!" A blush gave Nasty a fascinating extra dimension. "Sorry about the language. Take me up and introduce me to Fabiola."

Baskets of scented hybrid petunias and trailing ferns swung a little in the breeze. Polly registered their colors, and their heady smell, but didn't stop moving until Nasty reached around her to push on the brass door handle at TGIFriday's.

Noise, heat, and essence of charbroiled meat blasted her face. The instant they passed from the foyer through the second set of doors, a crowd of men about a corner table told her where she'd find Fabiola. Men flocked to Fab, they couldn't help themselves; yet she had never found one she wanted on more than a temporary basis.

"Follow me," she told Nasty, passing tables overhung with Tiffany lamp shades that allowed only a muted glow through colored glass. Perched on high stools, patrons watched banks of television screens around an elevated bar. Red light flickered in the face of an oversize clock.

"Hey, Polly! Come and join us."

She sought and found Art Loder's pleasant, smiling face at a nearby table. He sat with Jennifer, with Jack Spinnel, and several members of the crew. Polly squeezed Art's shoulder. "This place is bursting. Hi, guys. This is Nasty Ferrito. He owns a local dive shop. Nasty, this is Art and Jennifer Loder — our monsters. Jack Spinnel, writer, director, and producer. Willie Wonka — not his real name, I'll tell you about that another time if you want to know — Willie does magic with makeup. Seamus, and Caroline. Wardrobe and camera respectively. We'll come and visit

137

later. We're meeting my sister, Fab."

"The microbrew girl?" Art said, grinning. "Bring her over, too."

"Don't buy into it, Polly," Jennifer said. "He's been trying to get her attention ever since she came in."

Polly didn't miss Jack's cold stare — or the fact that it was directed at Nasty. "Later," she told Art. "Business first. Then pleasure. See you, Jennie."

Fab's clear voice rose from the center of the admiring group of men. Polly started burrowing a route between their bodies, then gasped when her feet left the ground.

As abruptly as he'd lifted her, Nasty set her down. The shutters had closed over his expression once more. He looked down into her furious face and snapped his gum.

"What do you think you're doing?" she hissed. "Don't you ever do something like that again."

"And don't you ever do something like that again."

"What —"

"Someone threatened to kill you today. Have you forgotten that?"

Her eyes stung. She hadn't expected her own reaction. Too many new experiences, some of them terrifying, some of them overwhelming in quite different ways, had come her way too fast. "I haven't forgotten," she said through her teeth. "How could I when you remind me about twice a minute?"

"How hard do you think it is to knife someone in a crowd?"

She felt her mouth drop open and was helpless to close it.

"You're a babe in the woods, Polly, baby. You don't get it, yet. And I'm not standing around waiting for you to get it when it's too late — when you're dead. Understand?"

"Well" — she blinked and swallowed — "unlike some people, I'm not used to thinking about people with knives."

"Do you understand me, Polly?" The unrelenting tone of his voice spit out each word.

"Don't call me baby again."

"Do you —"

"Yes. Yes, I understand. I want to talk to my sister, and there's a group of people around her table. How do you suggest I get to her?"

Nasty regarded her steadily and moved his gum around. "Stay close to me." Clamping a hand at her waist — surely more tightly than could possibly be necessary — he turned to the laughing gaggle of men. In a loud, terse voice that could cut granite he said, "Listen up!"

Polly flinched, and jumped hard enough to jar her teeth together.

Silence fell. Not just on the men around the table, but on a good portion of the whole restaurant.

Fire overtook Polly's skin. She bowed her head.

"This lady's trying to get to her sister," Nasty

139

said. "Her sister's sitting at the table you're juicing. Do you mind?"

A low grumble started and stopped abruptly. Polly didn't dare check to see how Nasty had made them quiet again. Feet passed her, and jeans, and bare, hairy legs. Gradually the restaurant noise rose again.

"Polly, where the Sam Henry have you been?"

She raised her head and looked into Fab's startling blue eyes. "Trying to get through your crowd of admirers. Where else would I be?"

Fabiola tilted her head to study Nasty. "Hmm." Her straight blond hair swung away from one side of her face. "Nice. You can be very sneaky, sister, and very selfish. Are there any more at home like you, gorgeous?"

"Fab," Polly said, but only because she was expected to protest her sister's aggression. "This is Nasty Ferrito. He — er, I invited him to join us."

"Smart girl."

"Let's sit down," Polly said when it became evident Fab wouldn't remember to invite them. "I understand you spoke to Mom."

Fab bent forward over the table. "Keep your voice down," she said, sending significant glances in Nasty's direction.

"Nasty knows all about it. I think Mom's half-convinced he's the enemy."

Fab sat back again. To Nasty she said, "Are you the enemy?"

"Why, yes, ma'am," he told her. "Of course I'm the enemy."

"He's not the enemy," Fab said matter-of-factly. "Mom's in a real snit. How do you like my dress?"

"What dress?" Polly asked.

Fab checked the divided halter top on the minuscule red number she wore. "I'm decent." Long, red-nailed fingers passed under her very shapely bottom to a hem that clipped the tops of elegant thighs. "Everything's covered."

Polly smiled at her adored sibling. "Just, my dear. How can you blame men for falling all over you when you look like that?"

"I don't blame them," Fab said. "Who are you, Nasty Ferrito? Apart from being Nasty Ferrito? My mother and I think that's a wild name."

"I'm a dive-shop owner," he said calmly.

"And?"

"Former Navy SEAL. Montana son. Loner. A dangerous dude." He raised his well-defined eyebrows. "And a man with plans."

"Crumb — as my soft sister would say. A virtuoso of violence in the flesh. Counterintelligence and all that stuff. Inhuman, that's what they call you people. Hell — I mean, crumb, what are you doing with my little sister?"

"Put a sock in it, Fab." Polly fumed. "For the record, I'm older than you. Nasty *used* to be in the Navy. He teaches diving school now."

"Oh, sure." Fab slid slowly sideways in her chair until she could see all of Nasty. "When they talk about seven feet of whipcord, they're talking about guys like you, Captain Death."

Nasty's sudden laugh startled Polly. She was growing tired of being startled around this man.

"Captain Death?" he sputtered. "That's great. Geez, wait till I tell Roman that one. He'll croak. Nice to meet you, too, Fabiola Crow. You're beautiful, but not as beautiful as your sister. You're smart — but I doubt if you're as smart as your sister. You're sexy, but definitely not as sexy as your sister. Polly's the family diplomat, too. But you're a winner, Ms. Crow, and I think I'm going to like you."

This time it was Fab who sat with her mouth open.

Art Loder appeared at Polly's shoulder. "Introduce me to your sister," he said. "She's something."

"This is Art Loder, Fab," Polly said. "He and his sister, Jennifer, are the Main Monsters."

"Yeah," Fab said, with the enthusiasm Polly loved in her twin. "You're fabulous. God, I wish I could move like you two."

"Thank you kindly," Art said. "I'd a sight rather watch you move."

They all laughed.

"Come back, Artie," Jennifer called. "We can't finish this argument without you."

Polly felt stared at and turned to meet Jack's eyes. He wasn't finding anything funny. He sent her a signal she didn't understand. She ignored him.

Jennifer said, "We've started a pool. You want

142

in? How many sports stadiums will there be in Seattle by the year 3000?"

Nasty stroked his jaw. "I can only count with my fingers and toes. I don't have enough. But then, who knows?"

"Right, mate!" Art slapped Nasty's very solid shoulder, and looked at his own hand. "Cripes. Go easy on the spinach, will ya? I need these hands."

"Artie!"

"Coming, sis. When you gotta go, you gotta go." To Fab he said, "Just let me know when you want to start tumbling lessons. Or dancing lessons. Yeah, how about dancing lessons? I'll make time to give you private sessions."

"I just bet you will," Fab said to the acrobat's departing back. "Pushy little fart."

"Fab."

"Not bowled over by the charmer, huh?" Nasty said, sounding preoccupied. His eyes didn't quite focus. "He's got a big head."

"International circus performers, isn't that what you told me, Polly?" Fab asked. "I've got to admit the guy's got some muscles in that cute red suit. He's got some other things, too. There's no way he could carry a concealed weapon."

"Fab."

"Oh, *Fab*," Fabiola repeated, grinning.

Nasty was restless. "What's with Domehead, Polly? Your producer friend. He's making holes in your back."

Nasty hadn't looked behind him once — as far

as Polly had been aware. How did he know Jack was staring at her?

"Is there anything you haven't told me about Jack Spinnel? That is his name?"

"That's his name," Polly said. "There's nothing personal I haven't told you because I don't know much about him. Professionally, he's had a number of successful children's series. And he's done one or two nature programs. Some gorilla stuff — the US studies, I think. Aborigines in the outback. A couple of critically acclaimed documentaries on South America."

Fab pursed her lips. "Hmm. Nice track record. Too bad he's such a prick."

"You don't even know the man," Polly protested.

"He's got the hots for you."

"That's stupid." And the suggestion had been made too many times to ignore, darn it.

The arrival of a waiter was a relief. She ordered a beer and potato skins. Nasty asked for Coke and fried calamari.

"Jackie boy doesn't want to share you with anyone, love," Nasty said when the waiter had left. "If he could figure out a way, he'd grab you and get you out of here."

Polly found her voice. "No, he wouldn't. You're seeing things — or making up things you can't see, or guess at." Gavin had spoken of Mary thinking Jack was involved with Polly.

"Am I, Fab?" Nasty asked.

Fabiola faced Jack's table. She lifted her wineglass and stared down into the pale contents. "I'd say Captain Death has great instincts," she said. "That guy's creepy, Pol. Nothing's moving. He's frozen with his eyes on you." She shivered and emptied her glass.

"Have you told him anything about what's going on?" Nasty asked.

"I haven't told anyone," Polly said.

"Venus couldn't have said something?"

"I know she wouldn't have had a chance to talk about the woman who called her. But if she'd told him about the answering machine threats —" He was trying to trick her into telling him everything. "There wouldn't be any reason to go to Jack."

"You know all about what's been going on, Fabiola?" Nasty asked.

"I know. Polly and I share everything. We always have."

"Do you think there's any reason why Bobby can't be kept safe here in Kirkland?"

"The guy on the phone did threaten him, or that's what Polly and I decided he was doing. He said he'd forgive her for the one mistake she'd made. If she got rid of it, or something."

Polly looked unseeingly at the beer the waiter placed in front of her. Nasty had successfully maneuvered Fab into telling him just about everything.

"And you and Polly decided this man meant Bobby?"

She needed fresh air.

"What else could he mean? What I don't get is

145

this woman who called our mother today. That's even more weird. I think the guy's got a woman who's afraid of him. You read about cases like that. These men get a woman, a wife, or a girlfriend, to do these things for them — help them get at another woman. The girlfriend or whatever is afraid to go against the man, so she goes along. Sometimes the guy's abusing the girlfriend's own kid. Can you imagine a sicko like that?"

"I don't have to imagine," Nasty said.

Polly looked at him. His voice didn't change, but it sounded as if he carried the experience of a very long life with him — and he'd been disgusted by a lot of that experience.

"Maybe I'd better ask some questions about your venerable producer," Nasty said. "I already know he thinks he owns you."

Polly rallied. "How could you know that?"

"I'll tell you when the time's right. For now, the less you know, the better. We'll make sure Bobby's safe," he said to Fab. "My partner's an expert in the protection game. You don't have anything to worry about there."

"Oh, I'm not going to worry about Bobby," Fab said. She looked at Polly from beneath thick, dark lashes. "It's my sister who may be in danger around here."

"Don't worry about Polly, either. I intend to stick to her day and night. I won't let her out of my sight."

"Like I said," Polly told him. "It's my sister who may be in danger."

Seven

She'd turned out all but the lights around the makeup mirror. Jack said she was too fat for the screen, but she wasn't fat. Mary Reese smoothed the loosely belted, white satin robe over her breasts. In the mirror, she watched her nipples push against the fabric, and wriggled on the small stool.

She wasn't fat. She had the kind of body men fondled in their dreams, the best dreams they ever had.

The building was empty. She'd hear his footsteps when he approached backstage, and the dressing rooms.

Mary picked up her watch from the dressing table. He was late. Bastard. He liked to make her wait. It excited him to think of her here like this, ready, and frustrated. He always said the waiting made her more inventive.

Tonight she intended to make him listen to her. Either he listened, and helped her come up with a plan, or she wouldn't put out. Of course, he was strong enough to take care of that . . . Mary pressed a hand between her legs and closed her eyes.

A draft hit her back before she realized the door had opened. "Mary, Mary," he said. "Nice of you to make sure you're well oiled for me."

She glared at him in the mirror, tossed her hair back, and pretended to be angry. "Well oiled for you?" She laughed. "Who needs you? I'm doing very well all on my own."

He closed the door. "Don't let me stop you."

"I didn't hear you coming."

"You were too busy."

"Go away."

"Maybe I will. Yeah, I think I'll just go away and find someone more obliging."

She pouted.

"On the other hand, I think I want to see you do it to yourself."

The idea appealed. "And then we can do it to each other," she said, the nerves that counted exposed, and begging for attention.

"We'll see."

"No, we won't." Peeved, she tightened the robe belt. "I don't feel like being told what to do. We've got plans to make. *I've* got plans to make. You're going to do what I want."

He approached and stood with his hands on her shoulders. "I don't like being told what to do either."

"Fuck you."

"You will, Mary. You will. But I want to watch you do it to yourself first. Come on." It was as close to wheedling as she'd ever heard from him.

Fixing her eyes on his in the mirror, she pulled the belt undone and parted the robe. Beneath it she wore a black lace teddy with satin ribbons holding it together between her breasts.

"Lush," he said. "You are so lush. Ice cream and big, dark cherries. And this hair." He ran his fingers through the red curls that brushed her very white shoulders. "I love your hair. All of it. Do it, Mary. I'm ready, but I want to watch you first."

"Why don't we —"

"Do it." A sharp tug on her hair underscored the menace in his voice. "Go on."

He excited her. Her breathing came in short gasps. Leaning her head against him, she let her knees fall apart. A slit in the teddy revealed the other red hair he was so fond of.

"God, you're something," he muttered.

She slid a finger through the slit and let her eyes close.

"Go for it, Mary. Go."

"No." A flush heated her all over. "Let's just get it on together."

"Don't cross me."

When he spoke like that, and looked like that — wild — he incited and frightened her. She'd defied him before, and the sex hadn't completely dulled the pain.

But it almost had.

Mary sprang from the stool and whirled away. "You can't make me do it."

"I'm not in the mood for games." He stood where he was. "Come here."

"You come and get me."

"Stupid, stupid, Mary. You don't know when

to shut up and do as you're told."

"Why don't you teach me?" she said sweetly, while her heart thundered, and sweat poured between her shoulder blades. She felt sick. "Come on. Teach me."

He moved as fast as she knew he could. Four steps and he reached her. Five steps and he slammed her against the wall.

Mary screamed.

"Shut *up*," he said into her ear. "Shut up, Mary."

"Kiss me," she begged.

"I don't like mouths. You never know where they've been."

"You're disgusting."

"We're very compatible."

Mary pushed on his chest.

He returned the favor until tears squeezed from her eyes.

"Are you ready to do as you're told?" he asked.

She nodded.

"Good." With a last pinch, he straightened and stood aside to let her pass him. "Back on the stool. I like watching in the mirror."

A thrill mounted under her skin. She returned to the stool and sat down, spread her legs, parted the fabric of the crotch in her teddy, and stimulated herself. Long, slick strokes. Her hips rocked.

"Pretty," he whispered, coming to stand behind her. He reached down and undid the satin ribbons. A swift tug and he had what he wanted.

Hauling the top of the teddy open, he revealed her heavy breasts.

Mary's vision blurred. She let her head fall forward.

He raised her chin. "You told me you wanted to be an actress."

She nodded, working harder, faster.

"Knowing how to put on the greasepaint is important to actresses." He wouldn't release her chin. "You've got to draw attention to your best features."

"Let me go."

Slowly, he passed a stick of violet greasepaint around first one nipple, then the other, making garish circles on her translucent, blue-veined skin.

"Stop it," she whined. "It's hard to get off."

He ignored her, picked up another stick, and added a turquoise line around the purple. "So pretty," he murmured. "Hurry up, Mary." Leaning over her, he pulled the slit open wider and clamped his hand on top of hers, guided her.

"I don't like that."

"But I do. D'you know what these are?" With his free hand, he tweaked a nipple. "Targets. Be quick. I'm ready for target practice."

Her stomach rolled over and she tasted acid. When she tried to pull her hand away, he snatched her fingers, and pumped them back and forth until she cried aloud.

"Good," he whispered against her ear. "Very good. Now, Mary. Now!"

She came. With a shriek and a dim spear of

humiliation, she came beneath her fingers, and his, while he watched her helpless bucking.

What she saw in the mirror then wiped away any trace of embarrassment. She fascinated him. He couldn't take his eyes off her body.

She didn't like the painted circles.

"Better?" he asked. When she nodded, he said, "But it's not enough, is it. It's never enough for people like you and me. Get up."

Dimly, she looked up into his face. Satiation spread its dreamy lethargy.

"Up," he ordered curtly. But he didn't wait. Instead he moved beside her, gripped her waist, and hauled her to sit on the dressing table.

Mary plucked at his shirt. "Come on," she said. "Come to Mary."

Very deliberately, he pulled her arms away and took them behind her back. He held her wrists together and studied her breasts. "I hope you've learned your lesson," he said, picking up another stick of paint and applying a third circle. Yellow this time. "When you want to grab attention, my love, just show off your tits."

Mary squirmed. The result was to grind the bones in her wrists together.

He tossed the greasepaint down and picked up a stiff liner brush. "For the finer touches," he said, concentrating, dipping the bristles into red lip gloss.

"You'll bruise me," she said, struggling against his hold on her arms.

Then the pointed brush made contact and the

pain didn't matter. "Yes." She strained toward him. "Yes, yes." Each stipple was a delicious dart.

"Bull's-eye!" His mouth and teeth replaced the brush with shocking suction.

Mary gasped, and cried out. She wrapped her legs around his waist and moaned. He sucked long, and hard. Her back met glass. The naked bulbs sent shafts of heat into her shoulders.

"See," he said, raising his face. "Trust me. Invention is my thing." His mouth glistened.

"Did you see him tonight?" Mary asked.

His face twisted. "Shut up!" The sting of his fingers on her cheek brought tears to her eyes. "I'll deal with it."

She didn't care how dangerous it was to press him, she had to have what she needed — his promise that they would win. "Was he with her?"

"You stupid, stupid woman. Stupid, selfish bitch."

He used a finger to wipe an oval of white greasepaint around the perimeter of her lips.

She felt his fingernail dig into the skin and winced. "Don't. We've got to talk about this. You're protecting her. I'll see them both in hell before I let —"

Black. Black silenced Mary. A wide swath of black liner, pressed so hard the inside of her mouth ground into her teeth. His eyes glittered. Fear fluttered in her chest, her stomach.

There could be no going back. "She's in the way."

"She's the least of our problems. A nuisance. Nothing else."

A single powerful lift and she thudded to sit on the stool once more. He stood beside her and made sure she saw what he'd done to her face. Great, garish clown strokes painted a huge, downturned mouth. The red gloss smudged out from the centers of her nipples, bleeding into the violet circles.

She heard him taking off his clothes but couldn't look away from her distorted image.

Then he probed her lips and Mary watched how he entered her mouth and withdrew, only to push ever deeper inside.

His buttocks tensed. "Work it, love. Hold me."

She closed her eyes and did as he asked — and sweated while he grunted. His body fascinated her. When he came, and let out a shuddering sigh, she fingered his butt, groped blindly for the rigid backs of his thighs.

"Great," he said, panting. "You follow directions well, kid."

"I'm not your slave," she told him, turning her face aside and wiping her mouth. "Now it's my turn. But I want to know what comes next with the other." All of this was a pastime, a game while the most important game was played.

"Leave it to me," he said. "This isn't your problem. I've got everything under control."

"You don't get it, do you," she hissed at him. "You're not in charge here. You're not the one who makes the decisions or hands down the instructions. I am. When are you going to get it right?"

He dragged her to her feet and shook her. "I've got it right. You're going to stay out of my way. You're going to stop giving me orders. And you're going to be where I want you, when I want you — with the information I may want."

"The hell —"

The next shake jabbed the backs of her calves into the stool. "You were saying?" he asked, menacing, keeping her off balance enough to make her try to scramble upright.

Excitement made her bold. "Get rid of her."

"Don't be crazy. You think we need police swarming around?"

"All you have to do is make sure she goes missing. And stays missing."

"Not until I do what I'm here to do."

She would not back away from this. "I want that woman a long way away."

"Just because you're jealous? I don't give a shit about how jealous you are. I'll do what I've got to do."

"And then she'll be out of the way?"

"Leave it to me."

"Damn you! Get tough before it's too late. I want it done."

"When I'm ready. When the time's right."

"I want —"

"Shut *up.*"

He flung her around and bent her, facefirst, over the stool.

Mary flailed, and tried to grab at him but he was too strong. With little effort he parted her thighs and wedged them apart with his knees.

Holding her down by the neck, he swept a circle on her bottom. This time she couldn't see the color of the greasepaint.

"Don't! I hate you. You're going to wish you hadn't done this."

"Don't you remember telling me I could do what I like as long as I made it different?" The paint stick clattered on the dressing table. "Didn't you say you get bored easily?"

"Let me up!"

"Targets, pet. Just making sure I know what to aim for here."

Mary tensed. "Use something. I don't want to bleed."

He laughed. "Do you think he does this with her?"

"She hasn't got what I've got." She braced her weight on her hands against the floor. Her breasts, with the grotesque designs, swayed. "It'll all come apart, I tell you. If we don't stop them, everything I've made will be destroyed. And I won't be the only loser."

"I'm going to stop them, Mary. My way."

"My stomach hurts." She smelled the grease remover before he slathered it over her. "You're going to suffer for this."

"Not at all. I'm going to love it. I bet he thinks she's more fun to do it with than you. Different, but more fun."

The cream didn't blunt the pressure of his first thrust. "You're sick," she shouted at him.

"And you love it." He began to use the clever power of his hips, and croon, "Give-it-to-me, baby," falsetto, and in rhythm with his onslaught.

Mary held her breath and gritted her teeth. Her time would come, her grip on ultimate power.

"I'm taking us to heaven, sexy Mary."

"Oh, yeah," she whispered. "Fucking heaven, Art."

Eight

"Can you tell me you want me to go away and mean it?"

With her door keys in her hands, Polly looked at her feet and tried to think.

Nasty didn't touch her. For that she was grateful. It would take so little to send her into his arms.

"Can you?" he repeated.

She shook her head no.

He hesitated just long enough to let her know he wasn't totally sure of himself. "Good," he said. "Because I'll go if you want me to. But not before I take a look around your place."

"You scare me when you talk like that."

"Pretending we don't need to be cautious won't make the danger go away."

"Maybe there isn't any danger. They say people who make crank calls don't usually follow through."

He took the keys from her and unlocked the front door to her third-floor condominium. "That's the case when the crank's picking random numbers out of a phone book."

"Well —"

"Your crank knows who you are."

She started to enter the condo, but Nasty held

her arm and put her firmly behind him.

"If this person didn't know who you are, he — or she — or whatever, wouldn't have called your mother in Bellevue."

He was making her more scared by the minute. She said, "The police don't seem worried."

"The police aren't falling in love with you."

Polly stood still in the mahogany-paneled foyer of the condo. He said things like that, and kept right on walking and looking around, and opening doors, as if all he'd spoken of was the weather.

"What if I don't want you to fall in love with me?"

"Tell me now." He passed her and opened the door into the master suite, where she slept.

Hesitantly, she followed him. He crossed her precious Nepal carpet in sumptuous blues and greens that lay atop dark wood floors. Her four-poster bed draped with lengths of jewel-toned silk held his interest for too long.

"Don't you want me to fall in love with you, Polly?"

"I don't know. I haven't thought about it."

While she leaned against the doorjamb, Nasty examined her bathroom. "I think of you as honest. Painfully honest," he said.

"Thank you."

"I think you've given it a lot of thought."

She frowned.

He slipped open clear glass doors to a huge shower with dual showerheads. "Whether or not you want me to fall in love with you. You've thought about it."

"You don't need to open doors you can see through."

"I would if I was getting in," he said, with not a trace of a smile. "Are you going to answer my question anytime soon?"

"I doubt it. I'm not ready for this. For the first time in my life, I'm in control of what happens to me. As much in control as a human being can be. I don't think I can give that up."

"And you think loving a man would mean you'd have to give up your independence."

"Why are we talking about this?"

"Because I want to. I admit I started it. This is a great place. Rich."

Polly trotted behind him from bathroom, to bedroom, to closet, where he toured her clothes. The foyer again, the kitchen, steel and black and businesslike, and made for the skills she still loved to use when she had time.

"I never knew anyone who could really cook," Nasty said.

"Surely your mother could."

His eyes caught hers briefly and passed on. He didn't respond.

Bobby's red, white, and blue room passed inspection. Every closet got a quick perusal. "Nothing," Nasty said, returning to the living room overlooking Lake Washington. "There's no doorman downstairs."

"No. But you can't get in without a key."

"I think I should stay here with you."

She looked at his hard profile. "I've got a son. He wants to be here with me."

"There's room for three of us."

"There are only two bedrooms."

His gaze at her was impassive. Uncompromising. Nasty's was not a face made for softness.

"Thanks for coming back with me," she said when she couldn't stand the aching silence. "I'll lock up as we leave. I've got to get the car out and get Bobby."

"I'll bring him back."

"I think —"

"Don't."

Polly took an uneven breath. "Don't what?"

"Don't think. Not about this. We may be over-reacting. I hope we are. But for tonight let me bring Bobby home and make sure you're both safe here."

Arguing wouldn't budge a man like Nasty Ferrito. "All right. Thank you."

"Your bed's too big for one person. One small person."

She took her keys from his hand and tossed them on a pier table. "If you're suggesting what I think you're suggesting, it's obvious you were never a parent."

"Nope. Never was."

"I've got a seven-year-old son. I don't share my bedroom with men."

"Not while Bobby's in the house?"

"Not" — she flopped onto a curved gray couch

— "I don't share my bedroom. Period."

Nasty chewed his gum between his front teeth. He sat beside her. "Good. That's what I hoped you'd say."

"Would it be your business if I'd said otherwise?" She sounded snappish, but he had no right to feel possessive.

He took a long time to answer. His long, broad hands hung between his knees. As relaxed as his posture appeared, an energy flowed from him. He looked sideways at her. "Is there anyone else, Polly?"

She hadn't expected that. "No."

"You don't want a man in your life?"

The questions were too hard, too hard because she didn't want to think about the answers. "I'm still working at feeling I've made my way back. All the way back."

"From where?"

Polly rubbed her arms. The cotton dress wasn't warm enough anymore. "Lots of kids rebel. Some rebel more than others. I did. And I made a mess of myself."

"You're not a mess now. You're a success."

"Do you feel you've got your life completely under control?"

He flexed his jaw. "I think I've come to terms. Isn't that kind of the same thing?"

"I don't know. I'm not an expert. I only know I'm not sure I'm ready for a relationship — the kind of relationship you're proposing."

"What kind is that? Are you sure you know?"

No. "Maybe I'm reading too much into everything you say — and do."

"Or maybe you're not reading enough into it. What I've told you isn't some sort of line. I never felt this way before — ever. When I was an active SEAL that took up everything. Before that — before that I didn't know what I wanted, except out. I wanted out of my old life. I'm not pretending there haven't been women. Good women. But they weren't you, Polly."

She drew her feet beneath her on the couch and wrapped her skirts around her shins. "Okay. We're too old to be coy. I think about you. A lot. I wonder what you're thinking about, what you're doing. I see your face. I get feelings about you."

He put an elbow on the back of the couch and gave her his full attention. "Good feelings?"

"Confused feelings. The kind of feelings I'm not sure I've ever had. And they may be feelings I can't afford to have, about anyone, right now. I won't do anything to unsettle Bobby. I won't bring someone into his life — and if you were in my life, you'd be in his — I won't do that casually. I can't take the risk."

"Would it help if I admitted this is one risk that scares the hell out of me, too?"

"I already figured out you're making up the steps to this dance as you go along. You can do that. I can't. I'm not ready to try."

He brushed a finger back and forth along her forearm. "Can we get back to the feelings you get when you think about me?"

"I'm not going to kid around. I'm sexual. When I think about you I get sexual feelings — and other feelings. They're all muddled up and scary."

"And that's bad?"

"I can't cope with it now."

"So you're going to walk away." His voice went flat. "Just walk away and tell yourself you're not missing a thing."

"Oh, no," she told him softly, capturing his finger, then his hand. "I'm not going to tell myself I'm not missing a whole lot if I say good-bye to you. But I just can't go into a casual, feel-good relationship. Now, and maybe never. Once I could have, but I've changed."

"I like who've you've changed into."

"And I like you," she told him rashly. "I do. I never believed in instant attraction — I probably don't believe in it now, but there's something about you and me — together. It isn't simple."

"It's very complicated," he said, watching her bend his palm back and trace the lines. "If it wasn't complicated, this wouldn't be so damn tough, would it?"

And it was tough. And she was dealing with escalating threats. Too much for one woman who yearned for peace. "It's getting late. Bobby should be in his bed."

"Yeah." He picked up a phone from the sofa table and dialed. After a brief interval he said, "Dust? Nasty. How's Bobby? Yeah. I'm going to bring him back. No, don't wake him up. I'll do

164

that when I get there." He hung up and returned to staring straight ahead.

"You don't have to put yourself out for us anymore."

"I'd consider it a favor if you wouldn't make another comment like that."

His words stung. "I didn't mean to sound ungrateful," she said.

"Gratitude isn't what I want from you. I want a shot at making something work between us."

"And I can't . . . You already gave me your laundry list of events for the night. You've accomplished everything but taking me to bed."

"You make that sound so grubby."

"Put the way you put it, it sounded grubby."

"Damn!" The flash in his eyes made her skin prickle all over. "Pretty words aren't my thing. But I'm honest. That's what I want. I want to take you to bed. I think we'll be great together."

Anger rushed at Polly. "Great together? I wonder if there's somewhere to look up that phrase and what it means. For us. Probably that parts of your body fit well with parts of my body? Is that what you think? And then you'll get to feel really great?"

Without warning he picked her up and sat her on his lap. When she tried to get off he shifted her again, to sit astride his thighs with her face close enough to his to feel his breath.

"I absolutely hate physical violence." She'd been there and done that — and didn't intend to go back.

165

"I hate it, too — unless it's necessary."

"It isn't necessary now."

"I'm not being violent."

"That's a matter of opinion." His thighs were large, and hard — and Polly could feel that they weren't the only large, hard thing about him.

Nasty kept his grip on her waist but made circles on her ribs with his fingertips. "I'm not being violent — I never could be with you. All I want for you is safety and happiness. This — holding you like this is completely selfish. The kind of selfishness you probably believe is all I think about. I want to feel you, and look at you. And I want your complete attention. Bobby's fine where he is. He's asleep, and he's got the best bodyguard in the world."

"And you want me to go to bed with you."

He shifted his hands to her face and brought it even closer. "If you wanted to go to bed with me, that would be terrific. I'd carry you there right now. But if you actually want to be with me at all, I'm over the moon, sweetheart. You said you think about me, you have feelings about me. Do you want me to tell you what I think and feel about you?"

She didn't trust herself to answer. Neither did she attempt to climb from his lap.

"If we're careful not to do anything to upset Bobby, and if we're careful not to hurt each other, too — can we at least see if we enjoy each other?"

He was hard — and growing harder.

And she ached. And she was wet — and aroused beyond wanting to turn back.

"We could enjoy each other, Xavier."

His eyes snapped to hers.

"Can I call you that? I like it."

"I don't care," he said, sounding as if he cared very much. Finding out why went on her list of "must knows."

"We could enjoy each other a whole lot," Polly said. "Even from a distance we knew that. That's what brought you around the dock each day when you knew I'd be there. And it's what made me keep going out to the docks and looking for you. Call it chemistry. Call it lust-at-first-sight. We came; we saw; we wanted."

"You have a way with words," he murmured. "I've always had trouble saying what I think."

"I haven't noticed that."

"I don't seem to have the usual trouble with you." He tipped her against him, turned her face into his neck, and smoothed the length of her back over and over. "Kiss me, Polly."

Kiss me, Polly. Such a simple request, with such complex possibilities.

Polly nuzzled his neck — and felt a tremor within him. She braced herself on his shoulders and raised her face until she could look into his again. He closed his eyes, and she surveyed the harsh, almost Slavic angles in his features. Uncompromising. But his eyes, turned to the amber she'd come to expect, had closed in a signal of submission. He gave up the power to her. The decision for what happened now he'd passed into her hands.

Polly rocked forward just enough to touch her lips to his. She heard him sigh, felt him sigh. Grazing lightly back and forth, she tasted mint on his lips and pulled back. "Gum," she said. "I'm kissing a man who's chewing gum."

Nasty laughed. He had the kind of face laughter suited too well. She was grateful he didn't do it often. And then she was unnerved by that gratitude — because it meant she wanted him too much, wanted him for herself.

"I swallowed it," he said and tapped the end of her nose.

"The gum?"

"Uh-huh."

"It'll stick your insides together!"

He laughed again. "Shut up and kiss me. I was just really getting into the mood."

She glanced significantly downward, and said, "I'd say you've been in the mood."

His laughter died. "I thought I told you nice girls don't notice things like that."

"You mean they notice, but they don't say anything. We'd better be grateful we've both got clothes on."

"Think so?"

This time it was Polly who closed her eyes. She closed her eyes, tucked her fingers into the hair on either side of his head, and brought her open mouth down on his.

She'd never kissed or been kissed like this before. He coaxed her to follow his lead, to use her lips, her teeth, her tongue. Music was part of her, part of her heart, of who she was. She felt music now like a rhythmic hum, a warm hum that vibrated her nerves.

Nasty tilted up her chin and buried his face beneath her jaw. He spread his hands on her shoulders, his fingers and thumbs extended as if he was afraid to close them in case he hurt her.

"That was lovely," she told him, her voice thick. "I love kissing you. You make me hot all over."

His chuckle had nothing to do with mirth. "Hot, huh? My dear Polly, I'm on fire. In fact, parts of me are going to explode shortly."

She blushed and enjoyed it. "Do you think we should turn the heat down?"

"Do you think we're hot because of the furnace?" The dips above her collarbones stole his attention. "You don't think it's that old thing called passion?"

"Arousal?" she suggested.

"You're so much more succinct than I am. I was going to suggest we may be overdressed."

"I don't think I could trust myself if we took our clothes off," she said. How funny that sounded.

"You can't know how happy I am to hear you say that."

"We're talking a lot, aren't we?"

"Nervousness causes that sometimes."

She took a breath that pressed her sensitized

nipples against her lace bra. "Have I made you nervous? I'm sorry."

"Not quite the kind of nervous you're thinking of. At least, I don't think so. I'm going to take off my shirt before I die."

"Of course. Would you like to go into the bedroom?"

Nasty regarded her solemnly. "Very much."

She stopped breathing. "Just take it off here. It'll work just as well."

"Why don't you take it off for me?"

"If you really want me to."

"I really want you to."

Polly undid the buttons carefully, concentrating on each one. When she reached the waist of his jeans, she frowned.

"Pull it out," he suggested.

She drew back.

"The shirt. Pull the shirttail out of my jeans."

"Of course." Hurriedly she did as he asked. His cuffs were rolled up. She opened the shirt and stopped again. Leg men. Breast men. Butt women. Various other kinds of women. She'd never considered what turned her on but maybe she knew now. Polly Crow could very well be a chest woman.

"Problem?" Nasty asked.

"Your chest."

He drew his brows together and looked down at himself.

"Your chest makes me feel . . . Oh, this is awful. It turns me on — just looking at it. We'd better stop this."

"Oh, no, we hadn't." Leaning forward, he took the shirt all the way off and threw it aside. "A man has to maximize his assets. If my chest is what it takes to convince you we're meant to be an item, I'll go without a shirt permanently."

Overcome by what she felt, and by what she'd said, she curled into him and hid her face in his shoulder.

"Hey!" Gently, he settled a big hand on the back of her head and stroked her hair. "What's this about?"

"Nothing."

"Nothing? You're trying to make sure I can't see what you're feeling — and you're doing that for no reason?"

"I'm embarrassed."

"Okay. Let me help you out. There's nothing about you that doesn't give me a hard-on. Feel better now?"

She scrunched up tighter.

"If you promise not to scream, Polly, I'll help you cool off. I could take off your dress, and whatever else you're wearing, and you wouldn't feel nearly so hot."

Her yelp didn't make her feel any less foolish.

"Is that a no?"

"Yes," she told him, her voice muffled against his wonderful, naked chest.

"Yes? Yes, you want me to take off your clothes."

"No."

"I was afraid of that. Polly, you can just cuddle

up against my chest and think sexy thoughts. That's fine. How would it be if I said sexy things to you just to help out."

Torture. This was some type of fantastic torture, and she was addicted to her torturer.

"I'll assume you're agreeing. I'm a man who makes a habit of doing what he says he'll do. I told you I was going to take you to bed tonight. I still intend to take you to bed — unless you absolutely forbid me. If you do that, I won't."

Things like this didn't happen to Polly Crow, social dropout made good. The new Polly Crow sang songs to children all over the country, and was held up as an example of motherhood, warm cookies, and cold milk, and how all the good things went together to make children feel safe and secure.

"Right beneath your round bottom, where your panties cover the important bits, my jeans are the only thing keeping me from slipping inside those panties, and inside you."

She shuddered. Those bits between her legs contracted. They ached, and the ache spread upward and outward.

"But your friend Belinda gave me the benefit of her bag of Inspiration. Foreplay. I'm into foreplay, Polly. How about you?"

She was dying.

"You, too, huh?" he said. "I'd like to undo your bodice. Could I do that?"

He didn't wait for her to agree. Instead he determinedly levered her hunched form from his chest, set her fists on his hips, and undid the row of small buttons between her breasts. "White," he said, revealing her modest lace bra. "Pretty. I bet you'd be more comfortable without it. Your breasts look as if they'd enjoy being held by me a whole lot more. Do you think they would?"

When he'd threatened sexy talk, he'd meant it. "Where does it undo?"

"At the back," she heard herself say, with a sense that she'd become someone else entirely.

Frowning with concentration, Nasty considered his next move. He slid the sleeves of her dress far enough down her arms to make her movements difficult and reached around to unhook her bra.

"I told you," he said, sounding triumphant when there was an instant loosening of the lace. "You'll be more comfortable." He slipped his hands down, beneath the fabric, to cup and lift her breasts.

Polly saw how tanned his hands were against her white flesh. Desperate to be free to react, she struggled to get the bodice of her dress all the way off.

Nasty helped her. He stripped the bodice to her waist, removed her arms from the sleeves, then got rid of her bra.

He held her legs just above the knees and looked at her breasts. "Dreams come true," he said. "You've got perfect breasts. Exactly right — for me. Everything about you is exactly right for me." As if to prove his point, he fondled her, smoothed her, pushed her breasts together and pressed his face into them. He licked and kissed, not missing an inch of pulsing skin and flesh.

Polly wriggled. She plucked at his shoulders and dropped her head back. He didn't miss an inch, but he didn't take her nipples into his mouth. He drove her mad, but he had to know that.

"Lie down," she ordered him.

His eyes opened, but didn't completely focus. Sliding sideways on the big couch, he did as she asked, scooting until he stretched out on his back.

Getting rid of the loose dress was easy. It settled on top of Nasty's shirt and her bra. Wearing only a pair of wispy, white bikini panties, she mounted him again, straddled his belly this time.

Xavier Nasty Ferrito made sounds she'd remember but never be able to describe. Polly stopped him from reaching for her. She laced her fingers with his and raised his arms above his head.

"Polly," he murmured.

"I'm in charge now. Trust me. You'll like it."

Rising to her knees, she rocked her body enough to make her breasts sway just out of reach of his mouth. Nasty made jerking attempts to capture first one, then the other nipple.

"Aaah," he yelled. "Gimme, gimme, you little devil."

"You had your chance. I thought you didn't want anything you haven't already had."

"I want everything I haven't already had. Then

I want it again. In my mouth, sweetheart. Please, I'm a starving man."

And she was a sexually starved woman. Polly knew that truth about herself. Fact was fact, and she wasn't a child — or even a virginal girl. She was a woman who needed a man — this man.

"Polly!"

Smiling at him, she lowered herself until the tip of his straining tongue made the lightest, most exquisite contact with a pebble-hard nipple.

Once, twice, three times she managed to repeat the torment — torment too painfully sweet to bear any longer.

But then the choice was no longer hers. Nasty rose from the couch, breaking her grip on his fingers, and reversed positions. He played with her breasts until she shrieked for more, or for mercy, in turn or all at once.

"My pants hurt," he announced. "Polly, my pants are agony."

"Take them off," she told him. "Now. I wouldn't want to break anything."

He stood up, a golden man, his strongly muscled chest sprinkled with gold-tipped, dark brown hair, the same dark hair he revealed when he stepped out of his jeans.

His penis rose, heavily veined and massively engorged, from a thick nest of hair.

"See anything broken?" he asked huskily.

"What I see is very dangerous. And we're still talking too much."

"You mean you'd rather just do it and not talk about it?"

"I mean I want to do it, Xavier." She couldn't look away from his penis. "But what we want, and what ought to be can be really different."

"Come here."

She let him take her hands and pull her to her feet.

"Can you tell me — other than Bobby — can you tell me what's holding you back?"

Polly couldn't make words for the half-formed fears and feelings. She shook her head. "Kiss me, please. Make me stop thinking."

The tenderness of his embrace surprised her, and it only served to deepen her need for him. His kiss was a delicate caress. She stood on tiptoe and locked her hands behind his neck. Back and forth he skimmed his mouth, skin on skin, tip of tongue, to tip of tongue. The hair on his chest grazed her touchy nipples.

From the solid pressure of him against her belly, she could only guess what it must be costing him to stand still and simply hold her.

"You are the sweetest thing that ever happened to me," he told her. "I wasn't looking for you. It never struck me someone like you might exist. But there you were."

The gentle passion in his voice unleashed a fierce tenderness in Polly. "And now here we are. Look at us."

She felt him smile against her lips. "That sounds like a great idea. At least, looking at you.

But you're not ready to make love, are you?"

How could she not be ready?

"You want the sex, but you don't want to feel the connection."

"You make me sound awful."

"I'm trying to understand, Polly. And to let you know I want to understand." He sighed. "God, it's tough. I didn't know how badly I needed to be here like this until now."

Nasty's touch drifted over her shoulders, started down her spine, hesitated when he could spread his thumbs to tickle the sides of her breasts.

She wiggled, and gasped. "We're tormenting each other."

"Can you think of a better way to be tormented?"

"No." She stroked his wide shoulders, pressed even closer. "I don't think you're losing interest."

He laughed shortly. "What do you expect?"

"I'm not a tease."

"Neither am I." He reached her bottom and followed the cleft slowly enough to drive her mad. "I'm just a man."

"Just?" Wrapping her arms around his waist, she echoed him, move for move, and dropped to her knees. "You're anything but *just* a man."

Polly held his penis in both hands.

He gasped and said, "I don't think you'd better do that."

"I'd like to if you'll let me." With a sense of

unreality, she pressed him between her breasts.

"Polly! Please, Polly!"

Slowly, she rubbed the tip over her nipples. His thighs tensed as if he was afraid of falling. "Is it okay, Xavier? Can I do this?"

"Because you feel you owe it to me or something?"

"Because I want to." She could hardly breathe. "I want a lot more."

"But you've got the kind of will most men and women would kill for, and you won't let yourself go."

"Maybe. I'd like to bring you pleasure."

When his fingers pushed into her hair, she filled her mouth with him, held his distended testicles and used her teeth lightly. His groans drove her to an edge she didn't have the strength to resist.

She wanted to feel him inside her.

But if she did, he'd claim part of her, and she wasn't ready to let even the smallest bit go yet.

His hips moved. Polly closed her eyes and tasted the salty beginning of his ejaculation. She'd never wanted to do this before.

"Don't stop," he cried. "Don't — stop!"

She didn't stop. She made her mouth a receptacle for his passion, his drive. His power flowed into her and she took it willingly, and heard his shout of release, and felt the savage spasms rip through him. And she did her best to catch him when he was spent, and slid down until his knees met hers.

Her best was useless. Xavier Ferrito was a very big man. They toppled sideways. He hauled her into his arms and settled her on top of him, his chest rising and falling hugely.

Now there seemed to be no words left.

They rested like that, entwined on the soft gray carpet, damp with perspiration, fighting for breath, their warmth the warmth of one, until he made a deliberate move.

Purposefully, he rolled her to her back and stared down into her eyes. "I'm going to have all of you, you know."

Polly didn't answer. She couldn't look away from him.

"Not tonight. But soon. You're going to be mine."

Still she couldn't say a word.

The little white panties were defenseless against his swift tugs. Nasty lifted her legs as if they weighed nothing, and draped her knees over his shoulders.

Polly kept on watching the changing depths of his eyes.

"The loveliest thing." His gaze went to her breasts and he leaned over to suck each nipple to a tormenting peak.

He slid one thumb into the slippery folds between her thighs, found the straining spot that made her cling to his hair, and quickened the escalating throb of the climax she had to have.

She tossed. Abandoned. This was the woman

she'd always been afraid she could be. The mind-less tossing away of herself when she hadn't yet been a woman didn't count. It had meant nothing — except as a measure of how little self-esteem she had.

"I've waited for you." Nasty's chuckle, deep in his throat, sounded eerie. "How about that. And I didn't even know you existed."

"I'm glad I do," she said, disembodied now, all nerves and senses and sensations now. "And I'm glad you . . . Xavier!"

The convulsion of erotic tissue silenced her. She raised her hips, helpless to stop the gyrations of her body.

He replaced his thumb with his mouth and tongue.

The sound that Polly heard, a sound from her own throat, came from far away. A scream. She blushed inside.

His tongue made a parody of what he longed to do with his penis. Pushing in and out of her, curling around the center of aching pleasure that had become what she was — her entirety.

He flicked his tongue over the place. Flicked hard. Again and again — and she came apart.

"I want you," she said in a tiny voice. "Make love to me, please."

"I am making love to you. I've been making love to you."

"You know what I mean, what I want."

"I know." He held her until the waves of fabu-lous pressure subsided. "It's what I want, too, but not tonight, my love."

"Xavier?"

"Not tonight. Not until you tell me you want to make love *before* I make you forget you don't want to."

Nine

Not until you tell me you want to make love before I make you forget you don't want to.

He'd left a presence behind. Where there had been only the comfortable silence to which Polly was accustomed, an energy remained.

When Nasty returned, he'd bring Bobby in and make sure they were safe. His words, not hers. He wanted to stay here with them.

Impossible.

Polly walked slowly from the foyer back into the great room. How would it be to share all of your life with a man you loved?

Love?

Now she was using that word so many tossed around. Often a meaningless word. Sometimes a destructive word. And, occasionally, the dearest word of all.

The dearest word of all.

She was falling in love with Xavier Nasty Ferrito, ex-Navy SEAL and enigma. Even the idea that she might never have met him made her stomach fall away.

If he would give her time — he said he would — and she would give herself time, this could turn out to be what she'd waited for all her life, without knowing she was waiting at all.

If he would give her time, and if the "could come to love," didn't turn into "it didn't happen."

The intercom buzzed. Polly hurried to snatch up the phone, "Nasty!"

The line was so scratchy she barely heard him say, "Buzz me in. Forgot my car keys."

"Here you go." The crazy leaping of her heart, the instant dampness on her palms as she hung up, were best left unexamined.

She did manage to fight the urge to rush out and meet him. Instead she opened her front door and went to locate the keys. Looking at the couch caused a weak rush. She still felt him, tasted him.

By the time the front door slammed she still hadn't found the keys. "Did you take them out of your pocket? I don't see them."

The foyer light went out.

"Nasty?" She went tentatively toward the front door, skirted the wall that separated the living space from the foyer. "Nasty?" The door must have swung shut before he came in.

Polly went to turn the light back on.

She never made it.

An arm closed around her waist and clamped her to someone who stood behind her, someone tall enough to move the top of her hair with his harsh breathing.

She scuffled to keep her footing and pulled at his hands.

His fingertips drove into the soft tissue beneath her rib cage. Drove deeper, and deeper.

"Please," she said frantically. "Who are you? Let me go."

He dragged her backward into the living room and kept on dragging, switching off lamps as he went.

Polly fought. She jabbed her elbows into him. He grabbed a handful of her hair and twisted, crammed her head forward so hard her chin hit her chest. Bile burned her throat.

A floor lamp between the piano and the window provided the only remaining light. Polly tried desperately to see the man, but she was no match for his strength. Once again he used her hair to force her head down until she felt her neck would snap.

He didn't *say* anything.

She screamed.

The hand that covered her mouth was encased in rubber, thin black rubber gloves. Polly smelled the sickening scent of them and gagged.

Her assailant jerked her upright and pulled until she lost her balance. He held her with grinding force, crushing her ribs and her breasts. His arms were covered with what looked like rubber, too.

A diving suit.

He wore a black diving suit.

Like Nasty, only not like Nasty. A different feel, different scent.

This man wasn't Nasty, he couldn't be. Why would Nasty do something like this to her?

Polly mumbled against the hand. Slowly, the pressure on her face eased. "Who are you? Why are you doing this to me?"

Her feet left the floor. He swung her over his shoulders and slammed her down on the carpet. Her head hit something hard, and she bounced with the force of the impact to her back.

"Scream again and it'll be the last sound you make."

A whisper. It was *him,* the man who'd been watching her, and leaving messages on the answering machine.

Polly blinked against exploding pain in her head. She looked up — into a blinding beam from the creature's head. A lamp on his head — like a miner.

Or like a deep-sea diver.

The remaining lamplight in the room cast a fuzzy outline around a sleek, powerful body. Then the final lamp went out, and she was alone with the darkness and the shifting white beam — and the man's vague shape.

"Why are you doing this to me?"

The beam hit her squarely in the eyes.

"What have I done to you?"

Closer again. He came closer.

Polly scooted away, into a table beside the couch. A lamp overbalanced. The weight of its angled armature brought it down on top of Polly. She heard her crystal dragon shatter against the wall at the same time as a hard metal edge gouged her scalp.

Another scream rose, but she clamped a hand over her mouth and managed to choke it down.

"Do you want money?" she asked.

He kicked her stomach.

Winded, blind with fear, she huddled on her side.

Unwavering, the beam remained on her face.

"Tell me what you want."

Not a sound.

When he moved again, it was so swiftly Polly had no chance to anticipate what he would do. Not that she could have resisted. He pushed her onto her face and settled a foot in the middle of her back.

She cried, she couldn't stop herself from crying. Her lungs squeezed against her ribs. Her breasts ground into the carpet.

His only sound came with the faint grunts that accompanied each fresh insult upon his victim. Methodical. Economical. Practiced. An expert at meting out pain. Cruel.

Swiftly, he pulled her arms behind her back and jammed them upward until she had to muffle her screams in the rug. She rocked her head from side to side and tears poured from her eyes.

He was breaking her bones.

As abruptly as he'd grabbed her arms, he released them. They remained where they were, heavy, aching, numb.

Using a handful of her dress, he hauled her to her feet. Buttons tore loose and she felt air on her chest.

All the darkness shifted. Light and darkness whirled.

Polly's arms hung useless at her sides. He shoved her forward through his precious beam, toward her bedroom. When she would have faltered, knuckles between her shoulder blades jabbed her on. When her legs threatened to give out, a punishing pinch to her buttock sent her stumbling onward again.

The next pinch was harder.

She sobbed silently, choked silently on her own mucus and saliva.

He would rape her. And murder her.

If she was going to be violated, and to die, she had nothing to lose. Polly flung around, flinched at the sound of her dress ripping. "Okay," she yelled. "Do it, bastard. Just do it! You've had your fun. I'm scared out of my mind. Satisfied?"

A series of short punches to her throat propelled her through the bedroom door.

She retched.

His next punch was to her sternum.

An expert. A man who knew how to inflict pain.

Fighting for each rasping breath, she staggered into a bedpost. She opened her mouth but couldn't form any words.

The bedroom door crashed shut. The beam swept one way, then the other. He was searching the room.

Searching for what?

"Why? —"

"To make sure you don't forget," the awful whisper told her.

She hadn't expected a reply. "Don't forget what?"

"What you've been told."

Nasty would be back soon.

How long ago had he left? It felt like hours. Polly knew it could only be minutes. Whoever was with her must have waited for Nasty to leave.

He'd bring Bobby back.

She cast about wildly. Not Bobby. Bobby mustn't see this — see her like this.

Bobby didn't have a key. They'd have to call up.

"A friend of mine's coming," she said. "He'll be here any minute."

The beam drew closer.

"If he finds you here, he'll kill you," she said.

And closer.

Her throat hurt. Her body hurt. Her arms ached. Where the lamp had hit her head, the tightly stretched flesh stung.

He stood so near she felt his heat, she felt the heat of the beam on her face and closed her eyes, waited.

"You haven't done what you were told, have you?"

Polly tried to cover her face.

He smacked her hands away, and whispered, "Have you?"

"I don't know what you mean." The remnants of her dress hung from her elbows. "I don't know. I don't know you."

"I told you what you had to do. You had to be

good. But you've been with that man."

Denying that Nasty had been here would be useless. "You mean Nasty?" She managed to giggle. "He's just a friend."

"Did he fuck you?"

The crude, rasping question made Polly flinch. "How shall I punish you?"

Finish it. Now.

"Shall I make you ugly? If you're ugly, he won't want you anymore."

Despite trembling legs, she stood straight and gathered her dress about her as best she could.

Something glittered. A silver sheen spun along what he held. Polly knew it must be a knife.

Nasty would blame himself.

The certainty came so sharply she blinked back tears. He would tell himself he shouldn't have left her alone, yet she wasn't his responsibility.

This . . . *thing* wore a wet suit. Like Nasty. Because he intended to put the blame on Nasty? Or because a dive into the lake would clean away all evidence of whatever he intended to do to her.

"If you don't stay away from him, he'll die."

Polly shuddered. What did it mean?

"Listen." The blade flashed.

Throwing up her arms, Polly couldn't smother this scream. The sound erupted in her head, in her ears.

"No one will hear you."

She kept her arms over her head.

"Where shall I cut you?"

Polly sank to her knees.

"Because of him, you will die. But he will also die — because of you. You are death to each other."

The cold touch on her back could only be the knife blade, the flat of the blade, sliding downward, under the fastening on her bra.

"And the child will die, too. Because of you and the dive boy."

Bobby. "I won't see Nasty again."

"No." Still whispering, the voice became serene. "No, of course you won't."

A single slice loosed her bra. A snick, another snick, and the straps fell apart. Holding her forehead to the floor, the attacker went to work, sliding his blade through fabric with calculated strokes until Polly huddled, naked, among the ribbons of her clothes.

Steel, so smooth and cool, rested on her back.

"I can come to you when I please. Whenever I please."

Let it be over.

"But I could kill you now. Easier. Yes, easier to kill you now. Your friend will be back soon, you say? Good. I'll wait for him. Someone must let him in if you can't."

She didn't want to die. But if she did, Bobby would be looked after. As long as Bobby was kept safe from this monster.

"Kill me and go. No one will ever find you. Nasty's clever. If you wait for him, you probably won't get away. He will punish you. He isn't afraid of anyone."

"There is no man with blood who doesn't bleed."

She must persuade him to go before Nasty brought Bobby back. "Nasty will know something's wrong even before he comes up here. Kill me and —"

"Shut the fuck up!" The whisper broke, rose to a grating shriek. "Shut, up," the voice ended in a whisper once more. "I've decided what will happen."

"Please —"

"Shut up, or I'll cut your eyes out."

Polly swallowed vomit.

"Shut your goddamn, sniffling mouth!" The toe of a hard shoe connected with her side. He kicked her twice.

She braced for the knife.

Then the tears came, the sobs she couldn't stop anymore.

Polly stayed where she was, folded into as small a ball as she could make. She covered her ears to close out all sound, shut her eyes tightly to obliterate the reality of this terror.

She heard her own drumming heartbeat, saw flecks of red behind her eyelids. Her blood roared in her head and ears, roared to fill every space.

The phone rang.

"No," she murmured. They must not come up here. "No, no, no. Go away."

It rang again.

"Don't." Shudders racked her in waves. Her arms still throbbed, and her side where the intruder had kicked her. Every inch felt bruised.

Again the phone rang.

Polly rocked, and moaned. The darkness hammered her — darkness and fear, and the certainty that he waited, knife poised, to hack her to death, to kill Bobby, and, if Nasty wasn't ready for the attack — to kill Nasty, too.

Ringing. Ringing.

It stopped.

A voice. Rather than risk talking himself, he'd let the answer machine pick up. She hummed loudly to close out the sound of her own voice reciting the message. The man would open the door now and wait for Nasty and Bobby to come up.

Polly listened to silence, felt the pressure of another presence, heard the build of soundlessness in a void.

Seconds passed.

He was waiting, too.

She knew then what he planned, to use them — each of them against the other. Keep one at bay with the threat of stabbing another, then stabbing anyway, until only one remained.

The one remaining would be Polly. He would kill Nasty first because he'd have to, or face a fight to the death when she and Bobby were dead.

She beat the carpet with her fists.

Why?

A cool current slipped across the floor, curled over Polly's wet face.

He had opened the front door, just as she had

opened it thinking it was Nasty who had returned.

But he couldn't have opened the front door because he was here with her. She held her breath and listened — opened her eyes.

A hint of light tinged the darkness. Not the white light from his beam. This was as if it glowed from somewhere else in the condominium.

Cautiously, she raised her head. The bedroom door stood partially open. The light she saw shone through the living room from the foyer. From where she lay the front door was out of sight.

She could see the foyer mirror. Polly sat up. A shadow — a suggestion of a shadow — touched the edge of the glass. She rubbed her stinging eyes. Not even a suggestion of a shadow now.

"Get away!" There was nothing she could do but try to save Bobby and Nasty. "Run. There's a man here. He's got a knife."

She panted, expected the creature to descend upon her.

No one answered.

"Nasty! Get Bobby away from here. Please!"

A tall shape launched itself across the threshold, smashed the door all the way open against the wall.

The lamps beside her bed flooded on and she peered through her matted hair at Nasty. He braced a gun in his right hand and made sleek, sharp sights around the room. Nasty, but not the Nasty she knew. Remote didn't describe his face now. Not even cold. No feature moved except his eyes, eyes turned to amber ice.

"He's got a knife," Polly whispered. "He wants to kill us all."

"Stay down."

With only a flicker of a glance in her direction, he moved smoothly through the room, repeating his slammed entry into her bathroom before turning his attention to the closet.

"Where's Bobby?"

Nasty didn't answer. Like a powerful wraith he skimmed the room and left. Polly sat with her knees drawn up, the ragged shreds of her clothes tumbled about her.

She heard doors bang in other rooms, then, so clearly she flinched, Nasty's loud, "Shit!"

Polly almost made it to her feet before he erupted back into the room and swept her into his arms. Swaths of red slashed his high cheekbones. He set her on the bed and stripped away the tatters of cloth. His hands were gentle but firm as he examined her.

"Please," she begged, feebly batting at him. "Don't."

"Did he cut you?"

"I don't know. Bobby —"

"Bobby's with Dusty. I shouldn't have left you."

"You were going to get him." Her jaw clenched.

He looked into her face. "I turned back. This is what I do — what I trained to do. Instincts. Do you understand?"

She shook her head. She didn't understand anything but that she felt his anger.

"I felt" — he smoothed her hair away from her face and some of the icy control slipped — "I felt you needed me. My mistake was trying to fight what I felt — and not making you do what I wanted to do in the first place."

"He pretended to be you."

Nasty pulled the quilt around her. "He beat you."

Polly leaned against him.

"Your head. It's still bleeding."

"A lamp fell on me." She giggled. "He made me smash my dragon."

"It's okay, sweetheart. It's okay."

Polly giggled afresh, and hiccuped. "And . . . and he cut up my clothes. And he said he would kill Bobby, and —" Her laughter sealed her throat. She bumped her face against his chest and moaned.

"And? What else did he say? Did you see his face?"

"No."

"Did you recognize his voice?"

Yes.

"Polly, did you know him?"

"I think he's the man on the answering machine."

"Why did he leave?"

"The phone. When you called up to be let in."

"I didn't call."

She looked into his face.

"The downstairs door was blocked open. I just came in."

"But the phone rang." Bursts of trembling shook her. "It doesn't matter. It stopped him."

"Thank God," Nasty said. "He won't get another chance at you."

She would not sacrifice him to save herself.

He slid a knee onto the bed and sat where he could look at her. "Darling," he said tentatively. "Hell, I've never been this scared, or this angry." Gently, he tipped her against him and smoothed her hair over and over again. "You're going to be okay. I've got you now."

And she almost believed him. Polly turned her face into his chest.

"We're going to have to call the police."

She nodded.

"They'll ask a lot of questions. And they'll want you to be examined."

Polly shook her head.

"I'll take you. And I'll stay with you, if you want me to."

"He didn't rape me."

She felt him let out a big breath. "For that, I'll always be grateful," he told her. "I couldn't stand to think of you going through — that. And I don't know how easily I'd live with so much hate."

"I think I'm going to cry." Her throat clogged. "I want my robe."

Nasty stopped her from getting off the bed and brought her blue terry-cloth robe from the bathroom. With sensitive efficiency he removed the quilt and helped her to get comfortable.

She wrapped the robe more tightly around her.

He paced, stopping from time to time to study her.

"I'm okay," she said, still shaking. "I can tell the police everything. You don't have to stay."

"I'm staying."

"I've got to get Bobby. He'll be worried."

"No kid was ever worried with Dusty. He's every kid's dream grandpa."

"You've already done too much for me."

"I haven't even begun to do things for you. You're going to be my life's work, Polly Crow."

And if she gave in to what she wanted and accepted that wonderful offer, she'd kill them both. "Don't be silly. You've got a business to run. This is something the police will have to deal with."

"They'll go through the motions. But you'd better get used to knowing I'm never too far away to hear you breathe."

"Xavier —"

"That means I'm going to be very close. All the time."

And if she didn't refuse, that could mean she'd be very dead anyway. "He said I had to do what he wants me to do."

Nasty came to stand over her. His lips curled away from his teeth. "You only have to do what you want to do. What did the sonovabitch say to you?"

"He . . ." She wanted to trust love, and to trust it with this man. To send him away would be to send a part of herself away. "He wants me. That's all. He just wants me for himself. He's mad."

"Shush," Nasty said, gently touching her cheek. "It's okay. I'm here with you now, and I'm not leaving."

Polly smiled at him. Her stomach knotted so tightly she felt sick again. "Nasty, will you let me tell you the way it is? Without interrupting."

The downturn of his mouth was mutinous but he gave one short nod.

"I'm afraid to let you stay."

"I'm not leaving."

"You said you wouldn't interrupt. I'm just as afraid to let you go." She had his entire attention. "And I want you as part of my life. I'm so muddled up I don't know what decision's the right one. There isn't a right decision. Whatever I decide is going to kill one or both of us."

"Could you make that a bit clearer for me?"

"When you said the man who's been making the calls isn't just a crank, you were right. We know that because he was here tonight, and I think he came close to stabbing me to death. He made it clear that if I don't stay away from you, he's going to kill me. And you. And Bobby."

"Sonovabitch," Nasty said distinctly.

"But he wants me. He's going to find a way to get me, I know he is." Panic surfaced again. "If he does, I might as well be dead anyway."

Nasty visibly gathered himself. "He isn't getting you. First, I'm calling the police. I should already have called them."

"Don't leave me!"

Something close to rage convulsed his face before he controlled his emotions. "You're not in danger now, Polly." But he took her hand and led her into the living room. "Sit here while I make the call. Then you can give me instructions on how to make you some of that tea you love. It's supposed to be good for calming people down, isn't it?"

Her smile felt good. "Uh-huh. They say it got the British through the Second World War."

Nasty wrapped her in his arms, and she felt him tremble. "Tea it'll be, although our friend is going to need more than tea for the war I'm going to put him through. There's a message on your machine."

Polly glanced around and saw the flashing red light.

Nasty pressed the "play" button.

"Oh, dear," the whisperer said. "And I hoped you might have understood that I will not tolerate this behavior. But you've defied me, again. Well, I'm a forgiving lover, my love, but don't push me too hard. Stay away from him. This is number two. And the rest is up to you."

"It wasn't him." Polly sat down on a chair with a thud. She pointed at the machine. "He left a message while . . . That man was here when the call came."

"Stay calm," Nasty said. "I'm going to call the police now."

"How many people are threatening to kill me?"

Ten

Mary Reese was a Class A bitch. Nasty listened to her as he browsed the shelves at Totem Book Shop. "Remember we're doing you a favor," she told the owner. "You need us. We don't need you."

The woman Polly had introduced at TGIFriday's — Caroline — with one lighting assistant, operated the sole camera for what was to be a short segment aimed at reinforcing the wonders of bookstores.

"We're on a tight schedule here," Mary Reese snapped. "Let's move it. Polly, ask your friend to wait outside. He's in the way."

"Chill, babe," Jack Spinnel said. He aimed a conspiratorial grin at Nasty. "Plenty of room."

Nasty didn't trust Jack's newfound charm.

"The hell there is plenty of room," Mary said. "How come we've got to drag some of these assholes onto the set when they're supposed to be there, but they're all hanging around here when we don't need them?"

"Language, my pet," Jack said mildly, indicating several local children who'd been brought in to take part in the scene.

As far as Nasty could tell, the only redundant cast member was Gavin Tucker, who showed absolutely no reaction to Mary's barb. He hung around Polly — hung too close for Nasty's comfort — and found reasons to touch her.

The two acrobats held an impossible position beside small chairs provided for the children. Each standing on one hand, they propped their knees and feet against each other with nonchalant ease, while turning the pages of books.

Seated in a chair, Polly prepared to read a story on camera. Dressed in bright pink, she smiled as if she'd had a great night's sleep, rather than suffered a vicious attack and spent hours with the police before returning to the condo to clean up.

Nasty stared at her until she looked back. Her smile faltered, replaced by an unmistakably intimate glance that filled him with triumph.

Gavin Tucker moved between them and bent over Polly, spoke to her in tones too low to hear.

"Get your goddamn —"

"Mary!" Jack said, aiming a ruefully apologetic grin at the shop's pretty blond owner. "We're all a bit uptight this morning, Dorothy," he told her. "You'll have to forgive us. You can cuddle Polly later, Gavin."

"She shouldn't be here at all," Gavin said, turning on Jack. Gone was the languid pose. "After everything she's been —"

"That's enough," Jack said, visibly gritting his teeth. "We're all together in this. A solid front. The less said, the better." He inclined his head significantly toward the owner.

Gavin appeared ready to argue. Instead he blew at the limp brown hair that flopped over his forehead and ambled out of camera range, muttering as he came to stand beside Nasty. "You were there, then," he said, his voice dramatically lowered. "You got there afterward?"

The fact that Polly had chosen to share last night's events with the cast of the show didn't thrill Nasty. "Yeah."

"Keep your voice down." Gavin propped a shoulder against a shelf and studied the book Nasty held. "You into South America?"

"I used to be."

"You been there?"

"Uh-huh." End of topic. "Polly says you're great to work with." When he wasn't a pain.

The painter didn't hide his pleasure. "Polly brings out the best in everyone. She's a natural. But I guess you know that."

"Sure," Nasty agreed, not at all sure he knew Gavin's angle.

"So what really happened last night?"

Nasty looked past the other man and through the store windows. Sunshine bounced off the tops of cars filing into the back lot of a nearby strip mall. "Whatever Polly told you happened, happened," he said.

"The guy" — Gavin came closer than Nasty liked to be to any man — "you didn't get a look at him?"

Shouting interrupted them. Mary Reese banged a clipboard against her forehead. "Wake

203

up, Jennifer, darling. You're supposed to be bloody moping now, not prancing. You're expecting to be made fun of because you don't read as well as the others."

"Bloody moping," came a husky female voice from inside one of the monster heads. "Anything you say, Mary, babe." The acrobat seemed suddenly to melt. She descended to the floor and lolled. "Better?"

"Silence," Mary fumed. "And watch the babe, bit, *babe*."

"Things are going from bad to worse around here," Gavin murmured. "I don't mind for myself. I'm used to it. But Polly's a shooting star, a fragile shooting star, and she hasn't been around the block like I have. This pressure could break her spirit." Serious brown eyes regarded Nasty.

He felt tense. Not frustrated from dealing with a man he disliked, but on edge without being sure why. The air seemed thinner, hotter — tropical.

Tropical?

"You know what I mean?" Gavin asked.

"What did you say?"

"Polly. She's under too much pressure, and not everyone's as keen for her to succeed as I am — if you know what I mean."

Did he know? "Why don't you explain?"

"There are some who think they'd do a better job hosting the show than she does."

Nasty frowned. "Like who? There's only one

other woman in the cast."

"You've got it."

The female acrobat remained slumped on the floor. "Jennifer Loder, right? Polly says she's a good friend."

"Polly's too damn trusting."

He couldn't argue with that.

"Mary's picking on me, Art," Jennifer complained theatrically. "I reckon she doesn't love us anymore."

The other acrobat batted her playfully. "Who couldn't love us, sis. We're irresistible."

"Hear that, Mary?" Jennifer said. "You gotta love us."

"Was it your idea for Polly to tell the world what's been happening?" Gavin asked.

Nasty's back turned clammy. He undid another button on his shirt. Damn, but he didn't have time to be sick.

Gavin nudged him. "I'd have thought it could be dangerous to spread it around. Might make this crazy do something stupid — even more stupid."

Good old Gavin had a brain or two. "It wasn't my idea. And I thought she'd just told the show insiders, not the world."

"In theory. If I were her, I wouldn't trust everyone who qualifies to keep their mouths shut."

"She decided she needs your support. And she doesn't want to keep explaining me away."

"Planning to stick around a lot?"

Nasty didn't meet the other man's eyes. "I'll

do what I think's necessary." He got a fleeting impression of trying to see through darkness, of someone calling him.

"How did you go from voyeur to sidekick?"

Nasty did look at him then. "Voyeur?"

Gavin chuckled. "Figure of speech. I'm not the only one who knows you've spent time watching Polly from your little rubber boat. Maybe you should be making sure no one questions your motives."

"I'm Polly's friend."

"New friend."

"Good friend."

Something different entered Gavin's eyes, and it wasn't friendly approval. "Okay. Good friend. So how badly was she worked over last night, *good* friend?"

"Whatever Polly's told you is what she wants you to know."

"He roughed her up?"

"You could say that."

"Would *you* say that? Or would you say he did more than that?"

Nasty wanted to believe the man was concerned for Polly. Instinct picked up something other than concern, something closer to prurient interest. "There was no sexual attack." Not the complete truth, but what Polly would prefer to be generally accepted.

"Is that the official story?"

"It's the story." He'd chosen the direct approach for this first morning — an open presence.

From here on it might be better if he was less evident. "You're not in this segment?"

"No. I'm here for Polly, like you."

The inference wasn't subtle. Gavin Tucker would prefer to be the one watching over Polly. "I'm sure she's grateful for your support."

Laughter riffled among the children seated at Polly's feet. She appeared to be performing an imitation of a bored turtle — in pink.

"Isn't she something?" Nasty said.

Gavin's response accompanied a lascivious grimace. "You might be able to say that. I certainly can't — yet."

"What does that mean?"

Laughter came too easily to the Gavin Tuckers of the world.

"Hell," he said, elbowing Nasty lightly. "You know what it means. I'd be lying if I said I didn't want a piece of her."

In this instance Gavin might do himself a favor by lying. "Polly isn't a woman who gives out *pieces*," Nasty commented.

"Except to you? She's already put out for you, hasn't she?"

"Do you like the way your face is arranged."

"I'm not afraid of you, fucker."

"You should be. Touch Polly, and you'll find out why."

The children laughed again, and Polly began singing. Down and Out joined in, harmonizing while they set up an exaggerated swaying behind her.

"It's time," Jennifer Loder said, wiggling her fingers at the small audience. "Time to do our thing, kiddies."

Polly gathered the kids around her and encouraged them to clap.

Sweat breaking out on his brow shook Nasty. He took a stick of gum from his jeans, unwrapped, and slid it between his teeth.

Animosity — no, too weak — hatred emanated from Gavin.

Too bad. Gavin wouldn't be a problem. Nasty understood weak, twisted people. Their very desires were what stopped them every time.

The ankle wound hurt as it hadn't hurt for months. Nasty shifted his weight. What the hell was going on with him?

"I'm going to make sure you aren't welcome on the set again," Gavin said very softly.

Nasty didn't say anything. The pain intensified. So did the flow of sweat. He blinked as it stung his eyes.

There was something here — something he ought to be able to place.

"Time," Jack Spinnel called. "Time, people. Good job."

Nausea joined Nasty's other discomforts. He slid the book back on a shelf.

Darkness. Heat.

He'd lost his gun, but not the knife.

He was remembering when it happened! The night in Colombia when someone tried to kill him. He'd eventually played dead so well that they'd left him to drag his smashed ankle back to the waiting chopper.

"You do know I mean what I say?" Gavin Tucker asked.

"What?" Nasty looked at him blankly

"Polly won't do anything to jeopardize her part. It means too much to her. You're a liability. You'll have to go."

"You stupid sonovabitch," he said, swallowing. "Get away from me while you still can."

He'd been taken by surprise. Everything should have been right on target — smooth. Then the figure had appeared through the undergrowth, beckoning. And he'd had to take the chance. Wrong chance. It had cost him his ankle — and his career.

It had cost the other bastard a back and shoulder wound that probably meant he was no longer singing in the church choir. Nasty would have given big odds that the guy bled to death.

Polly rose from her chair. She bent to hug one child after another. The owner of the bookstore chatted with Jack and Mary.

"Play time." Jennifer whooped and tore off her costume head. A few seconds later the children were taking turns being Main Monsters.

"Polly isn't your type," Gavin murmured. "Or you're not her type."

What was it he couldn't recall? Most of that night had become a blur.

"She's an artist — a performer," Gavin said. "You may be able to get inside her pants, but you'll never get inside her head."

Nasty straightened and faced the man. Shielding what he did, he found Gavin's "artistic" right hand and put a light lock on the wrist. "Outside," he said shortly. "Now."

"My hand!" Gavin hissed. "You're hurting my hand."

Tightening the lock was second nature. "Outside."

His face deathly pale, Gavin backed up. The moment Nasty released him, he shoved his hair out of his eyes and rushed from the shop.

Nasty was close behind.

"You're dangerous." Gavin fumbled for his car keys. "Damn dangerous. And I'm going to fix it so Polly knows I think so."

"Are you sure you want to do that?" Nasty moved menacingly close. "Do you think I'll bow out if you do?"

"Men like you are used to this, aren't you? Using your brawn to smash your way in where you don't belong. Women fall for it. Men don't. It's time someone stopped you."

Nasty looked over his shoulder into the bookstore, then at Gavin again. Pieces of a night he'd tried to forget were pouring back. The doctors had talked about the brain's ability to block out trauma; they'd said he'd probably never remember more about what had happened.

Gavin gave him a final, malevolent stare, and climbed into a vintage red Morgan.

Polly appeared beside Nasty and asked, "Is everything okay?"

"I hope so."

"Did you and Gavin have a spat?" The energy she'd found to do the show had fled. Signs of exhaustion showed on her face. "You two looked like circling animals in there."

"Thanks."

She looked hurt, and he hated himself for that. "Let's get you home," he said. "You're dead on your feet. So am I."

Dead on his feet, and more convinced he should listen to his legendary instincts than he had ever been.

"Nasty."

"Uh-huh."

"I'm scared."

Absently, he put an arm around her shoulders. "Where did that come from? I thought you said you were cool with everything."

"I lied. I've got this . . . this *feeling*. It's not going to stop. Whoever he is — they are — they're going to keep coming after me."

"You aren't alone." He began to sweat again. "I'm with you now."

"They'll wait. It won't matter how long they have to wait. When they decide it's the right time, they'll find a way to get at me. There's something out there." She stood with her shoulder against his side. "I won't have to ask you to go. You'll want to. Either I'm completely nuts, or I'm on a collision course with real evil."

He took a moment too long to gather her in his arms, but he prayed she hadn't noticed. "You don't get over what happened last night that easily. Let me worry, okay. I'll make sure nothing touches you."

She felt it, too. Not just coming their way, but right where they were. What they called, *the presence of evil.*

"You will do exactly as Festus and I tell you, Polly." Belinda's hair fascinated Nasty. Today she wore it gelled into kinky curls that made a black halo at least a foot in radius around her highly colored face. "And you, too, Nasty. A most commanding name, that. *Nasty.* One could not ignore a man with such a name. You and Polly are in my care. It has been ordained. Venus phoned me, thank goodness. She must be calmer. I could scarcely understand a word she said. But I phoned that nice Dusty Miller. He will pick her up and bring her here to the shop."

Nasty had wanted to collect Bobby from Dusty and take him and Polly away. Only Nasty knew there could be no *away.* The line had been drawn here, and here it would all end.

"I only came because you sounded so upset when you called," Polly told Belinda. "We shouldn't stay."

"But you have to," Belinda insisted. Adorned with black, sparkle-dusted gauze, she billowed before them through the shop and up a flight of spiral stairs. "You both look desperately *depleted.*

Festus! Come here, Festus. Come out of your wretched dome. Help me with Polly and Nasty. We'll sit in the roof garden. I've locked the shop. Venus knows to ring the residence bell."

Overcome by a sense of the unreal, Nasty held Polly's hand. She clutched his fingers. There were questions he ought to ask her, but he didn't want to hear the answers — not if they were what he expected them to be.

They followed Belinda through several dark, sparsely furnished rooms, and out onto the roof.

Cacti crowded a small garden on top of the building that housed Another Reality. Hundreds of cacti. More varieties than Nasty had ever considered might exist. Many bloomed, their unreal colors made more vivid by the layer of fine, white sand spread over the area.

Polly smiled faintly and averted her face.

He squeezed her fingers.

"You will sit here, Polly," Belinda said, firmly separating their hands. "And you over there, Nasty. You must both lie down and experience the healing powers of my garden."

Protesting that he didn't want to be separated from Polly by several yards of sand might make him sound unbalanced. He didn't want to be separated from her — ever.

Polly accepted her friend's autocratic directions and allowed herself to be guided to a rattan chaise. Nasty subsided into one just like it, right down to its purple-and-gold-striped pillows.

Belinda folded her hands beneath her bosom

and breathed deeply. She closed her eyes, and said, "Cleanse yourselves. We must gather the power needed to combat what we do not understand."

"Mom shouldn't have called you," Polly said, sounding miserable.

"Hmmm." Belinda rocked. "This creature who calls and tries to bend you to his will is to be understood, not feared."

Nasty sat forward on his chaise and studied the woman.

"He has succumbed to his deepest passions, and those passions have made him desperate."

"Belinda —"

"No." The woman interrupted Polly and went to ease her down onto the chaise. She stroked back her hair and kissed her brow. "You will not upset yourself further. Festus and I are experts in these matters of focused fascinations. We shall concentrate our power and decide how to assuage the hunger without depleting your strength."

Purple lingo had never been Nasty's forte — spoken or interpreted. But if he got the gist of this garbled message, the lady wasn't talking about knife-wielding wackos in wet suits. She still thought the problem of the day remained with passive telephone threats.

"Did Polly's mother explain exactly what happened last night?" The habit of gathering absolute information didn't die easily.

Festus emerged, a thin, gray-haired figure — also in black.

"Please calm Nasty for me," Belinda told him. "He is agitated. Venus spoke of a great deal of trouble last night. I wonder if Polly — and I understand perfectly, my dear — but I wonder if she is losing objectivity. Could that be so?"

"No." Nasty frowned Polly to silence. "No, Polly's perfectly objective. But things are under control." He didn't want her panicked more than she was already panicked.

"Of course they are." Belinda perched beside Polly on the chaise. "Forgive me if I sound like a mother hen, but Polly has become as close as a daughter to me. She is the gentlest of spirits."

As if he needed to be told. "The gentlest," he agreed, looking at his gentle spirit's troubled eyes.

"This man who makes these objectionable calls is harmless," Belinda said. "He may even be a true admirer. These things happen. He could be concerned for your goodness, Polly. He could believe that he has a mission to assist you to remain pure."

The turn of the conversation put Nasty on edge. "When Dusty gets here with Venus and Bobby we'd better get you to bed," he told Polly. "You're exhausted."

Festus hovered near the open door into the apartment over the shop. Nasty glanced from the man to a large, glass dome situated on what appeared to be a single, third-story room. "Your stargazing quarters," he said, indicating the dome. "Nice setup." Surely the city lights must prove a hindrance.

"Nice enough," Festus said. "Speak to that husband of yours, did you, Polly?"

She hesitated, then appeared to make a decision. "Sam Dodge isn't my husband, Festus. He never was."

"Hush," Belinda said loudly. "And you, hush, Festus. Some things do not need to be spoken of."

"Bobby's father and I were not married," Polly persisted as if driven to confession. "Sam was never interested in having children. When I became pregnant with Bobby, Sam told me to choose between him and the baby. I chose my baby — naturally." Then she looked at Nasty, looked at him hard.

"Naturally," he said softly. In other words, she was reminding him that Bobby was first with her.

Belinda wound and unwound her fingers. She ran them over her skirts as if drying her skin. The color in her cheeks grew even brighter. "You will not do as you're told, Festus," she said. "I warned you not to pry, but you didn't listen. You have forced Polly to speak of things that need never be said. You have humiliated her in front of her new friend. You —"

"I already knew Sam Dodge wasn't Polly's husband," Nasty said, trying for a bland tone. "She doesn't have anything to be embarrassed about. Will we hear that bell from here?"

"I'll go down and wait," Festus said, and fled back through the door with obvious relief at escaping Belinda's wrath.

"For Bobby's sake" — Belinda turned up her palms — "if not for your own, it would be best not to speak of his, er, condition."

"You make illegitimacy sound like a disease," Nasty said, not regretting his words. "If it is, it's not fatal. Not immediately, anyway. My father was an occasional visitor. His last name wasn't Ferrito."

"Oh, my dear," Belinda said in hushed tones. "How generous of you to try to soften this for Polly."

Nasty decided Belinda was never going to be one of his favorite people. "I think Polly is the most wonderful woman I've ever met. She doesn't need me to help her feel good about herself."

The woman regarded him from beneath lowered lashes. "You're right, of course. My reactions are because I am so concerned for her in these troubled times. Will you help me persuade her to look for the good in what this man says to her on the phone. I truly believe — given what Venus has told me about the messages — that he means Polly no harm."

"For God's sake!" He rubbed his jaw. "Sorry. I'm tired, too, I guess. But you don't know Polly was attacked last night, do you? Physically attacked?"

Belinda's bewildered expression took in first Nasty, then Polly. "Attacked? Who attacked you? A *man?*"

"Yeah, a man," Nasty told her. "Who the hell

do you think it would be?"

"What man?" She never looked away from Polly. "Tell me at once. Who is this man? How do you know him?"

"I don't know him."

"He got into her condominium. He hit her. Show Belinda the cut on your scalp."

Polly shook her head. "I don't want to. I don't want to think about it anymore. He grabbed me from behind and turned out all the lights so I couldn't see him."

"And?" The whites of Belinda's violet eyes grew prominent. "What did he do to you? Oh, please, what did he do?"

"Stop it." Nasty stood up. "This isn't helpful. Come on, Polly. We'll wait for Dusty and Venus outside."

Belinda rose as if to ward him off. "How dare you presume to interfere in matters you cannot possibly understand as I do! This is a matter of the heart, to me — of the spirit. Polly and I have a connection that is quite different from any you may pretend. I have encountered her on an astral plane of which she is yet to be aware. It is entrusted to me to guide her to safety."

"Too bad you missed out last night," Nasty said, his patience shot. Somehow he'd get Polly out of here without insulting the deluded lady further. "Sorry if I'm a bit short. It was a long night, and it's been a long day. And it isn't over yet. So, if you'll excuse us."

She breathed deeply, and drew herself up very

tall. Her expression became serene. "Polly," she said calmly. "Of course. I was troubled, but . . . Oh, yes, I was trying — the weak, earthbound part of me was trying to deny the warnings of my spirit. I deceived myself with the pretense that when I felt you were in trouble, it was merely our well-meaning whisperer. Oh, I shall have difficulty forgiving myself. I had only to listen and be sensible enough to know that the pain I felt was from your body as well as your mind."

The pain Nasty had begun to feel was somewhere else. "Yeah, well, thank you very much for the fresh air and insights."

"We'll have some tea. I know what it should be."

Polly's white face sickened Nasty. "We'll go home," he told her. "I'll take you home."

"Stop," Belinda pointed at him. Her long forefinger ended in a broad, blunt fingernail. She turned the finger on Polly. "There was sex, wasn't there? You were . . . You were forced to have sex."

"No," Polly said faintly. She went to Nasty's side. He saw the rapid rise and fall of her breasts.

"You must not lie to me. I cannot help you heal if you hide your shame."

"Stow it," Nasty said through gritted teeth. Damn, she'd driven him to lose his temper. "Give it up, lady. Practice the mumbo jumbo somewhere else."

"Mumbo jumbo!" He was treated to another sighting down her finger. "I see what you cannot possibly know I see. I see *you*. She was attacked by a man she could not see. Forced to have sex with a man she could not see."

"I was not forced to have sex." Polly pushed past Belinda and made for the door. "I couldn't see who attacked me, but he didn't force me to have sex."

"You wanted to have sex?" A whirl of black gauze swished between Nasty and Polly. "Oh, my poor girl. How could I have failed to understand at once. Of course. You did what your flesh drove you to do, but then you were ashamed. And this story is your sad way of trying to deny your own lust. We are your friends. We accept you as you are. Admit the truth of what you have done."

Nasty dodged Belinda, grabbed Polly, and rushed her inside. "Don't listen, sweetheart. She's lost it."

"You'll forgive me," Belinda said, only steps behind them. "And Nasty will forgive you. I knew about Bobby. Of course I did. And I knew your appetites still demanded satisfaction. You did not need to cover your excesses by inventing a story of rape."

Eleven

"She thinks I made the whole story up," Polly said. "Not the whole story, just the part about being attacked against my will." She and Nasty had gathered with Dusty and Venus in Dusty's living room. Bobby, who now had his dog, Spike, with him again, had been settled in front of the television in Dusty's bedroom.

Splendid in yellow tights and an oversize lime green sweatshirt — with matching headband — Venus hovered beside Dusty.

Nasty stood by the windows overlooking the terrace, and the lawns descending to the lake.

"What if they all think what Belinda thinks? The cast as well?" Polly moved behind Nasty. "You were talking to Gavin. What did he say?"

"The man's an ass."

She rested her forehead on his back. "He thinks I encouraged some stranger to beat me up? What kind of logic is that?"

"That's it!" Venus raised her hands. "I shall deal with these people myself."

"No, you won't," Dusty said. "Sit down. I'll pour us a drink."

"Thank you," Venus said. "But I won't be dissuaded. I'm a mother — and I'm a mother at one with the earth, and who understands the rightful order of things. It isn't right for a good, kind, gentle woman like my daughter to be accused of such outrageous deceit."

"You're right," Dusty said. He poured several glasses of Wild Turkey and took one to Venus. He shooed her into an overstuffed chair upholstered in daffodil-strewn yellow chintz. "You're absolutely right, but there are times when we've got to let the fools hang themselves, right, Nasty?"

"Right."

Polly got the impression Nasty wasn't hearing much of what was being said.

"We know we've got a problem on our hands, right, Nasty?"

"Yeah, Dust."

"But our bases are pretty much covered now. Bobby's a great kid, and he'll be with me. If he's not with someone else we can trust to do anything that's got to be done to look after him."

"You're a wonderful man," Venus said, her face filled with admiration. "We must always celebrate the day you came into our lives."

"I'm the one who's got to celebrate," Dusty said in his rusted voice. Every time he looked at Venus his eyes lost focus, and his mouth fell slightly open.

If she weren't so frightened, Polly might start to worry about her mother's apparent infatuation with her new friend. And Dusty's clear reciprocation of the sentiment.

"We can't allow ourselves to be diverted,"

Nasty said. He crossed his arms and braced his legs apart. The muscles in his back bunched under Polly's brow. "We've either got more than one faction at work here, or one very clever group set on making us believe there's more than one."

"But what do they want?" Polly raised her head and declined the drink Dusty offered her. "Why would anyone single me out for this?"

Nasty took a glass from Dusty. "This isn't anything you've ever had experience with before. You're going to have to let me deal with everything."

"But —"

"No," he said, cutting her off. "I mean it."

There was a great deal she wanted to know about Nasty. His anger, the anger she felt in him, made it tough to ask questions, but she had to. "When you were in the Navy you dealt with some bad people, I expect."

Dusty and Nasty barked with laughter at the same time.

"I'll take that as a yes," Polly said, feeling miffed. "You can't expect people who never had anything to do with that kind of thing to know exactly what you did."

"There's no need for you to know about it," Nasty said shortly. He turned from the window and looked down at her. "But you do want to know about me, don't you? More about me?"

He could fluster her with only a glance. "Don't you want to know more about me? Or more than you've been able to find out so far?"

"I already know what I need to," he told her simply. "I'll learn the rest as we go along."

Venus made a choking noise but Polly ignored her. "You assume so much."

"Yeah. It's a habit, but I base it on —"

"Instinct," she finished for him. "Bully for you. My instincts aren't so great."

"Nasty's are great," Dusty remarked. "He'd still be doing his thing if he hadn't had a bad break in Colombia."

"That's history," Nasty said, sliding to sit in a director's chair and draping one of his legs over a wooden arm. "I made a bad call and got shot. The end."

She did want to know more — she wanted to know everything about him. And she wanted to convince herself that her motives for taking him into her life weren't based only on what Belinda so accurately called lust. Or the need for the support of a strong, dauntless man when she felt so threatened.

"You do know Belinda was suggesting I was the man with you last night?" he said, swinging his foot. "She'd dreamed up some concoction about me sneaking up on you, then you deciding you liked the idea of sex with a rapist."

"That's disgraceful," Venus said, and swallowed a huge gulp of bourbon. "You must be mistaken. Belinda is a very special, very intuitive woman."

Polly couldn't look away from Nasty's eyes. "If she's so intuitive, you'd have to believe what she believes. Nasty's right, Mom. She did kind of hint that it could have been him last night." But Belinda didn't know how it felt to be in Nasty's arms, to be touched by him, and to touch him. If there was any violence in his lovemaking, it was the violence of his passionate tenderness.

"We gotta have a plan," Dusty said, coughing. "Smoke 'em out. Never could abide waitin' for the other side to make the first move. That's what did Nasty in. Not that he had a choice when —"

"Not now," Nasty said brusquely. "I've got some thoughts on all of this. I need a little time to work them through. In the meantime, Polly and Bobby can't be left alone."

"Bobby's with me," Dusty said. "How about you, Venus. Maybe you should stay here, too."

"I have my classes to conduct," Venus said, but she smiled a little girlishly, Polly thought. "And I'm responsible for running Hole Point. I can't let Bliss and Sebastian down. If I have even a hint of trouble, I'll call you for help at once. And the police will be checking in regularly."

"They'll be checking my place regularly, too," Polly commented. "I'll be fine."

"As long as you don't have a visitor when the patrol car isn't cruising by," Nasty said. He stood up. "Dust, I need to go to the *April* for one or two things."

Dusty cleared his throat and nodded. "Sure. No problem. Think we should see if Roman can make it over from Montana? Might be good to have another pair of eyes."

225

"I've got eyes," Venus said, widening hers.

Nasty's gum snapped. "Not the kind of eyes Roman Wilde's got. Maybe, Dust. But not yet. Not until I figure out if what I'm thinking is on the money. I'll be right back. Nobody goes anywhere until I am."

He left swiftly, without a direct word to Polly. She felt his absence immediately. Her breathing quickened, and her heartbeat. "He could be in danger because of me," she said. "You should go with him, Dusty."

She was rewarded with another harsh laugh. "Nasty don't need a baby-sitter."

"I was thinking of a bodyguard, not a baby-sitter."

"A bodyguard for the best bodyguard in the business — one of the two best in the business. Nope. Don't think so. But I would like to see Roman walk through the door. They made one hell of a team."

The light was failing. A willow at the shore cast a dim, swaying silhouette against a livid evening sky. She peered through the gloom until she picked out Nasty striding along the floating dock toward his boat.

He was putting his own safety on the line for her. She owed him honesty about everything she felt — and feared. She owed him the truth. There was more than a chance that she was falling in love with him, too, but there was also a chance that she might not be if they hadn't come together when she was needy.

Polly didn't want to need a man. Any man. Or she hadn't wanted to need one.

Then there was Xavier, Nasty Ferrito, offering friendship, offering passion, offering protection, offering — love, maybe.

And she needed him.

But she would not use him.

He'd made it clear he wanted her to stay here with Venus and Bobby. Because he'd gone to do something that could threaten her life? What about his life?

She couldn't stand waiting, and not knowing he was safe.

"I'm going to make myself some tea. Is that okay with you, Dusty?"

"Swill," he muttered. "If you can find some, of course it's okay with me."

Polly left the living room and hurried to the kitchen. She didn't put on the kettle for tea.

She shouldn't go against Nasty's instructions. He'd say she was foolish.

If it was safe for him to go out there, it was safe for her. If it wasn't, then she wanted to know, she wanted to be there for him.

Letting herself out of the house via the door from the mud room, she bent low and slipped along the edge of the terrace.

Nasty would be furious with her. She didn't care. This was one rash, out-of-character move she had to make.

Darkness fell fast now. As she jogged down the paved steps to the docks, she kept her eyes on

227

the uneven ground beneath her feet.

The sounds she made on the wooden planking of the dock seemed thunderous. Despite the noise, Polly ran. A formless premonition fueled her. The police had been able to do nothing but ask their endless questions, write their endless notes. She couldn't blame them. What had she been able to tell them that might give them a clue to whoever had decided to make her his victim? They'd taken the answering-machine tape, but as good as told her it was useless.

Lights glittered on the waterfront. Music shaded the air from the cabins of boats moored at docks to the south and from restaurants and cafés with windows open to the night.

Not a single light shone aboard the *April*.

Polly hesitated when she reached the side of the boat. Water sucked and blew under the sleek hull. Overhead, wind vibrated the naked masts. Lines creaked.

Scents of pitch and varnish and polish on brass wafted on the current that whipped Polly's skirts.

And captured inside the night and sea sounds was a silent core more still than any she had felt before.

Not even a deck flood.

He didn't want to attract any attention.

The hull rose above the level of the dock. Polly located a short ramp running to the gunwale and walked aboard. She tiptoed, and felt foolish, yet could not bring herself to do otherwise than step carefully.

The hatch to the saloon had been closed. She located a handle and pulled. It opened smoothly, and she climbed swiftly down to where she saw a glow coming from Nasty's cabin fore. Heavy cloth shades had been snapped over every port, hiding his presence from the outside world.

She heard him moving about, heard metal on metal, and a rhythmic clinking as if he counted items dropped from his hands into a pile.

Polly found her voice and whispered, "Nasty? It's Polly."

The clinking ceased.

He appeared in the entrance to the cabin. With the light behind him she couldn't make out his face. She didn't need to see it to feel his anger.

"I have to talk to you."

"How did you get out of the house? You little *fool.*"

She froze. His reaction was expected, but it still stung.

"Polly, are you mad?" He came to her so quickly she had no time even to step backward. "Impetuous. There's no room for you to be impetuous now. Do you understand me?"

"I had to come."

His fingers closed on her arm and he spun her around him. He bounded up to close and bolt the hatch, then returned to her. Now she saw his face. Shadows flung dark gashes beneath his cheekbones and into the slanted lines of his eyes and brows. He bore down on her.

"I've been wrong," she said clearly, holding herself straight, and as tall as she could. "I haven't examined what's happening to me with you. That's not fair."

"What's not fair is for you to put at risk the very thing Dusty and I are fighting to protect."

"Me." She jabbed a finger into her own chest. "Me and my family. Why? We aren't your responsibility. We met such a short time ago. Now you're putting yourself in jeopardy for me. I can't let you do that."

"You can't stop me from doing it. *I* can't stop myself from doing it. If you didn't want me at all, you'd have told me by now. I'm not falling for you in a vacuum, Polly. You're in here with me, fanning what I'm feeling."

"You don't know that." She turned from him and saw what it was that she had heard. "You already had a gun," she said, remembering him in her condo the previous night.

"Don't concern yourself with any of that."

There seemed to be an arsenal on his bunk. More than one gun. Ammunition. A sheathed knife. Other things she didn't recognize. And Seven curled in the middle of everything. "This is all part of what you were, isn't it?"

He didn't reply.

"You left that life behind. Now you think you've got to take it up again because of me."

"Can you face what may be happening to you alone? You've been attacked by someone who was armed and deadly serious. Do you want to be in the same place with him again, and *unarmed?*"

Polly could only look into his unblinking eyes.

"Facing up to force isn't a testosterone thing for me," Nasty continued. "It never was. The steps I'm taking to keep you safe are necessary. Do you understand?"

"Yes," she whispered. "Yes, I understand."

"Good. And 'this,' as you call it" — he indicated the hardware on the bunk — "is part of what I *am*. It's part of what I'll always be. No man lives by instinct and reflex and intense training — for years — and then switches it all off like a car at its final destination."

"You're a warrior," she said softly. "A man trained to fight and kill."

"I'm a man," he told her. "Just a man. Trained to fight and kill, yes, but not a man who wants to fight and kill. I only want to make sure I use my skills to safeguard those who can't protect themselves."

"Is that what you did in the Navy?"

He bowed his head until she could no longer see his face. "In the Navy I did what I was told to do. One more part of intense training. And doing what you're told to do is the one thing I expect of you."

"Oh, no," she told him. "I'm not a recruit in your battalion, or whatever."

He ducked his head and entered the small cabin with her. "You may not be a recruit, sweetheart. But don't fool yourself — you're in the middle of a battle. I just hope you listen up and help me make sure you and I win this one."

"You scare me."

"You've told me that before. I don't like it. But if that's what it takes to make you take what's happening very seriously, so be it."

Polly's temper flared. "Last night I was punched and pushed and . . . and, I had my clothes cut off by a lunatic. Do you think I don't already know I'm in trouble?"

His presence just inside the door made the cabin feel even smaller — and he filled all of it. "You may know you're in trouble, but you walked out here alone — in the dark. That was suicidal. Dusty thinks you're still there, doesn't he?"

"Yes."

"I'll give it minutes before my phone rings. If you think I get testy when I'm pissed, wait till you hear Dusty."

"I had to come."

"You had to do what was best — what was safest." He gripped the doorjamb overhead. "I'm no different from any other man whose . . . Any other man would react as best he could to protect the people he cares about."

Polly started to sit on the bunk, looked at the pile of evil hardware there, and changed her mind. "That's what I've got to talk about. Would we be getting so close, so fast, if I wasn't being threatened?"

"When you and I met for the first time, I didn't know you were being threatened."

"I did."

He frowned and swung his torso forward, flexing his powerful arms. "I don't follow you."

"I'd been getting those calls for several weeks. Then there was you. And you were strong and determined, and you knew what you were doing. And you weren't afraid — aren't afraid. You behave as if vicious people doing vicious things are part of your everyday life. You just *do* whatever you think it is you have to do about it. And —"

"Whoa." Releasing the jamb, he settled his hands on her shoulders instead. "Slow down. Cut to the chase and tell me what you're trying to say in a few words."

Tell him in a few words — think clearly enough to be brief when she longed, longed desperately to shut the cabin door, crawl into his arms, and stay there?

The power of her desire for him, now, here, stunned her.

"Polly?" He shook her gently and tilted his head to one side. "You're right when you say I behave as if this sort of thing was commonplace to me. That is what you were saying, isn't it?"

She nodded yes.

"Yeah. Well, it is, or was, and some old habits never quite die. The point is that I don't act scared because I've been here too many times before. But I am nervous for you. Not because I expect anything awful to happen to you — not now that I know how closely I've got to watch you — but because I hate what this must be doing to you. Let me take care of you, Polly."

"And that's exactly why I had to come and talk to you," Polly told him. With flattened hands, she patted his chest. "I will not use you. I don't want to use you. But I think that may be what I've been doing."

"Uh-huh?" His gaze settled on her mouth, and he rocked her back and forth. "Go on."

"You are the sexiest man I've ever met."

He cleared his throat. "Stop it. You'll embarrass me. What else?"

Polly smiled a little. "You can always make light of things, can't you? You're sexy and gentle, and you turn me on."

"Shucks, I'm sorry, ma'am."

"Be serious."

"Not on your life. Not if it makes you stop telling me what I want to hear."

This was harder than he knew, and the timing was all wrong, but she didn't seem to have any choice but to go on. "I haven't had a lot of practice telling men what I think. Not on a personal level. For Sam I was someone he owned. When he couldn't make me do what he wanted me to do — he told me to get lost."

All humor left Nasty's face. His eyes turned hard. "His loss. Your gain — and mine."

"There have been one or two men since then — nothing serious. They never meant anything to me."

"But I do?"

She undid a button on his shirt and smoothed the hair on his chest. "Yes." The weakening in her legs, the heat in her belly, were instant. This response she couldn't squelch clouded her judgment. "It's all muddled up. I think I feel . . ."

He slid his long fingers from her shoulders to her neck and rubbed his thumbs up and down beneath her ears. "What do you think you feel?"

"An emotional thing." She felt strange, almost disoriented. Too much had happened, too fast. "A *feelings* thing."

"A love thing?"

Catching her next breath, Polly met his eyes. "That's not fair."

"Why? I've already told you where I stand."

"And I've told you it's too soon for you to tell me that."

He concentrated on her lips, concentrated until he couldn't see them, because they were pressed to his own. Nasty kissed Polly softly, with quiet intensity that flayed her senses. "You can't get rid of me," he told her. "You've grown under my skin, and I like you there. Just let me call the shots for a while, okay? Let me take care of you because I can — and you may not be able to."

Blindly, she sought his mouth again. He made it too easy to stop questioning her own motives. He felt so good, so warm, so right.

"I'd better call Dusty and tell him you're with me," he said when they paused for breath. "I don't think I can go back just yet."

She blushed. "This isn't the time."

"For what?"

"Don't pretend you don't know." Her frankness astonished her. Glancing at him, Polly put a little space between them. "Couldn't a woman find a man irresistible because she needed him?"

His stillness returned. "Maybe."

"Couldn't I be attracted to you — want you with me, because I'm scared out of my mind, and I know you'll take care of me?"

"I guess." He watched her without blinking. "You could also be attracted to me just because you are — attracted to me. And the fact that I'm not afraid to do what's got to be done to keep one step ahead of the loonies is a side benefit. Doesn't that sound reasonable?"

Reasonable, yes. Certain, no. "I'm not sure I can trust what I feel. I wanted to come clean with that. I owe it to you. Until I met you I was sure I would always want to be independent. I've finally reached a point when I can take care of myself and Bobby without needing help from anyone. That's important to me."

"I can see that." He watched her mouth again. "Does that mean you'd decided you were never going to allow another man to be part of your permanent plans?"

She rested her fingertips on his lips. "I hadn't really thought about it. But then there was you, and I did. Before we actually met, I just liked looking at you. I liked the way I felt when I looked at you."

He blew on her fingers.

"But that's a sexual thing, Nasty. It's lust. It has to be when you don't know the other person."

He nodded his head. "It's the tits-and-ass re-flex."

When she gasped, it was his turn to go a little pink.

"Figure of speech," he said. "I mean that what a man notices first about a woman is her body — the way she looks. He reacts to that before he starts thinking about what a lovely mind she may have. You were doing the same thing — only as a woman looking at a man."

Polly lowered her eyes. "You've got a lovely ass." She raised her shoulders and gritted her teeth. "I can't believe I said that. Believe it or not, I'm a bit straitlaced, or I was."

"I think I believe it." Nasty laughed and caught her against him. "I'm corrupting you. But I've got one up on you. At least I watched the show and got very interested in the mind inside the pretty head before we met."

"Yes," she sighed, clinging softly to him. "Oh, yes. And I like what's inside yours, too. But I keep asking myself if I'd be as eager to wrap my life around yours if I wasn't desperate."

"Polly —"

"No." She put her fingers over his lips again. "No, please don't argue with me. You don't know the truth, not for sure. Any more than I do. It's unfair because we deserve a chance to find out if we could have something special."

"We already do." His eyes narrowed in a purely sexual way. "We have the makings of something more than special. First we get through the messy stuff, then we work on the other — us."

"I've made a decision." Pressing his arms back at his sides, Polly put space between them. "I'm going to deal with my own problems. With the help of the police — that's what they're for. With their help, I'll work my way through the business of this man who's obsessed with me. It's not something that never happened to anyone before."

"No."

"And when it's all behind me — if you still want to, that is — we'll see if we're meant to try being together in some way."

"No."

"Of course, if you . . . No?"

He picked up a handful of bullets and dropped them into a compartment in a leather case that stood open on the bunk. "No, you're not dealing with this on your own. With the aid of the police." A gun made of very light-colored metal fitted tightly into a velvet lined space that seemed made for it. "With or without your permission, I'm in this thing now, and I don't walk away from anything I've started."

"You didn't start it."

"That's not a sure thing."

The knife strapped onto his forearm, beneath his sleeve, and disappeared when he buttoned the cuff again.

"When did you get the first crank calls?" His voice held absolutely no expression. "Try to count back the number of weeks."

She thought about it. "Several weeks. Why?"

"How many? Ten?"

"Oh, no. Nowhere near that long. Three, maybe. Four even?"

"Think harder. For instance, how long ago did you first notice me around the docks?"

Denying that she'd noticed him some time ago would be pointless now. "Four weeks. It was on a Friday."

"Exactly right."

She snorted and settled her fists on her hips. "You can't be sure that's exactly right."

He raised his arched eyebrows. "Can't I? I think I can, love. On the Tuesday I poked around trying to see if I could catch a glimpse of you. On the Wednesday, I did. And on Thursday. Both days I was in the park when you walked out to the dock. The next day — Friday — I took the Zodiac over and hung around until you showed up. It was the first time you actually looked at me. For about ten seconds. I'll never forget how it felt."

Neither would she. "You aren't afraid to talk about things like this. A lot of men hide their feelings because they think they make them less — *manly*, I guess."

Nasty chuckled. "If a man knows he's a man, he doesn't have to be afraid to say what he feels. Polly, the calls started after the first time you saw me in the Zodiac?"

"Yes." What was he getting at? "A few days after, I guess."

"That's what I was afraid of. It could be that

239

I'm the reason for all this."

"No! Why would that be?" The jealousy she'd suspected?

He leaned against the wall and crossed his ankles. "If I am the reason, it'll become clear before too long. I thought about leaving — leaving town. Just in case I was putting you in danger, but —"

"No! You aren't." She stopped, with her lips parted, and stared at him. "Don't go."

He gave her a quizzical stare. "Not even if I'm bringing you the kind of attention no one wants?"

"You aren't."

"You're going to have to make up your mind what you want," he told her quietly. "First you're worried in case you're taking advantage of me, and you want to sort things out on your own. Then you're afraid I'll go away. What's it to be, Polly? What do you really want?"

"I'm muddled up." More muddled up than he could imagine. "I just wanted you to know that I'm not sure what I feel."

"Duly noted."

"I ought to get back. Dusty may not notice I've been gone if I'm quick. He's pretty taken with my mother."

"He'll notice."

She tingled under his gaze. "I'll go back."

"You won't go anywhere without me."

A few words shouldn't have such power to thrill, not when spoken in circumstances like these.

"I put a heavy flashlight on the table in the saloon. Take that — and the box beside it — while I finish packing this."

She slipped past him, pausing when he caressed her cheek. He dropped his hand, and she sped into the saloon. The flashlight and a heavy, black plastic box were exactly where he'd said they would be.

Anxiety over Dusty's reaction made her jumpy. And she wanted to be near Bobby again. She waited at the bottom of the steps and heard Nasty sliding doors in the lockers over his bunk.

Polly went up the steps and opened the hatch. The night was still windy, but warm. Stars winked in a sky banded with wisps of cloud.

On the deck the sounds of the boat's hull rubbing against fenders grew louder — no doubt because the wind had freshened even more.

With the big, black rubber-coated flashlight under her arm, Polly climbed to the dock and peered down at the luminous orange fenders wedged between the *April* and the wooden moorage.

"Polly!" Nasty's voice rose in a bellow from belowdecks.

Her stomach flipped. He could be so angry, so easily. "Here," she called back. "I'm here, Nasty."

She heard the scuffling behind her only seconds before she was knocked down. There was no time to cry out. An arm that felt like a steel hawser wrapped around her waist and picked her up. Whoever it was had waited in the darkness for

her to make the right mistake, and she had —
she'd left the *April* alone.

Another instant and she was airborne, airborne
in the grip of whoever owned the arm.

They burst downward through the surface of
the lake, ripped through water so dark it had
texture.

Cold texture.

Down, he drew her, down, and down. The
roaring blackness spun around her.

Pressure assaulted her eardrums.

Polly tore at the arm that held her, and kicked
at the legs behind hers. Her lungs burned, and
her nose and eyes stung.

Water pressed in on her chest and forced a way
into her mouth.

She drew in a breath and flailed. Never again,
she would never breathe again.

Twelve

The flashlight. Nasty regained his balance and realized what had tripped him. He turned to lean over the water between the dock and the hull of the *April*.

Polly had made it to the dock and dropped the flashlight.

Seconds ago.

And he'd heard heavy impact on the water. Even now a faint swell made the bow of the boat buck. He peered more closely at the surface — and saw bubbles.

Pausing only to kick off his deck shoes, Nasty dived into the lake and shot downward. Damn the darkness. Damn his carelessness for letting her out of his sight for even a second.

How long? A minute? Maybe a minute, but not much longer. Surely no more time than that had elapsed since he heard the splash.

He worked his legs, spun around, searched the opaque depths. Piles beneath the dock sent wavering shadows through the water. He heard the soft shush against the *April*'s bottom and the muted squeal of compressed fenders. The shape of a fish flipped past, and another, and another.

Thank God he could last so long between breaths.

243

His lungs expanded.

Again he twitched his legs, reversed directions, and struck out with his arms this time.

He swung a complete revolution, tracked in place, turned again. He felt the familiar cold concentration, and it comforted him.

A flash of something pale below him caught his eye. But then it was gone.

Then he saw it again — nearer this time. A pale, floating mass waving through the current. Nasty propelled himself toward it and grimaced as the mass took shape. Even as he'd forged downward, looking, a small part of him had hoped he was wrong. But it was the stuff of Polly's dress he saw billowing and flattening. Her hair fanned, then slicked to her head. She seemed to flail, just once, then curve backward, limbs flaccid, like an unconscious diver drawn to the bottom.

Nasty pumped his legs, and pumped again, and his fingers closed on her ankle. His second hand found her waist, and he didn't wait to find another purchase. Rather he released her ankle and aimed upward.

She neither resisted nor helped. His pulse pounded in time with his mounting desperation.

He broke the surface and gulped air. Shaking his head, blinking to clear his eyes, he hung on to the dock with one hand and used all the force in his body to swing Polly up. Even as he released her, his heart bounded at the sound of her coughing and choking.

He gripped the edge of the dock with both hands, but never made the first move toward hauling himself up.

Skillful fingers grabbed and lashed his ankles together swiftly, pulling him down at the same time.

Nasty heard running footsteps and yelled, "Dust! Dust! Here!" Then there was just enough time to fill his lungs with air before he submerged.

Instantly he jackknifed to fight his assailant. The opponent had the advantage. A loop of the same fine twine used on his ankles whipped around his right wrist, effectively tying him doubled over.

He made out the other swimmer. Black wet suit, including hood and gloves. Single tank. Equipped for speed, not endurance. Nothing was visible through the mask.

Nasty clung to the cold center of his concentration and waited the second it took for the man to try capturing the remaining free hand. Closing in, the diver pulled his knees to his chest and reached.

A blow to the man's throat sent him spiraling backward, clutching his neck. Nasty pointed his unfettered arm toward the surface and began to rise — too slowly — but to rise nevertheless.

After an endless, lung-crushing climb he felt his hand break the surface, felt air on his skin. The top of his head cleared the water.

A vicious tug on the line stopped, then held

him — just below reprieve.

Heat clawed at the edges of the still center of his mind.

So close.

Heaving, rotating, he wound his body in the twine. Once. Twice. Three times. And paused. He pulled his energy inside, captured his concentration, and got ready for the final effort.

His chest cavity sank in on itself. He couldn't hold on.

Elbows pressed to his sides, Nasty flung himself around in the opposite direction. Miraculously the line didn't snap taut again. Instead he'd made enough slack to allow him to arch into the clear, clean air, sucking life back into his lungs.

Triumph pummeled blood at his temples. He'd dealt the bastard a hard enough blow to shake him loose.

In that moment he saw the *April*, saw the dock — saw two silhouettes there. "Coming in," he called. "It's okay."

The line tightened again.

Automatically, Nasty took a breath.

This time he didn't see the other swimmer. This time the twine drew taut so quickly there was no time to react. He was dragged through the water, not down, but through — just beneath the surface.

Towed. He heard the echo of an outboard, the engine sound muffled as it reached him. He was tied to a moving boat. A fast-moving boat.

A slight slackening let him know they were

making a turn. He felt the blessed balm of air on his face, then the dragging speeded again.

Twisted son of a bitch. He intended to drown his victim — but slowly.

The knife was strapped to his left wrist. His one chance could be lost so easily. Already the fingers on his right hand felt useless.

Flexing his bound hand, he began to position himself to work the knife free.

Something scraped his back and he peered over his shoulder. A shadow moved just out of sight.

The net caught him off guard. Two swimmers came into view. The net they towed slipped rapidly over his bent form and closed, purse-seine style.

They secured their prize and swam swiftly out of sight.

Nasty floated upward and made himself relax. He relaxed and breathed deep, willing his heart to slow. His mind darted after clues. He didn't need clues now. He didn't have to care about the "why?" now. Only getting the hell out of the net mattered.

They were swimming back to the boat.

Getting out of the net could wait. Doing exactly what he'd set out to do before they'd "netted" him was his only chance. Cut the line — before they could throw the gears and shoot off again, dragging him in their macabre game.

With his knees to his chest, he pressed his left wrist into his right hand and tore his shirt cuff open.

The fingers on the bound hand didn't want to work.

How far had the swimmers gone?

How long was the line?

When would he be jerked down, and forward again?

One breath after another, he kept cleansing his air supply. And he fixed the handle of the knife in the palm of his hand, and wrapped his fingers and thumb around it.

A single backward jerk of his left elbow and the knife cleared the sheath.

He must not drop it.

How far?

How long?

When?

The heat started again. He willed it back.

All he had to do was transfer the knife to his left hand.

The sound of the engine changed, didn't it? Revved?

Forcing himself to concentrate, he took hold of the knife in his left hand and slowly released the fingers of his right.

He'd grabbed the blade!

Pain shot into his left thumb. A cloud spilled, a dark cloud. His blood into the water.

The engine did rev.

Slice the mesh at his feet. Slice the line. One, and, two.

A jolt shot from his heels, along his curved spine. Too late. He'd failed. They were towing him again.

The point of the blade was already caught in

the net. Nasty slashed, tore an opening big enough to bring a mass of nylon flashing into his face.

But he was through the first barrier.

One more aching, desperate lunge, and he could be free.

Thirteen

Polly kept the flashlight beam trained on the last spot where she'd seen Dusty.

Dimly she registered that bone cold had become part ache, part complete lack of feeling. Her body was heavy. Her brain refused to follow a single thought.

Xavier had saved her. She'd known it only dimly until she landed, choking, on the dock and saw him start to pull himself up.

But then he'd disappeared into the water again. That's when Dusty came running along the dock. He'd come quietly, and remarkably swiftly for a man of his age. She'd only begun to tell him what had happened before he silenced her and dragged off his shoes and shirt.

Nasty had shouted then, shouted to Dusty that he was okay.

She swept the beam back and forth, searching for some sign of either Dusty or Nasty. And she tried not to think of the extra time she'd wasted after Nasty surfaced. When he'd failed to swim in, she panicked and jumped into the water.

Stupid, stupid, stupid. As if she could find and save him. As if she'd forgotten she couldn't even swim. She had forgotten. And for the second time in half an hour she'd been saved from drowning

— by Dusty this time.

Polly hugged herself. Each second stretched, yet shrank. The moments seemed incredibly long, but they raced away, each one lessening the chances of Nasty and Dusty returning alive.

Once more she sought the spot, fifty yards or so out, where she'd last seen Dusty surface, then dive again.

At the most frail rim of her light, Polly saw a motion. She shifted the beam again and clutched the neck of her dress.

Two swimmers, two strong swimmers side by side, and closing in on the dock.

She took a single step backward, straining to see. Somewhere, either out there or closer at hand, was the man who had knocked her into the water and tried to drown her.

The two drew closer, and she saw that one was much longer than the other. His arms cut sleek troughs through the water. She dropped to kneel on planking. Nasty and Dusty. They were safe.

Nasty's voice reached her, "Don't move, Polly. Just sit there."

Dusty must have told him how she'd launched herself into the water, only to have to be rescued again. Perhaps now he'd decide he didn't need the kind of liability she represented. Not only was she on someone's hit list, but she couldn't be trusted not to panic in tight situations.

Dusty made it out of the water first and sank to sit beside Polly. Nasty dragged himself up and

251

stretched flat on his back, with the backs of his hands over his eyes.

"Hear anything?" Nasty asked.

"Nope." Dusty patted his buddy's leg. "They kept on going, though. The engine didn't cut out suddenly — just went out of range. Something fast."

"You okay, Polly?" Nasty turned his head and looked up at her. "We've got to get you dry and warm."

She shivered, but said, "We've all got to get dry and warm. Then we've got to talk — and go to the police."

"Maybe," Nasty said.

Dusty settled a hand on her shoulder. "We'll do the right things. Don't you worry about that."

"Maybe that man drowned." She didn't even regret sounding hopeful.

Nasty's eyes closed. "He didn't drown. He's going to wish he had."

Absolutely cold. Polly looked down at the closed eyelids of the man beside her and felt fear different from any she'd felt before.

She did love him. As surely as she sat trembling from cold and shock on the waterfront of the town she'd thought was her chance for complete happiness, just as surely, she loved Xavier Ferrito. And he was a very dangerous man. Dangerous, but not to her, not ever to her.

"Did the box I told you to carry go in the drink?"

It took a moment for her to register that he was

talking to her. "No." She bobbed up and re-trieved the container. When she fell, it had slid against a planter. "I've got it here."

"Good. Emergency provisions, Dust. Just in case."

"Yeah. Where's —"

"On board. I was pretty sure Polly'd gone in. I left everything."

Polly still held the flashlight. She trained it on Nasty and jumped when he flinched and threw an arm over his eyes.

"You're bleeding!" She knelt beside him and pulled his left hand into her lap. His blood seeped over her wet skirt. "Dusty, we've got to get him to a hospital."

Dusty lifted Nasty's hand and chuckled. "Yeah. Dusty's emergency room. Been some time since I performed kitchen table surgery, buddy. We'd better get the job done."

"I need to think."

"You can think while I do some embroidery on you. You're emptying out pretty good there."

"We've got to make plans."

"French knots and conversation. I'm up for it."

Polly didn't see the humor. She got to her feet and pulled at Nasty. "Come on. Please, come on."

A single tug landed her across his body. Seem-ingly unconcerned at the blood he distributed on her face and hair, he held her head in his big hands and stared steadily into her eyes. "I cut my hand on the blade of my knife. You know the one. You saw me strap it on. I'm not going to die from this cut."

"Well, you two lovebirds," Dusty said, "I'm going to have to interrupt here. Let me see the damage, buddy."

Nasty wouldn't let her go, but he offered up his hand and Dusty wrapped it in a strip torn from the bottom of his own T-shirt.

"Okay?" Nasty said, framing Polly's face again. "Can we quit fussing over a scratch now?"

Dusty grunted.

"Couldn't you allow yourself to be looked after? Just for once?" Polly asked.

He didn't as much as blink — or say a word.

"Let me up," she said in a small voice.

Dusty gathered the black box, took the flashlight, and moved apart from them.

"You don't understand, do you?" Nasty said, and she wished he still hadn't spoken. His deep voice had an edge of pure steel. "You see this thing in frames. In episodes. One little piece after another."

"No, I —"

"Yes. Yes, you do because you can't do anything else. I don't have the whole picture, but I've got a hell of a lot more pieces than you do."

"Is this a competition?"

His sudden smile revealed his strong, even teeth. It didn't even soften his eyes. "You have spirit, pretty Polly. I like that. But it can only be dangerous now — unless you keep it under control."

The warmth of his body slowly seeped into hers. She covered his hands on the sides of her head. "I'm not going to tell you again how much you're frightening me. I don't want to be a ninny who can't look after herself."

"You can't look after yourself. Not this time, baby."

"Don't call me that!"

His smile faded. "No. No, I'm sorry, I won't. You can't look after yourself this time. And that's not because you're weak. It's because what's happening is out of your league. It would be out of almost anyone's league."

"You think you know something about that man? You said he didn't drown."

"He didn't. He got away. He won't get away next time."

Her heart and stomach revolved. "Do you mean he won't be able to get away?"

Dusty's snicker sent shivers through her.

"There has to be a way to fight this without using violence," she said. Suddenly she longed for sleep.

Nasty sat up and held her so tightly she could hardly breathe. "We're not dealing with the world of *Polly's Place* and tidy, feel-good stories."

"You said you don't like . . . hurting people."

He stood, pulled her up with him. "That's not exactly what I said. Although it's true. I said I didn't like killing people."

"But you can do it if you have to?" The urge to cry came without warning. "That makes you a killer."

"Nasty —"

255

"It's okay, Dust. I can handle this. Go on ahead, and we'll catch up."

When they were alone, Nasty caught her chin between finger and thumb and tilted up her face. "Are you afraid of me?"

Polly swallowed. "I don't know."

"You mean that?" He raised one brow. "You really don't know whether or not you're afraid of me."

Her jaw worked. "You would kill this man, wouldn't you? If you caught him?"

"I'm going to catch him."

She had never been this cold. Very quietly she asked, "And you will kill him?"

"When this is over, I'll explain everything to you and you'll understand. I can't do that yet. But I know you feel something for me — a great deal, maybe. That's more than I've ever had from a woman before — from a woman I want."

"You make yourself sound so calculating."

"Maybe I am." He looked at the sky. "Call it a habit. You'll just have to help me soften up around the edges. You could make that a cause, or something. Soften up Nasty Ferrito."

"You're wet. And your hand needs proper attention."

"You're wet, too. We need to give each other attention. Lots of attention. I'm going to find a way to make sure we get the chance. You didn't tell me you can't swim."

She'd expected this. "It didn't come up."

"Yes, it did. I even asked you if you'd like to learn to dive."

"The answer's no." She laughed, and it almost felt good.

"You tried to come after me."

"Pretty stupid, I know."

"That wasn't the way it hit me. I'd say a person had to care a lot to try to rescue someone they thought was drowning — if they couldn't swim themselves."

He could tie her up in words so easily. "I guess you might be able to say that."

"Thanks," he said, with a mock punch to her shoulder. "Thanks, good buddy."

She couldn't allow herself to be diverted. "Nasty, I've got to know what you're thinking. About the other."

He found her hand and slid it down his body, down to his bulging crotch. "Any more questions?"

Her fingers closed convulsively. "Sex isn't a problem. It isn't the problem I'm talking about, and you know it."

"You asked what I was thinking."

Muscles tensed low in her belly and between her legs. "This," she squeezed him hard enough to draw a groan. "This isn't what you think with."

"If it is, we're in big trouble. It may be creative, but only selectively. Hell, Polly, you're killing me."

She tried to take her hand away, but he covered and held it where it was. "This wasn't my idea," she told him. "I've got a nutcase on my tail. You're making murderous noises about him, and I want to know how serious those noises are."

He released her hand and jerked her close. "You ask how serious I am? After what just happened?"

"It was awful."

"Awful? Geez, you've got an inadequate vocabulary. It was fucking deadly."

"Please."

"Oh, excuse me." Sarcasm oozed. "*Crumb*, but that was an icky experience."

"Don't laugh at me."

"Then don't say things that make me laugh at you."

She pushed at him. "Let me go. I didn't ask you to protect me. Please let me go."

He didn't.

"I'll go straight to the police and insist they take action. I'll tell them it's very serious, and they can't play a waiting game any longer."

"Polly, the police can't help."

Her throat ached. "They've got to."

"They *can't*." Keeping a firm hold on her, he started toward the *April*'s boarding ramp. "I'll pick up my things and get you back to Dusty's."

Desperation overtook Polly. "Tell me you aren't going to kill anyone."

"Venus will be worried out of her mind by now."

"Xavier? Tell me that if you catch this man — if you find out who he is — you won't really hurt him. He didn't hurt me."

"Yes, he did."

"Yes." She held his wrists and made him stop. "But even if you believe in taking a life, for a life — he didn't murder me last night. And I didn't drown tonight. He didn't kill me."

Young moonlight shone in his eyes. "You're so right. And if he gets another chance at you, he may not finish you then, either."

The steady thud of Polly's heart swelled. Her teeth chattered. "So why would you kill him? You wouldn't. Say you won't."

"Polly," he said. "Unless I've completely lost my touch with these things, he didn't kill you last night because he didn't want to kill you."

She watched his face.

"And he didn't make sure you drowned tonight because he didn't care whether or not you did."

"I would have if you hadn't saved me?"

"Probably. But I've told you it may not matter to him one way or the other."

"Stop it! Just explain what you mean."

"I already have." Wrapping an arm around her waist, he led her aboard. "If I knew why, I'd be closer to making sure one or both of us don't end up dead before our time. I don't. I am pretty certain it's not you he's after. I think this guy wants me. And he wants to take me alive."

Fourteen

"You're late," Jack said. He'd dozed while he waited for her. "Get in here."

The motel room door closed. "You order me up here to some godforsaken dump in the mountains — where I've never been before, by the way. Then you whine because I'm late?"

"Turn on the light," he told her. "We've got some things to settle first."

"First?"

"Turn on the goddamn light!"

"We've been through this," Jennifer Loder told him. "I'm better in the dark."

If he was a gentleman, he'd argue. He wasn't a gentleman. "Maybe I'd like to see that clever body of yours in action."

She laughed shortly. "But not my face?"

Jack didn't respond. Apart from some girl he'd sneaked into the showers at school, Jennifer was the only plain female he'd ever had sex with. But her body was fantastic. Supple and hot, so damn hot. She wound around him like a long, nymphomaniac snake.

"What's with the cheap motel?"

She wouldn't get anything near the truth on that one. "It's been a long time since I had a woman in a motel."

"If that's as much as it takes to give you your kicks, maybe I'm wasting my talents."

He was scared shitless. That's why they were in a no-name motel beside a mountain road — in the middle of almost nowhere. "I'll make sure you don't leave thinking you've wasted a thing."

"Unzip your pants."

He raised his arms and gripped the bed head. She was always like this. She called the shots, set the pace. Sometimes slow, and every way twice, sometimes fast — get it out, poke it in, and get it done.

"Did you hear me, Jack?"

From the start she'd made it clear that if he wanted her, wanted them to service each other with the kind of fanatical, impersonal intensity they both craved, it had to be on her terms.

"Did I get something wrong, or am I your boss?" he said, mildly enough.

"Shut up and get it out."

He wasn't in the mood anymore. "Sit down, Jennifer."

"I didn't drive for an hour on those roads to sit down. Not unless I sit on you. That'll be just dandy, mate. Otherwise, I'll say good night."

"You bitch. You know we've got trouble."

"You've got trouble. I'm all right, Jack." She laughed.

He didn't find her very little joke funny. Propping himself on an elbow, he groped for some of the pills he'd spilled over cigarette burns on the nightstand. He swallowed the pills with vodka, and closed his eyes for a blessed moment. The rush of power and excitement came almost instantly. "How about a little cocktail, Jenny? Something to help you keep me warm?"

"I don't need any help."

No, she didn't need any help. "Let me feel you."

"I want you to get rid of her."

Jennifer only cared about Jennifer. She saw the mess they were in from one viewpoint — her own. She didn't give a damn if everything he'd built got blown away. "It isn't that simple."

"She's in the way. She can make trouble. She's expendable. Any arguments so far?"

"What do you want me to do? Ask her if she'd mind taking a hike?"

"Yeah. I'd say that about covers it."

He felt fuzzy and warm — and turned on again. Jennifer roamed the musty room. He could see her shadow on the wall, then her reflection in a mirror, in the glass on a picture.

"I want to fuck, Jen."

"Weren't you the one who said we had to talk?"

"We can do both."

He saw her go into the bathroom. While he waited he popped another pill, with more vodka. "Jen! C'mere."

Water blasted in the shower.

"Crazy cow," he muttered, rolling off the bed. Staggering, he tore off his clothes on the way to the bathroom. "You're crazy," he shouted.

When he reached to feel for her, a swift chop

to his wrist sent him leaping away, clutching his arm and howling.

The shower curtain rattled aside. "Get in," Jennifer ordered.

He did as she told him and howled afresh. "Too goddamn hot, you sadistic — aah!"

She turned down the heat — a little. "I like it hot," she said, handing him a bar of soap. "And I like it slick. Use this."

His eyelids wanted to droop. He stumbled and caught himself against the tiled wall. "Get in here with me, Jen. I want you. You make me slick. You do it for me."

"When you promise me what I want — you'll get what you want."

"I can't think."

"Think about losing everything you've worked for."

"Stop it." He heard something tear but couldn't identify the sound. "What are you doing, Jen?"

"Persuading you, mate." Her strong fingers, closing on him, dragging it through a hole in the shower curtain, panicked him. "This is the best part of you, Jackie boy. The biggest part of you. Did I ever tell you shaved heads turn me off?"

"Women find it sexy." He heard the slur in his own voice. "Sexy."

"Some women, maybe. Not this one. If you didn't have such a big tool, I wouldn't give you the time of day."

He didn't like what she was doing. "Come in

here, Jen," he wheedled. "Let me hold you, baby."

"You're gonna love this, Jackie. It'll be the ultimate. Everything you want without even touching me."

"Not everything I want," he complained. "I like a lot of stuff you do. I like to suck your tits."

"Jack, Jack, you've got a foul mouth. We'll have to work on that." She worked on another part of him. If he didn't know it would hurt, he'd kneel in the tub and rest. She said, "We've got all night for fun and games, lover. I've only just started. But you've got to promise she'll go."

He tried to concentrate. "Get in here. I don't want the goddamn curtain."

"The curtain's getting hot, Jack. Soft." She held tighter and forced him backward. "But what Jackie wants, Jackie gets. You want me in there with you, here I am."

She stepped into the tub, using his dick to keep the curtain exactly where it was — between them. Strain popped cheap rings from the rail. Where they hit, they pinged.

"You're sick," he muttered, his hips rhythmi-cally jutting toward her. "Crazy sick."

"And you love it. Get rid of her, Jack. Now." She pressed her body against the soft plastic sheet, against him, and slithered over him. Her legs parted and trapped his. He felt her rub him into her, into springy hair and moist flesh. "She'll be the one to ruin it for us if she sticks around."

"I need her."

"You can pull it off without her. You're the inspiration, Jack. It's all you. It always was."

"Jen" — his knees sagged — "shit, Jen, I can't take this."

Her breasts dug at him. "You said you like these. Feel 'em. Squeeze 'em. Yeah, like that. Oh, yeah. Use your teeth."

"The sodding curtain —"

"Forget the curtain. It's perfect, Jack. You don't have to see me at all — you don't even have to touch me really."

"I want to touch you," he told her through his teeth. Then he bit a nipple and heard her yelp with pleasure.

She slid his cock back and forth between her legs, panting, and thrusting her breasts at him. Each time he felt the place he wanted to feel, she gave him a second to try groping his way inside her, then pushed him over her hot button again, seeing to her own satisfaction.

Jennifer leaned on him, trapped him against the wall with the fury of her attack. She was so strong. More shower curtain rings tore free.

She sobbed, high and thin from the back of her throat, then yanked him away so hard he yelled. Bending, she took him in her mouth and ran her hands beneath the curtain and behind his legs to squeeze his backside. When he shouted, she fumbled until she could pinch him.

"You are so sick," he yelled. "Finish it."

She was on her feet again, back to pleasing herself again. "You're a big man, Jacko. You

265

don't need her. You're the director, and the concept is yours."

"She'd have every right to go to the network — and the union." Jack groaned. "I'm coming, Jen. I want inside you."

"Soon." But for a few hooks, the curtain gave out and fell to bunch between their bellies. "Make sure she's got too much to lose, Jack."

"How?"

A relentless hand forced his head down. She slid her pointed breasts back and forth over his face, pressing a nipple into his mouth with each pass. "Whatever will hurt her the most, of course. Let her know that if she stays, she'll lose it."

"She's ambitious," he said when his mouth was briefly empty.

Jennifer convulsed. As always, she climaxed silently, spending all her release in the hammering of her hips against him.

"Now it's my turn," he told her.

"Convince her to take her ambition somewhere else. She causes trouble with the cast anyway. That would go against her if she brought a case. Do it, Jack. Tell her."

"You're missing something. I think we've got trouble we haven't even begun to guess at yet."

"Here's what you want," she said, positioning him where a single push sent him surging inside her. "Have fun, Jacko."

He grunted. The beating, cooling water washed his sweat away.

"Gavin —"

"Not now," he muttered. "Gavin's easy. If he drops out, no one will ask questions. He's got a history of moving on."

"If you'd let me finish, I was going to tell you to leave him to me."

Pressure mounted. Jennifer climbed on the edge of the tub, braced herself on the wall behind him, and spread her bent knees. "Work for it, Jack. It's always better when you have to work for it."

The curtain still hampered him. He stood on tiptoe, dipped and shoved, and grappled with her soapy body to keep his balance.

"Oh, yeah," she said, using her acrobat's body like a weapon designed for sexual torture. "Gavin won't be a problem."

"Can we save the talk for now."

"I multitask real well, Jack. I can take care of the little painter prick. No sweat."

"I don't want any mess."

"Trust me, Jack. There won't be. If there's any fallout anywhere, I'll handle it."

He was coming out as he should have been going in. He came on her thighs and made a grab for the rail. His hands closed on rusty metal, and he struggled to get back inside her.

Jennifer laughed. "The last living optimist," she said when his penis buckled.

The rail gave out and they slammed in a tangled heap on the bathroom floor.

Fifteen

He'd expected a call from Roman. "Dusty's an old lady sometimes," Nasty told him. "He had to fill you in on *all* the details."

"We always said a good woman was what you needed."

"While you and Dusty play matchmaker, I'm up to my ears in shit here."

"Anything new since the night before last?"

"No." He snorted. "I'm still getting my breath back."

"How's the hand?"

Nasty flexed his stiff, taped left thumb. "Dusty hasn't lost his touch. It won't fall off."

"You think it's the Colombian thing?"

"It doesn't have to be."

"That wasn't what I asked."

Nasty turned aside from the spreadsheet he'd been working on at Dusty's and looked through the open study door. Polly was working on a piece about sidewalk sculpture. Jack Spinnel had taken Nasty aside and told him he wouldn't let her out of his sight — and anyway, in broad daylight with Polly front and center at all times, they didn't have anything to fear.

"Nasty?"

"Yeah. I'm not sure if it's the Colombian thing,

but I think it may be. Makes sense it would be the last gig, doesn't it?"

"Revenge?"

"Seems likely. I've embarrassed them. I'm supposed to be dead."

Roman clicked his tongue. "You'd better watch your back."

"I'm watching all sides." Dusty had Bobby at the shop. Nasty had promised to go and pick the boy up before stopping by for Polly. "You'll like her, Roman. So will Phoenix."

"If you like her, we'll like her. You think they're using her to get at you?"

"She doesn't understand that."

"I didn't say she did."

Nasty thought about it. "Yeah. I think that's what they're doing. I probably ought to get her out of the way."

"Will she go for it?"

Would she agree to leave the show? "Probably not. She's afraid for Bobby, though. That might change her mind."

"You could be wrong, Nast." The Pollyanna role had never been Roman's finest. "Yeah, well — if it's the Bogotá group, we've got major trouble."

"And this time we don't have official sanction on our side," Nasty said before he noticed the collective pronouns. "I don't have official sanction on my side. You're real welcome as a sounding board, old pal. This is my problem, not yours."

"I don't remember you keeping your nose out of my business when you knew I needed help."

Nasty shifted a green glass dolphin on the desk. A gift from Phoenix, it made him think of her and smile. "Need is the important word. I'm not sure I need any help yet. If I do, I'll yell."

"Dusty thinks this is a big one."

Dusty definitely talked too much. "His judgment could be skewed. He's taken a fall for a belly-dancing teacher."

Silence followed.

Nasty grinned. He could almost see Roman's piercingly blue eyes narrow.

"A belly-dancing teacher," Roman said at last. "Is that what you just said?"

"You got it. Venus. Earth mother. She's pronounced Dusty a sunshine man living in a sunshine house, and he gobbles up every word."

Roman snuffled and broke into laughter.

Nasty chuckled with him. "Venus Crow is my Polly's mother. Interesting woman if you like that sort of thing."

"Your Polly," Roman said, as if not a hint of mirth had just issued from his lips. "*Your* Polly? As in, possessive?"

"Cut it out. I'm fond of her."

"That's not what Dusty said."

"All right." They'd never been coy with each other. "I may love this woman. Could probably love her — if I can figure out exactly what that means. But I don't think I'm good for her health. I'm almost sure I've brought her a lot of trouble.

Now I've got to figure out how to keep her out of harm's way without interrupting her career. And I'd kind of like to stay alive myself."

"I'll be there in a few hours."

Damn his careless mouth. "No, you won't. There's no immediate threat." Liar. "I overstated myself."

"You've never overstated a thing in your life, Mr. Ferrito. You're the tightest-mouthed bastard I know."

"I didn't think we were discussing my paternity."

"Don't change the subject. You could take them up to Rose's for a few days. She'd love the company."

He hadn't considered introducing Polly and Bobby to the folk at Past Peak. "It's a thought."

"If you're careful. Make sure no one gets any idea where they are, and they'll be as good as lost. Who did you ever meet who knows about that place?"

"No one who comes from Colombia," Nasty said, distracted. "Thanks for the inspiration. I've never had any flashbacks before." He hadn't planned to mention his eerie episode.

"When?" Roman asked. "You mean you've had some of that posttraumatic stuff?"

"Kind of. I saw it all over again. What happened — what I couldn't exactly remember before. I can't figure out why it came back except I was looking at some pictures of South America. Forget it."

"If I was there I could —"

"Shit" — Nasty looked at his watch although he knew what time it was — "I've got to get down to the shop. Dusty's expecting me. So's Bobby."

"Nasty —"

"I'll call if I need you. That's a promise. Do not come unless I ask you, okay?" He hung up before Roman had time to answer.

The phone rang while he was getting out of his chair. Let it ring. He shoved his keys in a pocket and retrieved his shoes from under the desk.

The phone kept on ringing.

Bobby had left his big gray mutt, Spike, with Nasty. He was a cat man, but this was an okay dog. He whistled, and the animal barreled from the kitchen, his big feet sliding on the quarry tile in the foyer.

Still the phone rang.

"Okay, boy," Nasty said, screwing up his eyes at the grating sound. Roman wasn't a man who gave up easily. "Let's go find your boss."

He went into the hall with the dog at his heels.

The phone rang again.

"Damn you, Roman Wilde." He turned back and snatched the receiver off the wall just inside the kitchen. "Yeah? I told you I'd call if I needed you."

"You stupid sonova . . . This is Dusty."

"No kidding."

"Come to Park Place. The movie theater. Bobby's missing."

Light rain fell. The tables and chairs around the fountain were empty. People filing into the movie theater watched Dusty and Fab talking with two policemen.

Nasty parked next to Dusty's camper — the very well equipped camper that had once been Nasty's — and got out of the Porsche. He dodged puddles and reached the foot of an escalator that rose to the second-story shops. Fabiola Crow hovered there, looking as if she'd like to leap onto the moving steps and escape.

Nasty interrupted the policeman who was speaking. "What was he doing here, Dust?"

"Going to the movies. What do you think?"

"I *thought* he was at the shop with you. If you'd told me that was likely to become a problem, the paperwork could have waited. I'd have looked after him myself."

Dusty's lips rolled in, and his eyes narrowed. He jerked his head several times until Nasty frowned, and said, "What? What's the matter with you?"

"Are you a friend, sir?" one of the policemen asked.

"Yeah, he is," Dusty said, bristling. "Bobby went to the movies. You can't keep a kid cooped up forever. He wanted to see a film —"

"I've got the message," Nasty said, cutting Dusty off. "I now know Bobby went to the movies. Thanks. Then what?"

"Are you here in some official capacity, sir?"

the second police officer said. He had a paunch and leather creaked with every shift of his considerable weight.

Nasty schooled himself to cool down. "Sorry," he said, almost choking on the word. "Bit of a shock is all. The boy's the son of a good friend."

"What's your name, sir?"

He gritted his teeth, mentally marked the time they were wasting, and answered the expected questions.

"Very good," Dusty said under his breath when the two officers had walked away. "Oughta get some sort of badge to go on your sash for that performance."

Nasty turned to Fabiola. In jeans and a blue T-shirt, with her hair pulled into a ponytail, and no makeup, she looked about fourteen. Fourteen and very frightened.

"I'm glad Dusty called you," Nasty said. She might be frightened, but not nearly as frightened as she had a right to be. "Polly's been through too much already. She's going to need your help with this."

"I called Dusty," Fabiola said shakily. "Bobby was with me. I asked if he'd like to go to the movies. It seemed safe enough. How could anything bad happen in a busy movie house in broad daylight?"

Oh, hell, it was tough dealing with people who probably still believed in Santa Claus. "You took Bobby to the movies? And you didn't think that was a problem, Dust?"

"No, I didn't," Dusty said, leveling a meaningful stare at Nasty. "Given what we think we know, it seemed like a pretty fair idea. That boy's getting scared out of his wits. My thinking was that there wasn't any need for that."

"Still think that way?"

Dusty looked away. "Seems to me we oughta be rethinking a lot of things. Seems to me your little theory's full of holes, buddy."

Fab's eyes stretched wider and wider. "What are you saying? You're talking about something I don't know, aren't you?"

Lies had their place. "No." Polly had agreed not to discuss the attempted drowning with anyone but the police. Venus believed she'd fallen in the water, then been pulled out by Nasty and Dusty. "I thought we probably wouldn't hear anything else from the guy who roughed Polly up. He'd gotten his kicks — or that's what I decided. This kind of shoots that theory."

"But you were having Bobby watched. If you didn't think there was any danger, why did you do that?"

"Because I don't like taking risks," Nasty said tersely. "But since you're admitting you knew we were trying to be careful, why did you decide to interfere?"

"Nasty —"

He waved Dusty to silence. "Okay, okay. We're getting carried away here. We're all worried about Bobby, so let's quit bickering and find him."

"I shouldn't have taken him," Fab said, her

eyes filling with tears. She was white and trembling. "It was stupid. I just can't seem to take all this seriously. I mean, Polly never did anything to anyone. She was pushed around a lot by other people, but she never stopped being . . . Polly. And Bobby is just a kid."

"Yeah." He put a hand on her back and walked her to the shelter of an awning. "Quit blaming yourself for being human. Help us reconstruct how this happened."

"The police will find him, won't they?" The dread in her eyes pleaded for hope. "He can't have gone very far."

"Did you actually go into the movies?"

"Yes. He wanted to go. As soon as I called him he got excited, and he was waiting for me when I got to the shop. We bought the tickets and some candy and went in."

Dusty kicked a cigarette butt aside. "Bobby went to the men's room," he said. "He never came back."

"I didn't notice he'd been gone a long time until someone wanted to sit in his seat. Then I was scared to go outside to look for him in case I missed him coming back in. He'd have wondered where I was."

"She finally went out and the manager had the theater searched. No Bobby." Dusty recited the events flatly. "He's been gone about an hour. The police are going to sweep the area and put out a bulletin."

"Back inside the theater," Nasty said. "I want

to take a look at the men's room."

"He might not have gone to the rest room at all," Fab pointed out.

"Dusty," Nasty said. "Talk to the kids in the ticket booth."

"Already did."

"Talk to them again. I want Bobby found before it's time for me to pick up Polly."

"She'll *die*," Fab said, visibly breathing through her mouth. "And it'll be all my fault."

He patted her shoulder awkwardly, but couldn't argue with most of her logic.

"It's hopeless." Her voice rose. "Where do you even start looking? He's been taken, hasn't he? That man's taken him. This is some twisted plan to make Polly come to heel."

Nasty only vaguely registered what she was saying. "Could be." He walked into the theater, ignoring the ticket taker's outstretched hand. He felt Fab at his heels, but strode ahead into the men's room.

With the aid of his fist, every stall door banged open hollowly against the walls, including one that brought a growl from a man inside. Two other men at urinals glanced at Nasty and zipped up fast.

"Nothing?" Fab asked as he returned to the lobby.

"Uh-uh." The ticket taker was a teenaged boy in a too-small white shirt with a too-big collar. "When did you come on duty?" Nasty asked him.

The kid's Adam's apple bobbed. "One."

"He was here when we came in," Fab said nervously. "You remember, don't you?"

"Sure I remember." The boy's reddened cheeks and awkward smile suggested he remembered Fabiola but was unlikely to have noticed a seven-year-old boy. "You're the microbreweries girl."

Fab turned a circle. "This is no good. The police will have covered everything here."

"This your other bodyguard?" the boy asked.

Nasty looked at him with sharpened interest. "What if I am?"

"Nothing. Just wondered. I thought maybe you were taking over from the other guy."

A glance was all it took to keep Fab quiet. "Why would you think that?" Nasty asked.

"Hey, I don't want to get into trouble. Not with guys like you."

"You won't get into trouble."

"I'm only supposed to take tickets." Truculence oozed. "They don't pay me to have opinions."

"Sure," Nasty said with a light punch to the kid's arm. "Maybe it'd be better if the manager asked you the questions. What's your name?"

"Brad." A deeper shade of red stained Brad's cheeks. "There's no need to tell the manager. The guy was late. He said he was supposed to be with her." He indicated Fab.

"Slow down," Nasty told him. "A man came here and said he was supposed to be with this lady?"

278

Brad studied his scuffed black tennis shoes. "I shouldn't have taken it. But it seemed okay. All he wanted was to sit and wait inside."

The small sound Fab made warned Nasty he could have another problem on his hands shortly. "You sit down over there," he told her, indicating a bench by the wall. "I can handle this."

When she'd gone, quickly and without argument, Brad produced two bills from his pocket. "He gave me this. He said he was a bodyguard, and he was late catching up with the woman he's supposed to guard. He said it would be all right as long as he was there when she came out."

"He could have bought a ticket," Nasty pointed out.

"There was a line. He said he didn't want to risk being in the line and missing her."

Nasty ran a hand through his hair. "Now let me see if I've got this straight" — he stepped aside while the boy took several tickets and tore them in half before handing back the stubs — "a man gave you money to let him sit in the lobby and wait."

"He didn't have to give me money," the boy said defensively. "I didn't ask him for it."

"Forget the money. He said he was that lady's bodyguard?" Nasty angled his head toward Fab.

"He never said whose bodyguard he was, but when the kid came out the guy talked to him. The kid who went in with her?"

Nasty chewed steadily while he thought. "Didn't the police talk to you yet?"

"Nah. I heard they were here. I been on break."

"What happened then?"

Brad shrugged. "The guy said he and the kid needed to go out and get something. Said they'd be right back."

Polly felt edgy. Mom had said Fab took Bobby to the movies, but where were Dusty and Xavier? "It's nice of you to drive me," she told Jennie Loder, who edged her conservative navy blue BMW through nose-to-tail traffic on Lakeview Drive. "But I could have walked."

"I needed an excuse to talk to you. With all you've been going through, I haven't felt I could take up any time."

"You can always talk to me," Polly said. Jennie was reserved, but she'd shown herself a willing ally on the show, and Polly liked her.

"How d'you feel about Mary Reese?"

The topic surprised Polly. "Okay, I guess."

"I think she's a bitch."

Polly laughed. "Don't like her much, huh?"

"You could say that." Jennie chuckled. "Seriously though, Art and I think she's a problem. This job means a lot to us. We've kicked around the world a lot hoping for a break like this. Mary could scupper the works."

Bobby was the focus of Polly's concentration. She wanted to be at the movie theater when the show let out. "You don't have a thing to worry about. The show's a huge success. It's so big I have to pinch myself sometimes."

280

"It's big because of what it is. The way it is. Mess with it, and it'll fall apart."

"No one's going to mess with it, Jennie. Relax." Walking would have been faster. Downtown Kirkland had become the place for kids to cruise — despite an anticruising ordinance. Fine rain wasn't deterring laughing crowds who spilled from the sidewalks and slowed progress even further.

"There's something with you and the diver, right, Pol?"

The Australian's accent inevitably made Polly smile with pleasure. "I'm not talking, Jen," she said, trying for a facsimile.

Jennie laughed. "Alrighty. Clam up on me. I'll take that as a yes. Mary doesn't like you, y'know."

"What?" Polly swiveled in her seat. "Mary doesn't like me? Where did that come from?"

"She's not married to Jacko, y'know."

"I do know that, yes."

"Can I trust you to keep mum on something?" Jennie glanced at her.

"Sure. You know you can."

The Australian screwed up her eyes. "I kind of like Jack. I could probably like him a lot."

Now Polly's interest was completely captured. "You've always said you hated the sight of him."

"Defense. I tried to hate him, so I wouldn't give in to what I really felt."

"Okay," Polly said slowly. "You've fallen for Jack Spinnel. What about him?"

Jenny shrugged. "Believe it or not, I think he's fallen for me, too."

"Geesh." The promise of fireworks lay ahead. "That'll mix things up. No wonder you aren't too fond of Mary."

"She and Jack haven't been getting along for ages. She demands everything of him — won't give him any space. And she's a maniac about sex."

Polly turned hot with embarrassment. "Yes, well, I suppose people sometimes fall out of love."

"Love!" Jennie guffawed loudly. "There's no love about it. Love's just a word, kiddo. She wants what's in his pants, and he's been giving it to her."

"Maybe the interest was mutual," Polly said mildly.

Jennie shrugged again. "Yeah. Sure. You're right, of course. I've never been the other woman, before. I'm a bit straitlaced when it comes to this sort of thing."

"Yes." What else was she supposed to say.

"I think the problem is that I've fallen in love with Jack. How about that for a corker?"

Sympathy blotted out any other thoughts Polly had had on the subject. "Oh, Jen, that's . . . I was going to say it's tough, but love shouldn't be a burden. You're in a mess, aren't you?"

When Jennie looked at her it was with eyes filled with tears. "Daft, right? I keep telling myself I've got to be patient. If it's meant to be, it will. But I'm serious about Mary wanting to change things, Pol. And this affects you."

"Me? How?"

"She wants you out. She thinks Jack's got the hots for you. According to Mary, Jack sleeps with every leading woman on any show he's directing. It's a lie, but she believes it."

Polly's stomach turned over. "Gavin said something like that."

"Believe him. He's an asshole, but he's got this one right."

"What am I supposed to do? She's Jack's second-in-command."

"Jack's top dog. He's god of the show. But I don't want to make it look as if I'm cutting Mary down because I want her out of his life. I don't think there's anything to be done at the moment except to watch ourselves. I think Jack's more than ready to kick her from here to China if she pushes him too hard."

"Park Place," Polly said as the center came into place. "The movie theater's in the corner."

"Yeah. I know. Pol, if there's any question, anything that doesn't sit quite right, tell me and Art, okay?"

"This is all I need now."

"Meaning?" Jennie steered into the parking lot and looked sideways at Polly. "Oh, sorry. Ah, hell, of course you've got your hands full already. You haven't heard anything else from that nutcase who broke in, have you?"

"No."

"You sure?"

Nasty had made her swear she wouldn't talk to anyone about the most recent incident. "Sure. Thanks for leveling with me, Jen. If Mary makes things rough, I'll tell you and Art. Not that I know what you could do about it."

"Quit," Jennie said shortly. "If she tries to get you out, we'll quit. And I bet we could get Gavin to come, too. Gavin's crazy about you."

Polly didn't touch that. "You make me want to cry. You're such a friend, Jen. This show's changed my life, and working with people like you is the icing on the cake."

When Jennie looked at her again, there were still tears in her eyes. "Feeling's mutual. I just wanted you to be on the lookout. But this is between us, right, Pol? Nothing said unless it has to be?"

"Nothing said unless it has to be," Polly agreed.

"I was worried about talking to you, but I'm glad I did. I don't always find it easy to make friends. So much time moving around since we were kids didn't allow for the buddy bit. Art and I only had each other."

Once Polly had tried to ask about the Loders' family, but the closed reaction had warned her to stay away from the topic.

"You like the diver, don't you?" Jennie smiled as if she expected Polly to avoid giving an answer again.

What the heck. "I do like him."

"More than like him?"

"I like him," Polly said. "He's different."

"You can say that again. He's bloody fascinating. Never saw a bloke with a colder face in my life. Still waters run deep, though, isn't that what they say?"

"I think so."

"Is he good in bed?"

Polly sat straighter. "How would I know?"

"Okay, okay," Jennie said, chortling now. "Have it your own way. But I bet he's not cold when —"

"Jen!" Polly put a hand on top of Jennie's. "Over there. By Park Place Book Company. Fab and Nasty."

"And the entire bloody Kirkland police force," Jennie said, swinging into a parking space. "Better not be any bank holdups this afternoon."

"Bobby's not there," Polly said, thrusting open her door. She ran, and shrieked when a car had to brake for her. She ignored the driver's yelled insults. "Fab! Nasty! Where's Bobby?"

Fab covered her face.

"Cool it," Nasty said. Muscles flexed in his hard jaw. "Everything's under control."

The police Jennie mentioned were dispersing to patrol cars and motorcycles. "Where's Bobby?" Polly repeated. Her throat closed. *No, not Bobby.*

Nasty closed his big hands on her shoulders and pulled her close so fast she lost her footing. He caught and gathered her against him. "We've got a little problem, sweetheart. But we're dealing with it."

Polly pushed against him. Her worst fear had

become real. Something had happened to Bobby.

"What's up?" Jennie joined them. She spoke to Nasty. "Something wrong?"

Fab had begun to cry.

"You're Jennifer?" Nasty asked.

"That's me."

"Could you do us a great favor and take Fabiola home? I don't think she should drive at the moment, and I can't leave. We'll get her car back."

"I'm not leaving Polly," Fab sobbed. "She needs me."

"She needs to be calm," Nasty said. "Jennifer? I'd really appreciate it."

"Anytime," she said. "Come on, Fabiola."

But it took Dusty, coming from the movie theater, to persuade Fab into the BMW. He spoke to Jennie, who sent Polly a worried look before slipping behind the wheel. Nasty gripped Polly even tighter. She felt his tension, but she couldn't concentrate on anything but her own terror.

"So," Dusty said when he reached the sidewalk, "do we do what the police say and wait at my place?"

Polly pushed at Nasty, pushed with all the strength in her body. "Where's Bobby? Let me go. Where's Bobby?"

He released her at once. "Bobby went to the movies with Fabiola. He left his seat to go to the bathroom and didn't come back. He was seen leaving the theater with a man."

It was true, Polly thought. That man, whoever

he was, had Bobby. Weakness loosened her joints. She felt herself start to slip.

Nasty caught her under her arms and picked her up. He took her as far as one of the tables by the fountains and sat her in a chair.

She rested her forehead on the table. "It's all because of me. He wants to get at me so he's taken Bobby. I feel so sick."

"You've got a right to," Dusty said. "I know you don't want to talk about this much, but we're going to work it through. Please trust us."

The two men sat, one each side of her, and rubbed her back.

"I must go to the condo now. He'll make contact there."

"I'm sure you're right," Nasty said. "But first we've got to have a plan."

"The police."

"They're on the case. There's too much hard evidence for them not to admit you're in trouble."

"Because my son's been kidnapped." She lifted her head. Fury pumped blood through her temples. "Bobby had to be kidnapped for them to take real notice."

"They wanted us to go to Dusty's," Nasty said. "I think he should go there. I'll stay with you."

Polly fell against the back of her chair and glanced around. She felt wild. A splash of bright yellow separated from the people milling in front of the movie theater. She clutched the edge of the table.

"Mom!" Waving an ice-cream cone in one

hand and a bulging sack in the other, Bobby dashed toward her. "Hey, Mom, you'll never guess what happened."

Sixteen

"Sam Dodge doesn't have the right to kidnap my son."

Nasty met Bobby's eyes. The boy looked away and buried his face in his dog's fur. He laced his arms around the animal's neck.

Polly couldn't stay in one place. She'd roamed Dusty's living room, sitting in one place, then another, since they'd brought Bobby back from Park Place.

"Feel like a walk?" Nasty asked her, attempting to load his words with the warning that she was pushing the boy too far.

"I'm not leaving him alone. From now on, where I go, he goes."

"What happened was my fault," Dusty said. "I shouldn't have let him go."

"How were you supposed to stop my sister from taking him to the movies?" Polly snapped. "It's nice of you, Dusty, but this isn't your fault or your problem. It's mine. And the police's."

Nasty didn't remind her that since they'd informed the police that Bobby had been with his father, and that he'd been brought back from, "just going for an ice cream," they were unlikely to jump too fast the next time she called.

"I went with my dad." Bobby's voice was muffled in Spike's neck. "He said he misses me."

Polly made fists. "He misses you? He —"

"Hey, Polly," Nasty said, stepping immediately in front of her. "You and Bobby need to have a long talk on your own. But you promised me you'd give me some advice on that other thing. Could we do that first?"

She hooked a strand of hair from the corner of her mouth. Her hand shook, and he knew she was as much angry as recovering from shock.

He raised his brows. "The papers I told you about are in my study."

Without a word, she left the living room and preceded him into the study where he closed the door.

"He never cared about him," Polly said, pacing again. "When I told him I was pregnant, he told me to get an abortion. Once. He saw him once, about four years ago."

"He came here?"

"I was working at Hole Point. The place my mother runs now. I don't even know how he found me."

If she knew what he felt, she'd either be confused or — as he'd managed to make her too many times already — frightened. He hated Sam Dodge, wherever he might be tonight. He hated him for having been part of this woman's life. He hated him enough to want to know they'd never breathe the same air. He hated Sam Dodge enough to wish him dead.

People who preyed on weaker people. People

who always had to win, no matter who else suffered. He felt hot. Sticky. His ankle hurt. He'd had the impression of a dark scene again earlier in the afternoon — when he'd been trying to decide how to search for Bobby. There'd been the sound of palm trees rustling and someone calling him. Then the flash of gunfire before he struck with his knife and saw blood gush from the retreating man's back. Then blackness.

"What is it?"

The sound of Polly's voice startled him. "Nothing," he lied. "I was thinking I wish I'd been the one who met you when you were a kid in need."

Her lips came together and trembled. She lowered her lashes. "When he came to Hole Point he wanted money. I had very little to spare. We got our lodgings for nothing. I did the cooking, and we ate there. Bliss paid me, too. She's always been so good to us. But there wasn't much left over."

"Damn him," Nasty said softly. He tried to hold her, but she shook her head. "He won't bother you again."

"He is bothering us again. D'you know what he told my little boy on the one occasion he saw him?"

"Don't, Polly, please."

"He told him he didn't like fair-haired boys. Bobby was blonder then. When Sam was leaving, Bobby followed him out and Sam gave him a candy bar — and a dollar of the money he got

291

from me. That's all he ever gave his son. Bobby's still got that dollar. I know because I know where he keeps it."

Nasty did hold her then. He took her rigid, shuddering body in his arms and hugged her. "I keep my promises," he told her. "I promise you Sam Dodge is never going to hurt you again."

"Bobby wants a father."

He smiled over her head, a smile formed from all the bitterness of too many years of trying to forget. "Every boy wants a father. And every girl."

"Sam's told him he wants to be a father to him. He's told him he wants us to be together. What can I say to Bobby? How can I make him understand, without telling him his father didn't want him?"

Her hair smelled of whatever faintly rose perfume she wore. Nasty rubbed his cheek back and forth over the top of her head. "I want to get you and Bobby away from here for a few days."

"The show —"

"Leave the show to me. I'll talk to Jack about it. I don't like the guy, but I think he's okay." He wasn't sure about anyone in this scenario. "I'm not telling him where I'm taking you, just that you need a little time off. These things happen. If you were sick, they'd film a lot of stuff they don't need you for, wouldn't they?"

She leaned more heavily against him. "Yes, I guess so." Gradually, her arms stole around him. "Bobby won't want to go. Sam told him he's going to call me and arrange to come and see us at the condo."

Nasty made himself ask, "Do you think he could have changed? Could he have realized what he's missed and want to try to mend fences?"

"He's seen me on TV and realized it means I've got some real money now. Sam doesn't know anything about love — or needing people for anything except what he wants from them."

He shouldn't be glad to hear her disgust for the other man. "Okay, sweetheart. Then I know what I've got to do."

She grew still.

"Dusty and I have a friend who lives not so far from here. In the foothills of the Cascades. She's very special. Different, but special. You and Bobby will enjoy being with her, and you'll be safe because Dusty and I can control things better there." He couldn't be totally sure of that, any more than he could be sure of keeping her safe anywhere, but at least he had a fighting chance of getting her away from Kirkland without anyone knowing where she was. That could be the key.

"I can't stop thinking about it," she said. Her fingertips dug into his back.

"Sure. Of course you can't. But once I get you away, you'll start to relax. Then we'll see what it takes to draw this guy out."

"Sam?"

"Sam and anyone else who thinks he's got a right to get in your way — or mine."

"Nasty, Sam's not a threat. He's . . . pathetic."

"But he makes you feel threatened."

She looked up at him and frowned.

Nasty closed his eyes and kissed her forehead. He ran his fingers into her hair. She began to have the expected effect on him. Never, he'd never been this susceptible to a woman before.

"You're different, aren't you? Different from other men?"

"Mmm." She was warm, and soft, and fragrant — and everything about her spoke to everything he was, everything he wanted. "We're all different."

She tilted her head to let him nuzzle his mouth down the side of her neck. "Not different the way you are. Xavier, you're a trained killer."

His lips rested at the base of her throat. He kept them there, but his eyes opened, and narrowed. Slowly making circles over her shoulders, he listened to her breathing, waited for what she would say next.

"You've killed people."

"I don't remember telling you that." He should have anticipated this. There'd never been anyone close enough to him to wonder what it meant for a man to be able to kill another man — for whatever reason.

"But you have."

She wasn't asking questions here. "Let's say I've done what I had to do in the line of duty."

"You aren't on duty now."

"Maybe not the way you mean. But I'm a man

who takes duty seriously." The instant he finished speaking, he knew he'd been too hasty. She was edgy. If he wasn't very careful, he'd lose her before he'd ever really had her. And he wanted her very much.

"I'm a peaceful person."

"So am I."

Their cheeks bumped. He looked into her eyes and at her mouth. Her chin raised slowly, as if she'd stop it if she could. But she couldn't stop it.

Air flowed softly from her lips to his. Nasty swept his mouth lightly over hers, and lightly again, and his eyes closed.

He was erect, and filled with possessive, protective tenderness at the same time. Controlling the urge to press for much more took inhuman effort. Her breasts teased him through her thin dress and his cotton shirt. Her hips, automatically tipping toward his, made him swallow a moan. She was testing, testing her own feelings — for him, and about what she thought he was.

A killer.

Nasty tore his mouth from hers and pushed his face into the curve of her neck.

She held him, and stroked his hair. "I want to . . . Xavier, I want to be with you. I *want* you. I'm just not sure I ought to."

"Hush," he told her, feeling for her mouth and pressing his thumb against her lips. "I know what you're trying to say. All I can promise is that I'm an honorable man."

"An honorable man who can justify taking lives."

For the first time since he'd been a boy looking at his future and fearing he saw nothing, Nasty wanted to shut out all feeling. "I can justify protecting those who need to be protected."

"And you want to protect me."

"I have to protect you. You need me."

She eased his face to hers and kissed him again, long and slow and deep. "I need you," she said, very quietly. "But what if what you are takes you away from me one day. Or if it ends up hurting Bobby."

"I'm never going to let anything hurt Bobby."

"But you can't promise that you . . . I'm not ready to say I can take what I can have of you, then get over losing you."

This was his crash course in the meaning of bittersweet. "Nothing's guaranteed."

Polly rubbed the backs of her fingers along his jaw. Stress and too little sleep had made their dark stains beneath her eyes. He couldn't be sure any longer, but he still had more than a hunch that she was paying for something he'd been part of.

"I could be an insurance agent. Or a shop-keeper — I am a shopkeeper in a way — and you wouldn't be able to be certain I was safe."

"You're no shopkeeper. You're marking time until you find something else that lets you push the edges of everything."

Was he? "Would it be such a bad idea to live

296

for the day? For a while? Could you try that?"

She shook her head and eased away from him. "I don't know. I've got to do something to get through these bad times."

"I'm not backing out of your life," he told her. "No matter how definitely you tell me to get lost, I won't."

"We could find out this is simple old infatuation."

"You might. I won't."

A pen rolled from the desk, and she gathered it up. "If I agree that it's a good idea to get out of Kirkland, my mother and Fab will have to be told — at least that Bobby and I are going."

"Of course." The shapes and patterns began to turn for Nasty. The men who had tried the underwater capture had been professionals. Sam Dodge played no part in that equation. But he couldn't be ruled out as a possible crank caller.

"Bobby has his heart set on having a dad in his life."

"You know as well as I do that Sam Dodge isn't here because he wants to be a father to Bobby."

Polly pulled the cap off the pen and made dots on her left palm.

"Sometimes it's kinder to be honest," Nasty told her.

"As in telling a seven-year-old boy that his father — the man he's fantasized about — doesn't give a darn about him? That he lied today when he said he did? Am I supposed to tell Bobby Sam

297

will use anyone to get money because he's probably still got an expensive drug habit?"

Nasty rolled onto his toes, testing his left ankle. "There are ways to let people down easy. Let me talk to Bobby."

"You hardly know him!"

"I'm going to know him very well."

She threw the pen on the desk and rubbed at the dots on her skin. "You're so sure you can have what you want. What you think you want."

"I know what I want."

"Look" — she scrubbed at her temples — "*Crumb,* this is awful. What shall I do?"

He didn't fool himself that she was asking him for any other reason than that there was no one else to ask. "Trust me. Trust Dusty and me. We'll get you and Bobby to a safe place. Then we'll figure out a way to pull in whoever's been terrorizing you."

Even the gentle swaying motion of her body warned him that she wavered between accepting his offer and rejecting it outright.

There was no choice but to press on. "And let me talk to Bobby a little. With you there, if you like. I think I can tell him a story that'll make him feel I understand some of what he's been going through."

"I can't agree to that unless I've got some idea what you intend to say."

He offered her his hand and closed his fingers when she took it. "I'm going to tell him how I got the name Nasty."

Seventeen

"Tell me."

He smiled faintly through the windshield of the Porsche.

Polly dug her chin into his shoulder until he glanced at her. "Tell me why you're called that. You're going to tell Bobby."

Nasty chewed his gum several seconds more before he said, "That's right. I'm going to tell Bobby. Later. Pack enough for a week, huh?"

"You said we were only going for a couple of days."

"I said a few days." He parked at the curb in front of her building. "But it could be we'll decide to stay longer. We might as well feel relaxed."

"Extra clothes are going to make us feel relaxed? Don't talk down to me, Nasty."

He pulled the key from the ignition and turned toward her. "Is it so bad to want to save someone you care about? From feeling what you feel? Which, in this case, isn't so hot?"

Polly held the door handle. "Have you told me everything?"

"What does that mean?"

"You're talking down to me again."

"Because I ask you what you mean?"

The lights of Carillon Point, a hotel and con-

299

dominium complex a block away, cast a wavering white shimmer on the lake. Polly blinked, and the shimmer lost focus. "I asked you if you're keeping something from me."

He took just too long to say, "No. I'm being cautious. Chalk it up to training."

Goose bumps rose on her arms. "Okay." She wouldn't get anything out of him unless he decided he wanted to open up. "I'll run up and grab a few things. I want to get back to Bobby."

"I'm coming with you."

Telling him she didn't want to be alone with him — and then dealing with his inevitable request to know why — would only make her more vulnerable to him. She got out of the car. If she had to fall for a man, why did he have to be a quixotic maverick with steel nerves? Why did Xavier Ferrito have to handle guns and knives the way other men handled screwdrivers? Why did he have to be comfortable dealing in death?

The next breath she took didn't get past her throat.

He joined her on the sidewalk and took her keys from her hand.

Footsteps approached and they both turned.

Polly felt Nasty make a subtle move and knew he'd reached for whatever weapon he carried.

"You used to be a whole lot easier to find, babe," Sam Dodge said, arriving in the light outside the door. "I've been waiting for you for hours."

"Not now, Sam," Polly said.

A big man, he wasn't as tall as Nasty, and his body had grown soft. "Sorry to butt in," he said, the easy smile as engaging as ever. "Your friend will understand if you tell him we've got important business to discuss."

Polly tensed, expecting Nasty to respond. When he didn't, her heart still didn't slow down. "I'm sure you want to tell me you're sorry about deliberately scaring me by taking Bobby away this afternoon. Apology accepted."

Sam took a pack of Camels from the inside pocket of a pale linen jacket. He tapped out a cigarette and felt through the pockets of dark silk pants for a lighter.

Polly's keys jingled as Nasty tossed them in his palm.

The lighter flame flared, illuminating Sam's flamboyant, sulky features. His hazel eyes sought hers. "Can we talk?"

The keys jingled some more.

"It's important, babe."

If she told Sam she might slap him if he called her "babe" again, Nasty would have an excuse to intervene. Polly didn't want to give him that excuse.

"Bobby," Sam said, and drew on the cigarette. His hair was as black and curly as it had been when Polly was a teenager. "We gotta put Bobby first now."

This time the keys rattled.

"Could we go inside?" Sam asked. "We don't want to discuss our son on the sidewalk, do we?"

Polly made up her mind quickly, and said, "Okay, but I only have a few minutes."

"Why?" Sam behaved as if she were alone. "You got a train to catch?"

"Let's get this over with." She reached to take the keys from Nasty, but he unlocked the door instead, pushed it open, and stood, staring into space, while she and Sam walked past him into the building.

Sam paused in the lobby. He flicked ash on the dark red carpet and rubbed it with the toe of one shiny loafer. "We wouldn't want to talk family business in front of strangers, would we, babe?"

Polly gritted her teeth. "You and I aren't a family. This is Xavier Ferrito. He's my friend. He'll be coming up with us."

With that she walked into an already open elevator and punched the button for her floor. Even moving with his deceptively lazy grace, Nasty joined her before Sam, who hooked back his jacket and stuck a thumb through a belt loop. He sauntered into the elevator and faced the closing doors.

Disaster had to be only words away.

Once inside her condo, Sam made little attempt to hide his curiosity. He looked around, picked up a small bronze of a zebra, and checked beneath its base as if expecting to find a price tag.

Nasty planted his hands on his hips and observed. His jean jacket settled comfortably on his big shoulders. Polly glanced at the left side of his chest and wondered if his mean gray gun was there. The neck of his white shirt lay open to expose tanned skin. The turned-back cuffs of his jacket sleeves rested casually against his wrists.

A picture of nonchalance.

A lie.

Polly wondered just what Sam would have to do to give Nasty a reason to explode into action, or simply to pull his gun.

"It's stuffy in here," he said, speaking for the first time since Sam showed. "I think I'll go out on the balcony for some air. Okay with you?"

Sam said, "Sure," before Polly finished opening her mouth.

If Nasty had a single thought of any kind, it made no impression on his face. He walked outside and sat in a chair, with his feet propped on the balcony railing.

"Guy's got a limp," Sam remarked.

Polly ignored him.

"When you got kids, you gotta be careful." He tilted his head significantly toward Nasty. "Know what I mean?"

"No."

"Sure you do. You were a lot of things, but you weren't dumb."

"Thanks. Want to tell me what the things were? The things I was?"

Sam dragged on his Camel and screwed up his eyes while he inhaled. "You don't wanna know." He glowered at Nasty's back again. "You always knew I was coming back."

Polly stared at him.

"Don't try pretending you're surprised, baby. It was you and me from the beginning for you. That's why you never took up with anyone else after I — after we split. You're trying to make me jealous. I can deal with that. Consider it forgiven."

"Forgiven?" What had seemed powerful, glamorous arrogance to a struggling teenager sounded like pigheaded stupidity now.

"I always forgave you," Sam said, raising his voice, visibly directing his comments toward the balcony. Nasty had left the doors open. He must already be able to hear every word. "You were young, and you came back to me each time."

The inference wasn't subtle. "Sam," she said quietly, "if you're suggesting what I think you're suggesting, it might be a good idea to back off. Now."

"Guys sow wild oats. Most gals don't feel the urge — you did." He shrugged. "I'm a tolerant guy. It wasn't easy, but I decided you were worth it. Once you were sure none of the others could give you what you had with me, you gave it up."

Polly looked at Nasty.

He didn't appear to move a muscle.

Sam snickered. "You were some handful. They all wanted inside your pants. Man, and they all wanted back in there — even when you let 'em know it was me or no one."

Heated blood washed Polly.

"You were stoned most of the time." Sam shrugged, and took another drag on his cigarette.

"You were a wild one. Whatever there was to experience, you wanted. So what? It's part of being young. And you've grown up."

"Thank you," she said through her teeth. "I don't want to continue this conversation. Don't go near Bobby again."

He smiled at her. "I've forgiven you for the way you cut me out of my son's life, too. I can tell you're different about children than you used to be. You understand how kids need two parents. You want that for Bobby."

"I want the best for Bobby. He deserves it."

"Sure he does. I do know he's mine, y'know. I did the math."

Polly was too angry to shed the tears that burned her eyes. "It's money, isn't it? It was always money. Everything you did was only for one reason — to try to get something for yourself. You came to me that one time at Hole Point, and it was for money. You were desperate, you had to be, because you've never wanted anything to do with Bobby. I wish he wasn't your son, but we both know he is. And I'm not going to bother to deny the disgusting accusations you've just made. Even if I'd wanted someone else, you'd have hurt me so badly, I'd have stopped wanting in a hurry."

A boat's horn sounded from the lake. Sam glanced through the windows. "It's all past. Over."

"You didn't want Bobby. You told me to get an abortion."

"Keep your voice down. Some things are just between two people. If Bobby heard that, he'd feel bad. Even though it's a lie."

"It's not a lie."

"If you need to believe it, okay. If it makes you feel better about causing the breakup, fine. It's dandy, baby — whatever it takes. But Bobby is my son, and I want him. I've missed too much of his life. These are important years — the young ones. You know he wants me, too. You should have seen his face when he saw me today."

She detested that Nasty was hearing all this, but she was also grateful not to be alone with Sam Dodge. "You've lost it, Sam. You haven't grown up. You haven't learned anything about the world."

"And you have? You're so smart and worldly?"

"Bobby's a little boy. You're right when you say these are important years. He's never had a father, and he fantasizes about what it would be like if he did. That's natural. But he doesn't know you. If he did, he wouldn't like you for long, would he?"

Sam's jaw came forward. "I want to be a father to my son. I want you, too, if you're ready to settle down."

A nightmare while she was awake. This was all a horrible nightmare. She considered and discarded responses.

"I'm not like other guys, babe. I'm not threatened by successful women. If you want to keep on with your career, it's okay with me."

"You're unbelievable."

Sam ground his cigarette out in the dirt around a potted African violet. "If this little burg's where you want to be, I can handle that. I can work out of anywhere."

"Work." Polly said the word, and tried it on while thinking about Sam. Not a match. "That could be tough. I bet they already have all the pushers they need in Kirkland."

"Still got the same wacky sense of humor," Sam said.

"You mean you've changed jobs? What do you do now?" Other than look for ways to get what he wanted for nothing.

He produced a pocketknife, flicked open a blade, and slowly cleaned his nails. "I'm a campaign organizer."

Polly had to think about that. "Gangs have elections these days?"

"Very funny," Sam said. "Charity campaigns. Big stuff."

Scams, Polly thought, but she didn't say so.

"Look, baby, I don't expect to put everything back together overnight. But we can do it. For Bobby's sake we can do it. Just believe in me this time, huh?"

"It's too late," Polly said, when she wanted to say it had been too late when they met — too late, and a mistake, except for Bobby.

"No, it's not," Sam said. "You just gotta give us time. Time and opportunity. We were great together. We'll be great together again. Hey, remember? Remember when —"

"That's enough."

Sam held up his hands and shook his head. "Okay, okay. I've come on too strong. You aren't used to the idea yet. You will be. I told Bobby —"

"Stay away from Bobby."

"I told him you and me are going to work at it. You should have seen his face. You can't take that away from him, Pol."

The sound she heard was Nasty, uncrossing, then recrossing his feet in the opposite direction on the balcony railing.

"I'm a very different guy than I used to be," Sam said. "Your buddy can come back in. Tell him to come on back. We need to be on our own, you and me. I got things I should've told you and never did. I want to tell you now, baby."

She wanted him to leave.

"You got it coming. You're special. I shouldn't have taken so long to let you know I think you're the best, but I had to do some growing up, too. And now I have." He spoke louder. "Come on in, buddy. Polly's got something to tell you."

If there were any way to make Sam disappear, she'd do it. Nasty rose to his feet and walked into the living room.

"What happened to your leg, buddy?" Sam asked. He shrugged out of his jacket and threw it over an arm of the couch. "Fall off your skis on the bunny hill? You look like a skier."

Nasty opened his stance and let his hands hang loose at his sides. He stared at the air above Sam's head and chewed, rhythmically worked the muscles in his jaw.

"You don't talk a lot, do you?" Sam said. He coughed, and cleared his throat. A nervous habit Polly recalled.

Nasty met Sam's eyes until the other man looked away and said, "Polly'd like you to go. We got things to talk about."

Only Nasty's jaw moved. His stillness tensed every nerve in Polly's body.

"Did you hear me?" Sam asked.

"Nasty's staying," Polly said, too loudly. The air sang with the promise of violence. "Sam's Bobby's father," she announced, and sucked in her bottom lip. Control threatened to slip away.

"Yeah," Sam said, sounding fatuous. "You only got to look at the boy to see that. I decided it was time to think about Polly and me. For Bobby's sake. And for Polly and me, of course."

She wanted to warn him. Didn't he feel what she felt? Didn't he sense that he was a hair away from a head-on collision with a killer?

Polly shuddered. "Sam —"

He cut in, "You waited for me. I knew you would. Damn, I shouldn't have taken so long to do what I always intended to do."

"Oh, please, Sam." Couldn't he see the ice in Nasty's eyes? Couldn't he see that stillness was readiness?

"Hey," Sam said. "It's okay, baby. Don't get

choked up on me. I know I almost lost a prize. You could have had someone else by now."

"She's got someone else."

Polly flinched. Nasty's statement cut like a sword edge swung through quiet air.

He raised his right hand, tapped his fingertips lightly on his chest.

Preparing to go for his gun . . .

Polly wanted to tell him Sam was helpless, that Sam only took on people who were smaller and weaker.

"What's with him, anyway?" Sam asked her, rubbing his palms together.

"Pick up your coat," Nasty said. "Take it with you. It's not my style."

"Smart-mouthed bastard."

Sam had no warning system for enemies like Xavier Ferrito. Polly took several deliberate steps to place herself between the two men.

"Don't you get it?" Sam asked. "You're in the way."

"Nope" — Nasty walked around Polly, walked toward the foyer — "I don't get that. But I did just hear your exit cue. Good night, pal. Go raise yourself some money somewhere else."

Sam turned an ugly mottled puce. "Where do you get off making suggestions like that?"

"Like you're chasing around after Polly because you need money? Can't imagine. Just came to me, I guess. Everyone says I'm intuitive."

Sam frowned. He clenched and unclenched his fists. "What is he to you, baby?"

"Her name's Polly. We're friends. Very good friends."

"How good?"

"Good enough. Come on, Sammy, come clean. You're in trouble, aren't you? Who's going to cut you up and feed you to yourself if you don't pay?"

Polly covered her mouth.

"Don't listen to him." Sam's color had fled, leaving him putty gray. "He only wants you for what he can get out of you."

Nasty laughed, a sound that should be unpleasant enough to send Sam running. "I want something from Polly," Nasty said, tapping his chest again. "But I want to give her the same thing. That's what makes me different from you. Let me open the door for you."

Spreading his arms, Sam appealed to Polly. "Tell him the way it is, baby. Tell him what we've been to each other. He doesn't get it."

"Out," Nasty said.

Sam reached for her. "Tell him he can't tell me what to do."

How could she ever have been impressed with him, so impressed she'd have done whatever he asked — except get rid of her baby?

When she didn't respond to him he turned to Nasty. "You can't tell me what to do."

"I am telling you. You can decide if you understand, or if you need some one-on-one help getting the message."

"I don't have to take this from you."

"Get out and stay out. Or I'll make sure you do."

Sam made a move toward Polly, then in the opposite direction. He looked sideways at Nasty. "Threats. You're threatening me. For God's sake, Pol. Can't you see what he wants? Guys like him don't spend time with women like you."

She swallowed. Her legs felt weak. This was Bobby's father, the man he wanted in his life, wanted to look up to. Whatever she did, whatever happened, her boy would be disappointed — at least until he was mature enough to see Sam Dodge as he really was. And then what? Would Bobby then wonder if having a useless father meant he was also useless?

"Did you hear what I said, Pol?"

"She heard," Nasty said. "She knows garbage when she hears it, you scum. She knows I want to spend time with her because she's sweet, and sincere, and funny, and intelligent. And she's also beautiful."

Sam combed his fingers through his hair. "Yeah. Yeah, I know all that. I was going to say it, but not with a goon like you listening in. Real men don't spill that kind of stuff in front of an audience."

Nasty strode to pick up the linen jacket. He slammed it into Sam's chest and let go. Sam grabbed it as it fell.

"You're lame," he said. "You got a bum leg. I can take you."

"Want to try?"

"Sam," Polly said, "I think you should go."

"And leave you with him? Like hell. These pretty boys make their way taking advantage of women. Where d'you get the war wound, pretty boy? Banging some bimbo on the slopes? Get carried away and fall off a cliff?"

Polly closed her eyes.

"That's it," Nasty said, so softly she barely heard him. "You don't talk that way in front of Polly. From here on you don't talk any way in front of her."

"Truth hurts, does it?"

"Sam, stop it!" Polly turned her back on both of them. "Don't you smell danger even when it's scorching your eyelashes?"

"Out," Nasty said. "This is your last chance."

Polly heard footfalls on the carpet, then on the tiled floor in the foyer.

"What if I say I'm not going?"

"You already tried that. Don't forget your jacket. We toss trash."

More footfalls. Reluctant, but heading for the door. Polly sent up a silent prayer of thanks.

"Don't think you've heard the last of this," Sam said. "No one pushes Sam Dodge around and gets away with it. Watch out for this guy, Polly. He's got you snowed, but he's no good. Don't worry, baby. I'll be in touch."

Polly turned around in time to see Nasty open the door and watch Sam come to a stop on the threshold. "I'll be in touch," he repeated. "You're getting upset. I can see that. You don't have to worry. I don't hit crippled ski bums."

"Great," Nasty said, edging the door closed in Sam's face. "I always try to be fair. An eye for an eye and so on. I took a bullet through the ankle. I was on duty at the time — Navy."

"Am I supposed to be impressed?"

"Nope. Just letting you know I'm like you — fair-minded. The guy who shot me, started running. It wasn't easy, but I ran after him — or hopped and dragged what was left of my other leg."

"I'm crying my eyes out for you."

"Yeah, I see that. That guy cried, too. And he kept on running — while he bled to death. I'd lost my gun, but I always manage to keep a knife handy."

Eighteen

Dusty didn't look up when they came in. Seated at the kitchen table with half-glasses a hair from slipping off his nose, he sorted through the pieces of a dismantled toy car.

"Where's Bobby?" Nasty asked. Polly didn't seem to hear or see anything. She hadn't since they'd left her condo with two bags, one for her and one for Bobby.

"Dust?"

"It's midnight," Dusty said. "I know when kids should be in bed even if you don't. He asked why he was sleeping here."

He should have anticipated that. "What did you tell him?"

"That someone's waiting to murder him at the condo." He looked from Nasty to Polly, and when she didn't speak, he said, "Yeah, well. That's what I thought. She's not with us, huh? Something happen?"

"Later," Nasty told him.

Dusty nodded. He selected a tiny screwdriver and went to work on the engine of the radio-operated toy. "I told Bobby I was baby-sitter while you two went out. And I told him he was going away for a few days."

"Hell, Dust! Why didn't you wait for me before

315

saying anything? He's only a kid. He might let something drop, and then we lose any benefit we hoped to gain."

"I told him he was going back to Venus at the Point." The tip of the screwdriver leveled in Nasty's direction. "I trained you. And don't you forget it. I'm not senile yet."

"We can't keep on taking advantage of you," Polly said abruptly. She'd changed into jeans and a yellow T-shirt and pulled her hair back in a rubber band. "You've both been really great, but this is all too much trouble."

"I put you in the room across from Bobby's," Dusty said, attacking the miniature engine again. "Top of the stairs. All the way to the end of the hallway. Bobby's on the right. He's already flaked out. You're on the left."

Polly glanced at Nasty, then at her feet. "The police would keep an eye open for us, wouldn't they? If I went home to the condo and took Bobby with me?"

"Sure, they would," he told her.

"But they probably couldn't stop something from happening."

"Probably not."

"I'm not good at being a nuisance."

"Tell her she's the kind of nuisance we eat up," Dusty said. "Tell her we bore easy, and she's saving us from doing something stupid to fill up our time."

Polly smiled a little. "Like what."

That smile made Nasty a happy man. "Like

316

thinking." He waited for her to look at him. "Thinking can be dangerous when you've got an active imagination."

"Yeah," Dusty agreed. "You wouldn't believe the stuff we can think up."

"You told Bobby he was going back to Mom?"

"Just in case he talks to someone who might talk to someone else. Until we know all the players, we can't afford to leave a trail of bread crumbs. That's why we're getting you out for a while. Waiting to see who looks for you should be real helpful. We want to be sure no one finds out where you are unless we want 'em to."

Nasty felt Polly's anxiety. "Bobby doesn't know about the calls, or the guy who attacked you. I think that's best."

Absently, she touched the place on her head where the lamp had carved its initials. "It is best. But how long will it be before he finds out anyway? I feel helpless. This is the first time I haven't been able to be sure he was safe."

"No, it's not," Dusty said. He took off his glasses and sent them spinning among the car parts. "He's with us. You're with us. You're both safe. You should get some sleep, so we can get away early. I can open a bit late — but I do have to come back and open."

"As soon as we head east Bobby's going to know we aren't going to the Point," Polly pointed out.

Using his best sage-elder voice, Dusty said, "I want you to stop worrying. We gotta take two vehicles. Bobby'll be with me. By the time we get to Past Peak he'll be so wound up about riding the ski lifts in summer, and fishin', he'll only half listen to why we changed plans anyway."

Nasty studied Dusty with fresh respect. He had a special way with children and women. Never put anyone down because they were weaker — Dusty had told him that early on. Look out for 'em, but let 'em do as much as they can. What they can do will help in the end.

"Quiet," Dusty said curtly, snatching up the portable phone before it finished the first ring. "Miller, here," he said, and listened. He met Nasty's eyes and the message passed: trouble.

"You sure?" Dusty said. "Maybe he just took a long walk." He listened some more before saying, "Okay. Yeah, I got it. If I hear from her, I'll give her the message. Try to relax in the meantime, huh."

By the time Dusty hung up, Polly was leaning on the edge of the table.

Dusty grinned at her, and Nasty barely stopped himself from groaning aloud. That grin said what he didn't want to hear — the trouble involved Polly.

"Your friend, Belinda," Dusty said. "Seems she and her friend had a spat, and he's walked out."

Polly straightened. "Festus? Belinda said Festus walked out?"

Dusty's eyes shifted away. "Not exactly, I guess. But she did say she doesn't know where he is. I told her he'll probably show up. These things happen. You'd better get some shut-eye, or you'll be wiped out in the morning. You've had a long day."

Crossing his arms, Nasty waited for the inevitable. It wasn't long coming.

"I *hate* it when people talk down to me," Polly said.

"She really hates it," Nasty said.

She glared at him. "I'm not a kid. I am in trouble, and that's hard — it only gets harder if the people you need to trust — the only people you have to turn to, maybe — if they lie to you."

Nasty nodded. "Polly isn't the type you have to shelter."

"Crumb. Will you let me do my own talking? Did Belinda call here because she was looking for me?"

Dusty assumed his wounded Schnauzer expression. "You can't blame an old man for doing his best to look after a couple of young'uns if he can."

Using the cover of patting his pockets in search of gum, Nasty hid a smile.

"Last I heard," Dusty continued, "that voodoo female was givin' you a hard time. Now she thinks she's got trouble, and she comes running to you."

"What exactly did she say?" Polly asked. "That Festus went for a walk and didn't come back?"

"More or less."

"I want to hear more," Polly told him.

Dusty raised a brow in Nasty's direction.

"Never mind asking Nasty what you should tell me." Polly backed away from the table. "Belinda's been good to me. The way she behaved the other day was out of character."

"She was a bitch," Nasty said, and gritted his teeth when Polly winced. "I should have said she's got a mean streak. Don't forget what she suggested."

"I intend to forget it if I can. I'm going to Belinda's."

"Stand by, Dust," Nasty said, following Polly from the kitchen. He caught up with her as she let herself out of the house. "Hold up, sweetheart. I'll drive you."

"I can walk."

He gripped her elbow. "If you don't want to be talked down to, don't make asinine suggestions." He marched her to the Porsche, unlocked the doors, and closed her inside.

The drive to Another Reality took only minutes. Before Nasty removed the key from the ignition, Polly was out of the car and ringing the residence bell. The door opened as if Belinda had been waiting on the other side, and Nasty had to hurry to stop himself from being shut outside.

Belinda ignored Nasty, and said to Polly, "I knew you'd come. You're too good to bear grudges. I wasn't myself the last time you were here. We've had a lot of difficult times, Polly, dear. Festus and I have had such trouble lately. The business hasn't been doing too well."

"I thought things had picked up since the TV slot," Polly said, walking ahead of the other woman and upstairs.

Belinda turned back. "Thank you for bringing Polly here. I'll take her home."

"That's okay," Nasty told her easily. "I don't mind hanging around. Who knows, maybe I can even be useful. Another pair of eyes can be handy when you're looking for someone."

Tonight Belinda wore her hair slicked back and wound in a knot atop her head. "This is a very personal matter. It's hard to speak freely in front of a stranger."

Twice in one night he'd been asked to get lost — both times for the same supposed reason. "Think of me as a wall, ma'am," he said. "No ears or eyes unless you say otherwise. I've had lots of practice."

Polly had also stopped. She sent him a glance that held the kind of intimacy that tightened his belly — and other parts. He wasn't cooling off on this woman. Nope. What he felt for Polly Crow grew more intense with every hour.

The three of them continued upstairs to the sparsely furnished sitting room. Sparse, but not cheap. Each piece had to have been chosen without concern for cost, or, in most cases, comfort. Dark wood abounded, and hard-looking animal-print upholstery.

"When did Festus go out?" Polly asked. "He's bound to come back when he's cooled off, Belinda. Frankly, I can't imagine him . . . Well, I'd have thought it was out of character for him."

Surprisingly svelte in black jeans and a black linen tunic, Belinda pressed her hands to her cheeks. "You were going to say you couldn't imagine him having the energy to walk out on me."

"No! Not that."

Belinda closed her eyes and swayed. "Perhaps not that exactly. But something similar. He fools people with his quiet act — and his distance. I'm so upset, I don't know what to do."

Nasty caught Polly's eye. She raised her shoulders.

"I should have talked to you about this a long time ago. I just kept hoping he'd take notice of me and stop."

"Stop?" Instantly Nasty was on alert. "Stop what?"

Very deliberately, Belinda turned her back on him. "I'd like to explain something to you, Polly. I can't if I have to worry about it being repeated elsewhere."

"Nasty isn't the kind of man who gossips," Polly said.

"Not that it really matters anymore. Most of it was so long ago, I'm the only one who remembers. And Festus. How could he be so foolish. We made another chance here. Now he's thrown it all away."

"Sit down," Polly suggested to Belinda. "You're upset. Let me get you something. Some tea?"

"I bloody *hate* tea!"

Nasty grinned — despite Polly's shocked expression. "How about something stronger then?" he suggested.

Belinda's response to that was to open a cupboard, whip out a bottle of brandy and three glasses, and pour hefty measures.

"Good stuff," Nasty said after his first swallow. "Doesn't the act get tiring?"

"Down there?" Belinda indicated the shop. "You can bloody say that again. I'm up to the bloody teeth with incense and crystals. It made a good enough cover for Festus. He could hide away in all that nonsense he's always liked. But I bloody detest everything to do with it, and now I'm getting out. Just as soon as I'm sure I don't have anything to worry about anymore."

"How about going a little slower?" Nasty suggested.

Belinda sipped her brandy. "I thought you were going to be a wall. No ears or eyes."

"I never said I didn't have a mouth."

That earned him a disdainful stare. "Festus is my husband. Did you know that, Polly?"

"I was never sure."

"Well, he is. And he's been good to me. Or he used to be good to me when I was young and didn't know exactly what I wanted out of life. That was before he started having his troubles."

A faint, acrid scent pervaded the space. Nasty identified it as an incense. The stuff Belinda "bloody" hated . . .

"We had to leave New York, you know."

Polly shook her head. "No, I didn't. I didn't know you were from New York."

"We had a successful business there. Wine importers. Then the other happened, and we had to get out."

Nasty chose a chair in a shadowed corner and sat down. He rested an ankle on the opposite knee and assumed his most useful gift — the ability to move nothing but his lungs. Sometimes he did it so well his presence was forgotten.

"A girl disappeared," Belinda said. She sniffed and turned her face away sharply. "They never found her."

Polly took the first sip of her brandy. Without makeup she appeared almost absurdly young. "Who was she? Someone who . . . Belinda, was this a girl who meant a great deal to you?"

"She worked for us." Belinda's low voice lost inflection. "A lovely creature. Adele. If she'd been a stranger, it wouldn't have mattered. Not as much."

"Losing someone we know is always a shock."

Belinda propped an elbow on the other forearm and tapped her teeth with the rim of her glass. For moments she seemed very far away. Then she said, "They were wrong, but they thought Festus knew something." Tap, tap. She made the glass ring with her strong teeth. "Or maybe they were right. I don't know."

Polly tucked back escaped wisps of hair. She avoided looking at Nasty as if she wanted Belinda to ignore him as much as he did.

"He's a convicted sex offender."

"Oh," was all Polly said, and her lips remained parted.

"He was framed, of course. And it's affected everything else we've done. He didn't do anything to any of those girls." She gulped brandy. "Just because he was kind to people, young people, they said he assaulted them. Those sluts were looking for a way to make some easy money. Every one of them. They gravitated toward him because they felt his kindness — his goodness. He'd try to counsel them, to help them. Then they'd trump up some story about him forcing them to have sex."

Nasty struggled against a desire to grab Polly and put her behind him. She was a big girl, and, at the moment, she was exactly where she needed to be — creating a focus for Belinda's fascinating diatribe.

"The things they said." A downward twist of Belinda's full lips accentuated the strength of her features, and the power of her personality. "Filthy things. Where would young girls like that learn such filth?"

"How old were they?" Polly's hoarse croak testified to how dry her mouth must be.

Belinda waved a hand and drank some more. "Old enough to know right from wrong. At least fifteen."

Acid rose in Nasty's throat.

"Because of what they said, Festus went to jail. But even that didn't make him free. He wasn't free of crimes he didn't commit even after he'd been to jail."

"Is there someone I could call for you?" Polly

asked. "Do you have family somewhere?"

Belinda's narrow green eyes shifted from their space study to home in on Polly. "I don't want family. I want Festus. He's the only family I've got." Her face crumpled. "We had to get out of New York because the police kept sniffing around. They were despicable. Adele probably got out of New York. Or she took up with some man who could show her a good time. Girls can be like that. Ungrateful. We did so much for her. She was almost like a daughter to us. Then she took off, and we were blamed."

"Belinda —"

"Festus had nothing to do with whatever happened to her. She's probably living somewhere now, and laughing at what fools we were. She took money from us, you know."

"She did?"

"Oh, yes, yes . . . yes." She sank to sit on an ottoman and buried her face in one hand. The all-but-empty glass dangled in the other. "I'm frightened for him. And I'm frightened for you, Polly."

Nasty gave up even the essential movement. Real men didn't need to breathe. He could feel the thud of his heart and the gathering of energy in his muscles and nerves.

"I'm sorry, Polly. I'm so used to trying to convince myself it was all a lie that I spew it out. I've practiced it over and over until I can recite it word for word."

"Recite what word for word?" Polly whispered.

The brandy in her glass trembled.

"What I just told you about Festus. I don't know if he was guilty of sexual assault with those little girls. He may have been, but he kept insisting I owed it to him to help him make a new life. And if he was going to do that, we had to make what had happened a lie."

Polly raised her eyes to Nasty's. He nodded slightly, and she gave him a wobbly smile.

"I don't know what happened to Adele. But I always suspected." Belinda shuddered. She sobbed and rubbed her face. "He was good to me. That's the true part. Festus kept me safe. I've never been completely stable. I fought mental illness when I was a child and a teenager. Festus looked after me."

What a crock. Nasty sucked in a breath. This was an act, it had to be. What he couldn't figure out was the reason.

Belinda got up. She sniffed and wiped her nose with the back of a hand. She swallowed the remainder of her brandy and poured more. "He probably killed Adele," she said brokenly. "I've never said that before. Not to anyone. But I've got to warn you."

The woman wandered erratically to a door and flung it open. "I've got to show you everything. The dome. Everything."

With a glance at Nasty, Polly went after Belinda. Nasty was right behind her. He reached for her hand and squeezed it. When she looked at him over her shoulder he kissed her cheek quickly and said into her ear, "Hang in with me, sweetheart. We've got to go through with this. Nothing bad will happen to you." The old rush hit, the pump of adrenaline in the face of potential danger.

Belinda led them up a short flight of stairs to a circular room with a glass dome ceiling. She flipped a switch and hooded lamps cast small pools of blue light at intervals around the area. In the center, a ladder rose to a wide seat that ran on tracks around an impressive elevated telescope.

"Crumb," Polly mumbled.

"He could revolve in any direction," Belinda said. "But he didn't bother."

Nasty frowned at her.

She climbed the ladder slowly. "Please try to forgive Festus," she said to Polly. "You'll understand when I show you."

Hesitating at each rung, Polly trod in Belinda's footsteps. When she reached the top, she sat beside the other woman on the green velvet seat and stared nervously down at Nasty.

He shut the door, turned the key that remained in the lock, then put it in his pocket before going after Belinda and Polly. He didn't attempt to sit, but remained with one foot on the ladder and one on the platform. His Sauer was within easy reach.

"Look through here," Belinda told Polly, then, "Don't try to move it. It's fixed in his favorite spot."

Polly put her eye to the scope and gasped. She drew back and sat stiffly, her hands pressed together between her knees.

He eased her along the seat and took a look. What he saw was no surprise. Good old, kind old Festus had made a habit of staring into Polly's condo. Through the skylight above her shower to be exact. "I couldn't figure out why he'd set up a telescope in this location," Nasty muttered. "Astronomers avoid civilization."

"The best way to get over it is to think that he's a bit sick," Belinda said. "And he didn't hurt you, did he?"

"Not yet," Nasty said. "And he's not going to."

"No." Belinda sounded subdued. "No, he won't. That's why I knew I had to tell you everything once he left. I don't know where he is. I think he's probably gone away from the area altogether. He's like that. He'll just pick up and go if something troubles him. I think he loved you, Polly."

Nasty felt Polly stiffen even more.

"If I show you the other things, you'll understand. Festus only wants to surround himself with beauty. He loves beautiful things."

She stood up and waited for Nasty to climb down with Polly behind him before following herself. Her movements were jerky now. And she smiled, a ghastly smile, first at Nasty, then at Polly.

Polly's pale face had set in rigid lines of control, but she no longer seemed afraid.

"Here," Belinda said, sliding open panels that concealed a compartment big enough for them all to go inside.

When she started to close the panels again, Nasty stopped her. "That shouldn't be necessary. We aren't going to develop any film, are we?" The compartment was a darkroom.

Belinda didn't answer him. She opened a file cabinet and pulled out a sheaf of large photographs. These she pegged, one by one, to a line.

"Xavier," Polly said. She backed into him. "It's horrible. Oh, no, no!"

Each shot was of Polly in her shower.

"You see?" Belinda said. She sounded excited. "You understand now, don't you? He loved beautiful things. So he watched you. He photographed you so he could look at you when you weren't there for him to watch."

"Sick," Nasty said succinctly. He averted his eyes. "Let's get out of here. The police will have to know."

"I don't want them to have pictures like that," Polly said. She stumbled past him, pushed him aside in her rush to get out of the darkroom.

Nasty didn't want the police to have them either, but there was no choice. "It's just work to them," he lied.

He wasn't surprised when she turned on him and said, *"Don't* keep talking down to me. I've told you I detest it."

"I showed you so you'd understand," Belinda said, sounding bewildered. "I thought you'd understand and forgive him. He didn't mean any harm."

"So she'd understand what?" Nasty said, finally giving the woman his full attention. He'd like to shake her. "What exactly did you set out to accomplish here tonight? If you really believe your husband has left for good."

"I don't know that," she wailed. "But I wanted Polly to know, so she'd stop worrying about things."

"You'll have to be plainer than that," he told her.

"How plain can I be?" Belinda turned back and brought her fist down on a telephone. "Don't you understand now? Festus made the calls. He called Polly's answering machine and left those messages. He must have. But he's gone now, so it won't happen anymore."

"That could be a big jump," Nasty said. "From telescopes and photos to telephone calls."

Belinda stumbled back into the room. "No," she cried. "It's true, I tell you. He's done it before. Always the same pattern. And I heard him!"

"You heard him making calls to Polly?"

Her head bobbed frantically up and down.

"A woman called Venus and asked questions."

Misery clouded Belinda's green eyes. "Me," she whispered. "He made me do it. But he's gone. You don't have to worry anymore. And you don't have to tell the police because it's over."

He saw Polly's wild expression, watched her

prepare to spill all the reasons why she did still have to worry.

"That's right," he said soothingly to Belinda while he kept contact with Polly's eyes, willed her to silence. "What a relief."

"Yes," Belinda said. "Polly can get on with her life again."

When he'd finally managed to pry Polly loose from Belinda's babblings and get back outside, they stood beside his car and he took her in his arms.

She hugged him and pushed her face into his chest where his shirt lay open.

He smiled faintly. "You do have a thing for chests, don't you?"

"Your chest," she mumbled, kissing him there.

His thighs tightened of their own accord. "Sweetheart, I've got some pressing reasons to want this — this whatever it is — to be over."

He hadn't intended to make a joke.

Polly didn't laugh.

"Do you understand what I'm telling you?"

"We still need to get out of town."

"You've got it." He wouldn't tell her what he now knew for sure. "We've got to make sure you're where I can control the situation. You're too much in the open here."

"Because Festus is gone from Another Reality, but he's out there. Nasty, the fact that he's made a major move probably means he's more dangerous than he was before, doesn't it?"

"Maybe." Definitely. "Or it could be that Belinda threatened him, said he had to stop. That could have made him mad enough to run."

"He could have decided to go away for good, couldn't he?"

"Sure he could. But we'll take a little vacation anyway. Rose is looking forward to meeting you and Bobby."

Polly got into the Porsche.

He fiddled with his keys while he studied the dark facade of Another Reality. Why did he get the feeling they'd just been fed a load of crap? If he had to guess, he'd say Belinda was still fronting for Festus. This had been an elaborate effort to get Polly back where she was vulnerable. In the condo, alone.

Sick.

The police would have to be brought up-to-date.

Too bad there was no point in mentioning to the police that what Belinda didn't know had made a suspicion a fact.

Not one, but two sets of maniacs were on Polly's tail. And at least two of the players had murder in mind — Nasty's as well as Polly's.

Nineteen

"I don't like this," Art said. "We had a deal."

Mary scrunched down in the seat beside him and let her head loll back. "We've still got a deal. That's why we're here. To make sure you understand what the deal is."

Early-morning wind whipped through the open windows of Jack's Mercedes. Mary hadn't asked if she could borrow the car. She'd insisted on Art driving because the thought of how mad it would make Jack was too sweet to miss. When the day warmed up, they'd put the top down. That's how they'd drive back to the studio — and make sure Jack saw them.

"Jack would be pissed if he knew I was driving his beloved car."

Mary laughed and turned her head to let the wind blow her hair. "I know. That's why you're in that seat. Keep going north. It's early enough to be no problem. By the time we get to Everett we'll still be ahead of most of the rush."

Art changed gears, put his foot down harder. "Let's get whatever needs to be said, said, okay? We've got a show to put on."

"We've got bits of a show to fill in around the edges of the hole where Polly belongs."

She had only slightly longer than expected to

wait for Art's response. "What the blazes does that mean? The hole where Polly belongs. She sick, or something?"

"Or something. We've got to find out what it is — the reason she's ducking out for a few days. Jack knows, but he's not talking."

"What makes you think Jack knows?"

"He got a call about three this morning."

"Interrupted your beauty sleep, yeah?"

She drew up her knees and squirreled around toward him. "We were in bed," she said. "We weren't sleeping."

"Too bad."

"You can say that again. The timing was lousy, but we managed to pick up where we left off."

"I'll just bet you did," Art glanced at her, and down at the short skirt that had ridden up to her hips. He patted her thigh and let his hand stray between her legs. "You could catch a cold, like that, gal. And put underwear manufacturers out of business if the trend catches on."

Mary giggled and trapped his hand. "I must have forgotten my panties. Just shows how much I've got on my mind these days."

"So what was the call?" He took his hand away.

She made no attempt to cover herself. Art's insatiable libido had been the first ally she'd identified since discovering that Jack's loyalty was unpredictable.

Art slanted her a scowl. "Who called?"

"Our sexy diver."

"Ferrito?"

"How many sexy divers do we know?"

"Personally, none. What did he want?"

"To tell Jack he was leaving town with our illustrious star."

Art braked so hard Mary thumped her wrists into the dash and waited to be smothered by an air bag. "Shit," she yelled when it didn't happen. "Get your foot off the brake before we get rear-ended."

"You've got to be joking." Blinking rapidly, breathing through his mouth, Art accelerated slowly. "That's not funny."

She looked at him with fresh interest. "I didn't know you loved Polly Crow so much."

"I don't give a damn about her one way or the other."

"So you always say. It didn't look like that back there."

He shifted quickly through the gears and took off with enough velocity to jerk Mary against the seat this time. "You shocked me. Who wouldn't be shocked? It isn't as if we've got a ruddy stand-in."

"We could manage if we had to."

"Oh, yeah? D'you want to tell me how?"

Mary began unbuttoning her blouse.

"Cut it out," Art snapped. "What's with you, anyway? We could have had this conversation in Kirkland."

"We could. I'm bored, and horny, and I want some fun. It's too hard back there. I've got us a place to go. You'll see, you'll like it. I also want to get a few things straight with you, Art."

He ignored her and overtook a truck.

"She's only gone with him to make Jack jealous."

"How do you figure?" Art cut in front of the truck again.

"D'you think for one moment that brainless stud of hers would take the time to call Jack at three in the morning if she hadn't put him up to it?"

"Where have they gone?"

It was exactly what she'd thought — Art wanted the little tease, too. Men always fell for the innocent act. "I don't know where they went."

"Jack would tell you. You can get anything out of him if you want to."

The thought that Art believed that pleased Mary. "He said Ferrito clammed up about where they were going. Just told him he and Polly were going away together for a few days."

Art fell into a silence.

She had to give him time to think his way through this. Then she'd go for what she wanted.

Grass in the wide verges beside the freeway was early-fall dusty, and brown. Dense evergreens made sure the state's name continued to fit. Night mist still clung to the valleys and blurred mountain vistas. God, she wanted to get back to California. And she wanted to take Jack, and a whopping success of a show, with her.

"I'm getting off at the next exit," Art announced. "We're going home. With any luck,

Jacko won't even notice we took his ruddy car."

"We're not getting off."

"The hell we're not, gal."

"If you do, I'll tell Jack."

He started to brake again.

"Get your foot off it," she told him calmly. "And quit panicking. We're going to pull this off. By the time we've finished we'll have everything we want."

The corner of his eye twitched. "I think we should get back to Kirkland. The shit's going to hit the fan over this. We need to be there to protect our interests."

"My interests are just fine," she told him, wishing she could believe it. "And if you stick with me, yours will be fine, too."

"Spit it out, Mary. I'm not a game player. You know that."

She pulled her blouse free of her skirt and opened one side. Concentrating on what she did, she tucked the soft fabric back.

Art looked at her, then back at the road. His throat jerked. "Cover that up," he said, but his voice broke. "Any ruddy trucker'd get an eyeful."

She stroked her naked breast. "Those poor men must get so bored. I'm just doing a little charity work."

Art's hands tightened on the wheel until his knuckles turned white. "What do you want?"

"I want you to do exactly what I tell you. Whatever I tell you."

He glanced at her breast again and shifted in

his seat. He checked the rearview mirror. "Button up, Mary. For God's sake."

Her response was to push the other side of her blouse away. She tilted her head back again and rested her right arm along the window rim.

"This guy's going to overtake us."

"Not if you speed up, lover."

Promptly, Art swerved into the fast lane. "Damn it, you're giving me a hard-on that won't quit."

"I've already done that." She grinned, and cupped him. "Ooh, maybe we won't make it to that place I told you about."

"Do up your blouse."

"Make me."

"I'm driving the damn car."

"The fuckmobile," Mary said, and laughed aloud. She sobered just as quickly. Business first, then on with the good times. "Jack and I have done it plenty in this car. I'll show you how in a minute."

On a downhill grade, the truck drew level, and Mary looked up at the driver. He stared straight ahead.

"You are sick," Art said with feeling. "You can't stop yourself can you?"

"And you're a little choirboy," she said sweetly. "A choirboy who enjoys target practice, among other things."

The trucker glanced down. Mary smiled and waved. As if it were on tracks, his head moved back and forth between his view of the road and her breasts. He held his tongue between his teeth.

"Christ!" Art said. "He's going to wrap that ruddy great thing around a pole. Is that what you want? Will that satisfy your ego?"

She sniggered. "Right now he's got a pole of his own to deal with." Deftly, she slipped a hand under Art's arm and unzipped his pants. Her hand was inside before he could try to stop her. "Drive, baby, and be glad you're the one in this car, not him."

"Stop it. I can't drive like this."

"Remember what we talked about the last time we were together — other than targets?"

He groaned, and his hips came off the seat.

The trucker kept dead level and Mary didn't need to see in the cab to know what he was doing with the hand that wasn't on the wheel. Sexual power thrilled her. She relished the way she'd learned to use it, and how immortal it made her feel.

She slowed down on Art. No point ending a perfect early-morning drive in a ditch. "I asked you a question," she reminded him.

His hips moved again.

"Patience," she told him. "I'm going to make you very happy, but we've got to clear a few things up first. I told you something had to be done."

"Yeah." He actually leered at the trucker, who showed no sign of missing any chance to eat Mary's breasts with his eyes. His tongue made repeated trips around his lips. "Look at that sucker. He'd climb right in here with us if we invited him."

Mary leaned out of the window and shouted, "Hi! Hey, you!"

"Knock it off." There was a threat in Art's voice this time, and she remembered how mean he could be.

The truck window rolled down, and the man inside shifted his baseball cap to the back of his head.

"Want to join us?" Mary yelled.

He laughed.

She abandoned Art's crotch in favor of lifting her breasts for the neighbor's greater benefit.

"You're going too far," Art told her. "You've *gone* too far. If we get a cop on our tail, he'll throw us away."

"Not if I get him to join our little party, too."

"This is all part of it for you, isn't it? This exhibitionism?"

"What was your first clue?" She jiggled her flesh and watched the trucker turn pale. She could almost see him sweat. "That's what made it so easy for us to work as a team, Art. We're both into alternative sex."

"I haven't forgotten what you want me to do," he said, making a grab for her blouse and missing. Instead his fingers closed on a breast. He let go immediately. "I haven't forgotten one detail. And you've succeeded in turning me so far on, I hurt. That means you'll get everything you want before I drive us back. Everything, and more. Can we stop this madness now?"

"Soon. I just want to make sure you don't back out, though." And she closed her fingers on his pulsing penis.

"Mary! We're going to have an accident, I tell you."

"I want you to forget what I said about Jennifer. It's not a problem. I talked to Jack about it, and he says she's so ugly, he has to screw her in the dark."

"The guy in the truck's beating off."

"Really?"

"How can he do that and drive that thing?"

"Talented, I guess. Or desperate. Don't think about what I'm doing. I'm only making sure we don't have to waste any time when we get where we're going."

"You don't have any proof Jack's sleeping with Jen."

"I have proof. I told you I did weeks ago. It mattered then, it doesn't now."

"I thought you were afraid it could get in the way of the show."

"No way. I was wrong about that. I wasn't wrong to worry about his infatuation with Polly. She's the real threat. He's trying to squeeze me out because of her. He's sleeping with her, too, but he's not admitting it. You should have seen him after that call. He was a madman."

"You've finished the trucker. He's pulling off."

Mary waved to the man again and blew him a kiss. "My good deed for the day. You should have

342

seen the way Jack performed after that call this morning. Like a rabbit. I don't want any of that wasted on that colorless little nothing. And I don't want her working on him to get me off the show."

"Why would she do that?"

"Because she wants him all to herself. And he's told her he doesn't need me, that he's the brain and the talent — as well as the money — behind the whole production."

"This show means everything to me, too," Art said. He covered her hand and squeezed it, and shuddered. "Jen and me need *Polly's Place*. We never had it so good before."

"You mean you never had it so good before you had me," she told him, doing her own squeezing. "When I told you to send Jennifer away, you said you would."

The Mercedes slowed gradually. Art let the vehicle float into the slow lane. The truck was way back now, on the wide shoulder.

"I agreed because you threatened to tell Jack about us if I didn't."

"How did you think you'd do your act without your ugly twin?"

"I didn't." He locked his elbows. "I intended to tell Jen to stay away from Jack. Then I was going to convince you that I could make sure she stayed away. I can do that, Mary. Jen wouldn't do anything to get in the way of this opportunity."

She pumped him ferociously. "You bloody little liar! I can't trust you."

He all but ripped her hand away. He twisted her fingers backward until she screamed. "You don't learn, do you? I've told you it'll be me who makes the final calls. And I've already shown you how much I can hurt you — anytime I want to. Jen's no bother, I tell you. Didn't you ever think I might have something on my sister? That I can control her? Didn't it cross your mind to leave things to me?"

Tears of pain squeezed from the corners of her eyes. "I don't leave anything to anyone. It's a mistake to leave the important stuff to other people. I learned that lesson the hard way. By losing."

He released her fingers and turned the Mercedes from the freeway onto a road through flat farmland. "This is going to be a new experience then, isn't it. Forget Jen. She won't be a problem from here on. If you had any sense, you'd shut up and let Jack have her. All the more of you for me."

Pleasure licked through Mary. He'd never said a word about really wanting her before. "Okay. Whatever you say. About her. But the other has to be done my way."

"Off with the old obsession, on with the new? Now it's Polly you're worrying about."

"I'm not worried about her."

Art nosed the car between tall bushes bracketing a dirt road. He drove even more slowly.

"Where are we going?" Mary asked.

"Never mind that. Finish telling me what to do."

"We don't have to have Polly. People come and go on top shows. Happens all the time."

"Not when a show is tailored around one person."

"She's no good in the part."

He snorted. "Every kid in the country thinks she's great."

"Polly's going to have to leave the show. We'll all be very sad. But it'll be another learning experience. How to deal with saying good-bye."

"Haven't we done that?"

"Not this way." She looked around. "We've run out of road." Scrubby trees made a tunnel over the car and the track ahead dwindled to a narrow path.

"Great, isn't it. I've always loved places like this. Like you're cut off from the world." He stopped the car and turned off the ignition. "Sexy as hell."

She wriggled and undid her seat belt. "Promise me, Art," she wheedled, getting to her knees on the seat and slipping off the blouse.

He closed his teeth on a nipple, and she shrieked with pure sexual ecstasy. "You're violent," she told him.

"Yeah. I'm violent. Violence turns me on. That's why we make a great pair — we like the same things. What am I supposed to promise you?" He hauled her scrap of a skirt up around her waist and slapped her bottom till it stung.

Mary made ineffectual grabs at his hand, thrusting her breasts in his face while she did so.

"You've got to promise to help me get what I want. I'll look after you, Artie. I'll always look after you. Take off your pants."

He paused long enough to undo his belt and push his jeans down past his knees.

"Lovely," Mary said. He was huge. Another thing that kept her coming back for more. Huge, and broad at the tip. She swung a leg over his hips and let him flirt against her while she grew even wetter. "Once Polly goes bye-bye and we all get over being so sad, Auntie Mary's going to write herself into the story. To help the kiddies understand how the world works."

Art laughed through gritted teeth. "Don't you think the sponsors might have something to say about exposing the little dears to this sort of thing?"

"Now!" She positioned herself and drove down, took him inside until their sex hair mingled. Art gave a keening cry, and she rose and fell on him again and again. "I'm going to take care of us. And I'm going to have Jack, too. And Jack can play around with your sister in the dark if he wants to. It'll give me something else to hold over him. He can't risk me leaking that to the papers. Jack who has twisted sex with a woman he won't look at with the light on. That might not play too well with parents in some parts of this country. Not wholesome."

"Shut — up," Art muttered, holding her breasts while he used his strong legs to do what needed to be done.

"Just give me your word, and I will shut up," she said grimacing with satisfaction. "You're going to find out where Polly's gone and make sure she doesn't come back."

His eyes opened. "What the . . . What does that mean?"

She smiled at him. "We're going to teach the children of America about death. You're going to make sure Polly has a fatal accident."

"Mad," Art said, and yelled as he climaxed. "You're ruddy mad. Who are you going to want me to kill next week? My mother?"

Mary spread her arms in glorious abandon and shimmied, bouncing her breasts before his eyes. "Don't be an ass, lover," she said, as she howled with her release. "Polly's the only one in my way. And you know you never had a mother."

Twenty

Nasty kept the Porsche's speed down and drove behind Dusty and Bobby in Dusty's sleek silver camper. All the way to the tiny town of Past Peak in the foothills of the Cascade Mountains, Polly had spared only brief glances for the beautiful scenery. The rest of the time she kept her eyes on the vehicle ahead. For Nasty to make such a point of wanting it where he could see it, there had to be the threat of danger every mile of the way.

"This place doesn't change," Nasty said when they drove through the center of the town. An abandoned railroad station stood to their left, and a row of single-story shops and businesses to their right. "Nice town. Nice people. The best. You and Bobby will have to come back when you can be free to wander around."

Polly's heart made yet another flip. Her life was becoming a series of fleeting, happy moments in one long, hellish episode.

"Phoenix used to work there." Nasty pointed toward the shop fronts. "Round the Bend. Trendiest little bar and diner in the west."

As they drove by, she located the sign. "Roman's wife, Phoenix? I thought she was a lawyer."

"She is. Doesn't practice. She had to live, and

there isn't much call for lawyers around here."

"Why would she settle in a place where it was so hard to find work?"

Nasty checked his rearview mirror — as he'd done about a thousand times since leaving Kirkland. "That's another story. She needed a break. The camper Dusty's driving was outside the Bend when it caught fire." He chuckled. "Fortunately I got the fire out before the whole thing went up."

"How —"

"Another story," he told her. "I'll tell you another time. Belle Rose — Rose Smothers's place — is about three miles on the other side of town."

"Roman and Phoenix are sort of larger than life to Dusty, aren't they?" Polly said. "Kind of a legend in their own time."

He chuckled again. "Dusty puts up a good front. Dusty the crusty ogre. But he's crazy about kids. Roman and Phoenix have two girls. Junior and Marta. Dusty's their surrogate grandpa, and that makes Roman and Phoenix okay, too."

"Bobby thinks Dusty's great."

"Yeah."

"I think you scare him a bit."

"I won't when he finds out what a marshmallow I am."

The laughter came before she could stop it. "Marshmallow?" Laughing felt good.

"Ask anyone I've known for a long time." He sounded aggrieved. "They'll tell you. That Nasty's got a loud bark. Doesn't mean a thing. He's a marshmallow. Ask Dusty."

"Maybe I should ask someone you've known for a long time who isn't your partner."

"Maybe." The silver camper made a right turn up a narrow road. Nasty followed. "I'm going to have that talk with Bobby. Things kind of got away from me last night."

Polly yawned. "Marshmallow and king of understatement. I think Bobby's the only one among us who slept at all. I'm still feeling sick about Belinda and Festus. Poor Belinda. She's really suffered."

Nasty pushed against the steering wheel, straightened his arms. He hadn't said much about what had happened at Another Reality. At his insistence, Polly had filed a complaint with the police. They'd told her she'd have to come back into the station to identify any seized materials. She'd agreed. But there had been no discussion between her and Nasty over leaving town as soon as Bobby woke up. They'd headed out of Kirkland by seven.

"It could have been Festus who knocked me into the lake," she said without deciding to say anything at all. "And he could have attacked me. He doesn't look it, but he could be one of those tall, wiry people who are very strong."

"Yeah."

The camper passed through an open white gate leading to a wide driveway. When the Porsche drew into the same opening, Polly read *Belle Rose* in wrought iron on the gate. "Sounds like the name of a Southern mansion," she commented.

"Or a description of the owner," Nasty said. He turned up the corners of his mouth at her. "Rose is from the South. She was her father's — her daddy, as she calls him — she was his only child, and he gave her everything. Except self-confidence. Rose is a very lovely, very reclusive woman. She loves people. She's going to want to keep you. Don't think I'm kidding — she will."

Polly wasn't sure she was keen on someone wanting to keep her, no matter how lovely and generous she was. "It could be that we're over-reacting. If Festus is responsible for everything, the police are going to track him down, and it'll be over."

"Sweetheart, if I could have one wish, I'd wish to find out that I'm overreacting. Until I know I am, I'd like you to let me play this my way. Okay?"

Argument wouldn't make a dent in his resolve. "Okay," Polly said. "But I can't be away very long. And I do have to at least call Jack and warn him. And my mother, and Fab."

"I called Jack early this morning — when we got back from the police station."

She turned abruptly toward him. "*You* called him?"

"Told him you and I were going away together for a few days."

"Xavier!"

His gum snapped, and she heard the force of his teeth coming together. "We've arrived."

She glanced at a fabulous, two-story white

house — Southern mansion-style from its columns to its extravagant veranda — and returned her full, furious attention to Nasty. "You told Jack Spinnel that you and I were going away together. As in *going away together?*"

"He may have made a leap like that. I told him you had some problems we wanted to work out together. If he made something of that, then you can't blame me. It's not my fault if his mind's on a single track."

Polly blinked. Sometimes the man stole her every lucid thought.

"Let's get inside. Rose will be wearing holes in her priceless carpets waiting for us."

"Of course Jack made something of what you said. The whole cast will think I'm . . . Well, they will."

"Think you're shacking up with me?" he asked in a helpful tone. "Maybe that would be a good cover. I still think someone's going to try to find us. When they do, I'll be ready, and then we'll both be able to sleep well." A smile flitted over his remarkable face. "And do other things well if I get my way."

Telling him he wasn't subtle was unlikely to move him. "I'm calling my mother as soon as I get settled."

"That's not a good idea."

"I'm calling my mother. And Fab. Unless you want them running to the police and reporting me missing. If I tell them they've got to keep quiet, or risk hurting Bobby and me — they'll keep quiet. In fact, they wouldn't tell anybody even if their toenails were being pulled out."

He leaned back and shoved his keys in the pocket of his jeans. "We've got to keep your nose out of the trashy thrillers you've obviously been reading. Pulling out toenails? We'd better buy you some good romances." His next smile was the most brilliant he'd ever shown her. "They might help convince you a good man is what you'd like to have in your life. You're right about Venus and Fabiola. Call them, but let me help you decide what to say first."

She got out of the car in time to see a small, bosomy woman with a curly, white-blond pony-tail rush down the front steps. While Bobby stood by and clutched Spike's collar, Dusty absorbed the woman's flying embrace with evident enjoyment.

"Rose?" Polly asked uncertainly

"God, no," Nasty said. "Nellie. Great woman. Runs Cheap Cuts in Past Peak. Beauty salon, I understand."

"She likes Dusty."

"Dusty likes Nellie. Come on." He held her hand and started forward, settled a hand on the back of Bobby's neck when he drew level. "This is going to be fun, Bobby. There's even a windmill here."

"Dusty said we'd go fishing," Bobby said. "Dusty said you can get fish this big up here." Bobby's arms couldn't spread any wider than he spread them.

"Uh-huh." A frown replaced Nasty's smile. "Did he tell you he'd teach you to wrestle grizzlies, too?"

"Nasty," Polly said, and nudged him in the ribs.

Bobby rolled his eyes. "It's okay, Mom. I know when I'm being kidded."

Dusty and Nellie waited for them on the veranda. Nellie looked at Nasty and sighed. "Same old story. The best ones are always taken by the time they get to me." Her crooked little moue endeared her to Polly. The very energetic hug she gave Nasty caused mixed feelings. When she reluctantly released him, she said, "Rose is . . . Well, Rose is Rose. She's been twittering ever since Dusty called to say you were all coming. I spend as much time as I can with her — especially when Tracy can't be here. You remember Tracy? Purple mouth? Nose ring? Doc Martens? She used to be a shampoo girl for me."

"I'm not sure I do remember her," Nasty said, so politely Polly craned her neck to see his face.

"Rose pays better, and she thinks Tracy's fads are great. You know how Rose likes to watch the world without getting too close. Tracy usually lives in, but she's in Seattle visiting her mother for a week, so I'm sleeping over nights to keep Rose company."

Dusty had already entered the house. Leaving Spike on the veranda, they went in, too. "How are Mort and Zelda?" Nasty asked. To Polly, he said, "They own that diner I showed you."

"Great," Nellie told him. She led the way into a spacious living room heavily scented by vases and bowls filled with pink roses. "Here they are, Rose. Doesn't Nasty look good enough to eat?"

Polly saw his face color and suppressed a smile.

A beautiful blond woman rose from an overstuffed couch upholstered in rose-covered brocade. The same brocade adorned a love seat and three chairs — and a chaise in a bay window. Small roses rioted over sumptuous drapes, and climbed heavy, slubbed wallpaper.

The picture should have been overwhelming rather than elegantly opulent. Elegantly opulent described Rose Smothers and her house perfectly.

Rose held a magazine to her chest. "You've come," she said. "I just knew you would. A gentleman's word is his word, and you are both such gentlemen. My daddy taught me to know a gentleman when I see him. And a lady." Her sweet smile lighted on Polly.

"You're looking lovely, Rose," Nasty said, surprising Polly again with his gentleness, his virtual courtliness. "You should wear lots of that color blue."

"You think so?" Rose swung a little at the waist, shifting the long skirts of a chiffon dress in two shades of blue. A satin frog closed the neck of a perfectly cut matching silk jacket. Her shoes were also blue satin, and she wore big blue crystal earrings.

Vague discomfort overtook Polly. She didn't

check her watch but figured it couldn't be later than eight-thirty in the morning. Rose looked ready for cocktails and the theater — or a presidential ball.

"She looks a picture, doesn't she?" Nellie said, apparently accustomed to her friend's eccentric taste.

"A picture," Dusty agreed, staring at Rose with open admiration. "She always does."

"Not quite like this, though," she said, holding out the magazine to Polly. "Maybe you'll be able to help me choose something really in style while you're here. I never quite know, you know."

Polly took the book and discovered it wasn't a magazine, but a sales catalogue. She also found herself looking at a model wearing a blue outfit identical to Rose's. Even the earrings and shoes were the same. And the blond model's hair was upswept, a thin blue ribbon wound into a braided chignon — just as Rose's was.

Rose had bought everything advertised in the picture — and copied the hairstyle. Polly handed back the catalogue. "You look better than the model," she said, meaning every word. More catalogues were stacked beside the couch — and another heap reached the arm of one chair.

"We need to get your guests settled," Nellie said in a rush. "Why don't I show them their rooms?"

The hairdresser's anxiety didn't need explanation. She was afraid Polly would notice the obvious — Rose Smothers was charming, but she was also eccentric and locked in her own world.

"Why, Nellie," Rose said. "I know they're tired, dear, but I won't hear of them not sitting down and joining me for tea before they do another thing. Do sit down, all of you. I don't believe I heard your boy's name, Polly."

Bobby, who showed nothing but his usual shyness at an introduction, suffered Rose's kiss to his cheek with only a restrained wrinkling of his nose. "My dog's outside," he announced. "His name's Spike."

"Most welcome, I'm sure," Rose said. "Nellie, you make sure Spike has what he needs, too, dear."

Nasty had subsided into the stillness that was part of him. Still watchfulness. He studied Rose, and the sadness Polly thought she saw in his eyes saddened her in turn. He cared for Rose Smothers the way good people care for good people. Nasty also regretted that such a lovely, charming creature was so ill equipped for the world.

"I gotta get back," Dusty announced, too loudly. "Gotta open that shop of ours, Rose. Nasty's and mine. The one I can't get you to come and see."

She fluttered a hand. "I'll visit one of these days. I've been so busy lately. You know how busy I am, Dusty. Phoenix calls every day, bless her dear heart. And I talk to the babies."

"Hey, Dust." The sound of Nasty's voice startled Polly. "Get Seven and take her in with you, will you? Make sure she eats. She gets funny when I'm not around."

"Sure I'll feed her."

"Seven's Nasty's cat," Rose said, seating herself at the bench before a white grand piano. "Cats love Nasty. That's always a sign of a good person — if cats love them. Cats and any animals. You come back soon, Dusty. Do you hear me?"

"I hear you, Rose," Dusty said. "I'll see myself out, Nellie. And I'll keep an eye out for Seven. Don't suppose you'd like me to check on that damn . . . I mean that boat of yours, Nasty."

"That'd be nice."

"That'd be nice," Dusty mimicked. "Never mind the damn . . . I mean, never mind the great big expensive boat. Doesn't give that any more thought than an IBS, property of the US government. But he worries his fool . . . He worries about that mangy, ungrateful cat, though."

"Don't speed on the way home," Nasty said. He moved close to Polly, and said in a low voice, "He always cleans up his mouth for kids, and Rose."

Dusty stopped in the doorway. He stared at Polly. "I picked up a little something to give to your mom. Because she helped me out that time. Would you take a quick look at it before I go — just to let me know if she'll like it. I haven't had much experience buying gifts."

"Except for kid gifts," Nasty muttered. "Ask to see the playroom sometimes."

Polly gave a half smile and excused herself. With a feeling of relief, she emerged from the

358

house into the brightening sunlight on the veranda.

"It's not her fault," Dusty said, coming to a halt at the bottom of the steps. "Her father sheltered her. From what we can figure, her mother took off with some man when Rose was a little kid and her father never got over it. He probably had some old-world notion about kids inheriting their parents' rotten traits."

"Some do."

"Yeah. But they don't always. And you gotta let people have a chance to live."

"She's young. Maybe she'll change."

He gave her a hard look. "She's not as young as she looks. At least, that's the way I figure it. And she's happy. Could be she ought to be allowed to stay the way she is. There's plenty of people hereabouts who think so. She'd do anything for a friend. Maybe we should say prayers we run into more people like Rose Smothers. Anyways, it's not my business."

"You're sure it isn't too much for her? Having Bobby and me here?"

"Look at her face. Look at the smile in those brown eyes of hers. She won't want you to go at all. She'll make you promise to come back and visit and you'll do it. Remember I told you that. And you'll come back to visit Rose. Everyone does."

Still uncomfortable, Polly shrugged and joined him on the gravel driveway. She started for the camper, but Dusty's arthritic hand on her elbow stopped her.

"That was a crock," he said. "What I told you about something for Venus."

Startled, she turned back. "I wondered what you were talking about. When you said she'd done something for you. I couldn't think what it had been."

"She'd do something quick enough if I asked." Defensiveness on her mother's behalf was the last thing Polly would have expected from Dusty. "She's a good woman, your mother. Generous. Spontaneous. Too many people spend a lot of time thinking before they do anything. That way they often never get around to it. When I get back to Kirkland I think I will just find something for Venus. Woman like that deserves a little thoughtfulness."

For the second time that morning Polly felt she'd entered the Twilight Zone. "I'm sure she'd be very grateful. Was there a reason for you to get me out here with you?"

He frowned. "Of course there's a reason. Why would I tell lies if I didn't have a reason."

"You wouldn't." She waited. When he didn't say anything more, Polly asked, "What's an IBS?"

Dusty's jutting brows drew even lower. "Why would you ask a fool question like that? Out of the blue?"

"Because you mentioned it," she told him, becoming impatient. "IBS, US government issue. You said —"

"All right. Sure I did. I was just checking to make sure you'd heard exactly what I said. Navy term. SEALs. IBS. Inflatable Boat Small. Standard issue to SEAL teams."

"I see." She didn't really.

"Hmm."

Polly cleared her throat. "Nice camper."

"Hmm."

"Nasty said there was a fire in it once."

"Stupid," Dusty said, his frown not even softening. "Stupid trick. Good job Nasty's quick. He's always been quick. He and Roman were the best men I ever trained."

She raised her brows in question.

Dusty reddened slightly. "I was their trainer. SEAL officers are always trained by enlisted men. It's part of the discipline. Same for all special forces."

The bond between these men made her a little jealous. How much room would any of them ever have for someone else? Out of habit, to mask any feelings that might show on her face, she made a study of her tennis shoes.

"I gotta get goin'."

"Yes. Thanks for helping bring us. I think it was easier having you with Bobby. He'd have nailed me with his questions."

"Nice boy," he said. "Needs a man around."

"Kids do," she said automatically.

"No disrespect, but I understand his father's not much good."

"No disrespect taken," Polly said. "Sam's a loser. He always was a loser. I don't want him anywhere near Bobby."

"Nasty'll make sure he doesn't get a chance," Dusty said. "That's what I wanted to talk to you about."

He had her entire attention. "About Bobby?"

"About Nasty. He's important to me."

"I know."

"Do you?" Sharp eyes bored into her. "I wonder if you do. What's he to you?"

She swallowed air.

"Just a man? Or something else?"

"We . . ." This wasn't anything she'd expected from Dusty Miller. "We haven't had a lot of opportunity to know each other yet."

"I think you have. I believe in instinct where people are concerned. So does Nasty. He had to make his own breaks. I don't suppose he's told you that."

"No."

"No. He wouldn't. But I know. He's sure of himself now. Comfortable. Hell of a SEAL, let me tell you. The best, him and Roman. This country's lucky to have men like them."

Polly regarded him, and said, "And like you."

Dusty waved a hand. "Never mind me. What's Nasty to you? I asked."

She pressed a forefinger to each temple. Even the fresh morning air didn't clear her head enough. "I'm not sure yet."

"Yes, you are. Either you want him, or you don't."

"Did he ask you to talk to me?"

"He'd kill me if he knew I was talking to you."

Kill. She wondered for an instant if she could talk to Dusty about her misgivings at the thought of Nasty being a man who had killed other men. Would Dusty understand why she trembled at the idea of making such a man a permanent part of her life, of her son's life?

"I want to know," Dusty said.

"Why? We're both grown-ups. You have to allow grown-ups to make their own way, Dusty."

He shuffled his feet. "I promised myself I'd always look out for Nasty and Roman if they needed me."

"You're loyal."

"So are they. So's Nasty. That's how he ended up with a shattered ankle and lying half-dead in a South American jungle."

"I'm not going to do anything to hurt Nasty. I . . . I care too much about him for that."

She received another brilliant-eyed stare. "Care?"

"Yes. Yes, I do care about Nasty."

Several seconds passed before he said, "It's going to have to be more than that. He let on how he told you he might be able to . . . well, to love you."

Sweat gathered between Polly's shoulder blades. She felt oppressed and excited, at the same time. "He did say that. He also told me afterward that he'd been hasty. I think —"

"I don't think he was hasty. He tried to back off a bit because he was afraid he might scare you off by coming on too strong. He told me that, too."

"Dusty, I don't think Nasty would feel good about us having this conversation."

"We're having it anyway. And I'm telling you one thing before I go. He's trying to hold back. I may not have a lot of experience with this sort of thing, but I know I'm right. Don't hurt him."

Polly glanced toward the house. "I couldn't hurt him. Men like Xavier Ferrito don't hurt that easily."

"They might if they did something dumb. Like love a woman who doesn't love them back."

"Dusty . . ."

He stared her to silence. "No. Hear what I'm saying to you. A man like him could hurt big time if this woman was the first and only one he'd ever allowed himself to love. Don't let it go any farther if you aren't ready for what it'll mean. It's all or nothing for men like Nasty Ferrito. He was trained to hate without holding back. But he trained easy because it was instinct for him. He'll be the same way about love."

Polly needed to sit down.

"If you can't handle that," Dusty said, "you'd better tell him to get out now."

Twenty-one

"No guest hosts," Jack told Mary. There had to be a way to distract her without drawing the attention he couldn't afford.

She hummed and began to dance, swirling her hair, shaking her hips, strutting between the abandoned cameras. They'd sent the crews home at noon, when Art and Jennifer Loder decided to scream at each other and refuse to continue.

Gavin clapped in time with Mary and laughed. "You've got to admit she's talented, Jacko," he said.

"You've got to be good to keep bread on the table in LA," Jack said, preparing for Mary's fury, but not caring. "If you're trying to make it in the business, that is. Mary found it helped if you could be on the table with the bread. Danced on a lot of tables in your time, didn't you, Mary love?"

She gave him the finger and kept on dancing. She and Art had shown up two hours late and in Jack's Mercedes. Mary had made some excuse about Art coming to her rescue when she needed to get away.

"Could we get it together here?" He pummeled his fist on a trestle table loaded with props. "We're going to have to use our time, people."

Her face flushed, Mary stopped in front of him. "The truth is we can't afford to *waste* time, darling. I say we go in tomorrow with a guest host. Me. Polly's sick. We pride ourselves on real themes, let's give 'em a real, real theme. Polly's sick and we're all worried about her but we're carrying on."

"No way," Jack said. This wasn't the first time Mary had paraded her ambition to be on the other side of the camera. "Forget it. End of topic. And we're getting behind, *darling*. We need to spend time on upcoming segments."

Dressed in street clothes again, Art strolled from the direction of the dressing rooms. "Sorry about that," he said. He was ruffled, had been ruffled since he'd finally showed up with Mary.

"Yeah," Jack said. Mary was sleeping with the guy. If he'd had any doubt, this morning's deliberate flaunting of their relationship had snuffed it out. "This is a small cast. I created it that way for a reason."

"You created it? You didn't have any help with the concept?"

He ignored Mary. "I wanted an intimate group."

"Oh, we're intimate," Gavin said, looking at no one. "Are we intimate? Oh, yeah, we're so intimate," he sang, conducting with a paintbrush.

"Polly's absence is unfortunately timed," Jack said. "We're going to have to put off what we had planned and work on some stuff we can plug her into later."

Jennifer joined them. "Polly's my friend, but I don't think she should have left like this. Puts us all in a bind."

"Shut up, Jen," Art said.

"Damn you," Jennifer snapped back. "Get off my back, will you? I don't need your bleeding permission to speak."

"Children, children," Gavin said, holding up his arms as if to separate them. "I've got a perfect idea. I know Jack and Mary are going to kick themselves for not thinking of this themselves." He paused for a dramatic moment, making certain every eye was upon him. "We'll do a piece on a trip to the circus! How about that?"

"Gavin," Mary said, the first to recover. "Be serious, will you?"

"I am serious." The man's eyes opened innocently wide. "Polly's sick and we're all going to the circus to keep our minds off being worried. Or . . . Yes, yes, I like this even better. Polly's not sick. We're checking out the circus so we can give her a surprise when we take her there. We could do all the side stuff —"

"Stuff it, Gavin," Mary said. Her lips came together in a tight line.

An outside door opened, letting in a shaft of bright, afternoon light. A man came into the building, and the light went out behind him. He stood where he was, just inside the door. Jack couldn't see who it was.

"This is a soundstage, buddy," Art called out.

"Cripes," Jennifer said. "For all you know it's

someone important dropping in."

"Afternoon," Jack said shortly. "What can we do for you?"

With his hands in his pockets, the man walked forward between scattered chairs and heaps of cables. "I'm looking for Polly Crow," he said.

"Aren't we all?" Mary said, not quite under her breath.

Jack narrowed his eyes to see the man. Tall, with black, curly hair, he appeared to be in his thirties. A body that had almost certainly been hard, had softened. The face was still dramatic in a disappointed way.

"Polly isn't here?" he asked. Then he thudded the heel of a hand into his brow. "Damn, where's my brain? She said something about not knowing exactly what she'd be doing this morning."

Cool premonition tiptoed up Jack's spine. "Polly told you that?" He felt trouble — more trouble.

"Yeah. I forgot. Is there a Jen Loder around?" The man's clothes were expensive, and he wore them carelessly.

Jennifer crossed her arms. "I'm Jennifer Loder. Why d'you want to know?"

The guy seemed oblivious to the subtle drawing together of the cast. Jack almost smiled. They fought with each other, but they belonged to a different — the same different — breed. When the breed felt a threat, they circled wagons against outsiders.

"I'm Sam Dodge," the man said with the kind

of smile that set Jack's teeth on edge. A smile that expected to get what it wanted. "Polly and me go way back. *Way* back."

"Yeah?" Gavin said. "*Way* back? Geez. That far, huh?"

All Gavin earned himself was another smile and a stare devoid of guile. "You've got it. That far. Could we talk, Jennifer? Polly's said a lot of nice things about you."

Mary moved beside Jack, and whispered, "Did Polly ever mention this clown to you?"

"I knew it!" Gavin said with gusto. "You love my idea about the circus, don't you, Mary darling?"

"Shut up," she told him with grim intensity. "I don't recall Polly mentioning you, Mr. Dodge. She's not here at the moment. Why don't you leave a note for her?"

Sam Dodge homed in on Jennifer as if Mary didn't exist. "You're from Australia."

"What was your first clue?" Art drawled. "This is a set, mate — a soundstage. You can't just wander in here."

Sam slipped off his gray silk jacket and slung it over a shoulder. He looked in several directions. "Doesn't seem to be much going on. I figured that. No light on outside."

"Did you enjoy Universal Studios?" Gavin asked with a faint, downturned smile. "I expect you saw the Phantom flitting around while you were there. And they told you all about the little lights outside the stages. Amazing, isn't it?"

Jack decided that if he were Gavin, he'd probably back off. Sam Dodge might be softer than he'd once been, but he didn't look like a man who'd be fun in the dark if he arrived unexpectedly.

"Polly and I were supposed to get together for breakfast this morning," Sam said. His glance in Gavin's direction was flat, cold. "She told me something might come up. I should have remembered that, but I didn't."

"You're Bobby's father," Jen said. Her arms were still crossed, and Jack noted how she flexed her fingers. "You took off with Bobby yesterday. When he was at the movies with Fabiola."

Dodge shrugged and laughed lightly. "I guess Polly told you about that. I honestly thought I'd have him back before anyone missed him. You know — no, you probably don't know how it is when you've got a kid you think the world of, and you don't get to see him often enough."

Jen stared at him blankly.

"Of course you don't. But Polly and me are going to change that. We're getting back together. Mainly for Bobby's sake for starters." The next laugh didn't ring more true than the last. "But for us, too. We'll just have to work things through."

"D'you always spill your guts to people you don't know?" Art asked, sounding too pleasant. "I don't see our Polly liking that one bit. Private, she is."

"Not about this. She's as excited as I am. We

370

talked all night. Poor kid's probably tired out."

The guy was inventing his story as he went along. And messing up as he went along, too. "You didn't try her place before coming here?" Jack asked.

Dodge hesitated before saying, "We were going to meet here. But I did try to call her. No answer. So I thought she was here for sure."

"She isn't," Mary said.

Jack reached for her hand and squeezed. There'd been an agreement among the cast and crew that no mention would be made about Polly's absence from Kirkland. Only Jack and Mary knew she hadn't left alone. Ferrito had been closed-mouthed about anything but the fact that he and Polly were going away for a few days — and that he didn't intend to say where they'd be. If the media got hold of any gossip about the nation's favorite star of a kids' show, there would be the kind of publicity Jack didn't want. Polly was squeaky clean. He intended to keep her that way.

Dodge continued to hold his ground, as if he could wear them down and make them tell him what he wanted to know.

"When Polly shows we'll tell her you came by," Jack said.

The ringing of a phone caused each of them to look around.

Sam Dodge swung his jacket forward and felt around until he produced a cell phone. He punched it on and said, "Yeah," and, "Hi, Bobby.

How's my boy?" He grinned from one member of the cast to another until he looked squarely into Jack's eyes. "Hang on a minute, son. I'll go out to my car where I can talk."

Jack barely stopped himself from grabbing for the phone.

"Why?" Sam said, frowning as he started to turn away. "No, no, don't hang up."

With her free hand, Mary gripped Jack's arm. He tightened his hold on her fingers.

"In the mountains? Sounds great. Don't you worry, your mom and I have talked, but don't tell her I'm coming. I'll surprise her." Dodge took Jack's pen from the table.

So much for Ferrito's secrecy.

"Doesn't matter, Bob. I don't remember numbers good, either. Rose's, right?" Dodge turned his back. He wrote on the flap of an envelope. "Something like that? *Belly* Rose's house? You're sure? Okay, okay. That's fine. This is going to be great. Not a word. You promise? Great. Bobby, where? . . . Oh, yeah, I know the town. It'll come to me. A railroad station. Old railroad cars. Yeah. Near a place called Bend? North Bend, maybe? Bobby? Bobby?" He removed the phone from his ear and looked at it.

"He's a liar," Mary murmured. "He couldn't have been with Polly all night."

"No," Jack said. "Don't worry about it. He's just looking to cash in on Polly's money. He won't get anything out of her. She's too smart for him."

"Look," Dodge said when he'd put the cell

phone back in his jacket pocket and torn off the envelope flap without asking. "I've taken up too much of your time. It's been great to meet all of you. Polly's talked a lot about you. When she shows up, tell her I was here, okay? Just in case I haven't caught up with her by then."

The guy actually thought none of them would figure out his game.

"Sure," Art said. "We'll tell Polly for you." He looked not at Dodge, but at Jen, who gave him a rare smile.

Sam Dodge left at a much more rapid pace than he'd arrived. Jack didn't wait for the door to close completely behind him before he said, "Okay, let's get on with it." He couldn't risk a discussion of what had just happened.

"Jack," Mary said. "That guy was lying through his —"

"None of our business," he told her, but gave her a quick hug. Peace was what he had to have if he was going to keep things on track.

Gavin picked up a second brush and tapped a tattoo on the trestle table. "Off to the circus, I say."

"What would that have to do with teaching kids about life?" Mary snapped.

"For some of us," Gavin said, "life has been a circus, my darling. In more ways than one."

"Bloody profound," Art commented.

Gavin waved his brushes. "Clowning, tumbling, high wire, trapeze. Think of the symbolism."

"You want to bring in a whole flaming circus?" Mary said.

There wouldn't be any circus segment, but the discussion served to keep agile minds off the subject of Dodge, and Polly. "A circus might have interesting possibilities," Jack said as if deep in thought.

"We wouldn't have to bring in a circus," Gavin said. "Our Aussie miracles can cover anything we need."

"I like it," Mary said, throwing herself to the potential winning side — as usual. "We learn the same values regardless of the type of life we lead. The circus performer's act becomes a parallel."

"Oh, yeah," Art said. "Honor and decency always win out, right, Mary?"

Jack didn't miss the glare Mary aimed at her most recent conquest.

"Trust, too," Gavin said. "I like this. I knew I could get in the mood of it. Trust will be the biggie. Art and Jen can do a knife-throwing act."

Art looked heavenward and shook his head.

"I mean it," Gavin said. "What takes more trust than standing there and allowing someone to hurl knives at you?"

"Drop it," Art said shortly. "We could work something out, Jack. The trapeze could be good."

"Knives," Gavin said. "I still say we do the knife thing."

Jen snatched one of his brushes away. "Why are you pushing this thing? Art and I don't do a knife act. We've never done one."

"We'd mock it up." Gavin made a grab for his lost brush but missed. "And we could be politically correct. You get to throw the knives, Jen." With his remaining brush, he pretended to aim at Art.

Art cried out and threw his forearms over his face.

"Jesus." Gavin took a step backward. "What's with him?"

Jennifer Loder went to her brother. "It's okay, Art." She caught at his sleeve and turned to Gavin. "Let it go, asshole."

"I only —"

"I told you to let it go. We lost a good friend, okay? He was knifed."

"How was I supposed to know?"

Jack smelled disaster. He smelled the disintegration of everything he'd set out to accomplish if he couldn't pull the power back into his hands.

Art dropped his arms. He went from a standstill into a series of somersaults and ended by vaulting, in a headfirst roll, over the trestle. "Gavin's a bloody marvel. That's how we'll play it, Jen. I'll be scared out of my ruddy wits and you'll win me over."

Jennifer laughed. She tossed the brush at Gavin and followed her brother's lead, tumbling and somersaulting as she went.

There was something that had to be done, Jack thought, and done very quickly. The surface shine on his cast didn't fool him. Cracks were appearing. He couldn't afford to allow *Polly's Place* to crumble and die — not yet. Soon it wouldn't matter, but he had things to accomplish first.

"Why don't we take a break," Mary said, leaning against him and looking up into his face. "Come on, Jack. Let's go home and kick back. We're both too wound up."

He considered, then said, "Mary and I are taking five, kiddies. Knock it off for a couple of hours, then meet us back here."

"Ooh, Jack and Mary are taking five for a couple of hours, kiddies," Gavin said. He caught Jack's eye, and added, "Sounds like a good idea to us, doesn't it? See you later."

Jack got Mary to the Mercedes before she started unzipping his fly. He drove with her head in his lap and managed to park in the slot under their condo building before she finished what she'd started.

Mary was always a good, predictable lay. Very predictable. She came. She slept.

He'd make sure she was exhausted enough to sleep long and deep today. And he'd be asleep beside her when she woke up.

Twenty-two

From the single room in the top of the unlikely windmill at Belle Rose, Nasty had an almost perfect view over the estate. Polly was with Rose, going through catalogues with every sign of enjoying herself.

Women were a puzzle.

Walking from one unglazed window to the next, he swept his glasses over the surrounding area. Nothing moved but trees and shrubs as they bent gently in the early-afternoon breeze.

The wisdom behind this move had been to draw the enemy into the open. And he would come — or they would come. Who the hell knew how many of them there were?

He'd made a mistake — a huge mistake.

The cell phone lay in the open lid of the case he'd brought with him. He'd be as secure using a phone as a radio from here.

He dialed, and before the first ring ended, Dusty picked up at the other end. "Room Below."

"I'm drawing trouble my way, Dust."

A slight pause. "Yeah. That's the idea."

"I've got civilians with me. Not a good idea."

"You're a civilian."

"Stay on track, Dust. If we could believe the

only target was Polly — and that the old loon, Festus, was our sole mark — dandy. But there were two divers that night. Two damn good, damn experienced divers. No rickety pseudowarlocks there. And they were after me. They tried to —"

"Do a purse-seine number on you," Dusty finished for him. "Turn you into a future fresh catch of the day. Yeah, I know."

"Neither of us are talking about it." Nasty kept his glasses trained on the house. "The South Americans. They promised they'd get me."

Dusty grunted. "You thought you heard the honcho say he'd find a way to bring you back. You were pretty much out of it with a busted-up ankle at the time. How d'you know it was him? Or that you really heard anyone at all? And how d'you know what's happening now is something to do with the Bogotá thing?"

"I know it was Emilio that night. I'd never met him, but I had heard his voice, remember. He thought I was already away, thank God. But he said he would find a way to bring me back. I think that's what's happening now. Part of what's happening."

"Did you hear any harps when the guy was promising you a return ticket to the big hacienda?"

"Don't kid around. If this is Emilio's gig, I should get the hell out of here and make sure I leave a trail."

"What changed your mind? I thought —"

"Maybe I'm not thinking as clearly as I should. I need to watch out for Polly. I've got to until I'm sure she's safe. But I won't help her or Bobby — or Rose — if I bring a couple of cartel shooters up here."

"Hold it." Sounds of Dusty pushing things aside came along the line. Then Nasty heard the doors at Down Below being locked. "Okay. Just want to be sure we don't get interrupted. Now you listen, and I talk. Got it?"

Bobby Crow emerged from the kitchen door at the back of Belle Rose. Spike shot into the open behind him and gamboled in circles. "Got it," Nasty said, distracted. "Bobby's a nice kid."

"What brought that on?"

"Forget it."

The boy meandered among rows of vegetables in the kitchen garden. He gathered stones and shied them, one by one, high into the air.

"Nasty?"

"Here."

"I'm gonna get hold of the guy who took care of things when we went to Montana for that weekend. When we went to see Marta after she was born."

Bobby wandered from the back of the house to the side closest to Nasty and sat down to take off his tennis shoes. The dog stopped running and padded up to sit beside his boss. "Why do that?" Swinging the shoes by the laces, Bobby got up and set off again, in the direction of a path through scrubby trees to the windmill.

"You're really thinking about taking off, aren't you?"

Nasty kept the glasses on Bobby and Spike. "I may have to. First I've got to figure out how to cover Polly and Bobby. He's on his way to my location right now."

"The boy?"

"Yeah. I need to pack up before he arrives. No point scaring him more than he's already scared."

"Okay. Just promise me one thing. Don't make a major move until you hear from me."

"Dust —"

"Let someone else do the thinking for once. Someone whose pants aren't cutting off his circulation."

"Dusty —"

"Be good to Bobby. He's a nice kid. You'll hear from me before dark."

Dusty hung up and Nasty knew better than to place the call again. If the bad-news feeling persisted throughout the day — and if he didn't get some flash from Dusty — he'd figure a way to cover Polly and Bobby and prepare to move on.

With the precision of long practice, he replaced his glasses and the phone in the lid of the case. He glanced at the disassembled rifle nestled in the bottom. He didn't have to hold it to sense its exact weight against his shoulder, to feel cool pressure on his cheek as he lined up along the sight. Please God he wouldn't have to use it at Belle Rose. He straightened and located Bobby immediately below.

A life without surprises, without the need to live by his wits, hadn't figured in Nasty's plans until the Navy had offered him their desk job. Then he'd had to face the future and consider what he would do with the rest of his life.

His scalp tightened. He hadn't faced the future. Even now he wasn't sure what he intended to do. Teaching weekend divers in a heated swimming pool wasn't going to cut it for much longer.

Hesitant feet brushed the wooden steps at the entrance to the mill. Set on a knoll, the blue structure had no real purpose other than decoration. Rose's father had built it because she'd told him she thought windmills were pretty. White flowers and green vines were kept freshly painted on the blades.

Spike leapt from the stairway. At the sight of Nasty, he skidded to a halt. Tail wagging hard enough to shift his entire rear end, he snuffled at the floor, then came to sniff around Nasty's legs.

"Hey, down below!" Nasty called out because he didn't want Bobby shocked by suddenly finding there was someone in the mill. "That you, Bobby?"

The footsteps stopped.

"Come on up. Wait till you see the view from up here."

"What's it for?" Bobby said, taking the steps quickly now. "It's the windmill Dusty talked about, isn't it?"

"Yup." Nasty watched Bobby's mussed towhead appear, and the boy himself. All arms and

381

legs, he was a thin boy, but tall as far as Nasty could figure. "This is the place. And it's not for anything but to look at. Rose had a dad who liked to do things to make her happy."

Bobby pulled at the neck of his baggy, striped T-shirt. "She asked for a windmill?" The shirt wanted to slide off one shoulder or the other. "Weird."

Nasty smiled. "I guess you could say that's pretty weird."

"Yeah."

A seven-year-old shouldn't be so serious. Unhappy even? "We're going fishing like Dusty promised." The feeling was foreign, the inexplicable affinity that made him say something he shouldn't say because he wanted the child to look carefree. "Maybe tomorrow."

"Mom could come, too?"

A child should not sound so flat, or look so apprehensive. "Of course your mom will come. She wouldn't stay behind. You know how she is."

"Yeah."

Nasty made a careful visual of the area around Belle Rose. If he used the glasses, he'd spook the kid. "Something on your mind?"

"Nah."

Amazing how one very small, very clear word could convey an exactly opposing message. "Want to tell me about it?"

The T-shirt wouldn't stay where Bobby put it. Finally he gathered the neck in one hand. "I want my mom to be happy."

Nasty stopped in the middle of taking a breath. "You love your mom a lot." They were the first words that came to him.

"She worries."

"Does she?"

"You're her friend." Bobby looked up at him, squinted against sunlight through an opening. "She likes you."

"Think so?" Pumping a kid, he thought ruefully. Pretty low stuff.

"Mom likes lots of people."

You deserved that, Ferrito.

"But not the way she likes you. She never talks to anyone the way she talks to you."

He hoped he looked grown-up, and honored, and a lot calmer than he felt. "I like her, too."

"She always took care of everyone. When we lived at the Point, she was the cook and Auntie Fab was the housekeeper. Grandma used to come a lot. But Mom looked after all of us."

Nasty thought he could read other meanings behind what the boy said. "Some people are like that. They're the ones who take care of other people."

Bobby had discarded his shoes — probably at the bottom of the steps. He tilted his head. "Do you have any kids?"

"No."

"Why?"

Apart from Roman and Phoenix's two little girls, one of whom was barely more than a baby,

Nasty's experience with children was about zero. "I've never been married," he said. He was going to have to work on his communication skills where kids were concerned.

"My mom and dad aren't married."

At first Nasty's mind blanked. Then he got the connection. "Well, I guess I meant I'd like . . . For myself, I'd like to be married if I was going to have kids." Oh, great. He was really doing a great job. He might as well tell the child he was a bastard, and that bastards were a bad idea.

The boy's pointed chin rose. "I would, too. When I have kids I'm gonna be married." His dog was beside him again.

Nasty caught a flash of red on the path to the windmill. He looked more closely and saw Polly coming toward the mill. She held Bobby's tennis shoes in one hand. Evidently he'd left them not on the steps, but where they'd let someone suspect he'd gone to the mill.

"You know my dad's in Kirkland now. He says he wants Mom and me."

"Does he?" Nasty gave Bobby his full attention. "Is that what you want?"

Two thin shoulders rose. "Lots of kids don't have a mom and dad — not together."

"But you wish you did."

"Yeah. I guess. My dad didn't used to want me."

In his mind, Nasty saw Sam Dodge's dissolute face. "Of course he did." What else could he say? He remembered Polly's description of the man's one previous visit to find her.

"He didn't," Bobby said. "I don't think Mom likes him. She got mad when he came before. I think she wants him to go away again."

"She'll do what's best." If he could believe he was best for Polly, he'd feel so good about that statement.

Bobby made a twisted wreck out of the neck of his shirt.

The red cotton dress Polly wore showed in flashes as she came closer.

Part of Nasty wished she would turn around and go back to the house. An equally insistent part of him longed for her to put an end to this conversation with her son.

"Mom told me you've got a funny story about your name."

"Hmm?" His focus grew sharp on the boy. "Funny? Oh, yeah — real funny. I sort of chose it."

"Your own name?" The brightness in Bobby's eyes was an improvement. "Cool. You got to choose your name. I didn't know you could do that."

"I didn't really. At least, not the way I make it sound. It was kind of a nickname when I was a kid and it stuck."

"You liked it?"

Two courses presented: truth or a lie. "I wanted to make a point. Dumb really. Some kid heard a man call me . . . nasty. The kid thought it was cute to call me nasty, too. Kind of, 'Here comes,

Nasty.' 'Yuck, Nasty's here, I can smell him.' You know the kind of thing."

Bobby's serious frown, the preoccupied way he shifted his feet apart, let Nasty know the boy knew very well how cruel children could be.

As she arrived at the mill, Polly passed from sight.

"I bet you were a big kid," Bobby said.

"Pretty big."

"You could have made the other kids call you whatever you wanted."

Nasty thought about that and smiled slightly. "Yes. In a way I did." He could almost see Polly standing at the bottom of the short flight of steps, listening. "If I had it over, I'd do it differently."

"I think Nasty's a great name."

He ruffled the boy's hair. "I think you're a great kid." A kid who'd done his share of hurting, and learned not to want the same for others.

"Why did someone call you nasty?"

"Because he thought I was, I guess."

"Why did you want to keep the name?"

Nasty glanced toward the stairway. Polly was down there, hearing every word . . . He ran a hand through his hair. This was a test. Polly was finding out how he related to her boy. "I didn't think too much of myself then. I was kind of hovering. Trying to be something, I guess. The nasty thing gave me something to be. They called me nasty, so I was. You said I was big — that I must have been a big kid. You're right. It took a while because it happened when I was pretty small. Maybe no older than you. But first I lived through what they called me. Then I grew into it." He wouldn't turn back now. "I earned my name. I was one mean son of a gun. No one got in Nasty's way."

"Didn't your mom get mad at you?"

Stopping this was a word away — maybe two or three. "I don't know what my mom thought. She worked and she slept. When she wasn't doing either of those things, she spent time with old friends." Men and booze — real old friends.

The boy's nose wrinkled. "That was tough, huh?"

"Yeah." A first. He'd never admitted to any feelings about his mother before today. "Not every kid gets a mom like you've got."

"My mom would have gotten real mad at the boy who called you names."

"It wasn't a boy. It was my father."

He and Bobby looked at each other. Nasty slid his gum into a cheek.

"You did something to make him real mad." A matter-of-fact statement from a child. Too bad the world wasn't filled with logical people like Bobby Crow. "He probably wouldn't have said it if he thought someone would hear."

"I made him real mad because I was born." Nasty laughed and the sound turned cold in his ears. "My father . . . Oh, it's history."

The boy kept right on watching his face. "He didn't want you?"

"He took off before I was born. He didn't know

I'd been born till he showed up years later looking for my mom. We'd left the ranch where I was born. I was playing on the sidewalk with some kids when he came. I heard a lot of shouting in the apartment. Then he came out and looked right at me. He said . . . well, good old Dad said a lot of things we don't have to repeat here. But he could look at me and pick me out of a bunch of kids."

"How?" Bobby gave up on the shirt and pulled it over his head. He tied it around his waist. "How could he pick you out?"

"Unfortunately I look just like him." Not wanting to, unable to stop himself, he saw the man his father had been through the eyes of the boy Nasty Ferrito had been that day. "He hated me. On sight. He asked me what my name was."

Disbelief rearranged Bobby's expression. "He didn't know your name."

"No. And when I told him, he said, 'Xavier'? and laughed. Then he said, 'What kind of fancy name is that for a nasty little bastard?' I went through a phase when I wished —" Geez, he'd been about to tell a seven-year-old that the man he was talking to had once been ornery enough to think it would be just fine if the world came right out and called him bastard on a regular basis.

"We're both bastards," Bobby said, and pressed his lips tightly together. "I know what that means."

For a few desperately intense moments Nasty

had forgotten Polly. He studied the sky outside. "We're both important," he said. "You're very important. Your mom thinks you're the most important guy in the world. I know because she told me. But I know how you feel sometimes. I've been there. You can talk to me about it, and whatever you tell me, I'll understand." This time with the child hadn't been planned, but it had been inevitable. If there was any hope for bonding between the two of them — among the three of them — it could only happen with truth as a foundation.

In the silence that followed, Bobby wrapped his arms around his ribs and screwed up his face.

"Something else on your mind?" Nasty asked. He expected to see Polly tiptoeing away again. He didn't.

Bobby blew up his cheeks and let the air out in a puff. "I'm scared."

Nasty hadn't expected that. He gave a big, phony grin. "Why would you be scared? You're on a trip. We're going to have a lot of fun —"

"I'm not a little kid. I know when people aren't saying stuff. Something's happening, isn't it?"

In this instance, Bobby *was* a little kid. "Nothing you have to worry about."

"But you and Dusty took Mom and me away because of something. You wouldn't just bring us here for a vacation. My mom should be doing the show. She never said anything about taking a vacation — not till I woke up this morning."

If Polly wanted to contradict him, she would.

"Your mom's real tired. She works hard, and this chance to get away came up. So she said she'd like to come with me and meet Rose."

The anxiety didn't leave Bobby's face. "Why didn't you and Mom let me drive with you?"

He'd never underestimate this young man again. He pointed at Spike. "The backseat of the Porsche's not big enough for you and him — not comfortably. And Dusty wanted to come up and visit Rose. They're old friends."

"He hardly stayed at all."

"Yeah." Had he been this sharp? "But he wanted to do it just the same. And he'll be back when he can get someone to look after the shop."

"Uh-huh."

Like mother, like son. They both had a thing about being talked down to. "With you gone, Dusty has to do everything himself. But we've got a man who can come in."

"Dusty said you're a lousy shopkeeper."

He controlled a grin. "I know. I just can't seem to learn. We'd better get back before your mom misses you."

"Because she's scared something could happen to me?"

Nasty gave him a thoughtful stare. "Your imagination's running away with you. Come on, Spike. How about a walk, fella?"

One of those words brought a giant bark. The dog rushed ahead and downstairs. When Nasty and Bobby arrived outside, Polly stood a little distance away with her son's tennis shoes in her hands.

"Hi, Mom."

"Hi, Bobby." She didn't smile. "I found your shoes." She held them out, and he took them.

"We were admiring the view." Nasty looked into her eyes. He swung his case. "I was going to take some pictures. The light's wrong. Bobby can hardly wait to go fishing tomorrow."

"Can't he?" To Bobby she said, "Nellie and Rose are waiting for you. They've got a surprise."

"Oh, sure," Bobby said, not quite pulling off bored disinterest. "You want me to go so you can talk to Nasty on your own."

"Bobby," Polly said — with a note of warning.

Her boy muttered, "Okay," and took off toward the house, his dog beside him.

"He's a great kid."

Tears gathered in her eyes. "The best. I heard what the two of you said."

"I thought you had."

"You told him all that to make him feel better."

"He asked questions. I told him the truth. At first I couldn't figure out why it seems so important to me for him to be happy."

She tilted up her face and sniffed. "It's because you're trying to make the child in you happy. The child you used to be."

"I'm not into psychobabble." But he was a careless fool with his mouth sometimes. "Don't cry, Polly."

"I ought to cry. My son isn't happy, and it's my fault. Parents should be able to make their children happy."

He took her tense, trembling body in his arms. She tried to pull away, but he wouldn't let her. "When you said he was the best thing that ever happened to you, you meant it. And you were right."

"Uh-huh. But I wasn't the best thing that happened to him. I gave him half of what he deserves to have."

Nasty tipped her against him and cradled her head. He rocked her gently. "He deserves the best, and he's got it. You're under a lot of pressure, or you wouldn't be doing this to yourself. One great parent is a whole lot better than two parents who don't get along — or one parent who wants you and one who tries to pretend they do. Hell, Polly, these are some of the things you people spend whole shows getting across to kids."

"So why don't I have it all straight myself?"

"You're doing fine. We'd better get going before Bobby forgets his surprise and decides to come back for us."

Polly looked up at him her eyes washed clean and bright, bright blue by the tears that were on her cheeks. He kissed the space between her brows. When he raised his face, her eyes were closed.

"Hey," he whispered. "It's easy, y'know."

"Mmm?"

"It's easy. What's happening to you and me."

"You'll have to explain that."

"Falling in love."

Her eyes snapped open.

"Like falling off a log, kid. That's about how hard it's been, isn't it?"

Her teeth dug into her bottom lip. "This isn't the time."

"Sure it is. We don't get to choose the time. That's one of the things that makes it so easy. We don't do much, and it just happens to us."

"Xavier . . ." She paused, her lips parted.

He chuckled. "I never liked my name till you started using it. When you feel really close to me, you call me Xavier. It sounds great."

"You assume an awful lot, Xavier Ferrito."

"Do I? Yes, I guess I do. I assume you love me, too."

"People don't do this nowadays."

He ducked his head until she looked at him. "What don't people do nowadays?" he asked her.

"The chaste falling-in-love thing. A few kisses. The odd touch. Then they're in love."

"A bit more than the occasional touch if I remember correctly," he pointed out. "But you're showing your ignorance, sweetheart. Obviously you're hopelessly out-of-date. We're doing the chaste — the more or less chaste falling-in-love thing, aren't we?"

"You're pushing me."

"Aren't we?"

Polly undid several of his shirt buttons and slipped her hands inside. She stroked his chest, moved in close, and rested her mouth on his breastbone.

Shaking her carefully, he spoke into her hair. "Answer me. We're in love. You know it, and I know it. Don't we?"

"Yes," she whispered. Her mouth moved to one of his nipples. With the very tip of her tongue she teased him. "Oh, yes."

Nasty settled his hands around her neck. Controlling the urge to crush her to him was tough. He rubbed his fingers up and down the back of her neck. "You are a chest woman, okay, sweet Polly. And I love you."

She became absolutely still.

"I love you, and I want you with me. We're going to work that one out."

Her hands fell slowly to his waist. "I think I'd like that. But I've got some things to get through first."

"Anything that affects you, affects me." It was true. Every other thing in his life might be on a vaguely uncertain foundation, but not this. "Festus could have taken off. We may never hear from him again. But if we do, I'll be right there."

"Nasty, I don't think it was Festus who attacked me at the condo. And I don't think he was the one who knocked me in the water."

"Just let me do the thinking."

"No!" She backed off, and he saw pure fury in her eyes. "I thought you'd got the message about treating me like a child. I'm not your responsibility. You can't kiss it and make it better for me.

I've got to think about Bobby."

"We'll both think about Bobby."

Shaking her head, she walked backward. "I want you. I want you so much. But I will do what I think is best. If that means I need to go away, I'll do it."

"Polly —"

"I won't do something dramatic like sneaking away without you knowing. I'll tell you I'm going. But it won't do you any good to try to stop me."

"The hell it won't." He caught one of her hands. "No. You understand me. *No.* You are not to even think about going anywhere without me. Got it?"

"I'm going back to the house. Those two nice women must really wonder what the deal is. Two complete strangers dropped on them like this."

He knew a flash of fear. The sensation stopped him. "Rose is no stranger to trouble. She's had her share." This was why he'd chosen to be alone for so long. When you had no one who waited for you, no one you waited for, the only time you were afraid was when you looked at the wrong end of a weapon.

Polly pulled on his hand. He started walking, kept on walking with her beside him. "Promise you won't do anything dumb."

"I'll do what I think is best. I can't stay here. It's not right."

"Please, Polly. I hate to use this, but it's true anyway. If you leave, Rose will think she's done something to upset you. Dusty told her you've been working too hard and need a rest. She's doing what she does so well — making you comfortable. And she's loving it."

She didn't appear to be listening. "Bobby will be safer if I'm not with him."

The next phase of his new sensations hit. Panic. "Safety in numbers. Remember that? And you'd never be able to rest unless you could watch over him yourself."

"Would you do something for me?"

"Anything."

"You watch over him. Just till this is over. I know you can keep him safe — but not as long as I'm a magnet for trouble."

A magnet? She thought she was the magnet? He almost laughed. "Dusty's coming back. I don't think there's anything major to worry about, but I do understand where you're coming from. Let's wait for Dusty and make some decisions then."

"Because you know this is bigger than we thought, don't you?"

He sure did. "No. I think it's all going to blow over. But you won't believe that until it happens. There's Nellie. Wave. I don't want her to sense anything. She's not as tough as Rose."

"Rose is tough?" She said it as if she thought he was mad.

"In her way. She's a bright woman who knows she's got hang-ups. She copes with that." And he'd seen her hold up under pressure in the past. "Wave."

Dutifully, Polly waved at Nellie, who stood on the veranda. "There you are," she called when they drew closer. "Bobby said you were coming back from the mill."

He shaded his eyes and smiled at her. "Let me guess. Rose is ready for some tea, and she's missing us." To Polly he murmured, "Something you two have in common. You're both tea lovers."

"There's a phone call for you," Nellie said. "He said he'd hang on while I came to find you."

Nasty looked at Polly. "I bet that's Dusty." They hurried after Nellie, who went inside the house.

He picked up a telephone receiver that lay on a delicate table in the hall. "Hello." No one answered.

"Is it Dusty?" Polly said.

"I don't know. He hung up. What did he say, Nellie?"

"Nothing really," she told him. "He didn't ask for you. He wanted to speak to Polly."

Twenty-three

So she'd told a lie. Or he might consider she had. But when she'd told Nasty she wouldn't do anything major without telling him, she'd meant it. That was before the call — and the evening of waiting while nothing happened. Nothing but Nasty getting a call from Dusty, which he'd taken in private and showed no sign of telling her about.

You did what you had to do, and she needed to put distance between herself and Bobby. She trusted Nasty to do what she couldn't ask of her mother. He'd keep her son safe.

Crumb, he'd be furious when he realized what she'd done.

He'd just have to be furious.

Thank goodness the evening had been short. Rose playing her white grand piano. Nellie listening and smiling. Nasty secretly making funny faces at Bobby, who had coughed a great deal.

The house was utterly still. Rose had given Polly a sweet room beneath the eaves with twin dormer windows overlooking the front of the estate. A light down quilt and rose-scented linens turned the double bed into a soft bower against one wall. Too bad Polly couldn't relax and enjoy the sensation.

Bobby slept on the floor below, with Nasty in

the next room. Rose had a suite at the opposite end of the house, and Nellie was using a room near her old friend.

After changing into jeans and a T-shirt, Polly had slipped beneath the quilt and waited for this moment. The few essentials — money, credit cards, driver's license — were in the pocket of her windbreaker on a chair by the door. She wouldn't take anything else. With luck, she wouldn't be missed even first thing in the morning. If someone came looking for her, they'd assume she'd gone out for a walk.

She threw back the quilt, mussed the rest of the covers, switched on the flashlight so thoughtfully provided on the bedside table, and pushed her feet into tennis shoes. The batteries must be conserved. Polly turned off the light and tied her shoes by feel in the dark.

Treading softly, she crossed to the nearest window and peeked out between the airy, floral drapes. Her tummy squeezed. So dark. She'd decided to walk into Past Peak and go to that diner to make a call for a taxi. Nasty had said Rose's house was about three miles out of town. Now that she'd made the trip, she knew that all she had to do was get to the road outside the estate — Mill Pond Road — turn right to 202, then go left into Past Peak.

Simple.

Simply horrible, darn it. She didn't even know where to tell the taxi to take her.

Back to Kirkland?

To Hole Point and her mother?

To Fab's place?

She crossed her arms on the wall near the window and rested her head. What would the police say if she asked them for help? They'd want to know what had changed since she last spoke with them. She had nothing concrete to tell them.

Belinda might be able to help. At least she could tell Polly if Festus had made contact.

"Go," she whispered to herself. *"Just do it."*

Polly pushed away from the wall and turned around — and a big hand, pressed over her mouth, stifled her scream. Her knees buckled, but she wasn't allowed to fall.

A painfully solid arm around her body, and a big, hard hand over her mouth, kept her on her feet.

"I think I've made my point," Nasty whispered into her ear. "Every thought you have walks across your lovely face. I'm getting very good at knowing what those thoughts are."

She shook her head.

Nasty rested his jaw against her temple. "Yes, Polly. *Yes.* I am a professional. I was a professional. I was trained to sniff trouble in the wind — and to see it in the crook of a finger, or the flicker of an eyelid. When you said good night to Bobby, you're eyelids weren't just flickering, kid — you were blinking so rapidly I wasn't sure you'd see enough to make your way up here."

Polly mumbled into his palm.

His breath was warm on her skin. "Screaming

would be pointless. You're among friends. My friends. Do we understand each other?"

She'd like to cry. Now that would be really stupid. She nodded yes, and he removed his hand at once. He didn't release her.

Polly stood still, her face close enough to feel the subtle shift of blood and breath beneath his skin.

"I'm so pissed at you, lady."

She winced.

"What the? . . . What did you think you were going to do out there?"

"Nothing," she said, very, very quietly. "I was just taking a look out of the window."

"You are a rotten liar."

"I am not. I never tell lies."

"Exactly." He shook her once, and held her so hard, with both arms, she could scarcely take a breath. "You are a rotten liar. As in you are no good at telling lies. A woman who gets out of bed to look out of the window isn't usually already dressed. And she doesn't usually stop to put on shoes and tie them real good and tight."

She began to shake. "How do you know that?"

"You interrupted my nap."

"Nap?"

"The one I was having when you threw back the quilt."

"You couldn't know I'd done that," she said, incensed. "Don't make things up. Where . . . Where were you?"

"You got out of bed and put on the flashlight.

Then you turned off the flashlight and tied your shoes in the dark. Never mind how I know, or where I was. I was waiting for you to do what you did because I knew you would. I saw you making your plans downstairs."

Anger totally replaced shock. "Congratulations. It's nice to know we train our armed forces to gang up on innocent people."

"One man can't be a gang."

"I have every right to get out of my bed and look —"

"Hush," he said. "Don't raise your voice. You told me you wouldn't try anything without talking to me first."

"I knew you'd say that."

"You lied to me."

"I knew you'd say that, too. The situation changed. When I said what I said, I didn't know that crazy man had already found me."

She heard his teeth come together, and the way he expelled a breath — hard. "Damn it, Polly."

"I've got to make up my own mind about —"

"No, you don't." He gripped her shoulders. "What the hell do you think you're playing with here? Some asinine monster characters from the show? This is for real. This is insanity."

"I know —"

"No, you don't. If you did, you wouldn't even consider putting on the martyr act."

Polly tried to draw herself up. "I'm not a martyr."

"You would be if you went out there and ended

up dead. What about us? What about Bobby and me? Don't we matter?"

She mustn't cry. "I was going because of . . . Okay, it was dumb."

His hold on her relaxed slightly. "Yeah. Real dumb."

"I'm sorry."

"Good." He stroked her arms. "Oh — oh, damn it all. You're shaking. Are you cold?"

"Cold?" Polly covered her own mouth then repeated softly, "Cold? Crumb! I'm absolutely terrified. Shocked. It's shock that's making me shake. If someone crept up on you in the dark, you'd shake."

"I never found that particularly helpful."

Wild laughter threatened. "You're like something out of a film. One of those films about men with black stuff on their faces who run around in jungles. Wading through mud with a machine gun held over your head. *Shaking wouldn't be particularly helpful?*" She did laugh then. It bubbled up in bursts that racked her.

"Okay," Nasty said. "Easy does it. It's okay, sweetheart. We'll consider this a useful exercise, shall we? Come on, sit on the bed."

"We'll consider this a useful exercise?" She laughed afresh. "You — you're not real. Watch it!"

He lifted her, and twisted them both, and — with the sensation of flying — she landed on top of him on the bed.

They lay there, quiet, listening — each to the

subtle living sounds of the other.

"How did you do that?" Polly asked when she couldn't bear the silence any longer.

"I don't remember."

Her face was inches from his, but she could see nothing but the glint of his eyes and teeth — and the suggestion of sharply defined bone. "Your ankle's pretty much perfect again, isn't it?"

"It'll have to do."

More silence.

"You're beautiful, Xavier." Where did words come from?

"Only you would call me beautiful."

"Why?"

"Because no one ever loved me the way you do."

Her heart had stopped. Of course it had. There was no way it could still be beating.

"You don't decide, do you, Polly? You just say what comes to mind."

"When I'm with you. I think you give me some kind of drug when I'm not looking."

She felt him chuckle, felt the vibration in his chest. "Truth serum," he said. "Shucks, and I didn't think you'd ever catch me."

"Truth serum? You make up your mind I love you. Then you tell me I love you. You don't know that, Xavier."

"I'm sure you're comfortable," he said. "It's a bit of a tight fit for me sideways on a double bed."

She let her face fall against his neck. "If you

think lying on top of a very hard man's comfortable, think again."

His body jerked beneath her.

"What?" She raised her head and tried — a totally wasted effort — to shake him. "What are you laughing about?"

"Oh, there's just something about the innocent way you walk into some things. Sorry I'm too . . . uncomfortable for you. We'll fix it."

Without giving her a chance to comment, he made another seamless move. Polly came gently to rest between the wall — and Nasty.

"You're not going anywhere," he said. "Not tonight. Not ever. Unless I'm with you — until this thing's over."

Polly tried to order her thoughts. "This isn't what I'd planned."

"Evidently."

"I was going to put some distance between Bobby and me. I really do think that's a good idea. He'll be safer away from me."

"Very reasonably put. At this point, if Bobby's in danger, he's in danger — with or without you around. I don't think he is."

Polly stiffened. "I'd better go down and check on him."

"Dusty's got the watch."

She tried to see him. "Dusty's back here?"

"Yes. We'll take it in turns to get some sleep."

"This is your turn."

"Was. I don't think it's going to happen, do you?"

A flush stole over her. "It's okay now. I promise I won't try anything else silly."

"You think I'd believe you after the stunt you just tried to pull?"

"I was confused. I'm not confused anymore. What I tried to do wasn't too smart."

"Admit you love me."

"I shouldn't have shoes on. They'll ruin the quilt."

"I've got shoes on, too. I don't care. Quit changing the subject."

"For a quiet man, you can really run off at the mouth."

"Oh, nice. One minute you tell me you love me, the next minute you insult me."

He muddled her up. "I didn't tell you I love you."

His hand settled on her neck. He played his thumb along her jaw, across her ear.

"Well, I didn't," she said. Even her whisper was breaking up. "I didn't."

"Do it, then."

"You didn't want to get out of the Navy."

"No." He sighed. "But I didn't want the desk job they offered me after my ankle was shot up. Now I'm getting used to the idea."

"Why are you?"

"You're pushing me." Warm, clean breath preceded his lips by only a second. He kissed her chin, the corner of her mouth, her jaw — her ear. And he held her tighter when she shuddered. "But I want something from you, and I'll keep on answering questions till I get it. That's why I'm finally settling down with the idea of being a civilian for the rest of my life. Because of you. I want you — to be with you. I'll be good for you — and Bobby. You won't regret loving me."

"When you were injured someone was trying to kill you."

He growled softly. "I'll wear you down. Yeah, someone was trying to kill me. Some people. Bad people."

"And you killed them."

"One of them. The one I managed to reach with a knife. There are still too many left. Too many drugs making too much money for people like them. Not just in Bogotá — or South America in general. In just about any country you want to name. But I've done my bit for the cause. Other men have taken over. I've got to spend my time looking after the woman who loves me, now."

She found his mouth with her fingertips. "The woman who loves you? What about adding that she's the woman you love, too."

"Oh, I do love her, too. I've already told her that."

A cotton T-shirt felt so nice layered on Xavier Ferrito. "You've got such a body," she told him, and rolled her eyes in the darkness.

"You've got such a body, too," he said promptly. "See, I told you I wasn't going to get that sleep, didn't I?"

"You're presumptuous."

"How can I be. You just told me you love me."

"I did not."

"You can't back off now. You wanted me to tell you I love you, too, and I did."

"I —" Somehow none of this was funny. "This is very serious stuff."

He nuzzled his nose and mouth into her shoulder, just above the saggy neck of her T-shirt. "Very serious. I'm going to have to get my act together."

Polly breathed through her open mouth. "What does that mean?"

"No more drifting. I'm going to have to grow up and decide what will be best for my family. Have you ever thought you'd like to live on a ranch?"

He was going too fast. Or deliberately trying to confuse her. "You've got a dive shop."

"Dusty's got it. I've got a financial stake, and I fool around. Suddenly I've got ambition."

"You've killed people."

He grew still. Then he slipped an arm beneath her and gathered her up until she lay half on top of him again. "I was a soldier. Can you think of it that way? A soldier following orders. That's the only way it works. If you're a soldier and you don't follow orders, you can bring down the people on your side."

The full-up feeling swelled again. Full-up and ready to overflow into tears. "I hate violence. And there's Bobby. I worry —"

"Bobby will be himself. He's going to make you

408

a proud mother. He'll probably drive you nuts first — the way he's supposed to — but what I have, or haven't been, won't change him. Although he'll know the man his mother loves is honorable and expects honor in others."

"Politics," Polly said.

"Huh?"

"Go into politics. You are so sincere. You could be handing out drugs yourself, and the pope would believe it was for the good of mankind."

"I'm telling the truth, my love."

Much more of this and she'd forget all of her reasons for not wanting to love him. "You're exciting. I'm dull."

His lips parted on her neck, and remained parted.

"A man like you would get so sick of a scared little rabbit of a woman who" — she steeled herself — "who can't swim because she's afraid of the water. It's because there are things down there."

"We're going to take these points one-by-one. But we're going to have to take them quickly."

Polly blushed — again. "Of course. I'm keeping you up."

His chest vibrated — again.

"What?"

"You are unbelievable — but you do have a way of getting right to the point. You are not dull. You're a gifted — an incredibly talented singer. And a personality. I guess that's what you'd call

409

it. The lingo's pretty foreign to me, but the woman who loves me will help put that right."

He was steadily turning her resolve, what resolve she'd ever had, to mush. "We shouldn't have shoes on. We'll ruin the quilt."

"We already did that one. You are so lovable on that screen. No wonder you amaze so many people. They can't believe someone wholesome can compete with what kids are *supposed* to prefer. Crap."

"I'm hot."

"Me, too, sweets. Oh, me, too."

He was playing with her. "No, I'm not. I was just saying that to change the subject."

"That is the subject, sweetcakes."

She didn't know whether to laugh or punch him. "Don't ever call me that again. Not if you want to live."

"And I thought I was the horrible killer here. What things down there?"

Things. "Oh, down there. In the water. There are things down there. I could always feel them sneaking around, lying in wait. Slimy things."

"Like me?"

"You're not slimy. You're lovely."

"Thanks. So are you. Swimming pools aren't usually stocked with *things*."

"We didn't have any swimming pools around when I was growing up." She'd prefer not to pursue the subject of her lean childhood.

"Fair enough. I'll help you get over it. You must be able to swim."

"I *must* not. And I'm not going to. End of topic."

"For now. Tell me you love me."

She was hot — hot enough to melt. "Shoes shouldn't —"

"Forget the shoes," he said, stroking her face again. "Men don't expect women to call them beautiful. Or lovely."

"Any woman who saw you —" *Learn to think first, speak after thinking.*

Xavier followed his fingers with his mouth, followed down her neck, beneath the T-shirt to her shoulder. "Any woman who saw me, what?"

She was only a mortal woman with mortal reactions. Wanting a man this much came from just being human. "Naked," she told him, and tried to bow her head.

"Oh, you do know how to cool a situation down. And I thought you hadn't noticed."

"You didn't have any clothes on." The squeakiness of her voice made her feel foolish. "I didn't know what to do. Stay, or go."

"You stayed."

She didn't have to see his face to know he was silently laughing at her. "You'd have stayed, too."

"You really looked, then, you wicked woman you. I'm glad Seven covered all the naughty bits."

Polly clamped a hand over her mouth to stifle laughter.

Keeping his face buried in her shoulder, he found a way under the T-shirt to smooth her back.

"Naughty bits?" Polly managed to say. "She didn't cover anything quickly enough."

"No wonder you could hardly wait to get your hands on me the next time. Pretty impressive, huh?"

A quiet wrapped her, wrapped her inside. Quiet need, quiet certainty — quiet, demanding, gathering desire. "Did you mean it? What you said?"

"That I love you, and that I'm going to stick to you from here on? I meant it? Did you?"

"You knew what I was asking you without —"

"Don't . . . Don't, Polly. Not anymore. I can't keep this up."

"I can't either." Pushing herself up, she settled herself on her elbows and rested her forehead on his. "I love you."

His hand stopped moving on her back.

"I never loved a man before. I know because I've never felt what I feel now before you."

"Polly." He made her name a caress.

"Can you stand it if I say something really sloppy."

"Please. From you, I'm going to be crazy about sloppy."

An urge to crawl all the way on top of him shook her. "Okay, here goes. I never loved a man before because I hadn't met you. So I couldn't, could I?"

"We understand each other so well. What do you think about ranching?"

She kissed him — hard. And kissed him again

412

— not so hard — opened his mouth easily, explored his tongue with hers — so very easily. Falling. The bonding of their lips drew her into a fall. She collapsed onto his chest and heard a groan deep in the back of his throat.

Gasping, she pulled back again. "Stop trying to force yourself into decisions you don't have to make in a hurry."

"Whoa. Such a long sentence. How'd you do that when all you want to do is get inside my clothes."

"Stop!"

"Sorry. I meant all I want . . . Forget it. No, don't forget it. I'm prepared."

She flattened herself on top of him and hugged hard. "You embarrass me."

"I embarrass me sometimes. But I thought you'd like to know. Ever since I knew you loved me, I've been prepared."

"Don't say it again," she told him in a small voice.

"Would you consider having more children?"

Polly closed her eyes, squeezed them tightly shut. "Do you have to deal with the whole thing right now? All of it?"

"You love me?"

"Yes."

"That'll do for now."

"Kiss me."

He lay absolutely still for a moment. The next moment he lifted her from him and set her on her back and sat up beside her. She saw his white

T-shirt shimmy upward over wide bands of muscle. And she saw the shirt fly through the air. She'd grown more accustomed to the darkness. His skin glistened faintly.

"Hot," he said, turning and bending over her. "That's a bit better. And I know how you feel about chests."

"Only your chest," she told him, aware of a possibly terminal shortage of air.

The touch of his lips on hers was so light it tingled. He held still, his mouth barely meeting hers, while tension built. Polly felt the crushing in of pressure and knew he felt it, too. She rolled her head, carefully, slowly, from side to side under Xavier's and heard another stifled groan.

At his sides, the skin was smooth. His back rippled beneath her hands. His chest pressed hers. She wanted to be naked — skin against skin with him.

Framing her face, holding her head still, he kissed her with power, and with finesse. He kissed her and murmured formless words that inflamed her — formless words that meant more than any she'd ever heard.

"You're crying," he whispered.

"No, I'm not."

His lips and tongue settled briefly on her left temple. "Yes, sweetheart. I taste your tears."

"I'm happy. I so happy, I'm scared."

"It isn't going to go away." Again he found her mouth, kissed her deeply, tenderly. "This love won't stop, Polly. I know it."

"Because of your famous instinct?"

"Mmm. Yeah."

"I'm too warm."

"What d'you want to do about it?"

"Take off my shirt."

With his face resting beside hers, he sighed. "If everything stopped right now, it would be fine with me."

"You don't want me to take off my shirt?"

She heard laughter in his voice. "I want you to take off everything. And if we never leave this room again, fine. That's what I meant."

Xavier took off her shirt. And her bra.

The air was cool but didn't ease the burning in her breasts. Neither did the big man's careful, clever fingers, or his mouth on her nipples.

Polly drove her elbows into the soft mattress, let her head fall back — tried to press herself deeper into his mouth.

He did nothing in a hurry.

Almost lazily, he rose and swung a leg over her until he knelt above her. He took her mouth, then kissed each inch of exposed skin, with concentrated care. Spreading his hands over her ribs, he slid gradually upward to span the undersides of her breasts.

"Xavier. I love you." How easy it was to say it. "You're going . . . No, I can't think. I love you."

"You and I are in love. And I never even knew what I was waiting for until there was you."

She felt her own wetness, and the throbbing ache between her legs — and the searing openness of nerve between breast and deep in her belly.

Xavier pushed her breasts together and buried his face between them. He took first one nipple, then the other, into his mouth and brought her writhing off the mattress again.

A shard of reason tried to insinuate itself, and she turned her face toward the door.

"Locked," he told her, and returned to driving her mad.

Power must be exerted according to ability. Polly unsnapped the waist of his jeans and drew in an audible breath.

Xavier made a harsh sound. He stopped moving.

"Hard," Polly muttered. "You give new meaning to the word. This must be painful."

"Less painful now," he told her. "This kind of pain I could come to need. All the time."

"You'd kill us both." He filled her two hands and she felt the pulsing of blood, the readiness of male seed. "I want you."

He undid her jeans and worked them down her legs, taking her panties with them.

The jeans made it past her knees before she made him help her free him almost as much as she wanted him freed.

Naked would take too long.

He dealt with the condom while she tried not to listen.

They both guided him to her, but then Xavier gently pushed her hands away.

Polly tensed for the stretching, the forcing she'd

welcome. Instead, he only nudged himself just into her entrance. And spreading his knees, he held himself there, and kissed her breasts again, curving over her, taking time she knew cost him dearly — as dearly as it cost her even as she loved him for it, reveled in it.

The pad of his thumb settled inside slick folds and moved in tight inflaming circles.

"Xavier!" She choked back a sob. "Oh, please."

"Shush, sweetheart. This is good. It's all good. Take it."

Polly took it with hips that wouldn't remain on the bed. She took it, and took it — and gritted her teeth with the pure, scalding ecstasy of it.

The circles grew even smaller, even tighter — and broke the center of the white-hot tension that kept her hovering short of climax. Before she'd finished keening out her satisfaction, while wanton gratification still gathered in erogenous skin and tissue, Xavier thrust his penis so deep inside her she convulsed with shock at the invasion.

"Okay?" he asked quietly, waiting with more of that control no man could be expected to find, not now.

"Okay," she murmured, and raised her hips toward him. "Love me, Xavier."

He gave a single, keening cry and lost the battle with himself. Too few strokes, and he muttered something she couldn't make out. He muttered, and emptied, and Polly couldn't stop the fresh tears. She pushed her fingers into his thighs, guided his legs until they rested between hers.

"Too fast, damn it," he said, breathless.

"That time," she told him. "Stay right where you are for just a little while, and we'll do it slower."

"Oh, sweet Polly."

Seconds passed, and minutes. He stroked her breasts — lazily at first. Then less lazily.

She felt him begin to tighten within her. "It's magic. I told you this would work."

"Geesh. Can we just stay like this forever?" His teeth came together audibly. "Can we do this again and again."

"And again," she said, squeezing her muscles around him.

"Mercy! Have a little mercy, my love. We're going to take our time, remember."

Polly squeezed some more. "I think it's out of our hands. Don't worry. We just need more practice. Sooner or later we'll get it right. I think it's the tennis shoes."

"Huh?"

"The tennis shoes. There's something about making love with your pants around your ankles. Very sexy. Makes it tough to be restrained."

"Oh, yeah." He gasped and fell into the rhythm she set. "Sexy, sexy. So sexy."

"Feels kind of forbidden."

"Yeah. *Polly* — I'm coming apart."

"Oh! Yes. *Yes.* Tennis shoes forever. You can't take your jeans off with tennis shoes on."

Twenty-four

He turned over and sat up.

Zero. Dead, cold zero sleep, to snapping awake. In less time than he knew how to measure.

He frowned and listened — illuminated his watch face to check the time. They couldn't have fallen asleep more than half an hour earlier. Polly breathed softly and deeply beside him.

Nasty smiled and bent to kiss her bare shoulder.

A sound had awakened him. A sound and a presence. Not here, not in the house, but outside.

Careful not to disturb Polly, he got out of bed and crossed to the window — and heard rain on the glass. He grimaced. The sound of rain had been rare in recent weeks, so rare he hadn't slept through it as he usually would.

It had rained that night in Bogotá. Warm rain, steaming earth, leaves that shone in the darkness and dripped on him as he crawled beneath them.

Out of habit, he was careful to stand beside the window, flat to the wall, and to lift the drapes so no movement could be noted from the outside.

Floodlights sent out beams at intervals around the house, cut a swath of light that faded into a wall of blackness some yards away.

The floods went out.

Nasty rolled away from the window. The lights

were one of Rose's more recent innovations. She was proud of them. They were left on all night, not for safety — which was why Dusty had persuaded her to have them — but because they made the house "look pretty."

Damn, he should never have let his guard down, not for a second, while he knew there was danger. He did know there was danger. It hadn't made any of the expected patterns, but it hovered. Without the incident with the divers, he'd have said the entire affair had an amateur stamp. But there had been the divers.

He saw Polly move just before she said, "What's the matter?"

"Probably nothing." This was the tough part. He wasn't sure how someone like Polly would react to confronting an unseen force. She'd come through a near drowning without breaking — endured the attack at her condo without completely falling apart. "I need to get to Dusty's location. I'd like you to dress — quickly — so I can leave you with Bobby."

The bedding rustled. He saw her put on clothes as she found them. He grabbed his jeans and pulled them on, and his T-shirt. His knife and its sheath were with his black nylon jacket, close to the door. His Sauer was just under the bed.

"Is someone in the house?" Polly whispered. She sounded steady.

"I don't think so. I do think we could have trouble."

"I want to get to Bobby."

"You will. I'm going to put Rose and Nellie with you, too."

"Should I have a gun? I expect you've got —"

"No. You don't know how to use a gun. And you won't need one." He hoped to God he was right. "Ready?"

She touched his back, and said, "Yes. Just tell me what to do."

As he opened the door, he saw the on/off flick of a flashlight. Dusty had arrived at the bottom of the stairs leading to the two third-floor rooms above a central gallery on the second floor.

Nasty put Polly behind him and slipped swiftly down beside Dusty.

"Could be nothing," the older man said.

"You let me go past my watch."

"I didn't know wake-up calls were part of the deal these days."

He deserved that.

"I heard something before the lights went out," Dusty said.

"That makes two of us."

"Someone threw the circuit. The box is in the laundry room. I left it."

Nasty nodded. "Good move."

"There's no obvious evidence of entry, but someone came in. I'd lay odds they went straight back out."

"To draw us outside," Nasty said. "Go in with Bobby, Polly. Try not to wake him up. Easier that way. Dust, I'll stay here while you get Rose and Nellie."

Dusty was already on his way, keeping low to skirt the gallery that was open to the foyer below.

"The dog doesn't bark?" Nasty asked.

"Usually. If a stranger comes."

Nasty considered. "He's not on home ground. I guess that could make a difference."

"I think he'd bark if someone new was in the house." She sounded relieved, and he hoped she'd stay that way.

"Good. Go in there now." He turned the door handle silently and opened just enough space for her to slip through. He caught her arm and bent to kiss her mouth. "This is probably a false alarm."

"I love you, Xavier."

He smiled. "I know. The feeling's mutual. Always will be."

"Please don't go outside."

Another foreign experience. Someone worried about him for other than practical reasons. "Spike didn't bark," he said lightly. "Don't worry. I'll just check around to be sure."

"Someone turned off the lights."

"Maybe they were never on."

"Damn it, Xavier. I'm not a kid. You and Dusty just talked about the lights going out, and the circuit being thrown."

He would need to keep a few steps farther ahead with this woman. "Okay. Sorry. Where are they?" he asked Dusty, who returned without Rose or Nellie.

"Won't budge," he said irritably. "Fool

422

women. You can't reason with 'em. Rose says she and Nellie are staying put in her rooms. We're to let them know when this *foolishness* is over."

"Shit," Nasty said with feeling. "You'll have to stay central. I'll be as quick as I can. Polly — in and close the door."

"No." Panic was there now. "You can't go outside. How do you know what's there?"

"He doesn't," Dusty said for him. "This is just precaution. A check around doors and windows inside to make sure there's been no entry. A —"

"No need to go into the minor details," Nasty said quickly, afraid Polly would freak out.

"There certainly is a need. Dusty's already established that someone came in, Xavier."

Dusty made no attempt to stifle a snicker.

Nasty said, "We're wasting time."

"Then he'll make a circle around the outside of the house. And when he comes back, no one will know he's moved — inside or outside. Will they, *Xavier?*"

"His ankle," Polly said. "He doesn't do this sort of thing anymore."

Nasty swore under his breath. "That's enough, Dust. Save the fun for later. Think of soft landings, Polly. And tennis shoes. I'm not a complete cripple yet."

He left visualizing the expression on her face and drawing satisfaction from knowing he'd at least got the color right. He didn't need to see the blush to be sure it was there.

The inside check was accomplished rapidly and

without incident. Rather than a door, he chose a window in the pantry as his route outside. The chance that he was dealing with professionals was better than fifty-fifty. Still, he had nothing to lose by hoping whoever was playing unpleasant games was too green to expect a man to crawl through a window rather than open a door and walk out.

He landed softly behind bushes in the bed that ran along the back of the house. The hood on his jacket unfurled to cover most of his face, as well as his head. With the collar closed tightly, he was virtually invisible. For once he blessed the rain that turned earth at his feet to mud. Bracing himself on the side of the house, he scuffed the slimy mix over his white tennis shoes.

No identifiable noise reached him, other than the steady drum of rain on the glass roof of a nearby greenhouse, and the shifting of leaves and branches — and small life — in trees and bushes.

If someone was waiting for him to make a move, they'd be in close. He had no way of guessing what location they'd chosen — or even if they were still in the area. He did what he'd been trained to do in similar circumstances — crouched and moved swiftly, not thinking about percentage chances anymore, just moving and making repeated visual checks behind him.

The rain grew even heavier.

Distant lightning swelled in a brief silver haze and faded quickly. A faint crackle of summery thunder was a long time coming.

He reached a back corner where trees came all

the way to the house. The scent of soaked pines and mulch flooded the air.

Nasty stumbled, and stopped. His heart pummeled his ribs. The ground was torn up here. Using even his hooded flashlight wasn't an option. He sank to a crouch and felt the soil. Practice allowed him to find what he'd expected: footprints. But not a single set. More than one man had tramped — recently — in the dirt beneath a window into a small storage room. He looked up. The window wasn't open.

Whoever had been here had either made it inside and closed the window — or left. He had to know which, and the only way to find out was by using the light.

With the Sauer in his right hand, he took the flashlight down to ground level and switched it on. A brief swing of the beam along the side of the house and back told him the story.

One intruder had come, gone in through the window, and left. That would be the man throwing the circuit to get Nasty outside. That was a given now.

The guy had started away, but someone else had shown up, bringing him back. There'd been a scuffle, and the two had left, one man pulling the other.

Straightening, he slid the switch off almost immediately and stared out at the wall of trees.

"Yo, Nasty."

He whipped around, gun braced, before the whisper completely registered.

"Friend," Roman Wilde murmured. "Easy."

Nasty lowered the gun, and the man he'd trust with his life — and anyone else's — arrived beside him. They stood silent, shoulder to shoulder.

Dusty would have some fast talking to do. Later. Nasty used the flashlight again, and turned it off again the instant he'd traced the marks in the earth for Roman to see.

Without a word, they put distance between them and struck out into the trees. Radio contact would be nice, but Nasty didn't have to see his friend to feel his presence, and to know he did exactly what must be done.

Civilians didn't do dark real well. Another point in favor of a pro. He narrowed his eyes. The smell was different, but he felt again the brush of other plants, vine-draped plants, on his skin. There had been no light that night either.

Another sizzling stroke of lightning struck — much closer. For an instant a suggestion of a glow penetrated the trees. It faded before thunder rushed in its wake.

Nasty crept onward, placing each foot, heel and toe, progressing so slowly his nerves jumped with tension. They could use an entire damn unit.

The next ripple of lightning came. For several seconds white light painted a path between the trees, over fallen trunks and jagged snags. And it touched something that moved.

Then all was blackness again.

Thunder roared, so close the ground trembled.

Nasty pulled his left sleeve high enough to expose the handle of his knife and stroked the trigger of the Sauer. Someone was ahead of him, and it wasn't Roman. Roman wouldn't be upright and in motion when lightning hit.

As swiftly as he dared, Nasty went forward. The lightning had provided a rough mental map of the immediate terrain. He reached the first fallen tree he'd seen and touched rough, wet bark. He wouldn't fire first. Neither would Roman. But if the mark gave one tiny excuse, the rules became the ones Nasty knew best. He unsheathed the knife and went forward with it in his left hand. On the night he'd lost his job, pain and shock had also cost him his gun. His knife had become a precious companion he had treated with utmost respect ever since.

He stumbled over something and flailed.

An arm surrounded his neck, clamped it in the crook of a steel-hard elbow, and jerked him backward. "No sound." The man behind him whispered against Nasty's hood. "Very quiet, very careful. No problems."

The cold clarity he needed slid around his brain. No time for cursing whatever wrong step he'd taken getting to this point. He dropped his right hand to his side.

"No," the voice said, at the same instant as unyielding metal slammed into the back of Nasty's hand.

He kept his grip on the gun. The second blow knocked it free.

"Better," he was told softly. "We will move

backward a few steps, then turn to your left."

There had to be a reason this joker wasn't putting a bullet through his head. He allowed himself to be guided back a step, another, another. Then he lifted a foot and brought the heel down on the toes of the man who held him.

A muffled cry escaped and the grip on his neck loosened a fraction.

Nasty twisted around and tossed his knife from his left to his right hand.

"No!"

Darkness collected and changed shape. A head and shoulders came at Nasty, connected with his belly. He grappled and cocked his arm, ready to strike with the knife.

The other man dropped. Nasty heard him roll and made a circle, knife singing through the air as he turned.

"Not again," came the whisper. "Only once for that. Now you pay."

He'd been right. This was Bogotá payback time.

The sound of an engine startled him. It grew louder, then cut out. A car had driven up the driveway.

Again he swung around.

A forced, rasping whisper, "It's time. Long, long past time."

The memories broke over him. *"It's time, friend. We've been waiting for you — and now we have you."* And there'd been gunfire. And his ankle exploded.

Low to the ground, the shadows coalesced. He lunged, but the shape dissolved.

A single, yipping yell sounded, and the night burst to life. The thud of feet, the rush of wind and rain against a powerful body.

Roman had closed in.

The fight was short and vicious. It stopped when Nasty fell over what he knew was a body. "He's down," he shouted. "Light, Roman."

A beam hit what lay at Nasty's feet.

They both dropped to their knees.

A man lay on his side, his head turned into the mud as it shouldn't have been able to turn.

"Shit," Roman muttered.

Nasty looked at him, and then at the trees on all sides. He took his flashlight and searched.

Lightning broke again, farther away again.

Another crackle came. Branches breaking. Crashing as someone made an escape.

"Shit!" Roman said, not lowering his voice this time. "The bastard got away." He looked at the man on the ground. "And he left us a present. This is the one who got dropped by the house. D'you know him?"

Supporting the lolling head, Nasty rolled the body to its back. A wound opened the neck from ear to ear. With a gloved hand, Roman wiped mud from the face.

Nasty focused his beam. He glanced up at Roman. "Poor creep."

Roman raised one dark, arched brow.

"I don't think our present is going to help us

much," Nasty told him. "Something tells me this guy's luck has always been bad. Mostly his own fault. Allow me to introduce you to Bobby Crow's dad — Sam Dodge."

Polly waited until Dusty, swearing so volubly she was grateful Bobby was deeply asleep, clumped downstairs in the wake of Rose and Nellie. At the sound of a car arriving, Rose had come from her room talking serenely about how quickly "the dear sheriff" could be relied upon to respond to her when she called. That had been minutes after Polly heard Dusty talking to a man she hadn't heard coming up the stairs. She assumed he'd come up the stairs since he'd suddenly been there, speaking in low tones, using a word that stood out from the rest — Nasty. Then the conversation had stopped. She'd decided the second man had left.

Now they were all somewhere downstairs, and they would soon come looking for her and Bobby. They'd find Bobby and take good care of him. If Nasty had come back, he'd have checked on her. That meant he was still out there. Polly wouldn't wait any longer to make sure he was safe.

She told Spike to stay, slipped from the room, and closed the door softly behind her. Swiftly, she made her way to back stairs that led down to a passage outside the kitchen. In some earlier age the servants must have slept in the third-floor bedrooms and used these stairs to go about their duties.

The kitchen was in darkness. Rose and the others would be in the living room. With the big flashlight from Bobby's room in hand, Polly let herself outside and flinched when rain beat her face.

She'd heard thunder but hadn't even thought about rain. Her T-shirt was instantly soaked, and her jeans. Water dripped from her hair down her neck.

If she called out, the sheriff and Dusty might hear and try to stop her.

Nasty was out there somewhere, and she refused to allow him to be alone — risking his own safety because he was worried about her.

The floodlights could have gone off for any number of reasons. That's what they'd decide. And it had to be Festus who'd found out where she was and managed to locate a telephone number.

Festus was sick. He was not a life-and-death threat.

The police were in the house. Even a crazy man would run away now.

"Xavier!" Polly started forward, shining her light first one way, then the other. "Xavier, where are you?" She didn't care how mad he got at her. There was no way she'd allow him to risk falling down in the dark because of her.

He could hurt his ankle again.

"Xavier! Where are you? The police are here — they'll want to talk to us." She stepped gingerly on mushy grass. He could be anywhere out here.

"Rose called the sheriff. He's with her now, and Nellie. Dusty's there, too."

She'd go to the front of the house.

"Stay where you are."

Nasty. Relief made her weak, and giggly. He wasn't far away — in the trees. She trained the flashlight on tall, straight trunks, and ran. "You stay where you are. You'll fall over something in there. Wait till I get to you. I've got a flashlight."

"Do not come any nearer."

She stopped, frowned, set her lips firmly, and carried on. "Stop giving me orders. And playing these silly games. You're going to have an accident."

The rumble of more than one male voice reached her, but she refused to listen. Scrambling, climbing over fallen limbs, she hurried in the direction from which she'd heard Nasty speak.

When she saw him he wasn't alone. He came toward her with a tall, dark-haired man beside him.

"Who is he?" Her voice rose to a silly squeak, but she didn't care. "Xavier?"

"Xavier?" the other man repeated, smiling. "This must be your Polly." He was exceedingly good-looking.

"I told you to stay with Bobby." Xavier closed in on her, his face set in unkind lines. "What are you doing out here?"

"The police are in the house. So is Dusty. Bobby's safe. I had to be sure you were safe, too."

"You should have done what I told you to do."

She smarted. He bore down on her. The other man avoided looking directly at her. "This isn't a naval maneuver," Polly said when she found her voice again. "And I'm not one of your men. That means I heard your lecture on following orders, but it doesn't apply to me. Who is this man?"

"Roman," Nasty said. "Roman Wilde. A friend of mine. We were SEALs together."

She studied Roman Wilde's face and concluded he wasn't just handsome, he was formidably handsome. "Don't they allow any ugly people in the SEALs?"

The two men looked at each other. It was Roman who laughed first. "She's funny. I think you found a keeper, Nasty. I always knew you would in the end."

Her light picked up something else, something on the ground a few yards behind Nasty and Roman. Someone. "Who is it?" she asked in a tiny voice. "Is he dead?"

Nasty strode to put an arm around her shoulders. "This isn't for you to deal with, sweetheart. I'll get you back to the house. It's just as well the sheriff's here. It'll save us some time."

"Who is it?" She clutched his sleeves. "It's someone I know, isn't it?"

"Let's go in the house."

Polly dug her heels into the thick layer of wet pine needles that covered the earth. She shrugged away from Nasty's arm. When he moved, she raised the flashlight and trained the beam on the fallen figure. Thick, dark hair curled despite rain and mud. Even at a distance she knew the face. Sightless eyes aimed in her direction. The slack mouth hung open, and a ghastly neck wound gaped above a blood-soaked shirt and jacket.

"Oh, no." She pushed Nasty's restraining arm aside. "Oh no, Sam. You didn't deserve this."

"No," Nasty said. "No, I don't think he did. He was in the wrong place at the wrong time."

"Get someone," she told them. "I'll stay with him."

Roman said, "I'll go. Be right back."

Polly forced herself to look away from the horrible wound in Sam's neck. "Who would do that to him?"

"We're going to find that out," Nasty told her. "I want you to go with Roman. I'll stay and wait for the cops."

As he spoke, he replaced his knife in a sheath on his left forearm.

Twenty-five

"Rain messes with the blood and stuff," the sheriff said, talking to Roman as the two came into Rose's kitchen.

Nasty watched Polly's face, her downcast eyes. He'd been watching her since they'd finally returned to the house. Dawn showed signs of breaking, although the downpour continued.

Polly had worked hard to avoid looking at Nasty.

Sheriff Bullock was a short, wiry man with the ready tongue of kindly, small-town law. He remembered Roman from his previous time in Past Peak. Once he'd discovered that Dusty and Nasty had also been SEALs, the investigation had become an endeavor among friends.

"Lucky we could get a medical examiner up here so quickly," Bullock said. "Not much happens around here. Clancy Depew's our coroner. He's a dairy farmer. Good guy for most of what we need, but not for that." He jabbed a blunt thumb over his shoulder.

"That was Sam Dodge," Polly said coldly, but without spirit. "He wasn't much of a person, really, but he was a person."

"Yes, ma'am," Bullock said, rolling onto his toes. "Old friend of yours, you said."

"Not exactly. We knew each other a long time ago."

"Addict then, too, was he? The M.E. mentioned tracks in the guy's arms. Old and new. A mess of tracks. I reckon it was something to do with that. Probably killed because he owed money. The M.E. said he thinks the victim was unconscious when they used the knife on him."

Polly sucked in a breath.

Nasty couldn't believe the man would spill information that way. He was grateful Bobby was still in bed, and that Rose and Nellie had been easily persuaded to return to their rooms.

Too bad Polly refused to budge, even after she'd been told she wouldn't be needed again for a while.

"How about some tea?" Dusty got up from a chair near Polly's and went to fill a kettle. "I bet Rose has got some of that nice herbal stuff here somewhere."

Nice herbal stuff? The last Nasty recalled, Dusty considered tea "swill."

"Hit over the head, he was," Bullock said, leafing through his notebook. "Dragged off into the trees before they slit his throat."

Polly let her head hang forward. She sat with her knees drawn up, her heels on the rungs of the chair.

And she thought he'd taken his knife to that piece of garbage. Nasty pinched the bridge of his nose and felt Roman's sharp eyes on him.

"They're taking the body away," Roman said

when Nasty looked at him. "The property's been cordoned off. There's another team out there. They think our man made his way to the southern edge of the estate, then to the road. Probably had a vehicle parked beside the main highway."

"How did Sam get here?" Polly asked.

They'd already been over this. "We don't know yet," Nasty said quietly. "His car hasn't turned up."

Sheriff Bullock put his notebook in a breast pocket. "I need to go into the office and make some calls. When Rose wakes up tell her not to worry. We'll take care of everything for her."

Dusty said, "Thanks," as he rummaged through cupboards for his herbal tea.

"You're sure this mystery man is the one who killed Sam?" Polly asked. "Without finding him, or knowing exactly where he came from, or where he went?"

"Oh, yes, ma'am," Bullock said comfortably, buttoning down his pocket flap. "Roman here saw him. And Mr. Ferrito. He attacked Mr. Ferrito, here. And he left quite a trail through the trees. You know what they say — even if a killer doesn't bring anything to the scene with him, he leaves something behind afterward." The sheriff delivered his borrowed wisdom with solemn sincerity.

Fortunately he couldn't see how Roman raised his eyes.

The man left by the kitchen door, and they listened to the clip of his heels on the path toward the front of the house.

The kettle boiled. Dusty poured water into four mugs and passed around a floral-scented brew. On any other occasion Nasty would have laughed. He didn't laugh now, only made himself sip the disgusting stuff.

"Time you got some shut-eye, Polly," Dusty said.

She didn't answer.

"Okay," Roman said. "What's your best guess, Nasty?"

"Bogotá," he said shortly. "Dodge got in the way."

Polly set her mug carefully on the table. "This man who got away killed Sam. You're all sure of that?"

"Yes," Roman said. He put his mug down, too.

"Why didn't he kill you the same way?"

In other words, she really didn't believe them. "Because he wants us alive," Nasty told her. "Actually, it's me he wants, not anyone else. He got to me first, and made it away after Roman arrived."

"The man who called here asked for me."

"I don't think that —"

"It had to be Sam. He came looking for Bobby and me. Wouldn't it be a big coincidence for someone else to come on the same night?"

"Not necessarily," Dusty said, grimacing into his tea. "Definitely not in this case. We got a good idea what's going on, and Nasty's right, Dodge was unlucky. He got in the way."

"Tell me what you know, then. The three of you. What you're not telling that sheriff, or me."

Nasty exchanged glances with the other two men. A case could be made for there being no reason not to tell Polly, but they wouldn't anyway. The habit of keeping information on a must-know basis died hard.

"You won't tell me anything," Polly announced. She gave Nasty's hands — the dried blood — a long glance. "You ought to wash. I expect you got that on you when you found Sam."

"No, he didn't," Roman said, so forcefully Nasty stared at him. "Not all of it. You should wash up, Nasty. Looks like the guy left quite a gash there. You need to take better care of those hands, buddy. I'm going to call Phoenix, then see if I can get some sleep before the questions pick up again."

"I'll come with you," Dusty said, all but rushing to join Roman. "I'll have a word with Phoenix, too."

"Subtle," Polly said as soon as the other men were gone.

"What does that mean? Or I should say, what do you mean?"

"Making excuses to leave us alone."

He pulled up a chair and sat down on the opposite side of the table. "You'd have to be a fool not to feel the tension around here. And I'm not talking about anyone's reaction to Sam Dodge's murder." Very deliberately, he laced his fingers on the table in front of him. "You think

439

I'm some sort of monster."

She swallowed, and her chin rose. "I don't know what to think. Sam called here, then came —"

"It didn't have to be Sam who called. It could have been the man who killed him." How could he make her stop looking at him that way without going into minute detail about things he'd rather not say aloud? "It's perfectly possible that whoever made that call asked for you because he knew you were with me. If he established you were here, he established I was here, too."

"He didn't kill you, though," she said. Shadows underscored her blue eyes.

"Because he wants me alive," Nasty said patiently. "It's a long story, but if I'm right — and Roman and Dusty think I am, too — then this started in South America when I was shot. I was supposed to be dead, and when I wasn't, I caused a man named Emilio — a drug lord — to lose credibility. This is the way I've pieced it together, and I could be wrong. But tonight a man told me I'd got away once and it wouldn't happen again — or words to that effect. He could only have been talking about my escape in Bogotá."

"Why would you be there? I didn't know our troops did things like that."

"You'd be surprised what our troops do," he told her, unable to keep cynicism out of his voice. "Talk to Dusty and Roman when they're in a talkative mood. The night you were pushed in the water there were two divers, not one."

"Divers?"

"One pushed you in and dragged you down. It had to be that way. He didn't care if you drowned or not as long as I went in after you. Two of them tried to get me in a net." He didn't feel like spelling out every detail. "If they'd wanted to kill me, they could have. They didn't even try. They wanted me alive. You were right when you said the man could have killed me out there tonight, too. But he didn't, did he? He knocked the gun out of my hand, and that's what did this." He flexed his right hand and closed his fist, opening a short, deep wound across his knuckles.

Polly burst into tears. She crossed her arms on the table and buried her face. Her back jerked with each sob.

Exhausted, Nasty got to his feet and took his chair beside hers. He patted her shoulder, stroked her hair. "You've had a rotten time of it, sweetheart. I'm sorry about Sam Dodge. Not because I think he was a good guy underneath it all, but because he was Bobby's dad, and your boy's going to take this hard."

She kept on crying.

"And I'm not sorry we're going to have to confront the fact that you think I'm a killer."

A sob caught in her throat, and she raised her head just enough to turn and look at him.

"You saw me sheathing my knife. You saw blood on my hands. And you decided I'd cut Sam Dodge's throat. You thought I could do that because I didn't want him anywhere near you."

"I guess I did."

"So you don't know me at all. And you don't understand that someone can do what they have to do under official orders, but that they have the same standards as any other decent civilian when they aren't under orders."

She shook her head. "I want to understand. You haven't helped me much. When I was attacked in my own home I needed to talk a lot more about it. You had other things on your mind. You just wanted me to do what you told me."

He hadn't thought of it that way.

"Why did you wait till now to tell me about the divers? I didn't see anything. I can't swim, remember? I was too busy getting used to the idea of drowning. You wouldn't talk about that, either."

"It's conditioning, Polly. When you spend years keeping things to yourself, you don't suddenly open up like a gusher every time something happens."

She took a paper napkin from a holder on the table and wiped her face. "Crumb, I'm a horrible sight." She blew her nose and pressed two fingers into her eyes. "All of this is happening. It isn't over."

"No. But it will be."

"I was so confused about being pushed into the water. It didn't seem to fit that Festus would have done it."

"He didn't."

"And Festus wasn't the man out there tonight?"

The idea was ludicrous. "No. Look at me, please."

Polly reached to take his injured hand in both of hers. "Let me get this cleaned up."

"Look at me."

"I'm sorry." She raised her eyes slowly. "How could I think you'd be capable of something like that after . . . ?"

He let her falter.

"Can you really blame me completely, Xavier?"

Maybe he couldn't. "Trust takes a while in the building. Just the way getting used to a complete change in lifestyle takes a while. I want to take however long it needs."

She got up and led him to the sink. Warm water stung the wound on his knuckles, and he yelped.

"It's got to be cleaned," she said, sounding serious but grinning at the same time. "Grit your teeth. You can do this."

He did grit his teeth, and said, "How about you?"

"I can't do anything but go along with whatever comes. With you."

" 'Course you can't."

"Don't start with the pigheaded stuff again." Blotting the jagged cut with a towel, she looked at him. "How am I going to break this to Bobby?"

"Carefully."

"That's not helpful."

"Sure it is. Bobby never really knew Sam, but he's canonized him in his mind. It couldn't be right to drop the entire truth on a seven-year-old."

"I can't pretend Sam isn't dead."

"No. I'm not suggesting you do. But you can say he had an accident and died. You don't have to pile on all the gory details. Best keep him here for a few days until things blow over. If we don't, he'll see it on TV — we wouldn't be able to stop him."

Tapping rattled the back door.

Nasty stuffed the towel into Polly's hands and raised a finger to his lips. Taking his gun in hand, he stepped to the door, and said, "Yeah?"

"Gavin Tucker. I'm looking for Polly Crow. The cops told me to come to this door."

Polly and Nasty looked at each other. Nasty tucked the gun in his waistband and opened the door.

"Geez, Polly," Gavin said, sparing Nasty only a brief glance before loping into the kitchen. "Are you okay, babe?"

"I'm fine. How did you find me?"

Gavin's long, pale face showed signs of fatigue and . . . fear? "I heard it on the early news. Just a snippet about a guy called Sam Dodge being murdered up here."

Nasty screwed up his face. "You couldn't have heard that."

"The hell I didn't." Pushing back his thin, brown hair, Gavin draped an arm around Polly. "Local sheriff gave sketchy details. That's what they said. Sketchy. Hah! He did everything but give the address of this place. No problem there, though. Anyone in the studio when Dodge came by yesterday could find out where you are if they want to."

Gavin didn't waste any time explaining himself. Bobby had called Sam Dodge's cell phone while the man had been at the studio asking questions about Polly. Bobby had told him roughly where Dusty and Nasty had taken him — and Polly.

"Another reason not to tell Bobby exactly what happened to his father yet," Nasty said. "He's sensitive. It wouldn't take much for him to decide it was his fault."

"You sure you're okay, Polly?" Gavin asked, giving her the kind of possessive look that churned Nasty's insides. "I'm worried about you."

"I'm managing. There's some weird stuff going on, but I'll get through."

There wasn't a graceful way to tell Polly not to say anything else to Gavin Tucker.

"I just cannot sleep." The door to the rest of the house swung open and Rose came into the kitchen. "There's too much going on here. And now I know what went on out there, I'm beside myself, Nasty. You should be resting that ankle." She pointed a perfectly manicured nail at his leg.

"This is my friend, Gavin Tucker," Polly said. "He's on the show with me, Rose."

Rose, in flame orange silk lounging pajamas, concentrated briefly on Gavin. "Of course he is. He's the man who paints those wonderful pic-

445

tures for the rest of you to use as scenery for all your sweet story lessons."

The sight of Polly's openmouthed surprise amused Nasty. "You mean to tell me you've been watching TV, Rose? And I thought you prided yourself in never wasting time on that nonsense."

She flipped a hand at him and scuffed to the refrigerator in gold, backless sandals. Her heavy blond hair curled about her shoulders. "You know perfectly well I only say that because it pleases me to put on airs sometimes. I've got a great big television set in my bedroom. In a tasteful cabinet. I watch *Polly's Place* every afternoon, and I just *love* it." She took a carton of milk from the refrigerator and pointed at Gavin this time. "Have you ever considered painting scenes in people's houses? I think you should. Of course, they'd have to be very expensive, but they'd be custom art, and they'd be very sought after."

"I hadn't thought of that, ma'am," Gavin said, fascination with Rose quite evident in his brown eyes. "But if you'd like me to paint something for you, I could probably manage that."

Nasty rubbed his aching eyes, using the opportunity to hide a grin. Whatever Rose wanted, Rose got — she always had.

"Why, thank you." Rose's smile was brilliant. "Did you hear that, you two? *The* Gavin Tucker is going to paint me a scene right here in my little old house. I spoke to Phoenix." Rose had a way of running one subject into another.

"How is she?"

"Just fine. And the babies are just fine. But Phoenix is worried about you, Nasty Ferrito. After what Roman told her, she's real worried."

"Maybe hot milk would help you sleep," Nasty said hastily. Who knew what Rose might have overheard? "I'll get you a pan."

"Don't you change the subject. Polly, you're going to have to make sure this boy takes care of himself."

The furrows in Gavin's brow didn't upset Nasty.

"I'll try," Polly told Rose.

"I'm glad all of them are out of the SEALs, I can tell you. When I think of all that terrible drug stuff down there in Colombia I could just *die,* with fright."

He must stop her from saying too much "Um, Rose —"

"Roman told Phoenix he and Nasty think whoever killed that poor man was really looking for Nasty on account of something that happened in Bogotá. He did tell you about Bogotá, didn't he?"

"Yes," Polly said, taking great interest in folding the towel into small squares. "Do you have some first-aid supplies."

"In the cupboard by the sink, dear. On the left. Sheriff Bullock's such a nice man, but he wouldn't know anything about drug cartels, do you think, Nasty?"

"Rose, Mr. Tucker stopped by to check on Polly — to make sure she's okay. Perhaps we shouldn't bore him with all this talk about old business."

Rose poured a glass of milk and went toward the door again. "Well, I certainly wouldn't want to bore him, would I? I'll be seeing you, Mr. Tucker. We have a date to do some painting, remember." She wiggled her fingers at Gavin.

"A date," Gavin agreed. He seemed agitated. Once Rose had left, he faced Polly and Nasty. "Just after Sam Dodge's visit to the studio Jack announced we should all take a couple of hours off. He could hardly wait to get out of there."

Polly found what she was looking for. "Jack can be like that. You know he has his moods. I think he needs to get off by himself sometimes."

"But he told us to be back in a couple of hours."

"Yes." She opened a bottle of iodine. "What's your point?"

"Mary came back in a foul mood. Doing her muttering act. You know what I mean. Carrying on about knowing Jack was up to something. I know you don't get it, Polly, but Mary thinks there's something between you and Jack."

"She's paranoid."

"I agree. But that doesn't change anything. The point is, you were gone, and then, apparently, so was Jack. I think Mary decided he knew where you'd gone and joined you."

Iodine soaked into Nasty's wounded knuckles, and he hissed at the pain. "Did Mary say anything to Jack when he got back?"

"He never came back."

Polly almost dropped the bottle. "Oh, that's . . . No, there can't be any connection. Call the studio, Gavin. Ask for Jack. No. No, call their condo first and talk to Mary. Make some excuse — say you need to talk to Jack. I bet he's there."

"He could be by now," Nasty pointed out.

Gavin walked to a phone on the wall and walked back to the middle of the kitchen. "South American," he said. "You guys think all this is tied in with something or other to do with South America? And drugs?"

No way should this conversation be taking place. "Evidently Rose drew some conclusions from a conversation she heard between my partner and a good friend of ours." Dusty and Roman would hear more about this.

"What are you thinking, Gavin?" Polly asked.

"Jack's made his name in children's programming — and documentaries," Gavin said. "Last year he won a prize for the one on drug cartels in South America."

Twenty-six

Dusty Miller deserved a medal. He'd taken Bobby fishing, making him a wildly excited little boy, and giving Polly the chance she needed to decide how to break the news of Sam's death.

Sitting on the veranda at the front of Belle Rose, with Roman Wilde, Nasty, and Rose, Polly niggled at the problem. In Sam's absence, Bobby had made him a hero. How could she create a balance between truth and fiction — and be sure her son didn't suffer?

"I told Nellie she ought to attend to her business," Rose said, rocking her bentwood chair. "She's very good to me, but I don't forget that she has her own affairs to deal with."

The two men made noises that suggested they'd heard Rose speak but hadn't listened to what she said.

Polly looked at the two of them. She'd noticed how they seemed to anticipate each other's moves — even thoughts in some instances.

She shouldn't feel jealous.

Roman's almost too-blue eyes met hers and he smiled. Good grief, there ought — as they said — to be a law, She smiled back and he got up to pace the veranda before leaning against a pillar and staring out over the lawns and the driveway.

His face showed that he'd lived and laughed — and maybe even cried some. She liked him for the way he spoke about his wife and their children. And she liked him because Nasty trusted him.

Nasty drummed the arms of his chair, then pushed to his feet and stood beside Roman.

Formidable.

You'd have to be a fool to get on the wrong side of a sixfoot-plus wall of all-male, watchfully restless energy. These two, one a big, tanned, dark-haired lately cowboy, the other Polly's glacier-eyed, silently alert shark in shark's clothing, should never be taken lightly.

She raked her nails back and forth on her jeans. What a shark. What a man. What a lover. Her skin throbbed instantly. Life had never been more complicated, but even trouble couldn't dull her feelings for this man.

"How long?" Roman said.

Nasty chewed steadily. "At least forty-eight hours."

"Maybe it won't take that long."

"Probably won't."

They spoke as if in code. "It's because you fought together, isn't it?" she said.

Both men looked at her. Nasty didn't just look at her, he looked into her. "Yeah. Sorry about that. We're deciding how long we ought to plan on digging in here."

"They're so clever," Rose said. "And such good friends. Good friends to anyone they care about.

Nasty and Dusty never let a week go by without checking on me. I'm a lucky woman. And Phoenix calls, too. I'm very lucky."

"You're very kind to put up with having your home taken over like this," Polly told her. "Especially by people who bring such trouble with them."

Rose pushed her rocking chair farther from the weak sun that had finally wiggled through the clouds earlier in the afternoon. "Trouble happens. I'm just so happy to have the company."

"What about Tucker?" Roman asked. He wore a denim shirt with cuffs rolled back over deeply bronzed forearms, and much-washed jeans faded into lines and creases. From discussion he'd had with Nasty, Polly had gathered his scuffed boots spent a lot of hours in stirrups.

Nasty's shirt hung loose and unbuttoned. He tucked his hands beneath it to rest on his hips. "Tucker," he said finally. "Yeah, there's Gavin Tucker, isn't there? I think the guy's okay. He's got a case on Polly, but who wouldn't?"

She wrinkled her nose at him, and Roman chuckled. "We know you do, buddy," he said, slapping Nasty's shoulder. "D'you trust him to do his bit with Jack Spinnel?"

"He'll call if the guy turns up."

"Do you think Jack could have come here?" Polly couldn't grasp the picture, not fully. "I know him. He wouldn't kill anyone."

"How do you know?" Nasty and Roman asked in unison.

She slapped her palms down on her knees. "Just because he did a documentary on drug cartels in South America it doesn't mean he's some sort of killer."

"Nope," Roman said. "But thanks to Gavin Tucker we now know the story dealt primarily with the Bogotá area. And it looks as if Spinnel could be even wealthier than he should be."

"He's got heaps of money," Polly protested. "He's done very well."

"Not quite as well as the kind of money we're looking at. That's your friend Gavin's conclusion, not ours."

"Gavin doesn't like Jack."

Nasty laughed. "Gavin hates Jack's guts. But that's because Gavin hates anyone who might get close to you."

She let that pass.

"We're going to hole up here for forty-eight hours, or until someone makes another move," Roman said, squinting. "Speculation's a good thing, but let's try for perspective, huh?"

"Perspective," Nasty agreed, and turned toward the driveway. "Company."

Tires grinding gravel, a police car nosed toward the house and swung to a stop.

A Kirkland police car.

"Kirkland?" Polly said, alarmed. "What would they come here for?"

Sheriff Bullock's familiar brown vehicle was only seconds behind.

Nasty pushed his hands in his pockets and went

down the crescent-shaped front steps to meet the officers from the first car. One man opened a back door, and Venus got out.

"Mom!" Polly shot to her feet.

Arms stretched upward, shaking her head, Venus rushed past Nasty to reach Polly. "My poor daughter. My poor, dear daughter. Oh, Polly, I can't bear it all. Such terrible things. And I thought my life was finally calm." She let her eyes drift shut and rested the back of one hand on her brow. "Serenity. I must have serenity. I must allow it to come to me."

Roman had joined Nasty and was in quiet conversation with the Kirkland policemen and Sheriff Bullock. "Mom, this is Rose Smothers." She smiled at Rose. "This is my mother, Venus Crow."

"I'm sure," her mother said. "Call me Venus. Oh, Rose, these are such difficult times. Do you have children?"

"No," Rose said. "I have never married."

The slight interval before Venus responded brought a grin to Polly's lips. "Yes, well, I have Polly and Fabiola. My twins. And I can tell you that being a mother is a trial. Frequently a great trial. Oh, I love them both, of course. And they bring me joy. But they also bring me pain." She scowled at Polly. "I should never have had to deal with the horror that confronted me today."

Venus wore full belly-dancing regalia. Crimson and gold. Her hair, coppery red at present, sprang away from her head in shiny curls.

"Will you excuse us if we leave you for a while?" Polly asked Rose, who studied Venus with discreet interest.

Venus refused to go into the house. She couldn't "be confined by captured air" and must remain outdoors. The farthest Polly managed to remove her mother was to a bench beside the driveway.

"Neither of you there when I need you," Venus said, fluttering with every move. "Fabiola. Oh, well, so important these days — both of you. She's on a shoot. Sounds so unpleasant. But she's gone and can't help her poor mother when she's shocked out of her mind."

"Mom —"

"Ooh, Polly!" Venus wailed, and fell into Polly's arms. "My poor child. I talk too much but it's only because I love you so much, and I can't bear that you have been exposed to depravity."

Foreboding chilled Polly. "Mom, please be calm. For me. Be calm and tell me exactly what's happened."

"I'm trying," her mother said in an unusually small voice. "Everyone thinks I'm flamboyant. And worldly. But under it all I'm really a little frightened of many things."

"I know." Polly patted her back. "I know, Mom. Relax. You don't have to pretend with me."

"That . . . that woman called me. She was hysterical. *Hysterical*, Polly. She screamed at me. She demanded to know where you were."

"Mom — ?"

"Where were you, she had to know. How could it be that she couldn't find you anywhere. Surely I knew where you were. Had something awful happened to you? Oh, my dear child, it was awful. I was so worried I went straight over there. I was afraid she was making herself ill."

"Mom —"

"Yes, yes, of course. Belinda. I'm talking about Belinda." She raised her head to look at Polly. "She told me about Festus. What he'd done. And she showed me . . . Well, you know. She said she'd shown you, too."

The thought of her mother seeing the photographs embarrassed Polly, then she remembered the police had taken all of them — also a horrifying thought. "She showed you the telescope?"

"And all those photographs. Disgraceful."

Polly sighed. She might have known there had been more than one set of prints.

"And she showed me the diving suit."

Polly drew back. "What are you talking about?"

"The wet suit Festus wore when he broke into your condo and waited there for you."

Festus. Festus after all. Polly looked toward the men in the driveway.

The sound of her mother crying astonished Polly. "Mom, it's okay. You did the right thing. You went to the police, and you had them bring you here. I'm sorry I couldn't tell you where I was going, but it seemed best for the police to be the only ones to know."

"But you don't understand," Venus sobbed.

"You don't know what it all really meant. How could you? She said she loved you!"

"Belinda's a friend, Mom. A nutty friend, but a friend, I think."

"She's not!" Venus took Polly by the arms and shook her. "You are too innocent, too trusting. She's a sick woman. She made that poor man make telephone calls to you and admitted it to me. Because she loves you it's supposed to be all right that she made Festus frighten you with dreadful calls. And when I said I didn't believe her, she brought out the diving suit and told me we all knew the man who attacked you was wearing one."

"No." Polly tried to free herself. "That's not possible."

"It is, I tell you. I can't go on. You have the policemen tell you. I called them as soon as I could get away."

"Did Festus come back?"

Venus broke into fresh gales of tears. "It's an awful, sick, sick thing. Talk to the policemen. I told her I couldn't remember your address. I said I had it in the car. If I hadn't, I probably wouldn't be here, now. I probably wouldn't be anywhere." She slapped both hands over her mouth.

From the corner of her eye, Polly saw Rose get up and start down the steps toward them. "Mom, Rose is coming. Quickly. Is Belinda coming here, too?"

"No! Talk to them." Venus pointed a shaky finger toward the men. "They'll tell you. She loved you, Polly. Don't you understand?"

She sat straighter. "You don't mean . . ."

"Yes, I do. The photographs were all over the walls in her bedroom. I thought I should be sick."

Polly was almost certain she would be.

"She wanted you. As her lover."

Settling Venus had taken more than an hour. In the end it had been Rose who managed to calm the other woman — with questions about belly dancing.

Closing the door of Rose's suite on the sound of Venus and Rose discussing lessons, Polly went in search of Nasty, Roman, and the police.

Both official vehicles had left.

Roman rocked gently in a hammock strung between the trunks of two apple trees on the side lawn. When Polly approached, he raised one eyelid to reveal a very-aware blue eye. "Don't wander off," he told her. "Better stay close to the house."

She was tired of being told what to do, and not being told why. "Where's Xavier?" she asked, more brusquely than she knew she should.

Roman lifted his head and both eyelids. "Over there." He looked past her and she turned around.

His shirt still flapping open, Nasty wandered from the back of the house. "You'd think he was taking a stroll," Polly muttered.

"Mmm." When she looked at him, Roman had closed his eyes again.

Determined to insist on getting back to Kirkland and the show and getting on with the business of living normally, she marched to meet Nasty. And as she drew nearer, she felt the familiar bump, bump of her heart.

"How's your mom doing?"

"Great. Thanks to Rose. I like Rose."

"We all do. She's the kind of woman who makes you want her to be happy. A good person."

"I suppose the police know all about it."

"Uh-huh."

"They told you everything?"

"Yup. Once Bullock started talking in front of us, everyone opened up."

She filled her cheeks with air and lost the battle not to stare at his chest. A few more seconds and she'd lose the battle against wrapping herself around that very solid, very . . . sexy chest.

"C'mere," he told her, holding out his arms. "I want to hold you, too."

She sent him an accusing glare. "Now you're reading my mind." But she went to him gladly and shuddered at the sensation when he embraced her. She settled her face on his warm skin, kissed that skin, and nuzzled her cheek against his chest hair.

"Belinda's in custody," he told her. "It isn't the whole enchilada, but at least it gets one part of the mess cleared up. I wish we could say we didn't have a care left."

"Have you considered that what happened last night could have been kind of random? Sam came looking for Bobby and me and ran into an armed burglar?"

"That would be nice," he said, without the enthusiasm she'd like to hear. "But no. It doesn't work. Sweetheart, I'm going to have to do something I don't want to do. I can't risk having you and Bobby near me."

Polly pushed on his chest, but he kept her where she was. "You can't get rid of me that easily," she said. "Bobby should be somewhere else. Safe. But where you go, I go."

The pressure of his chin on the top of her head tightened her insides. "Listen to me, Polly. I can deal with this. You can't. And now we know Belinda and Festus were your problem — and they're not going to be a problem anymore — it only makes sense to get you away from me so you don't get caught in the middle."

"I'm not going."

"No. No, I didn't make myself clear. Roman and I think you should stay here with Rose until the dust settles. They'll make their move quickly now. They have to. If they wait, they'll be afraid I'll either get away, or get to them."

"You don't even know who they are."

"I think I know where to find them. I'm going back to Kirkland."

She swallowed and felt ill. "You believe it's Jack, don't you? You think he's the one chasing you?"

Nasty eased up her chin. He kissed her gently, his lips only slightly parted. "I love you, Polly."

It took effort to say, "Don't change the sub-ject."

"I'm going to marry you."

Crumb, tears again.

"Trust me to be careful — and fast. And try not to think about Belinda and Festus. They were an aberration. These things are sick, but they happen."

"I guess they'll go after Festus, too."

Nasty's forehead furrowed. "Venus didn't tell you about him? No, I see she didn't."

Hope made Polly giddy. "They've got him?"

"Yeah." Nasty didn't send up any cheers. "They got him. Well preserved. Makes a guy suspicious of words like, " 'Till death do us part.' " Belinda locked him in their basement freezer — probably about a week ago."

Twenty-seven

"I'll be on the boat," Nasty said. "They'll like that — the idea of a chance to get at me alone."

The day was still warm, the earth moist. Dusty and Roman stood with Nasty between all-but-bare vegetable beds in the kitchen garden.

Dropping to his haunches, Roman picked stones out of the soil. "Do we have our signals straight?"

Nasty nodded. So did Dusty.

"Right. Then you'd better get going. It'll be easier if you do it before they come back." He glanced toward the windmill, where Polly had taken Bobby to talk.

"Poor little kid," Dusty said. "He's too good, y'know."

Nasty sidestepped a pebble Roman tossed at his shoe. "What does that mean?"

"Too tight. He's trying to make all the grown-ups happy. Doing what he thinks they want him to do. He watches to see which way the wind's blowing before he opens his mouth."

Like any intelligent kid who never really got to be a child. "Polly's done a good job with him, but it isn't easy — being a single parent."

Another pebble hit the ground at Nasty's feet. Roman grinned up at him. "Is she going to get some help with that?"

Dusty coughed and thumped himself on the chest. "Dumb question, Wilde. We gotta weddin' to plan for."

"Mind your own business," Nasty told them both. "You've been smoking again, Dust. You keep promising you'll cut that out."

"Yeah. We ought to get going. I'd like to be settled in before dark."

Nasty looked toward the windmill again.

"Go on," Roman said. "Go see how they're doing. We don't want your attention divided — not while we've got other business to deal with."

"Roman's right," Dusty said. "Go to Polly and Bobby. Probably not a good idea to slip out, anyway."

He didn't waste time talking. It was important to get back to Kirkland, but Roman was right about divided attention. Once into the trees, Nasty broke into a run. His leg only got stronger, and he took pleasure in feeling it respond almost like the old times.

Outside the mill, he stopped and looked up. The place was still, so still he had the disquieting thought that they might not be there.

He poked his head up the stairway and called, "Halloo up top! Anyone on the bridge?"

Scuffling preceded Spike's explosion from above. The big gray dog's rear end waggled from side to side as he shot down to greet Nasty. Scratching the animal's ruff, he climbed slowly upward.

Polly and Bobby sat, cross-legged, facing each other in the middle of the room at the top of the stairs. Bobby's arms were tightly crossed, his face pinched and serious. Polly made a valiant attempt to smile at Nasty.

"Hey, guys," he said. "Okay if I join the party? For a few minutes."

He thought Polly's mouth quivered before she pressed her lips together. "We're not a lot of fun to be with right now," she said.

"No one can be fun all the time." Bringing Spike with him, he sank to sit between mother and son. "Dusty and I are heading out in a few minutes. I wanted to let you know we're leaving. We're going to swing through Bellevue and drop Venus off on our way."

"Thank you," Polly said.

Bobby turned his face away.

"I told Bobby I've decided to accept Rose's invitation to stay here for a few days." Polly's voice sounded strained. "I'm going to have him show me how this fishing works. He learned a lot with Dusty today."

"I didn't hear what you two caught," Nasty said, wishing he could grab them both and take them away where they could put all this behind them.

Bobby shook his head.

"You didn't catch anything?"

Another shake of the head.

"I can't believe Dusty took you out all day, and neither of you caught anything. His reputation's

464

going to be shot. As soon as I get back, you and I'll go. We'll take your mom for luck. We're bound to catch lots."

"Maybe I'll be the one to catch lots, and you'll be the mascot," Polly said.

Bobby wiped the short sleeve of his striped T-shirt over his eyes. "My dad died."

Words deserted Nasty.

"We're having kind of a difficult time with this," Polly told him, and he saw her slow intake of breath.

"I'm sorry." Give him something to say that mattered.

"He had an accident," Bobby said. "He fell and got killed."

Geez. "And you're angry. Because you always hoped he'd come back, and you thought he was finally going to."

Bobby sent him a confused stare.

"Sometimes we want things so badly we start believing they're happening." Maybe he should just keep his mouth shut.

"My dad was coming back. He said so."

"Yeah." Nasty looked to Polly, but she shook her head slightly. "Your dad wanted to come back. I heard him say that, too."

Spike snuffled toward Bobby and licked his face. The boy put an arm around the animal's neck. "Mom didn't want him back."

"Bobby —"

"Bobby," Nasty said, cutting Polly off. "Your mom wants the best for you. She wants you to be happy. I know she thought it would be great if your dad could spend some time with you."

"She didn't love him anymore."

He saw glimmerings of the child's dreams. "You wanted your mom and dad to love each other. That's the best way, but it can't always happen."

Spike's thorough licking went unnoticed. "Mom loves you."

Polly bowed her head.

"And I love her," Nasty said firmly. "I can't take your dad's place. I mean, I can't be your real dad — but I can be there for you. I can be *here* for you."

The hunching of Polly's shoulders disconcerted Nasty. She needed his comfort, but he had to concentrate on the child. "This is an awful time. You've got to get used to what's happened. But you and your mom don't have to do it alone. That doesn't mean I can magically make all the bad feelings go away, but I can listen — and I can try to help."

"Are you and mom going to get married?"

"Yes," he said without hesitating. "Will you like that?"

Bobby frowned and wrinkled his nose. "What will I call you?"

He felt Polly looking at him and smiled. She rested a hand on her son's dusty knee.

"You can call me whatever you like." Rushing things wouldn't necessarily be bad, but it could be. "You think about it and let me know."

"If my dad didn't come to find me, he wouldn't have had an accident, would he?"

This is where the degree in psychology would help. "Your dad was a grown-up. He did what he wanted to do. He decided to go to Kirkland. What happened was nothing to do with you. You didn't tell him to come. If he'd come when you wanted him to, he'd have been with you a long time ago." He prayed he wasn't overstepping what the kid could handle.

"Give me a hug," Polly said quietly. "Mom needs a hug."

Bobby sniffed and swallowed — and got up to go and put his arms around Polly's neck. "Don't be sad," he told her. "Don't cry, Mom."

She shook her head and held him tightly. "I won't. I've got you, haven't I?"

"And you've got Nasty," Bobby said.

Nasty scowled at the fading light. Something had got in his eye. "Well, gang, I'd better get going before Dusty comes looking for me. Roman's staying a few days with Rose before he goes back to Montana. He, er, he should be able to get through his business here pretty quickly."

He and Polly looked at each other over Bobby's head. Damn the risk. He knelt and pulled them both against him. "You two are the best. You're the most important people around, d'you understand me?"

Polly rested her head on his shoulder and nodded.

Bobby faltered, then leaned on Nasty.

467

This was what they meant when they talked about feeling full up.

"Snap!" Roman slapped a card down and grinned with triumphant glee.

"Aw," Bobby complained. "You're gonna win again."

"Maybe I'm going to win," Rose said. "Snap."

"Ahhh!" Roman and Bobby yelled in unison.

Polly had begged out of this round. She got up and left the kitchen. The happiness she felt frightened her. A woman shouldn't have to be afraid to be happy.

All she wanted was to be with Nasty and Bobby. She'd never known the kind of peace and wonder she'd felt when he'd held the two of them in the windmill — and when Bobby had shown that he was ready to accept Nasty.

The grandfather clock in the hall chimed. She walked slowly past, counting to ten with the chimes. Bowls of pink and white roses scented the air.

Peace.

She opened the front door and strolled onto the veranda. The floodlights illuminated a wide margin around the house. A warm evening made the rain of morning seem imaginary. More roses in tubs carried their fragrance to Polly. Birds gave their night songs. Rose's daddy had created an idyllic setting for his beautiful daughter. Despite early opinions to the contrary, Polly had decided Rose was mostly content with her life.

How unreal to think that only last night Sam had died in the woods on the other side of the house.

Someone ought to mourn him. In his seven-year-old fashion Bobby would wrestle with the idea, but Polly wanted to believe he'd make peace with his father's death and move on.

She slowly descended the steps. This was the kind of night that drew people to the mountains. Warm, still, the sky big and dark, and sprinkled with stars — and clear as it was rarely clear in a city.

"Polly!"

Startled, she grabbed for a handrail and went backward up a step. The voice had come from beyond the floodlights.

"Polly, over here. Quickly. Oh, Polly, *quickly*."

"Jennie?"

"Yes." Jennifer Loder emerged from the trees on Polly's left, at the edge of the lighted driveway. She kept her head bowed and beckoned frantically. "C'mon, Pol. We gotta move fast."

Polly looked back at the house.

"Polly!"

Her pulse sped up. She hurried toward Jennifer, who drew back between the straight, tall trunks of Douglas firs.

"Cripes, Polly," Jennifer said when they were face-to-face. "What's been goin' on up here?"

Polly hesitated.

Jennifer put a hand beneath Polly's arm and drew her close. "That's rhetorical. Or mostly. I was there when that Sam came to the studio. Then Gavin told us all the ghastly stuff about last night. What a mess. And now this."

"This?" Polly echoed.

"Well — whatever your friend Nasty's got going. I didn't ask, I just did what he wanted. He does mean something to you, doesn't he?"

Polly's skin turned icy. "He means a lot to me. Is something wrong? Did something happen to him?"

"Damned if I know. He's alive and kicking, I'll tell you that. He came to my place. Mine and Art's. Said he'd just gotten back to Kirkland, and he was going to his boat. Wouldn't say why, or what was going on. But I could tell he was strung tight. You know what I mean."

Polly knew. She didn't feel like talking about it. "Why would he come to you?"

"I'm trying to explain that. He sent me on this cloak-and-dagger mission to get you. I didn't know how I was going to pull it off without — Roman, is it? Yeah, Roman, that's right. He wanted me to get you without bringing Roman on your tail. That's what Nasty said. I told him I'm not an errand girl, but he said you'd told him we were friends, and so on. You know how that goes. So, here I am."

Polly's stomach took another turn. "Nasty asked you to come and get me without Roman knowing about it?"

Jennie waved her free hand. "Hey, don't ask me to figure out the workings of a man's mind.

I'm only a woman, right?"

Polly didn't laugh. "How did he know how to find you?"

"Beats me. Look, if you want me to go back and tell him you don't want to play his game, I'll do it. You know I'll do it for you."

"How did he seem?"

"Seem?" Jennie's eyes glinted in the darkness. "Geez, damned if I know. Except he was rattled — I could tell that. You know how cool he is. Ice-man, I'd call him. But I could feel him jumping on the inside — and he said he needed you."

Panic made a rapid trip along Polly's nerves. "I ought to go in and tell them I'm leaving." Nasty needed her. Please don't let him be hurt.

"I agree. But Nasty asked me to beg you not to do that. His words, not mine. 'Beg her not to say anything to anyone,' he said. 'Ask her just to come with you and tell her it'll be okay.' Then he went tearing off again. So it's your call, girl."

Polly dithered.

"Oh, you're going to worry yourself sick," Jennie said. "This is a rotten idea."

But Nasty *needed* her. "He wouldn't ask this of me if it wasn't desperately important. Wait here." She turned and dashed back into the house, praying she wouldn't meet anyone before she could get out again.

She couldn't bear to think of worrying Bobby. By the phone in the living room Rose kept a notepad and pen. Polly wrote a short message to Roman and took the entire pad into the foyer.

Balanced beside a bowl of roses, it was bound to be seen.

When she retraced her steps she thought at first that Jennie had left. Then she appeared again and they ran through the trees to the end of the long driveway. Jennie's car was parked several hundred yards down the road, almost at the main highway. Polly had to run hard to keep up with Jennie's athletic stride.

Headlights swung toward them on the road leading to Rose's house. Jennifer pulled Polly into a crouch until the car passed, then they carried on.

The drive to Kirkland seemed longer than the forty minutes that passed before Polly saw the lights of the little city. She and Jennie had said little on the way, and, for Polly, apprehension grew with every mile.

At Peter Kirk Park Jennie turned left onto State Street.

"We shouldn't turn here," Polly said. "Nasty's moored at a private dock in front of his partner's house. North of the boat ramp."

"I said I'd take you to my place and call him."

Polly glanced at Jennie. "I thought he needed me as quickly as I could get there."

"I'm just telling you what he asked me to do. If you weren't my friend, I wouldn't be going to all this trouble."

"No." Polly felt uncomfortable. "I'm sorry, of course this is a big imposition."

Jennie and Art lived in a small rented house at

the end of a cul-de-sac. Jennie pulled her BMW to a halt in front of the garage and got out. Leaving Polly to follow, she hurried to open the front door and go inside.

On her few previous visits, Polly had become accustomed to the Loders' sparse furnishings. Jennie laughed at the couch and one chair in the uncarpeted sitting room, and called the decor, "Late We Don't Got No Roots."

Tonight Art sat at one end of the couch. He wasn't laughing. Polly didn't recall ever seeing him so morose. Or was that angry? Or just plain tense?

"Hi, Art," she said lightly. "Sorry to take advantage like this. Thanks for letting Jennie come to our aid."

He grunted and got up to shut the front door that opened directly into the room.

"I'll make that call, then. And get out of your hair."

When she reached for the phone on an arm of the couch, Art said, "Damn thing's out of order."

Jennie threw her keys on the mantel. "You're kidding! Try it anyway, Pol."

She did, and the emptiness of a dead line greeted her. "I'll get to a call box and report it for you."

"Sit down," Art said.

Polly started for the door. "You've done more than enough. Thank you both. I'll —"

"Sit down. Now."

Jennie put an arm around her shoulders and

473

guided her to the chair. "Art's bothered. Any little glitch, and he's bothered. Sit down. I've got a few things to do, then I'll run you to a phone."

"It's not far," Polly protested. She broke into a sweat. She had to get to Nasty. "I could walk to the boat. Honestly, I think I ought to go now. Nasty will be —"

"We don't give a damn what Nasty'll be," Art said, rising to his feet. "Jack's making waves, Jen. We've got to move. They're ready for us."

Bewildered, Polly curled her fingers over the arms of the chair.

"What about Mary?" Jennifer asked. "Did you do what we talked about?"

"I thought about it. No point leaving too much for the local law to use. They might not be as stupid as we think."

"Yeah? You think they'd put any of this together? We don't want to leave any tracks, brother dear. That means your Mary goes."

"She's not my Mary. And she doesn't know shit. Jealous bitch. All she wants is Jackie boy."

"The woman's dangerous, I tell you. You told me she talked about offing . . . Well, she didn't hesitate when she wanted to make sure I wasn't a threat. Or our friend, here."

Polly opened her mouth to breathe. She'd walked right into something awful. Polly looked from brother to sister. "What are you saying?"

"Mary thought you were sleeping with Jack. And she wanted you killed for that."

"Don't be ridiculous."

The back of Art's left hand, connecting with Polly's face, snapped her head back. "That was after she wanted Jen killed because she thought she was sleeping with Jack."

"Which I was," Jennifer said, still with a smile on her lips. "You're going to bleed on that pretty white T-shirt."

Shuddering uncontrollably, Polly touched her cheekbone, winced, and looked at blood on her fingers. She'd made a terrible mistake coming here. She almost laughed. Bleeding, bruised, trapped with two people who were discussing her death, and she was thinking in understatements.

"Go for Jack," Jennifer said. "Tell him we've got orders to move and we're to rendezvous here."

"Okay. I checked on Ferrito. He's still aboard."

"Nasty —"

"Shut up." Jennifer yanked Polly's hair, but looked at Art. "This is working, thank God. The boss won't be handing out any more chances, so don't fuck up this time."

Polly's scalp stung. She searched the room, trying to order her thoughts. She had to get out of here. She had to warn someone, warn Nasty.

Art looked down his nose at Jennifer. "Who fucked up last time?"

The expression on Jennifer's face didn't change. "Get going." She looked at her watch. "The window closes at four."

"What are you talking about?" Polly kept taking breaths, but her lungs didn't seem to expand.

"What's happening here?"

"Do me a favor by the time I get back, sis," Art said, pointing at Polly. "Make sure she doesn't feel like talking anymore."

Twenty-eight

"I don't hate you," Jennifer said. "I don't care enough to hate you. Understand?"

Polly understood nothing, not anymore, unless it was that she had to think, and think fast.

"You aren't important — except to help us get what we want."

"Why don't you tell me what you want? What you think I can do for you?"

"I don't hate you."

This was a crazy woman, Polly thought. Her stomach clamped down enough to hurt. Somehow she had to get out before Art got back.

"Once you've done what I want you to do, you'll have to go, of course. We couldn't leave you to tell the cops about us. We've got everything ready. They'll find out we had to go back to Australia for a family emergency. Only we won't be the Art and Jennifer going to Australia. They'll be the couple we've paid to do it. We've got other plans." Jennifer sniggered. "Y'now how you can be sure you're going to be offed?"

"Offed?"

Jennifer gave her a cold-eyed stare. "Killed. If someone with all the power and a lot to lose tells you everything that could finish them, you'd better have funeral plans made. It's a dead give-away."

"Is it?" Polly started to get up.

Jennifer pushed her back down.

"You could cause me a lot of trouble. You could ruin me, because I'm going to tell you everything. But then you won't be around to talk about it."

The woman before her was tall, as tall or taller than most men, and she was strong. "I can't fight you, Jennifer. And I can't make deals." Polly refused to show how terrified she was.

"Right, on both counts," Jennifer said. "Come on, I want to change."

"Why me?"

"Why me?" Jennifer undid the belt at the waist of her jeans and stripped it from the loops. "Poor little Polly. *Why me?* Because you got in the way, you silly bitch. All you had to do was play your part and keep your nose clean, but no, you had to get in the sodding way. Get up."

Polly didn't move.

The leather belt sang through the air. She screamed, and threw up her arms. Points on the metal buckle blasted into her head. The strap cracked on the backs of her hands.

Pain shot into her skull.

"Get *up*," Jennifer ordered.

Dizzy, Polly pushed to her feet. She crossed her arms, pushed her stinging hands into her armpits.

Jennifer reversed the belt to hold it by the

buckle. "Hurry up, pretty Polly." Using the belt like a whip, she flicked it against Polly's cheek, then, repeatedly, across her back and buttocks, herding her from the living room into a hallway.

At the door into a bedroom Polly balked. She turned blindly toward her attacker and lunged.

Jennifer's laugh echoed in Polly's ears. She laughed, and slammed a fist into the soft flesh beneath Polly's ribs — and brought the belt down across her shoulders as she doubled over.

Winded, stunned by explosions of pain in her chest and head, on her back, Polly curled up on the floor.

Jennifer kicked her temple, hauled her up, and threw her onto the bedroom floor.

"Stop it!" Polly scrambled upright and stood, swaying, blinking to clear her vision. "What have I done to you?"

"You were born," Jennifer said through her teeth. "You and millions like you, *pretty* Polly. And the men look at your pretty face and your helpless little body, and they want to look after you and drool over you — and they don't care if there's nothing in your pretty, *stupid* head."

"Jennifer —"

"Shut up! Lie on the bed. Go on, lie on the bed."

Polly couldn't move.

"You little idiot." A single, vicious shove sent the door rattling into its jamb. Jennifer shot home a bolt, flipped a hasp closed, and snapped a shiny, obviously new, padlock shut. "On the bed. You move, and you're dead." Her laughter now was high and jerky. "You don't move, and you're still dead. Get it? Move and you're dead. Don't move and you're dead. What you call a no-win situation."

The unmade bed, a nightstand with a black halogen desk lamp on top, and a row of open, overflowing suitcases comprised the room's furnishings.

Without warning, Jennifer lowered her head and charged. The force of impact took Polly's feet off the floor. Folded over Jennifer's head and back, she traveled backward to slap onto the mattress.

Dry heaves tore at Polly's belly and throat. The white light from the lamp bored into her brain. Sweat drenched her body.

"Don't you bloody puke in here," Jennifer barked. "Stupid bitch. Useless. What would a man like that see in a useless . . . Ah, it's not worth it. You can't get out, so don't try."

Tears mixed with sweat and burned Polly's eyes. Panting, she turned on her side and watched Jennifer go into the bathroom. There wasn't a phone on the bedside table. Moving gingerly, Polly lifted her head to scan the room.

"Get off the bed, and you're dead," Jennifer shouted. She laughed again. "Don't get off the bed, and you're dead. Get off the bed, and you're dead. Don't get off the bed, and you're dead. Oh, yeah! Oh, yeah, *pretty* Polly."

Two windows. The bedroom had two outside

walls at a corner of the house. Ugly brown drapes lined with foam hung unevenly at each window. Polly raised herself a little higher to get an angle on where the drapes didn't quite come together. If she could make it there, she'd have a chance of climbing out.

"Not if you don't want to die," Jennifer sang out, her head protruding from the bathroom. Her thin brown hair hung loose over a visible bare shoulder. "Go for the window, and you die. Don't go for the window, *and you die.* Start praying, pretty Polly. This is number four, and death is at your door."

"You?" Polly whispered. "You made those calls?"

"Only the really good ones," Jennifer shouted. "After I heard you get one of the heavy breathers. That gave me the idea. This is number one, and the fun will soon be done. God, it was so great. Never did get around to number three. Too late now. I heard all about the witch woman. What a laugh. I ought to send her candy for all the help she gave us."

Polly held herself still.

If she gave in, she was definitely going to die here. A woman she'd worked with, and laughed with — and called friend, would kill her tonight.

Hold on. It's never over till they call time. Fab used to say something like that when they'd been frightened kids in Venus's unstable days. Frightened kids afraid for their lives whenever Venus and one of her men fought while Polly and Fab held their breath, sick at the thought that their beloved, flighty mother would die. Fab would cry, but she'd comfort Polly at the same time, and tell her they just had to hold on.

Polly had cried, too, but she wouldn't give Jennifer the pleasure of seeing her cry tonight.

No one knew she was here.

Squeaky sounds came from the bathroom.

Roman would have found the note by now. Polly thought about what she'd written. It didn't say anything. Just told them not to worry — she'd be back. Roman wouldn't do anything to frighten Bobby and Rose. No, he'd do the sensible thing and wait — just as she'd told him to wait because she'd be with Nasty and there was nothing to worry about.

"Ta da!" Leaping into the bedroom, Jennifer turned a cartwheel without putting her hands down, and landed on the end of the mattress. "Look familiar?"

Wincing at the pain every move brought, Polly scooted as far up the bed as could. "Why are you wearing a wet suit?"

Jennifer's hand shot out so swiftly Polly didn't have time to react. The other woman's fingers tangled in her hair and twisted. "Up, up, up we get. The trampoline's great. Ever been on a trampoline?"

"No!"

Using Polly's hair, Jennifer hauled her to her feet, and bounced her. "This is a good start. No, a good end. Hah! Too late for you to learn to use a real trampoline. Bounce, pretty Polly, bounce."

"Let me go!"

"Beg."

Polly squeezed her eyes shut. Vomit rose in her throat.

"Bounce!"

Bearing down on the pain, swallowing repeatedly, Polly went limp, allowed herself to hang by her hair until Jennifer let her fall.

"Do as I tell you."

With her knees hugged to her chest, Polly remained where she was.

"I'm the diver. Don't you get it? I'm the ducky diver, ducky. We've played in a bedroom before — your bedroom. And I took you for a little swim, only you can't swim. I didn't think he'd bloody save you. You were supposed to drown that night, but fate smiled on us. He's too bloody clever for his own boots, that one, but we still need you. So he did us a favor."

Jennifer Loder was drunk on her own brilliance, and on her own madness. Polly's silence would inflame the woman more, but if she was going to die here tonight, it wouldn't be in shame at her own weakness. The window might still be her best bet. Maybe Jennifer would be distracted by something, and Polly could find a way to break the glass.

Releasing her hair, Jennifer pulled up the bottom of Polly's T-shirt and tore it open across her back. "Ugly," she said. "Polly's pretty white skin is all ugly and red." With her fingernails, she scratched a path up the prominent bones of Polly's spine.

Breathing through her mouth, willing herself not to cry out, Polly pushed her head between her knees to hold back faintness.

"Really ugly now." She unhooked Polly's bra, rammed a fist beneath her chin, and flung her to her back. "Really, really ugly."

Nausea broke in waves. She would not give up. She would not let this creature win.

"Here." Jennifer produced a phone from beneath the bed. "Do what I tell you, or you'll die." A huge, gaping grin stretched her thin-lipped mouth. "Do what I tell you, or you'll die. Do what I tell you, and you'll still die." She smacked the receiver against Polly's ear and jaw.

Polly hunched her shoulders and didn't attempt to hold the phone.

"Ballsy bitch," Jennifer said softly. "This is what you're going to do. You're going to call your sexy dive boy's number and tell him to stand by."

"No." Polly shook her head.

"Yes." With one sweep, Jennifer stripped her to the waist. "Yes. You'll call him and tell him to stand by. Tell him something unexpected's happened, but you can't talk. You'll call him back as soon as you can."

Polly grabbed for the remnants of her shirt, and her bra, but Jennifer tossed them to the floor.

"Make the call." The phone was ground into her face again.

"I can't do that."

"Do it."

Polly shook her head no. "I'm not making the call."

Shooting her feet from the bed, Jennifer dropped to sit beside Polly. "D'you like women?"

Polly narrowed her eyes to look at her.

"Do you?" Jennifer covered one of Polly's breasts and squeezed. "Come on. Don't tell me you've never been with a woman before."

The nausea swelled again, nausea and pure revulsion. The urge to rip Jennifer's hand away all but overwhelmed Polly. She sat still, stared directly into the other woman's eyes.

"I can do anything to you. You couldn't stop me. I think I'm going to see if you scream when you come."

Polly stared.

Jennifer slapped her face.

Polly forced her eyes open, and stared.

"Make the call," Jennifer yelled. "Art's going to get back with Jack. You'd better have made the call, or I'll give you over to Art and you'll wish you had. He's not a happy boy when things go wrong the way they did last night. And when he's not happy, he's mean.

"Art's been through a lot for me. For us. He had to play along with Mary Reese so we could keep tabs on Jack. Art deserves to get what he wants."

The next instant Polly heard voices and the sound of the front door opening and closing.

"Shit." Jennifer dragged a sheet from the mussed bedclothes and tossed it at Polly. "Cover yourself up. I don't want Jackie boy droolin' over you."

From the living room, Art called, "Jen?"

"Bedroom," she called back, and worked the combination on the padlock before unbolting the door.

Gray-faced, with sweat rings under the arms of his wrinkled khaki shirt, Jack Spinnel entered the room ahead of Art. He saw Polly and halted. Art gave him a shove from behind and closed them in. He produced a gun from inside his jacket and aimed it at Jack.

Jack's eyes widened. "What's the gun for?" He looked at Polly. "What's she doing here? I thought you said you were giving me the film and taking off. What am I supposed to do about her?"

"Nothing," Jennifer said, causing Jack to swing toward her. "Not a thing, Jacko. She's going to call Ferrito. He's going to rush over here to save his lady love. We'll be ready for him. She dies. You die. We take him to our rendezvous point. The cops find you and pretty Polly and decide they've got a lovers' quarrel gone wrong. Maybe we'll leave Mary alone after all. We were wise to make sure she never knew about Colombia. When the cops get to her she'll be singing her guts out about how that louse Jack was boinking his star. All neat and tidy. Art?"

"I like it, sis."

"You said you'd give me the film," Jack said, his face even paler.

Polly stared at him until he met her eyes. She tried to smile a little, to warn him that whether or not they liked it, they were on the same side. They were all they had.

His wild gaze slid away again. "I've done my part," he said to Art. "Now I get the film and get out."

"And blow the whistle."

He waggled his head from side to side. "Honest. No. Not a word, ever. I'll go back to Mary, and I won't know a thing about anything."

"No, no, no." Art brought a sneaker slowly, deliberately down on the toes of Jack's shiny Ferragamos. He stopped the other man from falling. "Stand up and take it like a man, Jack. You got your exposé, now you've got to pay back."

"And I smuggled all that dope into the States in my equipment. That was the payoff for the documentary."

"You've got it wrong," Art said, as if Jack were a mentally challenged child. "You got a fancy prize for the wonderful documentary. That means you still owe Emilio for not letting on about how you paid for the inside information. Now you're going to settle the debt."

Jennifer pushed the phone under the bed and walked behind Jack. She wrapped her arms around him and fondled his crotch. "I think I'm going to do something I've wanted to do for a long time."

These three had all played parts in a horrible scheme, Polly thought. She glanced toward the windows again, and at the lamp, and at the cord to the telephone. Surely someone would come if she threw something hard enough to break the glass.

"I found Ferrito, didn't I — and I staged a show near him so you'd be in place and above suspicion when Emilio sent word he was ready" — Jack squirmed and plucked at Jennifer's hands — "It wasn't my fault if he got out of your net. You should have had him.

"And I found out where he'd taken Polly for you. You messed up again. He gave Art the slip again."

"You were supposed to make sure he stayed away from pretty Polly as soon as we smelled trouble there," Jennifer said, and bit his neck. "She made it harder, Jack. Tonight she's going to make it easier — but only because we're good at rolling with the punches. She's wasted a lot of time for us. Emilio's not happy. He was ready to show his friends he can call the shots across the world whenever he wants to call them. You spoiled his party. Now he's got to have another one."

"Let me go," Jack said. "Give me the film and let me go."

Art turned to Polly. "He thinks we've got a film of him supervising our friends putting certain merchandise into his equipment. For shipment back to the States. Emilio said he'd give him the film if Jack would help us get Mr. Ferrito back. Mr. Ferrito did some terrible things in Bogotá. Terrible. He embarrassed Emilio, and he's just got to go back and say he's sorry."

"You want to take him back so they can kill him," Polly murmured.

Art's mouth fell open. Waving his gun, he swung from looking at Polly to gape at his sister. "I told you to make sure she didn't talk anymore. She just talked, sis. What are you going to do about it?"

Jennifer unzipped Jack's pants and slipped her fingers inside the fly. "Depends on what comes up." She snickered. "I'll either shut her up quickly, or not so quickly. I've got business to attend to here, first. Soon as it's done, she's done. Gag her. Call Ferrito and say Jack's out of his mind. Say he's always had a thing for her. Tell him Jack grabbed her from that house, but we came to the rescue. She's here, but she's asleep. Come and get her, baby! Better yet, Polly can tell him to come and get her. And she can say how good we've been to her."

"I won't call him."

"Make her do it, Art."

"He can't make me do it."

"Shut up, fool," Jack said. He hardly seemed aware that Jennifer was fondling him. "Keep quiet, or they'll hurt you."

"Touching," Art said. "I do believe he cares."

Polly avoided watching what Jennifer was doing to Jack. His breathing grew heavier. She turned hot with embarrassment.

"Ferrito made our lives hell," Art said. "Emilio expected Jen and me to make sure he never got out of the compound alive. We killed him. Or we thought we had. But the bastard didn't die, and we suffered for that."

Nasty had it right, he'd had it right all along. His only missing link was the identity of these two.

"We were in the circus," Jennifer said. "Till Emilio saw just how talented we really are. Cripes, I nearly had a flamin' cow when Gavin made that crack about knife throwing, Jacko. Art and me can throw knives. Boy, can we throw knives. And we can shoot. And get in and out of anywhere. We're bloody indispensable, we are, but Ferrito spoiled our record. Now he's going to go back for his own funeral."

Holding Polly's destroyed clothes aloft, Art pulled the phone from beneath the bed and thrust it on top of the mattress. "Jack abducted you. We rescued you. Come and get you. Make the call."

"He'll guess something's wrong. He'll know you'd have taken me to him if it wasn't."

"Why, *thank* you, Polly, love." Art dropped her clothing in her lap. "We're grateful to Polly, aren't we, sis? She's right, y'know. So here's what we'll do. You say Jack brought you here because he couldn't take you home to Mary — but we wouldn't go along. Tell him you're afraid to go anywhere without him."

Jack panted loudly and groaned.

"Kill me," Polly told Art. "Kill me now or kill me later. So what? Kill me if I do what you want, kill me if I don't do what you want. Right, Jennie?"

Jennifer said, "Smack the mouthy bitch."

Art obliged, snapping Polly's head around with the fist that held the gun. He hit so hard she fell forward onto her raised knees and closed her eyes. She tasted blood.

"Make the call," Art said tightly.

"I'll never make your call. And if you make it, I'll scream so he'll bring the police with him."

Art dealt her another blow, this one to the other side of her head.

"Leave her alone." Jack's voice was strangled.

"Oh, a gentleman," Jennifer said. "A gentleman with a little, tiny prick. Look, children. Look at Jack's tiny prick. He wouldn't look at me when we did it because I'm too big, and too bloody ugly. Now it's Jack's turn to be laughed at."

Polly longed to lie down, longed for the voices to stop, for the horror to be over. She longed to know Nasty would be okay and that he'd be there for Bobby. Then she could let go. Then it wouldn't matter.

"Dial the number for her, Art."

Dredging up her strength, Polly lifted her head and swept the phone from the bed onto the floor. She pushed it as hard as she could, and laughed when the receiver flew off and cracked as it hit a wall.

"Don't!" Jennifer yelled as Art leveled the gun at Polly's eyes. "That's what she wants. She wants you to kill her. I've got one or two things I want first."

Art kept on staring at Polly. "We had it in the bag," he said. "You know that, Jen. If Ferrito hadn't gotten the hots for this bitch, we'd be home free." Insane hatred threaded every word. His finger tightened on the trigger.

Jennifer's mouth pulled down at the corners. "Of all the rotten luck. They almost ruined everything for us. We can't go back. We've got to go on."

"I say we kill these two and run," Art said.

His sister laughed, a dreadful sound. "Like hell. How long d'you think it would take Emilio to catch us. No way, Art. We're going to win it all. Get Ferrito here. I want him to watch first."

Nasty pounded a fist into the opposite palm. Dressed in black, with a black stocking cap, he paced in front of the silent phalanx of police vehicles and men. They'd assembled at the end of the cul-de-sac where the Loders lived.

The threat of winter edged the night wind. From time to time a dark shape moved, but made no sound. The army of the law had moved into position without lights, and after the nearest neighbors had been evacuated to a safer distance. These people huddled in a group on State Street, where a crowd had begun to gather behind the police cordon.

A police radio van stood to one side. Outside the back doors, a man waited for the signal that an outgoing call was being made from the Loder house to Nasty's cell phone.

"What's taking so long?" Nasty muttered to Dusty. "Maybe we've got it wrong. Maybe she isn't even there. It didn't have to be Jennifer Loder's BMW. Whoever's got Polly could have taken her somewhere else."

"Bullock saw a dark BMW at the end of Rose's street. When Bullock got to the house, Roman found the note. Polly —"

"Yeah, yeah, I know. Polly had been there only minutes before. The note said she was going with me. A lie. And afterward, the car was gone. And I know the Loder woman drives a dark BMW. And there's a dark BMW right in front of the goddamn house now!" He couldn't stand the waiting. "They could be killing her while we speak. She could already be dead. The Loder woman, too, if she was a decoy with a gun in her back. I've got to go in."

Dusty grabbed his arm. "Keep your voice down."

The officer in charge approached. "Better cool it, sir," he said to Nasty. "We wouldn't want to alert them."

"I could be wrong. This may not have been an attempt to set me up. They may not try to call me."

"We're going to fan men out around the property and close in."

These people didn't know what they were dealing with. They didn't know that the people inside that house dealt in death the way Tully's dealt in coffee every day down in Kirkland. "Don't do that," Nasty said. "Let me go in alone."

"I can't do that, sir."

"If you don't, you'll walk into a bloodbath. You may kill whoever made the Loder woman lure Polly away in my name, but he won't leave Polly alive."

"This is it, sir," the man outside the van hissed. "Ringing now."

Nasty leapt into the van, tearing off his cap as he went. He donned the headset a radio operator silently handed him and sank down in front of a microphone. At his signal, the operator flipped a switch and pointed at him.

"Yeah," Nasty said.

"Is this Nasty Ferrito?" A woman's voice, but not Polly's.

"Speaking."

"This is Jennie Loder. Y'know, Polly's friend?" She didn't sound threatened.

"I remember you, Jennie."

"Polly's here. I've got a bit of a problem on my hands."

Nasty took a deep breath. It didn't calm him down. He let the appropriate second pass before saying, "Polly? There? Where?" He hoped he sounded suitably amazed.

"At my place. I'll give you the address."

He counted off another pause. "Polly's . . . Where is your place? Here in Kirkland, you mean?"

"That's right. Look, you don't have anything to worry about. She's sleeping now, but she's okay."

Sleeping? Or dead? He had to do this just right. "How did she get to your place." If he didn't ask the questions, they'd get suspicious.

"It's a long story. Best you come on up here. I saved the day, I'm glad to say. No thanks to Jack Spinnel. Never would have guessed he was crazy enough to . . . Well, I've already called the police. They're on their way. They'll take care of Jack. You can't swipe people and take them away just because you've got the hots for them."

The radio operator looked at Nasty. No distress call had been sent by Jennifer Loder to the police. The detective, who was also listening in, looked at Nasty and gestured for him to wind up the conversation.

"Thank you, Jennie," he said. "I'll be right there. Give me the address." He wrote it down.

"You're leaving now?" Jennifer Loder asked.

"I'll be there in about ten minutes." Less than a minute would be closer to the truth, giving him at least a chance at a surprise attack.

"Good on you." Jennifer cleared her throat. "We'll be waiting. Don't waste any time."

Nasty sat back. He squinted at the lit panel in front of him. *"Time. It's time. You won't get away this time."*

"We'd better get on with it, Mr. Ferrito."

He took off the headset. "What? Oh, yeah. Ready." On the street again, he replaced his cap. "Dusty. I want you behind me. Okay with you?"

"Mr. Ferrito, sir —"

"I know," Nasty told the policeman. "This isn't the way you're comfortable doing things. Please bear with me. I know what these people are. We trained in the same kinds of jungles." He'd almost died in their particular jungle, on a night when a husky voice had whispered, *"It's time. Checkout time."* And a flare of light had blossomed the instant before a bullet smashed his ankle.

"You okay?" Dusty asked, sounding desperate.

"Great. Have your men fan out, Officer, but please tell them not to move in until you get a signal from me."

The officer adjusted the gun at his hip. "We want you in a vest."

"We don't do vests," Dusty said. "They slow you down. Now we gotta go."

"You've got five minutes," the officer said, very quietly. "But I didn't tell you you could go in there."

Nasty left at once. Running, registering the protest in his ankle, he hugged scrubby bushes on two vacant lots to the right of the Loders' house. He made his way rapidly to an unkempt hedge bordering the property.

Dusty fell in behind him. "What d'you think?"

"I don't believe what I think," he said, moving again, skirting the hedge to come at the house from the back. He'd be expected to walk up to the front door and ask to be taken prisoner.

"What's that mean?" Dusty could still move out when he had to. "Tell me."

"I think I've heard Jennifer Loder's voice before."

"Revelation. You know you've talked to her."

"Not here. Somewhere where she whispered. I think she was in Bogotá. I think she was there when I got shot. She could be the one who told me they were waiting for me — right before I went into the open and, whammo. Out to pasture, here I come."

"Nah."

"I kept getting snatches of something. In the past few weeks. Since I met Polly. In the bookshop it happened. And a couple of other times. It was her. Always her. I know it now. There's a light in that corner room."

"One at the front, too," Dusty said.

They flattened against rough siding, bent low, and slipped rapidly to stand beneath the lit corner windows. Cautiously, Nasty straightened until his head cleared the level of the sill. There was a gap between the drapes.

He edged forward. A narrow slice of the room inside had the quality of too few parts of a jigsaw. At first he couldn't tell what went where. A bed. White light directed on the bed. He went a little closer. On the bed, a body swathed in a sheet, the sheet fastened with a belt at the bundle's waist. He couldn't see farther down than that.

It could be Polly. He quelled the urge to raise the Sauer and blast his way in through the window. Around the shrouded head, a strip of something had been tied, rammed in the mouth, and tied. A gag. You didn't gag a dead man — or woman.

Movement.

Into his view came the back of a man. Naked. He took another backward step. In front of him stood a diver.

Nasty froze. *Diver.* Jennifer Loder in a wet suit. She held a gun. Nasty recognized a Glock 19 and didn't envy the man who was feeling its cold barrel in a very sensitive spot.

Jack Spinnel. The naked guy's head was equally naked, almost more so as it shone with sweat.

The Loder woman was in charge, and her attention was splintered. Nasty ducked and ran on to the corner, turned, and came to a door with a window. Inside was darkness. Without hesitation, he worked the lock. An easy number. At least the hinges were oiled. Dusty came in behind him and closed the door carefully. Lives had been lost over lesser mistakes than letting a breeze slam a door.

The room they sought was only feet away. Voices came from inside. Jennifer Loder mocked and taunted Jack. Jack didn't whimper, or beg — Nasty liked him for that. He did take foolish risks. Calling an enemy with a gun an ugly cow might be a fatal mistake.

"You're going to get yours, Jackie boy," Jennifer said. "I was going to wait for Ferrito and let him watch the whole thing, but I think we'll have a quickie little number before he rings the old bell.

"Uncover pretty Polly's eyes. Hurry up. That's it. Carefully, does it. Okay, children, here goes. Jack gets to hump ugly Jennie with the lights on — and with an audience. If he can get the pathetic little bugger up. Oh, yeah! Look, violence turns him on."

Nasty knew the sounds he heard were of Jennifer getting out of the suit. "Wait here," he whispered against Dusty's ear. "I'm going in." He might blow it, but he couldn't wait for a better chance. Struggling out of the wet suit would impair her balance, and her concentration.

"You always said you wanted to do it with the light on, Jack, but you didn't really. You were glad you never had to look at me."

"You didn't want me to look at you," Jack said. "You know you're ugly."

The man had a death wish.

Beneath Nasty's weight, the door burst inward and parted company with its hinges. It fell across the foot of the bed. He vaulted to his left and crouched, the Sauer braced.

"Shit!" Jennifer Loder tried to tear the wet suit completely off with her feet. She still held the Glock. "You move and she dies." The gun was aimed at the bed where he saw Polly's eyes looking at him through a rent in the sheet.

Polly shook her head at him, shook it wildly from side to side.

Without warning, Jack moved. He lowered his head and ran, roaring, into Jennifer.

Nasty went for the Glock.

Loud, gurgling, choking sounds jerked his attention to Polly. She writhed, rocked her head to one side, bucked up and down.

She was choking. Her eyes turned repeatedly to her left. Nasty took a step toward her, and glanced to his right. Polly was warning him. He threw himself forward at the same second as Art Loder pulled his trigger. A silencer made sure his weapon produced only an almost innocent pop.

"Jen!" Loder's mouth fell open. His eyes strained wide open. "Jen!"

Jennifer Loder had dropped to the floor. She lay on her face. She didn't move.

Art Loder let go of a wolflike howl. His teeth bared, he lined up on Nasty.

Dusty hadn't lost his touch with his old Colt. A bloody mass blossomed over Loder's shirt. His gun slipped, slow motion, from his fingers. He buckled at the knees, and Nasty watched him die before he hit the ground.

Nasty looked at Dusty and pulled his knife from his forearm to cut the sheet away from Polly's head.

She stopped him from taking the sheet all the way off. "Not dressed," she croaked.

Nasty sank to the bed and pulled her into his arms. He felt the approach of silent men. The police would be on their way.

Grabbing up his pants, Jack Spinnel covered

himself. Then he slid down the wall and sat, his head turned away, saying nothing.

"It wasn't a man," Nasty said to Dusty. "In Bogotá. She called to me. Jennifer Loder. And she shot me."

Dusty made his way between fallen bodies to sit at the foot of the bed. "You don't know that. You can't be sure, just because —"

"I can be sure," Nasty interrupted. "I thought I'd killed him. Her."

"You did. You knew you had. With the knife."

"No." He pointed to Jennifer Loder, to shocking red scars sweeping in a wide arc around a shoulder blade. "I know my mark."

"Well, we finally finished the job." Dusty put his hand on Nasty's shoulder. It was over.

Twenty-nine

One each side of the bow, they leaned on the rail of the *April*. Early-morning mist floated inches above the water and curled up to all but obscure the dock.

A gull cried through the echoing almost day, and its cry broke somewhere out there, broke and faded.

"You ought to get some sleep," Nasty said. He felt his separation from her.

"So should you."

"I'm tough."

"So am I."

"You're turning blue — and various other colors."

"Don't be rude."

He chuckled and leaned out to peer into the clear water where it lapped at the boat's hull. "I was only talking about the state of your bruises." Backed by the veil of mist, the bowline reflected on the surface.

The blanket of moisture wrapped them in a damp chamber where sound issued and fell away as if it had never been.

"The doctor said you need to rest for a few days," he told Polly.

"He also said I ought to be concussed. People

with concussion shouldn't be allowed to sleep."

"He said you *ought* to be concussed, not that you were. You've been through hell, Polly. You need to give yourself a chance to get over what's happened."

She was quiet.

He looked at her. Coming to the *April* had been her idea. When the police had released them, she'd refused to go to her condominium, had declared that she'd only go there again to pack her things. And she'd said she would be looking for another place to live.

When they'd come aboard, with Polly wearing a sweater one of the policemen had produced, Nasty had told her to take whatever she wanted from his cabin. An ancient camouflage T-shirt in shades of green, brown, and beige had been what she chose. It sagged at the neck, flapped around her slim upper arms, and fell below her knees. It didn't do a thing for the purple marks on her face.

"The shirt lends an air of mystery," he told her.

"I like it because it's yours."

No snappy response came to mind.

"I hate to be repetitious, but I'm still jumpy."

"It's all over now. There's no need to be jumpy."

"That's why I am," she said. She put one sneaker on the other and rested her chin on folded arms atop the rail. "It's all over. I saw how you were last night. You did it all like . . . It was like going to the store is to me. You hold a gun the way I hold a purse. That was all natural to you. Most people's minds would switch off. Yours gets clearer and clearer."

"I seem to remember telling you — several hundred times — that I was trained to do those things."

"You were different. Cold — I mean really cold."

He had to smile. "Rather than just my usual cold?"

She turned her head and propped a cheek so she could look at him. "You aren't cold. Not really. But you're always going to think about the Navy as the best days of your life, aren't you?"

"I'm going to think about it as some of the most challenging days of my life. And some of the days when I did what I was supposed to do and did it well. Any human being feels good about something like that."

"There are going to be a lot more questions."

"Questions we can handle. I'd never have thought of Jennifer Loder. Not in that context. Every time I heard her voice I felt weird, but I didn't make the connection."

"What'll they do to Jack?"

Nasty drew up his shoulders. "Hard to say. He could probably buy himself a lighter sentence if he sang about the things he knows. He's going to do time. Possibly a lot of time."

Polly pushed her hands into her hair, sucked

504

in a breath, and removed them again, much more carefully.

"Go lie down," he urged her. "Sleep for a few hours. The police will want us again later. And your family will be clamoring to talk to you. Then there'll be Bobby needing you."

She straightened and backed up to sit, with a plop, on a hatch. "Festus dead. Belinda in jail. Jennifer and Art dead. Jack in jail. He only put the show on here to create a way to cover getting at you."

Nasty stared at her thoughtfully. "And if you weren't so irresistible, we might not be standing here today."

Polly raised her head. "Jennifer Loder said that. In a way. How could they have imagined something like you and me?"

He smiled. "Ironic. Wonderfully ironic." Irony that all but blew him away. "You saved me, sweetheart."

"You saved us both," she said.

They were silent for a long time before Nasty remembered to tell her, "Belinda bought that wet suit. The cops told me. She bought it from a shop in Bellevue — probably when Festus was already dead. Just to try to back up her story. She's so nutty, she must have kept convincing herself there wasn't anything going on other than the mischief she was causing."

A dressing covered much of Polly's left eyebrow. Another rested on her cheek. Sutures in a wound beneath her jaw showed dark against her unnaturally pallid skin.

"Please go to sleep," Nasty said.

"I'm scared!"

The passion in her voice shook him.

"I'm afraid, Xavier. It's over. All the stress, the fighting, the looking over our shoulders. Like someone burst a balloon we blew up too tight. Was our loving part of that stress? For you? You want me to go below and sleep. It's because you want to be alone, isn't it? Alone to think about what it all means now?"

"Polly —"

"Don't stop me. If I don't say it, I'll never have the nerve again. You aren't happy being a partner in a dive shop. You need something else, and you'll find it. Watching you last night, I knew you were never cut out to be a passive man."

"I'm not passive."

"I can sense how flat you feel. Everything's changed, and you aren't the same." She pushed back her hair. In the clouded light her eyes were the palest of blues. "I won't beg. I can't let myself. But I am going to tell you what's inside of me." Her fist went to her breast.

He raised his hands and let them fall. "You're afraid?"

"Yes. Afraid, and shaky, and kind of hollow. Empty. But I'm full, too. That's absolutely a mad thing to say, but it's true. I look at you and I can't find a way to tell you everything I think."

She was doing better than he was. "Try."

Her hands came together in fists. "You

wouldn't think of trying to help me, would you?" The expansion of her lungs showed how shaky she was. "I'm in your way. You didn't realize it before because you hadn't come face-to-face with what you have to have in your life. Not really. You need excitement and . . ." Her voice drifted away.

Nasty swallowed. "And?"

"And I understand," she told him, tipping up her chin and closing her eyes. "I wish you the best, my love. I wish you luck and happiness. But I'll always love you."

The hesitation, whatever had held him back, snapped. If he touched her, he might break her. The power of what he felt for her was stronger than any emotion he'd ever felt before. He took several steps toward her and turned his back.

"Oh, Xavier, you are so special." She had never meant anything as much as she meant those words. "I hurt inside. Oh, I hurt. I have to tell you that because you've given me so much. I used to think I'd never love anyone — that I never could."

"I'm afraid, too."

She hugged herself. "You'll know what you're supposed to do soon. I just know you will. There are so few men like you — you're very valuable, my friend."

"I'm afraid of losing you, Polly."

Words failed her. He'd said what she needed to hear, and sweet emotion stole her breath.

His spine was long and straight, his shoulders

so broad. Standing in front of her with his powerful legs braced apart he seemed a rock, immovable, beyond damage.

"We're afraid to believe our own luck, love," he told her. "That's it, isn't it? We've had more than our share of the other and managed to make lives for ourselves. Lives that didn't risk what matters most — the heart. Geez, I even know what that means now. But we found each other. And we loved each other — love each other. And we're so damned afraid to believe it won't get snatched away — like everything else we ever wanted this badly."

Polly stood up and went to stand behind him. Very lightly, she leaned on him, rested a bruised cheek on his shoulder. "That's it," she murmured. "That's what I feel."

He put out a hand, palm up. "Me too, partner. If you decide you can live without me, I'll jump in the lake."

Polly brought her palm down on top of his. She smiled into his shirt. "Jump in the lake? So what? You can swim."

"Wearing concrete boots."

"If I know you, you could swim in those, too."

"You have too much faith in me."

"I could never do that."

He pulled her around him until they were toe-to-toe. "Polly Crow, you're my hero. I need you. I'm always going to need you."

"Me, too. You're my hero. And all the rest.

You're the quiet one, but you do words better than me."

"Nah. I chew gum better than you, though."

"I don't chew gum."

"See what I mean?"

She looked up into his face. "I wish you'd hold me."

"Where?"

"Right here."

"No, I mean what bits of you do I dare touch?"

Polly laughed. "Just be gentle with all my bits, please."

"You hussy." Bowing over her, holding both of her hands, he kissed her lips softly, for a long, long time.

She saw his eyes drift shut and closed her own. When he raised his head and sighed, she looked at him again, and said, "I'd like to be with you forever."

"You will be. You don't get any choice."

"Will we be good at it? At being" — she wasn't sure what she should say — "at being there for each other?"

"At marriage, you mean? We're going to be great at it. Kiss me."

Easy request. He held her, and her skin stung everywhere he touched. A great sting she'd put up with for approximately a lifetime — if she could guarantee a long life. "Are you sure you won't suddenly come to and decide this is a bunch of sloppy nonsense?"

"Uh-uh." Crossed around her waist, his hands

tightened a fraction, drew her a fraction closer. "You've got to work at relationships. But if you want it badly enough, you do what it takes."

"And you don't go to sleep mad?" Polly said into his mouth.

"Or walk away from an argument."

"Or bear grudges."

"We're going to be so good at this."

She framed his face. "You are so gorgeous, Xavier Ferrito. Inside and out. I want my son to have you to guide him."

"Hey!" A deep frown drew his finely shaped brows together. "That's right. We're parents."

"Yup. Take me, take my son."

"Okay. Take me, take my cat."

Tears threatened. "I've always been afraid to be too happy. I'm going to work at getting over that. Sometimes this marriage thing won't be easy, but we'll make it through."

"Boy, you don't know how to let go and let it happen, do you? But I think you did just agree to wash my dishes."

"What!" Pushing on his chest, she leaned away from him. "Just a minute, here, buddy."

His angelic smile was almost believable. "You're going to like everything I do to you so much you'll beg to wash my dishes."

"We'll love what we do to each other." The humor went out of her eyes, replaced by a pledge.

Nasty understood that pledge. "I'm going to hold you to that, love."

"I'll hold you to it, too."

"Promise you'll trust me?"

"Always."

"This is what the guy sings about." He could only remember one line of the song, and it might not even fit so well. "The way you make me feel. Ten feet tall, or something. Bulletproof."

"Don't say that!" She swung him around and beat his chest with her fists. "Don't you ever mention your name and bullets in the same breath again."

"Okay. When?"

"Never."

"No. When do we do it? The 'M' word? We ought to be able to tell Bobby when we see him." He wasn't above blackmail to get what he wanted. "That'll be very soon, by the way."

"Soon as you like, I guess."

Exactly what he'd wanted to hear. "How about this afternoon?"

"How about as soon as we can do whatever we have to do first?"

"Put it there." When she shook his hand, he said, "We've got a bargain."

Applause broke out behind him. He looked over his shoulder at three pairs of eyes peering from behind the open doors to the saloon.

Polly covered her face and leaned on Nasty. "They were spying on us," she said, laughing self-consciously.

"No way," Dusty announced. "Just me because I'm the oldest. Roman and Bobby didn't get to look till I could tell them it was a done deal."

The employees of G.K. Hall hope you have enjoyed this Large Print book. All our Large Print titles are designed for easy reading, and all our books are made to last. Other G.K. Hall books are available at your library, through selected bookstores, or directly from us.

For information about titles, please call:

(800) 257-5157

To share your comments, please write:

Publisher
G.K. Hall & Co.
P.O. Box 159
Thorndike, ME 04986

CARMEL CLAY PUBLIC LIBRARY
515 E. Main St.
Carmel, IN 46032
(317) 844-3361

1. This item is due on the latest date stamped on the card above.

2. A fine shall be paid on each item which is not returned according to Library policy. No item may be borrowed by the person incurring the fine until it is paid.

3. Any resident of Clay Township, complying with Library regulations, may borrow materials

DEMCO